Gabriella
and
The Curse
of The Black Spot
Book 2 of the NuGen series

James Cardona

Gabriella and The Curse of The Black Spot

Book 2 of the NuGen series

ISBN: 978-0-9850284-7-3

This book is dedicated to those who shine light into dark places.

Table of Contents

Table of Contents

Chapter 1
The Void

Snatching the door handle, I enter the building and run up the steps two at a time, then three, leaping up to the second floor, rounding the staircase and as I reach the top I hear the door below open and the police entering and yelling, "Stop! Stop! Don't move! Stop right there!"

Ignoring their cries, I run down to the third door on the left, swipe the passkey that Dr. Duggan gave me, throw the door open and am immediately sucked into the room, tumbling head over heels.

Gabby, you can't be here. Again. No, not again. It has to be—it has to be a dream. You can't be here again.

My body is sucked toward the void entrance as if I am an insignificant particle being drawn toward an immense black hole and I hear the door bang open, in the distance, and it seems so far away, my escape, so far away. From a weird angle, head upside down and crooked, I see Kyle sucked in and the door slams behind him. I smash my head hard on the ring edge as my body feels like it is being ripped in two, a spike of mind-numbing pain in the center of my brain as I cross the threshold and then skid across the floor of the Void.

Welding goggles! Welding goggles! I don't have my welding goggles!

Sitting down, eyes clenched down hard, my body shaking, I holler, "Kyle? Are you in here?" My words are swept from the air and ripped out of my throat.

I take off my jacket and then my shirt, tear my

shirt into strips, just like I did last time, just like I do every time, tying one strip across my cut forehead and another across my eyes so that I can squint through them a little.

I stand up and call-out, "Kyle?" looking around, squinting, spinning in every direction, frantically. "Are you in here?"

My ears begin to ring for the silence. Turning, squinting, I make out the exit circle and start walking toward it. I reach the Portugal gate and look out at the frozen picture of Michael hovering over the control panel, hand still on the over-sized button, eyes looking at the gate as if he is staring at me staring at him, frozen, a tiny slice of time, a captured moment in time. I want to stand here forever, staring at him. I don't want the rest of it to continue because I know what happens next. I know exactly what happens next.

Suddenly, swirling around me, the smell of lilac. And jasmine. I turn, squinting, looking around for the clouds and the Void-man. Then cold. Oh so cold. I hate this part. I look around hurriedly because I know what is next.

Pfeeeetzz!

Something grabs me from behind, hands on my neck, strangling me, choking me and I can't breathe! It feels like death. And cold. Like darkness is easing into me through his touch.

"Get off me! Kyle! Let go! You idiot!" I shake my shoulders back and forth, trying to shake him off. He releases and is gone. Again.

I walk to the gate, determined to exit when just in front of me the white deepens to a dull yellow, then blue, then a deep indigo. It is Kyle's face, coming at me, I know it. I just don't know why. I feel nauseous, like I always do, but try to ignore it.

Out of the indigo leaps a metallic face, black and bronze and brown and silver and platinum, dull but shimmering, coming right at me. I step back then cold hands grab my shoulders, and the touch, his touch, brings a choking, stifling dread, and fear, and everything terrible and awful.

Wake up! Wake up! Gabriella, wake up!

Looking down at his hands, my skin fades silver where he holds me and—

I—

Feel—

So—

Cold—

"Let me go! Kyle! Let go!"

Light shines off his shady black face, the black of night, the black of decay and death. I can barely talk and I feel like he is draining me, as if life is being pulled out of me—

I feel—

Weak—

Suddenly—

I pull back my head and slam it into his, head butting him as hard as I can. I look down and there are splotchy black spots where he held me. My head is throbbing and the blood is dripping down onto my face. His form is black and dead and as his eyes move, I suddenly recognize him, recognize his former self and what he used to look like when he was alive, before he became night and darkness and death. I recognize the face I held, the face I kissed, the face I was to marry. Somehow I am drawn to him like a fly to blue light, knowing that he will kill me yet unable to pull away. I look down and see it spreading, like some splotchy, sick disease, spreading from where he held me. I touch my forehead and it feels so cold and I know it is spreading from there too. I am becoming night, becoming darkness and death. I feel sick and diseased but there is nothing I can do to stop it. It is the black spots. How could I possibly stop them?

A surprised look comes over his face as he begins to fade to nothing, the space where he stood fading back to white, right in front of my eyes. Gone.

I leap through the Void exit, fly out into the Portugal control room, skidding the side of my face on the floor and turn to see Michael staring down at me.

Then I wake up.

Chapter 2

Detectives

I shake from the nightmare as the pilot announces that we will be on the ground in Philadelphia momentarily. Smith and Mom are none too happy to retrieve me from Portugal. I am in big trouble. They will escort me from the airport to the police station in Princeton for an interview with detectives. I still don't know if I am going to be charged. Then I will go on to the Philadelphia Freedom debrief and that's another thing I am worried about. Will they kick me off the team?

We exit the plane and pick up Smith's car, everyone in an unnatural silence. Smith drives us out of the city, across the Ben Franklin bridge and up 295 North into Princeton and to the police station. Mom squeezes my hand as we exit the car and says, "Just tell the truth."

We enter the busy station, pass through scanners and metal detectors and then are shown to a very small room. Two detectives enter but only one of them sits, the one who does all the talking. I explain everything at least twice but he still doesn't seem to get it.

"So tell me this again. There's a big ring and you go into it?" The detective looks at me and winces.

He doesn't believe me but I am telling the truth!

Mom and Smith are with me but I am still too nervous.

I reply, trying to keep my voice from shaking, "All right. One more time. Michael opened the gate and I leapt in, trying to escape Kyle—"

"Michael's your boyfriend from... where again?"

I glance at Mom then back, saying, "He's not my boyfriend. I already told you that."

"Okay, okay. So then?"

"Michael opened the gate from the other side. No one was here on our side."

The officer replies without looking up from his screen, "And how did he know to open it?"

"I called him."

"So, you are running from this Kyle, so you say, and you call your boyfriend and tell him to turn on this machine to escape?"

Distress is in my voice. "He's not my boyfriend."

"Why didn't you call the police?"

"I don't know. I panicked, I guess. Kyle was in a police car following me. His lights were on full blast. The sirens blaring. I don't know."

The detective says, "Right, right, right. You were being chased by three police cars. It's in the report right here."

"I was scared. I don't know why I ran. I was afraid."

The detective scribbles more notes onto his screen. "Right, right. So let's get back to this. You go into this ring?"

"I was trying to get away from Kyle. He was going to hurt me. I just knew it. And Kyle was just too close; he got sucked into the Void after me and that's when everything got really weird and I had no idea what was going on. I still don't know what happened really."

"Right. Void, right. Listen, I'm just an old beat cop who's been around a little too long. You're going to have to do a little better than that. So, let's do this. Sit back, close your eyes and just tell me what happened."

I close my eyes and say, "The Void was all white, everywhere except the entrance and exit portals, like it always was when I went through, and I couldn't see anything since in my panic I forgot to grab my welding goggles. I bandaged my bleeding head by tearing my shirt since I banged it on the entrance ring and I wrapped an extra few strips of the torn shirt cloth around my eyes so I could at least try to see a little. I know Kyle got sucked in too. I saw him flying in after me but when I looked around.... no Kyle! Where was he? I didn't have a clue. I looked everywhere and every which way; I even called his name. Nothing. As I headed for the exit, assuming that maybe he really didn't make it in, a face suddenly came out at me—Kyle's face! That's why I know he was in there. He tried to stop me from leaving; I tried to fight him off, unsuccessfully, and I totally don't understand why he looked that way."

"Right. That's weird. Can someone corroborate any of this?"

I open my eyes and say, "Dr. Duggan. But it was different than the way he described it. The Void, I mean. Another thing that I don't know about. I remember Michael and Dr. Duggan both said that it was called the Void because everyone who traveled through it using the dimensional transport machine saw a light-eating pitch black darkness. That's what *they* said anyway."

"Right. Okay. Got it. Dr. Dooogan. Princeton professor, right?"

Smith interrupts, "It's Duggan. You know, like 'Dug', then 'Gan'. Dug—gan. There's a split second pause in the middle."

"Right. How do you spell that?"

Smith writes it down for him then the officer

continues, "So you think this Kyle who was chasing you is still in there?"

I answer, "Maybe. I guess. Michael shut down the machine and we didn't see him come out on the Portugal side. Your men were on the other side?"

"Yeah, yeah." The detective scribbles some more. "So you think he is still inside this machine?"

"In the machine? The machine is just a gateway. It opens up to another dimension. Duggan told me once. Like height and weight... no, that's not it. I think it's like height and width—they are dimensions—you can measure them."

"Right. Okay. Yeah, right. We will talk to him. The science doesn't matter to us too much though. We just need to get our hands on this kid. He stole a police cruiser, you know?"

"I know."

"And you two were engaged. You're sure you don't know where he is?"

"I told you already! He was trying to kill me! I don't know where he is! He wanted to run some crazy experiment on me. I was trying to get away from him."

"Right." The detective looks over at Smith and back at me.

Smith says, "Whatever happened, Kyle was not under any direction or authorization from NuGen. We actually have quite a few questions for him ourselves."

The detective looks out of the top of his eyelids at Smith then returns his gaze to me. "All right, Gabriella. So you think this Kyle is somewhere inside this machine. Err... some place that this machine leads to? And where is that again?"

"I wish I knew. Maybe he was on the dark side while I was on the light side? Maybe the machine opens up to more than one dimension and somehow he was in one and I was in the other and somehow he was able to push through? I don't know. It's just so weird."

"Right. Not exactly the 'where' I was looking for. I just need to track down your fiancé. You can help with that, right?"

I say, "You act like I am covering for him. I'm not! We were engaged. Okay, I got that. But not anymore. No way am I going to marry that guy! I'm not hiding him! Got it?"

"Right, right. Calm down. No reason to get upset here. I'm just trying to get the facts. That's all. So tell me again. You saw white and he saw black?"

I exhale, then reply, "Yeah, I guess."

"Any ideas why?"

"I don't understand it either. I was thinking like, maybe the Void changes depending upon who is in it? Maybe everyone experiences the Void differently? That it's somehow interactive? Maybe the Void is not really a *place*, but some kind of reflection of who you are when you enter it? I don't know. I wish I could talk to Duggan myself. I'm sure I have more questions than you do. Anyway, Dr. Duggan shut the project down and as far as I know Kyle is still trapped in there."

"Right. I don't think I have any further questions for now. As far as what we do with you, obviously you have lost your driving permit. You know what that means?" He asks.

"I can't drive."

The detective leans back in his chair and says, "You can't even apply for a new one until you're eighteen. And you're lucky that's all."

"I'm lucky?" I don't feel lucky. Actually I feel very unlucky."

"You're lucky we don't lock you up. There are a few people that have spoken on your behalf. Smith here is one of them. I'd say you're lucky—lucky Smith here knew the judge that was assigned to your case—lucky no one is pressing charges, the team, the University. We'll be in touch."

I don't know what he expects me to say so I let out a thank you and try not to keep my face expressionless. Clearly the detective thinks that I am a waste of his time.

As we start to get up to leave, he adds, "And if you decide that you remember something else or you decide that you know where this Kyle is, you call us right away, okay?"

Chapter 3

Limited Suspension

"Sit down and I will tell you how this is going to go."

"Coach, I—"

She quickly clips my words in the air, barking, "Sit down, I said!"

I shuffle over to the corner of the concrete-walled room and sit on the hard wooden chair. Coach Donavan steps forward, towering over me, glaring. Mr. Lyttle and Jerry step in the room, two of the white shirts from the front office. Lyttle immediately takes a seat against the far wall and whips out his screen; it looks tiny in his enormous palm.

"You don't know what you have done, do you? You don't know how bad you have screwed up this time?" Donavan bellows.

I want to answer. I want to say that I know exactly how bad I screwed up. I know I brought unwanted media attention on the team and this couldn't be good for Donavan's career. But I know better than to respond so I just sit there and stare up at her.

"Do you realize what the other teams are saying? Do you realize what the tabloids are going to do with this? I knew I shouldn't have let your little romance go on! You and your boyfriend, I knew that couldn't have gone well! And Cyndi and her guy too. I don't know what I was thinking!"

"It wasn't her fault," I say without thinking.

"Don't interrupt me! Sit there! Just sit there and don't say anything!" She paces for a moment then continues, "This is all over the media and the front office goons," she looks back at Lyttle, "no offense—are going to cook up something to swing this in a positive direction—"

Lyttle interrupts, "You are going to play ball with us, aren't you?"

"Of course," I say.

He nods and looks back down at his screen.

Coach Donavan continues, suddenly softer, "Gabriella, this is bad. This is very, very bad. You know, even though it might not seem so to you, I like you and have gone to bat for you in the past. You have no idea what the politics are like around here. There are one-hundred girls waiting in line to take your place and the bean counters in the front office wouldn't hesitate for a moment if they thought switching you out for some new face would generate more revenue for the team. You don't know it, none of the girls do because I insulate them, but I have saved your butt more than once."

I nod slowly.

Coach's shoulders slacken and she slowly steps back. "But this one, this one is out of my hands. I can't save you this time. This is too big for me and, I hate to say it, you're on your own."

Jerry steps forward and clears his throat as if he is about to read a prepared speech that he has practiced many times. "Gabriella Conceição, you are now hereby placed on limited suspension."

I thought he would have said much more and I have no idea what it means. "What?" I say. "What does that mean?"

Lyttle looks up and says, "Gabriella, you are

extremely lucky that you have a fan base that spends money. There is a direct correlation between your running times and merchandise sales."

Donavan looks through her eyelids.

Lyttle continues, "Err, it seems that girls aged twelve to eighteen quite like you and I estimated that letting you go would result in a 3% drop in t-shirts sales and a 4.5% drop in the very lucrative sweatshirt department."

Jerry quips, "Even if we get someone of equal or better talent."

Lyttle purses his lips and whispers which is odd since we can all hear him, "We don't want to do that right before playoffs."

I ask, "So what does my suspension entail?"

Donavan looks at Lyttle with a sort of confused look on her face. She must have thought that they were going to do something much worse.

Lyttle nods and says, "Effectively nothing. You can train, you can race, but the team needed to let the media know that you were being disciplined for this."

Donavan adds, "It does mean this though: One more screw up and you're gone." She sounds serious this time. Lost from her voice is the typical Donavan growl that I am so accustomed to.

I am on my last leg.

Lyttle stands, closes his screen and says, "Yes, what your coach says is true. Our numbers indicate that you can't stand anymore bad publicity. We forecast that it would affect your sales and that we can't have. Any questions?"

I stand and shake my head.

The two men walk out and Donavan turns to follow them. I try to stop her to apologize. "Coach, I want to tell you how—"

She turns and says, "Don't. Listen Gabriella, you're young and you made a mistake. I've been at this for a long time and I've seen a lot of good, well-meaning girls come and go. I've heard every promise and every apology that you can think of. Hey, you screwed up. You picked the wrong guy. I don't need to know anything more about it. I don't really want to hear your apologies. All I want is for you to perform. That will be enough of an apology for me. Start putting some points on the board and we will consider ourselves even."

She gives me her back and walks out of the room. I follow her and am just so thankful that I am still on the team but the moment is bittersweet because I feel rotten for what I have put the others through. Cyndi and Sidney both won't talk to me, and with good reason. The rest of the team probably thinks that I am a loose cannon and will try to keep their distance. No need to associate with someone who is ready to be let go. And Mom? That's a mess too. All I can do right now is do what Coach said. Keep my mouth shut and try to perform. But it sure does hurt inside.

Chapter 4

The Knee

"I'm gonna break your legs!" the short one says as she passes our bench. Everyone ignores it of course but her words are ringing in my ears. Something about the way she said it, as if she wasn't just antagonizing, like she really meant it.

The race starts and it is all of a sudden all too obvious exactly what she intends to do.

"Run! Get away! Get away from her!" Donavan screams as I launch off the benches with the rest of the team. We are right on the edge of the barrier line and somehow we all know what will happen next.

The black spot itches and ohhh do I want to scratch it sooo bad.

"Faster! Faster! Faster!" Donavan hollers, "Run! Move it! Get away from her!"

Nomi and Qi are running as fast as they can but the three-hundred-pounder is closing quickly. Across the rope bridge, quickly pouncing on the tilting balance beam and speeding toward the curved wall and water leap, they just can't seem to get away. Qi glances back at the last moment as the beast dives, wrapping her arms around the two, Nomi and Qi, her tackling them fiercely, knocking them off course with a grunt, the three falling in a pile of tumbling flesh, disqualified. The large girl quickly stands over the two looking down at them in condemnation and all I can think about is, "Eat or be eaten." It was Mr. Dunberry's lesson in 5th period

History class yesterday, a quick survey of Evolutionary Theory. The girl's stance reminds me of one of the pictures in his presentation, the one of the half-man half-gorilla. Eat or be eaten. Eat or be eaten. Survival of the fittest. Just animals competing to survive. Mr. Dunberry thinks that's what we are.

The beast of a woman flexes her arms as her sneer turns into a grin then she struts off course.

The black spot itches again. Don't scratch it. Don't think about it.

I know I can't touch it, not here in front of everyone, but I *really* would love to. Claw at it really. Even better, tear it off, rip it off, just make it go away. But all I can do right now is ignore it. I don't want anyone to know that it's there.

"No!" howls Donavan, pacing up and down the field, shaking her fists. "They *know* better than to run so close together!" Elektra, our last runner left on the course, flees from the two Sacramento runners. It's a race but the way those two are chasing Elektra it's as if they are trying to catch her, not pass her.

As they swing across the ropes and quickly balance across barrels, the two are catching up and the panic is in Elektra's eyes. Cyndi's hands squeeze the bench hard and I can feel it flex next to me. Elektra is all alone out there and there's nothing we can do about it. The Sacramento fans' scream is in my ears; they want blood.

Elektra dashes across the rope bridge just in front of our benches, wide-eyed fear stabbing at us, eyes screaming out, "WhatdoIdo? WhatdoIdo? WhatdoIdo?" as the Fire-Plug sweeps to and fro just inches behind her, a grin painted across her face, eyes staring at the back of Elektra's legs.

Elektra involuntarily releases a grunt as she swings

off the last rope and thrusts herself forward, trying desperately to accelerate, to get away, to somehow increase her distance from the Fire-Plug. In a short section of open track Elektra adds some distance. She has always been our fastest on open ground, but with three sections of obstacles coming up, our whole team tenses knowing that the Fire-Plug will catch her here, if at all.

Then it happens; she smashes into Elektra. For some reason my eye is drawn to the saliva glistening on her lips. Elektra buckles, her leg twisting oddly and for the briefest moment, holding under the Fire-Plug's weight, then SNAP! The crowd gasps as she quickly crumbles, loosening an ear-piercing scream. The Fire-Plug stands over her for a moment then walks off the field. Quick, nimble Elektra is nimble no more, her body lying bent and curled at unnatural angles, shaking, sobbing and screaming. A cold shudder runs down my spine as I realize that Elektra's leg has just broken.

The black spot itches again, burns really, and I reach my hand up to it, but no—I mustn't touch it. I force myself to put my hand down. It begins to throb in unison with the blood pulsing in my temple and suddenly I am sooo angry.

What is going on! Elektra? No!

The blood in my temple pulses harder and faster and I can feel the veins on the side of my head slowly elevating, forming lines on my skin. Rage fires through me and the black spot burns intensely.

Who do they think they are? That was intentional. I am not going to let that go!

Two men in white smocks stretcher Elektra off the field and both sides of the small stadium applaud respectfully for her. My lip quivers uncontrollably. Now I want blood. I want revenge. But I have no idea why I feel this way.

I don't say a word for the rest of the half as my gut twists and turns. The rest of the team is quiet as my mind replays events in my head over and over again. Last season Velocity and her two goons from the Brazilian squad broke my leg, intentionally I think, and watching what just happened to Elektra from this angle bubbles a little nausea into my throat as my knee tingles where it was broken. Glancing over at the rest of the team and their seeming disinterest, I wonder if they are morbidly thinking that it's all part of the sport. Or maybe they are just thinking about losing the game.

Is that what they are worried about?

I hope they are at least a little concerned about Elektra even though they don't show it. But me, like a simmering pot full of crab-boil, I can barely contain my rage and I can't stand the fact that they are so calm.

"You ready?" Cyndi says. Usually optimistic that one but the way she says it is cold and distant as if she still doesn't want to talk to me.

Didn't she see what just happened to Elektra? Why isn't she upset? Why isn't everyone ready to destroy this team? And on our own turf no less!

The Philadelphia crowd is chanting, "Free-dom! Free-dom! Free-dom!" their faces full of expectation. The tension in the stadium is palpable and the rest of the team is silent and wary. We are close to qualifying for the playoffs but that seems like a long way off right now.

"Yeah, let's do this," I say but I mean a whole different kind of "do." Pausing for a second, looking at my shoes, I mumble to myself, "hope I'm ready," then push off the bench. I look over at Sidney as I rise, sweat still beading on her shoulders from her warm-up striders.

She always knows what to do, I tell myself. She leaps up and the stands behind us instantly erupt.

"Gabriella! Be ready! Okay? I need some points out of you!" Donavan hollers, shaking me from my thoughts. It's starting to get old, rescuing the field team all the time, the *men* who are supposedly the *real* focus of this game, when they keep giving up points and winning right now is the last thing on my mind anyway. I want revenge.

We can only run three in the second half and we will be up against four runners from the Sacramento team. It's hard to tell who they will be, their sprinters or enforcers, as they are warming up all seven to confuse us. Can't blame them, we do the same thing. Our two enforcers are sitting and with Elektra out, we three are the fastest. Donavan said that we are going to try to out run them in an all-out speed race. I like to run fast but right now my gut tells me I could settle for an old-fashioned fist fight.

The men continue to play on the field near us as we three line up at the start of the track that borders the playing field, waiting for the Sacramento girls to come out, me barely able to cloak my rage, Sidney and Cyndi not saying a word, refusing to talk to each other in front of me, refusing to even acknowledge that I am standing right next to them. They both haven't forgiven me yet for not telling them about Kyle and letting them think that Sebastian was the one who hurt Cyndi.

I knew and I didn't tell them, that's true, but they are still refusing to listen to my side. They still refuse to hear me out. I wish they would at least let me tell my side of the story.

The black spot burns and I suddenly find my hand on it, caressing it, my lip quivering violently. Who needs them anyway. The skin circling the spot has somehow risen like the back of a scared cat. I consciously force myself to put my hand down and stop touching it. It's on the back of my neck but just under my shirt line and no one can know it is there. Let's get this thing on! I got blood on my plate today.

Antonio catches the green ball just in front of me, near the white line, throws it nearly across the field, quickly turns toward me, winks and says, "Hey, Gabriella," then runs off. The boys on the team are off limits according to Donavan. Coach Bustoff has a similar policy for his guys but it doesn't seem to stop anyone from flirting. And even though rage is coursing through my veins I totally don't mind his attention.

The Sacramento girls finally come to the start line and their meager fan's cheer is drowned out by the hissing and booing of the Philadelphia fans. I love Philadelphia fans. The Beast and the Fire-Plug from the first half are joined by two fresh sprinters. I intentionally sandwich myself between the enforcers and my tiny sprinter's body looks like sad, wilted lettuce between two pieces of bulging, marbled, rye and pumpernickel, yet it is all I can do to not push at them before the gun. I have no idea what I am going to do but my force of will tells me I can do anything right now. Eat or be eaten. Eat or be eaten. Eat or be eaten and I am hungry. Get on the plate girls because you are about to be served.

Their red shorts remind me that they are NuGen girls and it makes me hate them all the more.

It was NuGen that tracked us down in Venezuela so many years ago, NuGen that sent goons to threaten my father, to try to squeeze him for his research, research that Smith said was rightfully NuGen's property, goons that chased my father and killed him, well... made him crash his car anyway… well… I think they killed him… whatever happened… I don't know… no one does… but I hate them all the same. They killed my Dad! Stupid black spot. Stupid black spot. Stupid black spot. Aaargh! It won't stop itching and I just want to smash something!

Sidney looks impatient for the gun; she looks back at me, frowns and quickly looks away. She has her shell on and I still don't know how to break through.

Heat radiates off the two goliaths on either side of me, the Beast and the Fire-Plug. The gun fires suddenly and I push my arms off at the two girls as I haul into a full sprint trying to antagonize them. I am disappointed that they ignore it and I am off far in front of them.

Sidney, Cyndi and I fall into a single file line and quickly put twenty-five yards between us and the Sacramento girls. We fly across the rope swings, the crooked wall and the water leap and as I run up the warped wall and barely grab the ledge I look back to see that the two Sacramento enforcers are hanging back, waiting for us to complete our loop, obviously intending to throw us off course when we pass. We know we have to split up so Cyndi and I slow down and let Sidney get some distance. This lets the two Sacramento sprinters catch up and one of them passes me and comes up onto Cyndi's heels. I try to keep somewhat in front of my opponent and keep her behind me for the obstacles that have to be taken one at a time.

Just past the tilting balance beams, blue and yellow flashes past me.

I have to do something!

The two enforcers inch up in anticipation as Sidney approaches, sprinting hard and fast at the far edge of the path, trying to quickly blow past them. I know what they are going to do. They are going to smash Sidney!

No you don't; I am not letting that happen. The black spot is burning a hole in the back of my neck and I turn on every ounce of speed I have, quickly catching and passing blue and yellow. I am dogging the faster Sacramento girl's heels, the one just behind Cyndi, and the two enforcers have lost the tension in their shoulders and let Sidney fly past, knowing that the time is not right.

At the second pass of the crooked wall Cyndi looks back at me. It would be nice if she would acknowledge me, signal me, at least let me know what she is planning but it looks like it will be all one way for now. We used to run as a unit, Cyndi, Sidney and I. We didn't have to talk strategy before hand, we didn't have to yell out to each other on the course; it was just a look, a nod or a feeling. When one of us needed help, the other two instantly knew it and we were there for each other. Now I am all alone.

Cyndi tears into a sprint and I follow suit, quickly passing the other girl in blue and yellow.

The enforcers are looking back at their coaches and hollering, "What? What? Now? These two?"

Before they can figure out what to do we are past them. There is one lap to go. They will definitely be coming out on the next lap and I don't know what will happen. I know what they are feeling; I can see it in their eyes. I know what they are feeling because I feel it too. Smash something, break something, crush, kill, destroy. Eat or be eaten. Eat or be eaten. The black spot is burning, tearing, pulling, kill, kill, kill. I know what they are feeling because I want it too. I want to hurt something, someone, anyone.

Halfway through the final lap, black spot driving

me, me barely in control, like a spectator outside my body, watching, not understanding, I drive past Cyndi and yell up to Sidney, "Let me pass!"

Sidney glances back and frowns, not understanding, but slows up and lets me pass her. She says nothing as I fly by and she is right behind me, three meters back, watching my every step. Just as I reach the enforcers I see confusion on their faces. They know I am not the fastest yet I am in front. If they take me out their girls will never pass Cyndi and Sidney; if they don't I will grab three points for first place.

My eyes taunt them. Come on! Let's go! Let's see who breaks! I don't know what's driving me but I can't stop myself. This is suicidal! Gabby, what are you doing?

I fly as close as possible and leap toward them. One of them grabs at me trying to push past me as I am blocking their access to Sidney. Sidney flies by on the outer course edge and as the second one, the Fire-Plug, tries to step by me I stick out my leg to trip her. That's for Elektra! She leaps over it but it is enough to slow her down and Sidney escapes. The whistle blows and the Beast and I must leave the course. We are both disqualified.

Retreating to the benches, I briefly scan faces but none return my gaze.

Donavan shallowly says, "Good call, Gabby."

It is a 5-1 second half for us runners with Sidney scoring three points for first and Cyndi grabbing two points for being second across the finish but adding in with the men's performance it looks to be another loss for the Philadelphia Freedom.

The match ends unceremoniously and the dejected team waves to the fans without smiling as it retreats down the tunnel.

Slumping down onto the locker room bench, all my energy gone, my body completely drained like a long empty oil can lost in the corner of father's shed, all the rage and anger from half an hour ago wiped away as if it was never there, I can't understand what came over me and who was that person controlling my mind and my body. That wasn't me. No way. All I wanted to do was to destroy. To eat. To consume those girls like a hungry lion stalking a wounded calf. That's not who I am, is it? No way... Is it? No.

Eat or be eaten. Is that all that sports are? Some tamed-down version of survival of the fittest? Playing at the game of life in some sick exhibition of who should live and die? Mr. Dunberry thinks so. He said that sports started thousands of years ago as something warriors did to occupy their time while waiting outside cities under siege. The cities had tall walls, fortresses really, and the attacking armies would camp outside the walls and wait for the city's food supply to dwindle down before their final assault. Sometimes this could take months and what were these bored warriors to do? Play checkers? No way! They practiced all sorts of warrior-like things, of course; throwing their spears, hammers and maces; sword play and defense; running, jumping, diving and leaping. And wrestling? Of course they wrestled like caged animals. But who threw the javelin the best? Who could run the fastest? Who could leap over a row of bodies to reach his intended target the fastest? Practice quickly turned into competition. "Hey Achilles, bet I can throw this here spear farther than you can!" The birth of athletics was born in battle, born in survival, born in a life and death struggle. Eat or be eaten. That's what life is all about. At least that's what Mr. Dunberry said.

I wait for the rest of the team to exit, me moving

as slowly as possible at my locker which is easy since I am *really* sore, then trudge into the empty showers and quickly wash off the day's track grime, staring at the center metal pole, water on my face and hair, unmoving, keeping my back toward the wall so that no one will see the black spot. It doesn't itch now. The skin around it is not raised up like before either. Rinsing off the last of my soapiness I hear voices in the locker room and quickly towel off. I wrap my long brown hair in my mini hair towel and make sure the back of it drapes down to cover the black spot then exit the showers and enter the locker area.

Coach Donavan's bark echoes out of her open doorway, "I can't *bee-lieve* you agreed to that! John! What's wrong with you? You would have never stood for that ten years ago!"

John Murray answers through the screen, "I know, you don't understand. It's not me."

"Not you! I saw you standing right next to those Sacramento animals right before they went out and broke my girl's leg!"

"Michelle, It wasn't my call. In your heart of hearts you have to know that."

Coach Donavan is silent and I am trying to dress as fast as I can because I know I am listening to something that I shouldn't be. I am embarrassed to be eavesdropping but I can't help myself. Donavan and John Murray were both assistant coaches on the same team many years ago and apparently they were some kind of an item. Coach told me that she regretted letting things get in the way, things that seemed important at the time—don't they always—things that seem so trivial now, but time went on, they grew apart, and she lost him. I was hoping they would get back together. It would make the fairy tale in my mind seem complete anyway.

"Not your call! Not your call! So you just stood there and said nothing when you knew what they were going to do! Open your mouth and say something for once! Ugh! Now I remember why I left!"

I slip out so as not to be noticed and head into the parking garage.

Chapter 5

Dreaming of Blue

Mom is waiting in the parking lot, dozing in the driver's seat. The team always leaves long after the fans are gone and I am the last one out so she clearly has been sitting there for some time. Looking at her, guilt crashes down on my head like the mudslide that hit the favela back when we lived in Brazil. Blood flushes my cheeks. Why did I have to run from Kyle? Why did I have to take Mom's car? I lost my license and who suffers for that? Not me. Mom.

I scuffle across the parking lot, open the passenger side door and flop down in.

Mom puts the car in gear. "How'd it go?"

"We lost."

"I know. I heard on the screen." She pulls to the exit and waves at the attendant who opens the lift-gate. "I heard Elektra got hurt too. Is it bad?"

"No idea," I say in a monotone, trying to not bring up my injury last year. Mom pulls out onto the highway heading south. "I hope she's All right."

"Me too."

Mom pauses as she passes a few cars then asks, "Did it look intentional?"

"I think so." I know where this conversation is going and I don't know if I can head it off. Mom never liked the idea of me competing. She wants me married with a family, at home with kids. A job—sure, something to keep my mind fresh—but a career? No way! Mom wants a *traditional* life for me. Something that shows that she raised me right in spite of the fact that she was without a husband. Certainly not *this*. No one from her culture wants a wife in the spotlight, a wife with an important career or a wife with a big mouth. A wife should never overshadow her husband according to Mom. It would somehow take away his relevance. For Mom, a woman should know her place and wherever that is, I am certainly not there. Of course she never says any of this out loud, it is all communicated through inference and subtleties.

"Gabby, I know you don't want to hear this, but how much longer do you think you are going to run before you get hurt again?"

Trying to head off a long drawn out debate, I blurt out, "Listen Mom, I understand. I just don't see where this sport is going myself. Seems like the enforcers are getting more and more violent and for some reason the fans are eating it up. Too many girls are getting hurt but the league doesn't do anything about it because the ratings are through the roof. They're turning the Pre into a running Hockey fight and it makes me sick but for now this is what I am doing. I just want to keep competing, okay? I'll try to be careful." I look over at her and the way she looks at me and the worry in her eyes makes me love her so much. If she asked me again I would quit right now. Luckily she doesn't.

"Okay, Gabby. I understand. Just try to stay away from those big girls."

As Mom drives I knead my thighs with a roller trying to flush out the last of the lactic acid to minimize my soreness. Mom says, "Sore?"

"Yeah. And I have a Chemistry and a UNA History test tomorrow then straight to practice so I am going to be sitting in a chair all morning then running all evening which won't be good at all and I am so dreading it."

"Probably find out about Elektra tomorrow?"

"I hope she's All right. If it's a clean break and if they can set her leg right away and if they can bubble-plaster it and if they get the thermo-injections percolated she might be back in a week. Two weeks tops. A lot of *if*s. If not, the rest of the season is gonna be tough, big time."

"Well, you know you don't have to do this."

"Mom!"

"I'm just saying."

We pull into our driveway, get out of the car and enter the house. I crash into my bed and curl under the covers wanting to quickly fall into a deep, exhausted sleep but I find myself lying there, eyes open, incredibly tired, staring at the dark, listening to the crickets and night critters through the open window and wondering what my life is becoming.

The crickets are getting louder. Or maybe I am just focusing on them. In Biology class I learned that insects make all that racket to call their potential mates. Usually it is the male that makes the noise, flashes the lights, sings the song, does a dance or shows off his beautiful feathers or plumage to attract the female. Like skyscraper construction workers flexing their muscles as they hawk at pretty girls on a crosswalk, these bugs are out screaming for girls. The crickets make their racket by rubbing their hind legs together like the bow of a violin. I remember the young men in Venezuela, so crass and forward, like these crickets, calling to the ladies walking to the bus stop by our little clothing store, "Hey baby, baby, you lookin' fine!" They were quite ridiculous.

Young fools. I remember that the women always ignored them, and suddenly I unconsciously frown as Michael's young soft face and brown curly locks appears in my mind. And Michael, oh no, Michael. The only man I ever truly loved and I rejected him for Kyle. Will he ever forgive me? What could I possibly tell him? How can I get him back? Even him I lost. All alone, I am all alone. Every friend I have ever had and every person I have ever known is gone.

A slow tear leaks from my eye; I squeeze it out and let it fall onto the pillow. This is life, Gabby. A roller coaster, right? Not a fairy tale. There are no happily-ever-after. There is just life and we live it. Things happen and that's it; we move on. We don't fall on the sword and die, we move on. We live life.

I decide to not think about it just like I decide every night, every night since I escaped Kyle and the Void, every night since I got back from Portugal, every night since everything changed, every night that I spend by myself, lying in my bed, staring into the darkness, all alone.

My eyes flash open, cold sweat on my forehead, as the bluish-white glow radiates down from him, the Void-man floating above me, his face inches away from mine, too close, and somehow I am so very relieved to see him.

"Okay," I mouth, smile and then cautiously say, "Hi." I still don't know who he is, where he came from or what he wants with me but so far he's saved my life twice and I haven't had a chance to thank him.

He floats up, closer to the ceiling about three feet away and my heart flutters thinking that he is leaving. "No. Wait," I mouth, wanting desperately to raise my hand to him but somehow not being able to control it. I feel pinned to the bed and it is now that I realize that I am asleep. I must have dozed off. This is a dream, another one of my stupid dreams. He's not real.

He pauses, glistening blue eyes looking through me, and opens his mouth, his deep echo chamber voice resonating through me. "Meet me."

I try to nod, agreeing to anything just so he won't leave, then mouth, "Where? Meet you where?" There is so much I want to say to him, so much I want to ask him; I can't let him leave yet. Even though I know that he's just in my head, that he is some kind of fabrication of the randomly malfunctioning neurons in my sleeping, beta-wave brain, I still want him to stay.

"You will know when you find it."

Instantly I am awake and the room is black. The ceiling fan creeks a little as it wobbles slowly round and round. Touching my forehead, I feel no sweat even though I think I should since it was there in the dream and I want to be back asleep and in the dream, with the Void-man, to talk to him, to ask him, to thank him, to find out where he comes from and what he knows. I feel like all my questions are stuffed in my mouth and I curse myself for not blurting them out when he was there. I know he knows something. I wish I could really see him again. But that's impossible, I know, because Dr. Duggan shut down the project and there is no way into the Void and no way to see the Void-man. He is lost to me forever. And what I just saw, it was just a dream anyway.

Something tugs from inside my chest, a tuna on a fishing line, fighting, struggling, telling me to get out of bed, but I know I should try to fall back asleep. The line grows taut, pulling me to get up. The clock's dull red numbers say 3:00AM and as I swing my legs over and off the edge of the bed I can't believe that I am actually going to go looking for him. The Void-man is real, that much I know. The dreams, I am not so sure. Sometimes I think that I've got Void-man-itis and everything that is going on in my life brings him around but that can't be right, could it? My own personal alien, spaceman, dimension-traveler, ghost, spirit or whatever he is? And why does he look like my dead father? He doesn't sound like him or act like him. His voice, echoing like that, like there's more than one person in there—and his mannerism and word choice, no, he's nothing like Dad.

I slip downstairs, tiptoeing as if I was walking on rice paper, not making the smallest of sounds, and take minutes to slowly open the door. I can't wake up Mom. Once outside I slip into the backyard heading for the edge of the woods, my nightgown blowing in the breeze as night air raises goose bumps on my legs. I pause at the edge of the woods, wondering how I somehow knew to come this way, blackness before me, night sounds in my ears, crickets, owls and who-knows-whats making all sorts of sounds. I look back at the solitary lamp on the back of the short row of town-homes, a light indicating civilization, order, decency and normalcy, a light indicating how life is supposed to be, a light indicating my lonely life without Michael, Cyndi, Sidney, or even that nut I was going to marry, Kyle, a life all alone. I turn back towards the dark woods, staring into the blackness, the frightening unknown, the pitch-black insanity of thinking and believing that maybe the disembodied spirit of my dead father is somehow looking out for me, calling to me, in my dreams, calling me into the blackness of these creepy woods full of invisible animals making nighttime sounds, the insanity that the Void-man and I are somehow linked and that he wants to help me get through all the rough spots in my life, the insanity that anyone at all cares about me. You aren't actually going into those woods are you, Gabby? It was just another one of your stupid dreams, Girl!

The stillness of the back yard is unmoving and silent as I say out loud, "I can't believe I'm gonna do this," then turn toward the blackness and step in. Nervous and goose bumpy, I gingerly step over piles of twigs and small branches trying to keep to the soft, wet leaves and not make the smallest of sounds, trying to not snap the twigs as if doing so would alert some fierce predator of my presence.

"Hey, hey, hey, hey."

What was that? I turn and turn and turn looking for the source of the voice and all I hear is crickets and owls and all manner of creeping things. Was that a voice? Gabby, don't lose it now.

My eyes are adjusting, slowly, and I can see a little but everything is in black and white. Michael once gave me a ten-minute dissertation on how human eyes have two different types of photoreceptors, cones and rods and one is used for seeing color, I forget which, and the other black and white, and the color ones need more light to function and that's why when it gets really dark we can still see but we can't see in color, just in black and white and shades of gray. I am so happy for cones right now. Or is it rods?

There is a small clearing just ahead so I squat down behind a bush suddenly feeling nervous about stepping into the open, as if I am somehow more safe behind a little bush. I hope there's no poison ivy here. The black spot itches and I unconsciously find my hand on it, caressing it, and the flesh is raised again. Is there something out there? Is that why the black spot is bothering me? Michael would say that endorphins and cortisol are running through my brain and my blood stream and maybe the black spot is simply another reaction to how I'm feeling, just another psycho-somatic reaction. I can't believe his voice is so in my head. Gabby, you have to forget about him. I love him, yes, that's true, but that's just not enough. I can't have him.

Stupid black spot. I wish it would just go away. I wish it wouldn't itch so much. Spidey-sense? A reaction to my own body? Maybe it's a sickness, a Void disease. Maybe.

I can't believe I'm doing this! I can barely see the back of my house through the dense vegetation. Actually I can't see the house at all, just the rear light filtering through the leaves. Well, I know about where it is anyway.

Void-man? Where are you? I can't believe I'm doing this! It's three AM and I've got two tests tomorrow. Donavan is probably going to run us into the ground for losing and with Elektra out, at least for a few days anyway, it's going to be rough.

"Hey, hey, hey, hey."

Not that voice again. A dim blue glow fades just behind a fallen tree. There. What's that? The Void-man said I would know where I am when I find out where I am or something like that. I hate riddles and I *don't* know where I am *or* where I'm supposed to go.

The blue fades. The woods seem unnaturally quiet. Standing up and moving from behind the little bush, soreness briefly reminds me of yesterday's game. I clench my fists and shakily step into the clearing wishing there was just a little more cover. I prance to the fallen tree, peer over and spy the blue glow about thirty feet away fading between two tightly-spaced trees. I leap the fallen tree and dash toward them.

The black spot burns, itches and fires lightning down my back, my goose-flesh tingling and bumpy with fear, me not knowing where I want to run to first, toward the bluish-white glow and maybe some answers or towards the lamp glowing in our back yard.

There are pricker weed patches on either side of the two trees so I have to squeeze myself between them and just as I pass through the blue glow seems to fade away.

"That's great," I mutter and slowly spin around looking for where it might have gone when I realize that I can't see our backyard light anymore. A shudder tenses my shoulders. My watch says 3:20AM.

"Great, I have to get up in a few hours. Gabby, what are you doing out here?"

Then I realize that the fallen tree I just leapt over is gone and a slight dizziness grips my mind quick, hard and fast. Turning around slowly, looking every which way, slowly, turning around, turning around, turning around, every which way, things are different, I realize, different, different, different.

"Hey, hey, hey, hey."

A soft breeze caresses my check, softly, slowly, as I pause, stop and stand. Confused, I listen. Where? No. What? Then suddenly, jasmine, the smell of jasmine, all around me, and—is that? It is. Cloves, the smell of cloves wafting in and around me on the breeze, the soft, soft breeze. Turning around, turning around, looking, listening—this can't be happening—I can't be lost, can't be lost; I can't think. I can't stop the hoots in my ears as I turn, lost. No. No. I stop and pause. Breathe. Breathe. Breathe. Slowly, slowly, I turn, stop. Look. Turn. Stop. Look. Turn. What's happening? Where?

"Aaarrgghh!" Something touches my shoulder and

I leap back and turn, ready to run, ready to fight, ready to die in an all-out blaze of glorious punches, fists, arms, elbows and head butts when I realize it is him. It is the Void-man.

It's him! It's him! He is really here!

Standing in front of me, right there, just there, blue glow and all.

It's him. I don't know how he did it, how he escaped the Void, but it's really him standing there.

Or I am just going crazy.

Trying to shake away the nausea, trying to shake away the fear, the fright, the goose flesh and the cold sweat, swaying back and forth in the tree filtered moonlight; I finally, fearfully open my mouth, hoping that he is really, really there because I am so totally afraid that he is not. "Look... Okay... Just don't fly away... Okay? Don't leave me right now... because I am so freaking out. Okay?"

That didn't come out the way I wanted and he is just standing there, staring at me, looking like my dad, a blue glowing version of my dad, a spirit-like, ghost version of him with a completely blank, expressionless face.

"I... I just—" I stammer, then let loose in a flurry, trying to get it all out before he escapes, "I need to know who you are. I mean, I *want* to know. Are you my dad? Why do you look like him? You don't act like him. And how did you get out of the Void? Did you come from there? And why can I see you? Can everyone see you? Were you in my dream? Why do you keep coming to me? And Kyle? Where is he? Is he still in the Void? Are you locked out of the Void? Can you just please tell me something? Anything? Please, please, please I really, really need some answers so I can stop feeling like I am going crazy!"

I stop with a huff looking up into his face, my dead father's face, restored and young, like he was when he was in his twenties, when Mom first met him, long before I was born. He was so good looking and I never realized it.

"Listen." His voice is so loud that I think it would shatter windows if we weren't in the woods. It pulses through me.

I stare up at him for a good minute. Impatient that he hasn't said anything, I start again, "I just—"

He holds his hand up so I stop myself from speaking. He slowly lowers his arm and another long minute passes then he opens his mouth and recites, "You will find a partner in the place that you least expect it, in the lowest of lows, but it brings you to the highest of highs."

The words they shake through me, oddly, like waves. They have a quasi-periodic rhythm and somehow the reverberating pulsations of his voice cause the words to ring in my ears.

He pauses, staring at me, then continues, "There is a one who is a friend who would destroy you. You watch whom he follows and who follows him. He is not what he seems but you are not deceived. No, not deceived by the bouncing numbers or the shaded letters or the shaking digits or the random dots. He will chase you and chase you but you will hide very well, and it is your ability to hide that will allow you to hide your deepest of secrets."

Again he stops and stares.

I open my mouth, me shaking and sweating under the relentless barrage pounding through me, but before I can interrupt he holds out his hand and adds, "In this time of trouble, you will look deep. You will think hard. You will look down deeply and you will find strength within yourself. You will fight for it as a small sparrow, a sparrow that will become a mighty hawk."

He speaks these words, me barely able to breathe as each word shakes through me, shock-waves punching me in the gut over and over like an endless stream of North Shore waves pummeling a twisting, lost surfer who finally, thankfully, finds herself washed up on yellow sands, face down.

He says, "Above all and in the end, things cannot be as you would like and a supreme sacrifice you will have to make. A choice, a choice, a choice. It is yours to decide."

I falter, bending down to one knee. It's too much. In my head. Somehow, someway his words are rattling through me, in me, through my very spirit and my very being, as if they are somehow racing around inside of me, looking for a resting place, finding a place to adhere themselves to, bonding, becoming a part of me, like the childhood memory when I fell off my tricycle and dad ran to me and scooped me up, I can never, ever forget it. Shock-waves, pummeling me, echoing through my heart, my mind, my spirit, pulse over and over. I'm down on one knee, hand on the ground, eyes clenched down tight then, suddenly, it's over. I open my eyes and it's over. I open my eyes and—No way!—I am back in my bed! Nausea blankets my stomach as I roll over and look at the clock: 2:59 AM.

Sobbing, painfully, I think—I don't want to think —but I have to. I have to admit that it could have been just a dream. Another stupid dream! Not another stupid dream! No. No. No. That was just too real. It can't be… I don't want to think right now. It hurts too much. I don't want to think about anything.

But his words are still echoing inside of me. They are a part of me now.

Chapter 6

Freedom Finally

My eyes slowly peel open after a long restful slumber. Weekends, weekends, I love weekends! It is so scrumptious to sleep in. I love it! And especially after this week. It has been such a terror, what with the intense Ultraball training and competition schedule; three tests at school including Chemistry and UNA History on the same day—I got an A, yeah! —and a B, bummer! —having to deal with Elektra's injury and subsequently finding out that she will be out for several weeks; being told we will have to deal with her potential replacements; mentally preparing for their new egos and whatever baggage they carry around and that crazy dream-slash-mystery night-time experience with the Void-man and his cryptic message that I can't stop thinking about, can't forget and can't understand even a little bit.

Yes, thank God for weekends.

Slowly unearthing myself from my bed, slowly, slowly, rolling out from under the blankets slowly, I get up, clean up, and slide down the steps, trying to pick up my feet as little as possible, my fuzzy bunny slippers barely scraping the tufts of the carpet, only cracking my eyes open enough to skillfully guide my body down the stairs.

I slump down into the dining room chair next to Mom, her staring out into the backyard woods, like she always does when she has some deep thoughts that she doesn't know how to deal with, then she says, "I heard from Archibald this morning."

My ears perk up. Archibald? I never call him that. Sounds too weird. "So how *is* Dr. Duggan?"

"Fine... considering."

Considering he lost his entire life's work because of me. Once the news got out, Princeton shut down his lab. He lost all his funding. Thirty years work gone in one day. No knowing how it all ends. No knowing what went wrong. No knowing anything. Everything. Just. Gone.

"Yeah, considering," I say.

She looks back at me then shallowly smiles. There is no condemnation in her eyes, maybe a desire that things happened differently, but on her face it is obvious she has been down this road of mistakes, lost opportunities and disappointments before. She's never told me any of the stories of course—but she can't hide the look on her face.

"He's starting it back up."

"What? What do you mean?" I ask.

Mom takes a sip of coffee then replies, "He told me he got permission. Strict controls, of course. Just one operation as far as I know."

"When?"

"Today actually."

I leap up, howling, "I gotta go!" while running upstairs to change. Stopping halfway up the stairs, I turn and yell out, "Mom! Can you give me a ride?"

"W-Why?"

"Kyle?" I say as if it is so obvious I can't believe I have to say it.

She exhales, puts her hands on her knees and pushes up creakily. "Okay, let's go see."

We hustle up to get dressed and then to the car but Mom won't move fast enough.

"Mom! Let's go!" I whine.

We get in the car and Mom slowly puts on her seat belt, checks that her mirror is straight, adjusts her seat, checks her mirror again, checks her seat-belt again, checks her mirror again, then slowly looks over at me and says, "Ready to go?"

"Mom!"

Head tilted, she says, "Gabby, we'll get there but you have to put on your seat-belt."

I concede then fold my arms in my lap and look at the floor. If I hadn't lost my permit I wouldn't be held hostage like this. Mom's proving a point but I don't have to like it.

She backs out of the driveway and mashes the screen button as she puts the drive controls in forward and quickly selects Princeton's Particle Physics Laboratory, Dr. Duggan's lab and the home of the dimensional transport machine. One half of it anyway, the other is in Portugal.

Mom presses on the screen again as she powers onto the highway and Dr. Duggan's voice comes over the speakers, "Yes?"

"Archibald, we are on our way to your lab," mom says.

"Shenanigans. Now is not the best time. What seems to be the problem?"

"Gabby?" Mom waves her hand at me.

"Dr. Duggan? This is Gabriella."

"It's aaahh… nice to hear your voice." He sounds flustered. I know I am certainly distracting him. "What seems to be the problem?"

"I understand that you are starting up the

machine?"

"Shenanigans. Why do you need to know?"

I reply, "It's Kyle. If you were to start up the machine... We never found him, I mean he never came out—as far as I know—and—"

He interrupts me, "Yes, my dear. We are well aware of that and we have the situation under complete control. Is that all?"

"Yes, Dr. Duggan."

The screen connection terminates.

Mom leans the car toward the exit and says, "We can go home?"

"We're almost there. Can we just stop in for a minute?"

"It didn't sound like he wanted us there," mom says.

"Pleeease?" I am getting way too old to be pulling my little girl voice and Mom knows it but she doesn't turn off the highway.

As we get closer to the lab I breach another one of the subjects that mom never seems to want to talk about. "Duggan was an old friend of the family who used to work with Dad, right?"

She answers, "Not exactly. They didn't actually work together. They shared space at the University and their projects were in the same building. But that was a long time ago."

"Yeah," I say pensively.

"Feels like centuries ago. Feels like we were different people back then. So long ago. Before we moved to South America, long before the war, long before a lot of things."

"Must have been strange seeing him here. In UNA."

"Oh, but he hasn't changed. No, not one bit," Mom replies.

I say, "I thought he was a kook when he came to the house and the way he was sales pitching his 'new invention'."

"I think he came on too strong. He always has been the type to get really excited when he talks about his work."

"To be honest—wow, I didn't know I was going to say this—to be honest, I was kind of depressed at the time—although I would *never* admit that to anyone else —and you thought it was a great idea. I guess you thought it would get me out of the house so I would stop moping around?"

Mom glances at me then says, "You're a mind reader. You needed something to focus on and hey, why not? I thought you might be able to make some money at it too. And from a friend of the family no less. Someone we could trust."

"The only reason he came to me and offered me the chance was because of that stupid article in *Sports Illustrated*, right? You didn't have anything to do with it, did you?" I question.

"No, I think it was just the article. I didn't tell him to ask you."

Looking down at my feet, I feel like opening up more. It's not like me at all, but I continue, "At the time I hated that article. Funny too, when I think of it. It was that stupid article that, in a way, got my leg busted. It was that article, calling me *The Unmodified Girl* that turned the rest of the team against me, that turned the rest of the league against me, really. It put a huge bull's eye on my back. It was the article that got me injured and at the same time the article that got Dr. Duggan calling and the article that got me into his machine. Weird right?"

"Yeah."

I look up and say, "It was the article that got me in that machine and got me to Portugal."

"Don't remind me." Mom scowls.

"I know. I don't know what I was thinking. I took the chance. I did it. I went into his crazy machine. It was the article that got me into the crazy dimensional transport machine, into the Void and somehow got my leg healed. In a way, I lost my running because of the article and I got it back because of the article. The article, that stupid, wonderful article in *Sports Illustrated*."

Mom smirks. "Gabby, sometimes I think you link things together that have nothing to do with each other."

I look over at her as she drives. "I know, you don't think that the machine healed my leg."

"No, I'm not convinced but that's okay."

The car turns onto the tree-shaded lane, past the big white sign and up to the front of the nondescript concrete building, then we park. There are three police cruisers in the lot along with about ten other cars, more than I have ever seen in this lot back when I used to come here and certainly something serious is going on. I cautiously exit the car and Mom says, "Be quick. I am going to wait here," and she pulls up a screen game.

I enter the quiet building and scale the staircase. At the top floor several people are in the hall and they stop talking and look at my face and stare. As I reach for the door handle to Dr. Duggan's lab, a woman with black hair, maybe in her thirty's, says, "What do you think you are doing?"

"I need to see Dr. Duggan. I'm Gabriella Con—"

Before I can finish she clips my words in the air. "We *know* who you are. You *shouldn't* be here."

The others step closer. They were probably working with Dr. Duggan, grad students maybe, people who lost a great opportunity to do revolutionary science because of me, people who are currently not too happy to see me. I am getting really uncomfortable as they circle me and to defuse the situation I blurt out, "Look! I'm sorry about what happened but it wasn't my fault! It was Kyle."

A blonde behind me quickly squeals, "Typical! Not your fault! That's how all you celebrity types take it. You screw everything up and nothing's your fault. We should have never let you in here in the first place!"

Dr. Duggan opens the door and utters, "Shenanigans! What's this racket out here? We are about to begin. Oh you, Gabriella. What are you doing here?"

"Kyle? I wanted to talk to you about Kyle."

"Yes, we know. We have everything under control," Dr. Duggan says deliberately and allows the door to ease open revealing about ten police officers just inside along with a large staff of young-looking grad students at the controls. He looks back at his staff, back to me, frowns a moment, then mutters, "Shenanigans, you can come in. But stand in the back and DON'T SAY ANYTHING."

Ignoring the hallway crowd's laser-beam stares I enter the room and head toward the rear of the room, pressing my back against the plaster wall next to a metal bar bolted to the floor and feel very, very small and mouse-like. Everyone in this room hates me, I think, everyone except the police officers and they are probably just indifferent, just doing their assigned job for the day. They have probably been briefed but surely they have absolutely no idea what is really about to happen.

Dr. Duggan checks off items on his screen as various status calls are hollered out by the technicians.

The room looks dusty. It certainly hasn't been occupied in a while and a large pile of white sheets sits bundled in the corner. The metal ring, the gateway into the Void, sits on the far end of the room. Control elements, hundreds of them, border the outside of the ring. The devices have wires and tiny hoses that come out of their tops and are neatly bundled together with tie-wraps every few feet then routed along the edge of the floor near the wall and down the entire length of the room and over to breakout boxes which have wire bundles coming out of them and tied into the backs of the workstations that the grad students are monitoring. Most of it is cleanly wired and routed but it looks like equipment that the students put together. Another reason they must hate me. It's not like they just worked here. They *made* this stuff!

Duggan strolls over to the police officers and gives them some instructions that I can't hear but I don't have to because I know what comes next. They are about to start up the machine and the room is about to become real crazy. Duggan steps away and announces that final countdown will be within minutes. The officers look at each other and smile nervously and a few of them start looking around and jockeying for position next to the large metal poles. No one comes over to share my pole and I feel diseased.

Several of the grad students leave the room and the remaining ones, the ones behind the workstations, buckle themselves down into their chairs. Duggan takes a seat and straps himself in then looks back. The lead officer nods then Duggan's gaze moves over to me. He has a disappointed look on his face. I thought he would be excited to start the machine again but I suddenly realize that this is another reminder of what he lost. I nod.

He looks away, slowly, eyes toward the large, towering, metal ring and says for one last time, "Initiate!"

The grad students push buttons and mutter to each other over their ear-pieces. A whooshing sound permeates the air, making hearing anything else nearly impossible. I brace myself hard in the corner, both hands on my pole, and the police officers wrap their arms and hands around theirs. The ring pulses neon blue, sputtering initially as the controls on the ring clatter, then suddenly, the neon blue grows much brighter and a stiff wind sucks the air from the room throwing papers up and filling the air with all the loose dirt and stray particles in the room making it feel like we are in the middle of a Kansas dust bowl. Everyone's eyes are glued to the center of the ring and it's neon blue glow, the grad students, the police, me and Dr. Duggan, waiting expectantly for something to happen. The dust and papers begin to settle back down. We stare and wait. A few minutes pass and nothing happens. A few more minutes pass then Dr. Duggan, seemingly perturbed, announces, "Get the chair ready!"

The transport chair module is rolled out onto the tracks leading up to the ring by two students who are fighting to not be sucked closer to the neon blue glow at the center of the ring. It appears to be quite difficult work setting up the chair and I wonder why they didn't do it beforehand. It was the same chair that I rode on so long ago and it still has the seat belt that was later added to prevent people from intentionally leaving the chair and jumping off into the Void, people like Gabriella Conceição who ruined everything.

Just as the chair module appears ready to be sent into the Void a dark figure appears in the center of the blue. Duggan holds his hand up signaling for the students to wait then the figure grows closer, more defined and less fuzzy, a jet-black apparition, standing in the center of the ring. Stepping through the ring, the figure is suddenly launched through the dimensional gate, bounding through the air, across the length of the room, tumbling across the floor and striking one of the metal tracks with the side of his head. He's knocked unconscious and even though I knew who it would be, the only person it could be, I am still in a state of shock looking at his face. It's Kyle.

Duggan howls, "Shut it down!"

The students smash buttons. The blue glow, the wind and the howling noise die down. The police officers ease their grips on the long metal poles and quickly scoop up Kyle and drag him out of the room as the chief calls out a quick report on his screen.

I follow them out as close as I can and for some reason I feel like I have to get closer to Kyle. I have to see his face. I need to be next to him. The black spot is smoldering like a large warm hand on the back of my neck rubbing softly, slowly, massaging deep, deep, oh so deep and it feels oh so very, very good. I have to get next to him! I don't know why but it is suddenly just so obvious. I just know it.

They drag him outside, cuff him and prop him up against a railing. Apparently they are waiting for an ambulance. I stand as close as I can and I can't stop looking at him. I know the black spot is drawing me closer to him. What I want to know is why. There is no way I am going back to him. Never! But what I want, what I really, really want is to know what he did to me. What is this black spot? Why does it make me feel so weird? How do I get rid of it?

Kyle looks a little older and certainly haggard. Very haggard, actually. Worn. He was in that Void for months and since time moves much slower in the Void, that could have felt like years, maybe tens of years. Wow. Michael told me once that a person could go crazy in there like that. I wish I could pity him but really I don't. Maybe someday, but today all I want is answers. Well, I kind of want to punch him too but for now answers will do.

The ambulance pulls down the lane, lights blaring and stops at the building steps, the police chief waving at them to drive up. They smartly exit, open their rear doors and pull out a gurney and wheel it over to Kyle. They place him on it and strap him in as the chief speaks to one of the paramedics. The second paramedic waves something in front of Kyle's face and he suddenly bolts up. Several of the officers step back and place their hands on their gun holsters.

Kyle's eyes quickly dart around at the officers, the paramedics, down at the straps holding him down then he relaxes like air being released from a balloon. His eyes turn toward me and I know I need to be at the side of that gurney—now!

It is all I can do to repress the urge to run to him. Adrenaline is coursing through my veins and my heart is pumping hard and fast, harder and faster than at the peak of my pre-race warm up when I am so totally focused on exactly what I am going to do in a race. I know this feeling well but it is so much stronger! Bang! Bang! Bang! My heart is slamming hard and I want to run to him! I stand and begin to slowly walk, using every ounce of my effort to hold myself back, hoping no one will notice my movements. I glance over at our car and mom seated inside and she is watching me, her mouth slightly open, probably wondering what I am about to do.

As I reach the rear of the ambulance, me being drawn, a fish on a hook, dazed and hypnotized, an officer turns to me and says, "Hey! Where do you think you are going?"

Desperately I say, "Hi! I'm Gabriella Con—"

"We *know* who you are. Now move along."

"Please, I… Please, I just really need to talk—"

"Sorry, Miss. There will be no talking today. Now move along." The officer stretches out his arm as a barricade and I so want to leap over it. It would be child's play.

I can see Kyle, barely, through the wall of officers. He is only about three meters away but he may as well be still in the Void because there is no way I can reach him without doing something that I will totally regret.

The officer motions toward the edge of the building, saying, "Just stand over there."

I feel the black spot burning stronger and a feeling of anguish courses through me as an uncontrollable deep frown appears on my face.

Then I hear something wonderful! Kyle's voice! He clears his throat as if it is the first time he is about to speak in a very, very long time and says loudly but plainly and clearly, as if he is teaching a lesson to a small child, "Gabriella, you are a part of me. I am a part of you and we are all a part of this great nothingness. None of this exists. It's all an illusion. A dream. And your acceptance of that fact will be the beginning of your journey on the path." He then promptly lays his head back down and closes his eyes and I am left standing there with my mouth open.

The burning coming from the black spot dissipates

along with my desire to be next to Kyle as if I just pushed away from a very satisfying meal.

I watch as they load him into the ambulance and the motorcade files out of the lot then I drift back over to Mom's car, get in, buckle up and wait for the long series of Mom questions on the return trip home.

Mom waits until we are on the highway, mercifully giving me a few minutes to collect my thoughts, then says, "So—"

"So," I reply and then pause for a few moments knowing that it is a waste of effort to make her ask specific questions at this point. "So, they started up the machine. The police were waiting for Kyle. As soon as he came through they shut it down and everyone left."

"It looked like Kyle said something to you there."

"Yeah, he did. Some mumbo-jumbo about the world being an illusion? I don't know. It was all gibberish. I think he lost it in there."

"Huh? Do you remember what he said exactly?" Mom asks.

"Why?"

"I don't know. Just curious. No reason really."

"It was something like, 'Nothing exists?' Something like, 'Everything is a dream.' Uuuh, 'an illusion?' That's what he said, 'an illusion,' and then something about being on a path or something like that." I intentionally leave out the part about us being connected of course because no way do I want to talk about that.

"That *is* weird. Nothing exists, huh? I guess he did fall off his rocker in there. Maybe he hit his head?"

I respond, "He did hit his head but I don't know if that had anything to do with it."

Mom drives for a bit longer then continues, "Sad

too. I *did* like that boy."

"What? Mom! He was a psycho!"

"I know. But before all that. Before we found out he was a psycho. I liked him back then. He was such a nice boy. Too bad he had to go and turn into a psycho."

"Mom! He didn't *turn into* a psycho. He *was* a psycho. People don't go from being perfectly normal one day to being total psychopaths the next. He was crazy the entire time. We just didn't know it because he was such a good liar."

"I know, I know, Gabby. I'm just saying that I liked him before all that, that's all."

I obviously can't argue with that sort of nonsense so I let the car grow quiet.

Mom lets go of her dreamy eyed daze full of images of me being married and her arms full of grand-children and changes the subject, "You know Smith told me that Kyle would probably come out of there pretty crazy?"

"Well, he was crazy when he went in and he came out even crazier."

"Kind of the reason why I thought coming here would be a waste of time. Smith said we shouldn't bother listening to anything Kyle said anyway."

"For once I agree with him."

"By the way, Smith and I are going out tonight so you are on your own for dinner, okay?"

"Sure." Unfortunately I have gotten used to being alone even when I'm surrounded by people. It is starting to feel all too natural. "Where's he taking you?"

"Not sure but someplace nice, I hope. It's our anniversary."

"What? Anniversary of what?" I pivot in my chair toward her.

"He doesn't know anything. Don't tell him, okay? I want to see if he knows but today is one year since we met here in UNA."

"Sure, I won't say anything." Anniversary? I really don't care for Smith. He has too many secrets and I still don't entirely believe that he is interested in my mom for no other reason than her companionship. He's after something; I know it. "You two are growing close then?"

"No, just friends—for now." Mom smiles but I do not join her.

"Mom, I don't know how I feel about all this."

"Oh, Smith will never take your father's place. You know that."

"I know, it's just some things that happened, some things that Kyle said. I've never told you and I just—I just don't trust Smith."

"Gabby! You can't blame Smith for what happened with Kyle."

"No? According to Kyle, Kyle was simply Smith's pawn and maybe that's not true but who knows?"

"He said that? I wouldn't believe a word that boy said."

"In any case, on several occasions I spied both Smith and Kyle trying to get small pieces of my DNA, lip prints off cups that I had used, strands of hair and who knows what else they went for."

"Smith did that? Why didn't you tell me?"

"I, I don't know."

"Harmless though, right? He's just a geneticist. Maybe he wants to know more about you. Hey, maybe he can help you with your performance, your running?"

"I guess. But it *is* my DNA. He shouldn't just take it like that."

"True. But I don't think he would do anything—"

I interrupt her. "Kyle told me that Smith thought that Dad actually created me in the lab."

"Why are you still listening to anything that boy said? I can't believe that he said that! That's low. I told you before, you were born the old fashioned way."

"I remember. But it would make Smith wonder, I'm sure. I mean, it makes me wonder too. I am the only girl in the entire league that's unmodified and that's the only reason anyone knows my name. There isn't any reason that anyone should know my name—even the locals—any reason except for the fact that I have unmodified DNA. The modder companies must hate me, NuGen especially, since I blow a hole right through their sales pitch that being modified is somehow the only path to greatness. I must be costing them lots of money."

"True, but I don't think Smith would—"

"On the other hand, I have my doubts myself. What if it's true? What if somehow Dad did modify me without you knowing? Okay, maybe Kyle made it all up and Smith didn't say it, but what if I *am* the Holy Grail, the untraceable modification? What if Dad did cook me in the lab? You said you were sick a few weeks before your pregnancy and that Dad was by your side every day in the hospital. What if he did something to you then? If I'm modified but untraceable then there would be no modification fingerprints and my DNA would appear to be unaltered. No one would know. No one but dad and he's dead."

"Gabby? Are you serious? This is just such a conspiracy theory and this is so not like you."

"I know, but I still can't trust Smith. I bet he would love to run some of his nutty experiments on me. Who knows? Sometimes I think—"

"What?"

I regret saying anything. "Forget it. I'm just going crazy. Maybe it's the stress of the game."

"Tell me."

"Just don't get mad."

"I won't. Tell me," mom says.

"Sometimes I think Smith doesn't care about you or me; he just wants to solve this riddle. Sometimes I think that he's only dating you to get access to me. That we are simply a means to an end and as soon as he gets what he wants, he's outta here. I know it sounds crazy. It sounds crazy to my own ears and I can't believe I am saying it. I just hope he doesn't hurt you in the process."

"Oh, Gabby. You know I'm a big girl. I can handle myself. And this crazy stuff Kyle filled up your head with, don't think about it for another minute. Let me talk to Smith. I'll find out."

"But—"

"Oh, don't you worry. He won't know what hit him. I'll have him spilling his guts and he won't even know he's doing it. I don't think it's what you said, but if it is, I'll find out."

Chapter 7

Friends No More

I exit the car and Mom drives off as I stroll through the training center parking garage. I swing my duffel over to my right shoulder and pass-code into the team entrance then trudge through the dingy, sparsely lit hall. Just before I enter the team locker room I overhear Cyndi and Sidney laughing loudly through the door. I don't have to be psychic to know what will happen as soon as I open it but it can't be avoided. I pass-code in and they both turn, look at me and instantly lose their smiles. Cyndi turns toward her locker and busies herself; Sidney walks out.

I open my locker then look around the open door to make sure she is still there and that we are all alone. "Cyndi?" I say as I stare at the contents of my locker; soap, shampoo, deodorant, a towel and a picture of Michael.

She moves some stuff around in her locker as she ignores me.

I step out from the shelter of my locker door and look at her. "Cyndi?" I try to make my voice sound soft and soothing without it sounding too pleading, even though I would have no problem begging. I just don't think sounding like that would help.

She closes her locker and readies herself for training, matting down her shorts and flexing her leg muscles as if I am not even there.

"Cyndi? I just want to talk. To explain what

happened."

In a flurry she launches herself at me screaming, "FOR WHAT? So you can tell me you're sorry? So you can tell me he tricked you? You KNEW and you LIED! There's nothing for you to say to me! EVER!" Wet spittle is on her lips and I can see the strain in her little forehead and neck.

I recoil, not knowing how to respond, but I know I can't give up now. "Please. Just give me a chance—"

She sneers, turns, slams her locker, grabs her bag and quickly exits.

I open my locker and thrust my head against the hinge of the door. Gabby, get a hold of yourself. What did you expect? It's all true. You lied to your best friend. You are going to have to eat that.

I consciously stop myself from hyperventilating and change my clothes. I clean my red eyes and try to make it look like I just didn't get verbally smashed in the face and then head for the field entrance when Donavan steps out of her office and says, "Stay right there, Gabby. I am going to call a meeting."

A few minutes later the rest of the girls enter, Cyndi and Sidney, Max, Qi and Nomi. They congregate toward the other side of the locker area which makes me seem all the more like a pariah then Donavan steps out of her office along with two of the team staff, Jerry and Mr. Lyttle, and three girls that I haven't seen before. Donavan bellows, "All right! Real quick here! I just wanted to get you all together for a few words before today's practice. First off, I appreciate that all of you have been putting in all of your required training and for the NuGen girls that you have been meeting your performance and effort targets. All your numbers look real good! Of course that doesn't win games but at least it keeps these two goons off my back!"

Jerry interrupts with a chuckle, "That's right! Hahaha." His toothpaste-commercial smile broadens. "But we are going to win right? Hahaha. We have confidence in all of you girls and with one more win needed to cement our spot in the playoffs we feel real good about this lineup."

Lyttle just stands there taking up space. He is enormous.

It is clear that Donavan doesn't like Jerry or Lyttle or much of the front office staff but she gives them space and when it is obvious they have no more to say, she continues, "Okay! An update on Elektra! Looks like she might be out a few more weeks than we thought so with us so close to playoffs a decision was made to pull up some girls from our feeders. We talked about this a few days ago. So here they are!" She motions toward the three new girls then says, "Girls! Introduce yourselves to the team!"

A young thin girl, about my age and clearly a sprinter, holds her hand up and waves it bashfully then says in a high-pitched nasally, little-girlish voice, "Hi everyone! My name is Cassandra? Cassandra Stone? You can call me Sandy? Err... Please don't call me Sandstone?" She raises her voice at the end of every sentence as if she is asking a question and she enunciates every syllable discreetly like they are separate words, saying, "Sand—Dee," not, "Sandy."

She continues, "I ran for Chestnut Hill Academy? Well at least I did up until today. I am still in high school? Ob-Vis. And I'm so glad to be trying out for the team?" She ends with a giggle and since no one shares it she quickly loses her smile and steps back.

The next girl is clearly an enforcer which is weird

since Elektra was a sprinter and our strategy mainly involves being quick and fast and the team's only pure enforcer is Maxine. The new girl says, "My name is Greta. Some of you might remember me. I ran for Germany for the last six months of last season but they let me go when they decided to reduce their enforcers and pick up some sprinters. No problems, I got married and we moved to Philadelphia for my husband's work. Now that we are settled in, I am looking for another crack at it."

The final girl exudes confidence and it's as if the air changes around her when she speaks. "I'm Mercury. Mercury Jackson. I ran for RU, ahh, Rutgers University for those who don't know, not far from here, and will graduate this semester. The college season just ended so I'm in peak condition and ready to fly for the Freedom."

Donavan howls, "I determine who *is* and *is not* in peak condition! And don't worry! If you can't hold your own, all three of you, you're gone! Now for the rest of you girls you might be wondering, 'Why do we have three new girls?' and so here's the answer! The front office is contemplating some changes, especially after our poor showing in the Sacramento game and this is the result. One of these three is going to fill in for Elektra, at least until she comes back, but now here's the rub, when she does come back she is going to have to compete for her spot. And for the rest for you, I don't want you all to lie back either! The front office is thinking of some changes and that may involve some of you all too! If you can't pull your weight, you're gone! Everyone got that?"

We all nod and Donavan continues, "Now I'm sure you new girls know the rules and how we play but just in case you forgot to do some research on our team, listen up! Each team has a total of seven runners and we can run any combination we want in the two races, even the same runner twice, but only seven may run and only the first three across the finish line score in each race. Same as in high school and college. And of course the men's field team score adds in also which can make winning pretty unpredictable. And if you didn't know it, I don't like unpredictability! Right?"

We all reply, "Right, Coach!"

"Another thing. each of you, I am sure, wants to move up to the pros so you might find it weird that you are stuck in this cooperation-competition relationship. You want to be the next to move up so you're all competing against one another for that spot and trying to best each other. Yet at the same time you are all on the same team and should be trying to help each other win. Let me tell you, if I see that you are playing for yourself at the expense of the team... Cassandra, tell the team what you think will happen?"

"You're gone?"

"It's not a question! You're gone! That's all! Now let's hit the field!"

Donavan, Jerry and Lyttle file out. The look on the rest of the team's faces tells me that they all wouldn't mind it one bit if I got bumped off the team by one of these three sharks. The nine of us leave the locker room and file up through the long hall to the practice field. Sandstone squeals, "Ooohh, here we are! Here we are! I can't believe I am actually here! This is so-o-o cool!" She spins around looking at the field, the course and the stands.

Mercury quickly separates herself from the rest of the team and launches into a brisk warm-up run and she already looks fast. Several of the front office staff are in the stands scribbling notes on their screens which is odd since they almost never come to practice. The rest of the team slowly casts a wary eye at the stands and a realization overtakes them. They're going to rank us.

We are unnaturally quiet during the warm-up, everyone lost in too many thoughts to engage in idle chitchat. After the warm-up, Mercury finds a bench in front of the front office white-shirts and dramatically strips off her warm-up sweats—there is no way she could make that look spontaneous.

Sidney mumbles, "I am going to grind her into the earth."

Sandstone comments to no one in particular, "Wow! It is really *hot* in here!" And she is right although I didn't pick up on it until she said it. There is condensation on the glass and it is steamy in here. The front office guy's white shirts are starting to stick to their bodies and they look none too happy.

Donavan huffs then motions at one of the trainers who steps forward and says, "Good eye! Something new we are trying. We got our hands on some new research out of the University that indicates that low intensity training under high temperatures for consecutive days, err, say ten days or so—can increase speed by as much as 8%. It mimics high altitude training with much more predictability and without the hassle of having to fly out to Colorado. Of course that was a study using untrained, err, so-called 'normal' people, and err, you all are in peak conditioning, ahh, but we felt that if we could get a performance gain of even one half to one percent that it might be worth the effort so, ahh, what we are going to do is try to hold all of your body temperatures at least at —let me check here—100.5 degrees for at least one hour then gradually increase the time duration and then, ahh

—"

Donavan slices his words in the air. "Okay already! Enough talk! You girls are going to run in the heat! All right? Enough said!"

Donavan turns and points up at the stands and barks, "We're going to run a mock race for the *judges!*" She makes quote symbol motions with her fingers and we all know exactly who she is referring to.

No teamwork, it will be an all-out sprint with nine girls on the field. She gives Qi and Max and the new girl Greta the option of being enforcers and if they can take out the first few fastest they will be credited with points. The start line is thick with bodies and today there are no friends, no teammates and no breaks; it is an all-out war. My body trembles as a vision of my first major try-out in Brazil flashes through my mind. We nine are lined up where normally there would be six or seven or rarely, eight. Everyone knows the start will be key and we are all leaning deep, shaking our dripping shoulders, trying to stay loose.

The race goes quick and fast and us "old-timers" definitely have an edge on the new girls because they rarely change the obstacles on our practice field. Sidney is way out in front, followed by Cyndi then me but Mercury seems to be doing quite well as she is on my heels and I suddenly want to beat her more than anything.

I can't let her pass me!

Nomi is there and Sandstone too. But Mercury, no, I must beat her.

Then it happens. I let it happen. I want it to happen. I become the run. I am the run. The run and I are one. There is no more Gabriella. There is no more self. All that is left is the run. A frantic dis-association from my body? An over-concentration on every move? I don't know what it is or how it happens. I. Just. Run. All my human concerns fall away and I only place my body where the obstacles are not. I am the run. My mind is blank and I am no more. I run. From the left, just to the left of my vision, Sandstone dashes up alongside Nomi and they flash together, bounding next to me, in rhythm. Left foot, right foot, left foot, right foot, as if they are becoming the run, in unison, together, and they are subconsciously calling out to me to join them. Should I join in on their cadence? Just becoming the run, next to each other. Just becoming. Sandstone knows it; I can see now. She knows how to leave herself and become. Mercury is there too but she is not one of us. I can see that now. She doesn't know how to become. It is only the becoming that is important. We sprint together for some moments, in flawless formation, jumping a gap, then dodging barrels, then across ropes and up walls, one, two, three, we go. Ignoring the audience, the staff and even Coach because now, right now, we are the run.

Qi tries to race with us but then falls off the back so she switches to being an enforcer and pushes Nomi and then Sandstone out. I shake my head and fall back into competition mode and it is as if I have lost something, suddenly. I am no longer the run but a person running. Sandstone howls at Nomi as her eyes look over at Donavan, "Why did you get so close? Everyone knows you don't run so close near an enforcer!"

By now everyone is completely dripping in sweat due to the heat in the building. My eyes are burning from the salt and I can't stop running to grab a towel and my hands mush it around more. It takes everything I have to stay in front of Mercury and it is only my familiarity with the course obstacles that is keeping me a few feet in front of her.

Max sets her cross-hairs on Cyndi, slows as she approaches then lightly bumps her off course. They both walk off and Max sheepishly says, "Sorry, I had to."

Cyndi replies, "No problem, Maxie."

I wish she would say that to me.

It is clear that Greta wants to take out Sidney and everyone knows it. On the next lap Greta charges out of the safe zone and dives towards her but Sidney vaults her and is away. Greta stands in the center of the track, shakes the dust off her clothes and spits. I dodge past her and then Mercury right after me and it is as if we aren't even there. Her eyes are trained on Sidney. Greta leaves the safe zone and slowly jogs to the next set of obstacles as Sidney flies around the track.

I know what she is thinking. Take her out on an obstacle. No way would she do that! It's too dangerous!

Sidney traipses across the rope swings, over the water leap and up to the warped wall. Just as she races up the wall and reaches for the upper ledge Greta slams into her, grabs her legs and heaves her off course like an old discarded play-thing. Sidney flings off the course from eight feet up, bounces and rolls across the turf. Donavan blows her whistle and I am glad that I don't have to finish an all-out foot race against Mercury because I am not sure I can beat her.

After she realizes that Sidney is not injured she barks, "Greta! This is just a practice! What are you doing out there!"

The soaking wet team hustles in toward the benches and grabs some water. The front room staff pack up and move out apparently satisfied with what they have seen or maybe not able to tolerate the heat anymore.

After a quick break that seems like an instant we return to running drills and I take a moment to slide over to someone I have been wanting to talk for quite a while: Sebastian. He is lurking in the shadows near the left side field entrance propped up against a wall and when he sees me heading toward him he quickly stands up straight as if he is surprised that someone saw him there. Donavan would toss him out on his ear if she knew he was in here. I pop into a light jog and stop in front of him and then both of us duck into the corner where Donavan can't see.

I want to talk to him to get him to forgive me and maybe to get him to help me get my two friends back. I know I need to say something to break the ice and I have absolutely no idea what to say. "Hey Sebastian, long time no see." That was great! Idiot! What are you saying?

He looks down at me hard, then quickly back at the field then back at me, softer. "I guess you could say that. I haven't seen you since—" He looks away again as if I am an unwanted distraction.

Well after that stupid start I might as well just give him the truth. I heard somewhere that the truth sets us free, right? "Yeah, since—" Well, here goes. "I aaahh—I wanted to talk to you about what happened."

He exhales slowly then looks at me full on, right at my face, like he is looking through me, like he can somehow look into my soul, searching for some ulterior motive. The tension slowly leaves his face and he replies, "All right, I guess."

I know that he knows what happened. He knows everything and I don't really know exactly what to say, how to say it or why he is letting me talk right now. "I wanted to apologize to you. I wanted to just say—" I can't hold his gaze so I look down. "I wanted to say I was sorry."

I look back up at his face, and continue, "It was wrong. I know that now. Actually I knew that then. I just. I just. It was wrong, that's all. I should have told Cyndi the moment I found out that it was Kyle, not you. I had the opportunity. I just. I don't know why— I just. You know I can't blame anyone else but myself. I did a lot of things that I shouldn't have and—there's things that I should have done that I didn't. I just. I am just real sorry that I came between you and Cyndi. I lost one of my best friends and if there is anything I can do—well, there is probably nothing I can do since Cyndi won't talk to me, but, just let me know, okay?"

I start to walk away from his face set in stone so I don't cry in front of him when he unexpectedly calls me back. "Gabby. Hey. Listen. "

I stop and take a few steps back toward him.

He says, "I don't blame you really. Don't kill yourself over it. I forgive you. You were going through a lot and with Kyle manipulating you. I know he's good at it. I know that you were in love with Kyle and love can do weird things."

I wasn't in love with Kyle but I was going to marry him. Don't remind me again.

He continues, "He manipulated you and who knows what he told you—probably some crazy stuff— and even about me too—probably mostly lies, I guess."

Wow. He's fishing? Wonder what he is worried about me knowing. "Honestly he didn't say much. He told me that both of you were trained in that? Manipulation? By NuGen? And that you weren't a very good student."

He leans his head back. "He did, did he? Well let's

just say that I wasn't very good at *that*—hence, my assignment here." He looks toward Cyndi on the field. "But I am okay with it."

"He said something about you not being able to control your emotions and that's why you fell in love with Cyndi but I don't see anything wrong with that."

"Yeah." He looks back out to the field over my shoulder.

I share his gaze. "So do you think you two could get back together?"

Sebastian looks at me surprised then a knowing look crosses his face. "Not yet."

"If I can help. I will. Anyway, I got to get back."

As I hustle off, Sebastian says, "Hey, by the way, they are releasing Kyle today."

I spin on my heel, "What?"

"I don't know the details, just heard something at the office."

"Do you know where?"

"You should ask Smith. I think he will be there for the debrief."

Smith! Again!

"Gabriella, get out here! Enough goofing off!" Donavan howls.

I head back to the benches and wipe off my dripping forehead and arms and it feels like I just stepped out of the shower. I jump back into the intervals with the group but my head's somewhere else.

Chapter 8

Ex Nihilo

After practice I head to the lockers and immediately call Mom. "Hey, we're done."

"On my way."

"Mom?"

"Yeah?"

"I heard Kyle is getting released today."

There is silence on the line then she replies cautiously, "Gabby—"

I quickly cut her off, "Could you ask Smith? Where and when?"

"Gabby, I know you were supposed to marry him and… you know I feel so bad, responsible for what happened. I shouldn't have pushed you but don't you think you should let this go?"

"Mom, I'm not trying to get him back."

"I just don't want you to get hurt again."

"Mom, I won't. But thanks."

"I'll see what I can find out."

I clean up, shower and put away my gear and no one in the locker room will talk to me except Sandstone, and her a little too much. She makes me uncomfortable with the questions she asks when everyone else is within earshot. "Hey Gabriella! I can call you Gabby, right? Everyone else does? At least in the news? Good? Right?"

"Sure. If I can call you Sandstone."

She frowns. "I hate that name."

Her locker is next to mine. Too bad for her. She

doesn't realize that she is associating herself with the unwanted.

"Hey, I noticed you don't say much? Why's that? Don't like talking? Cat got your tongue? Oh, that's a saying here in UNA. Do they say that in Brazil? It means something like you don't talk much."

"You talk enough for the both of us." That sounded too harsh so I peek around my locker door and smile at her.

"Oh." She smiles back. "Yeah, I get that a lot. Don't know why. Guess that's just the way I'm wired? Can't shut up sometimes? Hey! Noticed the other girls don't talk to you much either? Why's that? Guess 'cause you don't talk back, huh?"

I can feel Cyndi's eyes on me from the other side of the locker room. "I... I... You don't want to know." I close my locker door and turn toward her. "Sandstone. Listen. No one on this team wants to be my friend. In fact, no one even wants me here. Your locker is next to mine so you started talking to me. Your mistake. If you want to make it here you should probably just avoid me like everyone else. You will be much better off."

Her mouth is open and for once she doesn't say anything. I turn, lock my locker and leave out the back entrance toward the parking garage.

I walk to Mom's car feeling awkward in my own skin. After having said out loud what I have been feeling these last few weeks it feels like it is all that much more real. Like having said it actually brought it into being, not that I was merely acknowledging something that was already there; I spoke and it suddenly popped into existence.

I stop at the passenger door and blow out my wind, trying to clear my mind, open the door, plop down in and smile at Mom as if nothing is wrong in the world of Gabriella Conceição.

Mom pulls out of the parking garage and points the car north.

"Where we going?"

"Well? You asked about Kyle being released. I called Smith and weaseled it out of him. And I knew you would want to be there so that's where we are going."

"Mom?"

She glances over at me and back at the road. "Yeah?"

"I love you."

She smiles as she drives. "I know."

We pull into the parking lot in front of a moderately sized red brick building. The parking lot is about half full and it appears that nothing special is going on. No news crews. No throng of NuGen goons. Just another day at the office. As we exit our car, Smith calls out to us, "Hey you two! I didn't actually think you would show up."

Smith and another man, a much older, wrinkly man with sandy blond, streaked hair and a thin, light beard saunter over and Smith introduces him. "Gabriella, Elia, this is my supervisor. Victor Chavez. Victor, I would like to introduce you to Miss Elia Conceição and her daughter, Gabriella."

Victor speaks with a raspy voice, "Pleased to meet you," and both my mom and I return niceties. We four turn toward the police department entrance and walk toward it.

Smith says, "I guess I know why you would want to see Kyle, Gabriella, but NuGen is going to have him first. I told your mom here that it would be a waste of time to come but she said that there would be no use trying to stop you," he pauses and smiles over at me as if he just told a joke and I wonder if he is saying all this for me or for Victor. "So it would be good if you two wait out of the way. The police are releasing him to our custody and after we debrief him, maybe in a week or so, you can vent on him all you like. For now you two are not going to be able to talk." He looks over at me questioningly as if he wants me to agree to what he said but I only give him back a blank stare then finally a nod.

You may be dating my mom but you are not my father.

Victor opens the large glass door and holds it for the rest of us and as I cross the threshold long bolts of ecstatic electricity fire out of the black spot and down my back, pulsing, firing in a seemingly random sequence. It feels so-o-o good! Kyle is close, too close; I just know it. My eyes dart around the room and everyone is moving in slow motion; square-jawed detectives with thick belts carrying coffee cups and worn, outdated screens, the plump and dopey looking security guard moving trays through the security scanner, and a few women looking business-like, full of self-importance, badges clipped to their hips and there, right there, sitting on the bench, staring at the industrial tile floor, it's Kyle! My eyes lock on him and the air is drawn from my lungs as the pulsing, swirling, magnetic draw of the black spot caresses my neck, telling me to become complete.

"Gabby? Are you okay?" Mom questions.

"Aahhh. Yeah. Yeah, I'm okay. It's just—I'm fine. I'm okay."

Smith looks at me with curiosity in his eyes and motions at a wall to the left of the scanners. Mom and I both retreat to the wall without a word and Smith and Victor proceed through the security scanners. They say some words to a bored and tired-looking man who must be seriously contemplating his present career choice who then passes them a screen which Victor promptly signs with the tip of his fingernail. They stand in front of Kyle and say a few words that I cannot hear while Kyle looks at them with a blank stare, promptly stands and leads them out through the security check point. Kyle does not look my way once or even acknowledge that I am in the building. As he gets closer, the pulsing coming from the black spot grows stronger and more irresistible. I can't take my eyes off him and he won't even look at me. I know Mom is watching me, looking at the side of my head anyway, and I can't help myself; I don't care what she thinks right now. I want to say something to him, anything, but all the speeches I have rehearsed for the last weeks have left me. He passes just in front of me and as he does he whispers, almost inaudibly, "Merge," without the least indication that I am just to his right.

Smith exits the building, followed by Kyle, followed by Victor and as Kyle leaves the wind is sucked from my lungs and I am suddenly angry and I don't know why. Angry at NuGen? Angry at Smith? Angry at Kyle? I don't know who or why but I could break something right now.

I push open the door and charge toward the three, smashing Victor out of the way and tackling Kyle down the concrete steps. I stand over him and scream, "Now you listen here! You've got some explaining to do! Who do you think you are?"

"Gabriella! Gabriella! Hold on just a minute." Smith places his hand on my arm. I snap my head towards him, pierce him with my eyes and snarl, "Smith! You don't want to mess with me right now!"

I can tell that he is looking back over my shoulder

at Victor who must be motioning at him because Smith lets my arm go.

I tower over Kyle and he looks so pathetic, lying there awkwardly on the steps. Covered in dust, he gazes down at the gray concrete in front of his feet, then up at me and speaks as if he is addressing all four of us, "You know I once was told that the world and all the universe and everything in it came from the nothingness. I remember NuGen wanting us to learn about many of the different religions, not so we would be religious of course, but so that we might understand cultural differences."

Smith's chest noticeably tightens as Kyle continues, "One of them said something like, 'The earth was without form and void and darkness was on the face of the deep. And the Spirit of God was hovering over the face of the waters.' Another, I think from one of the American Indian tribes, says, 'All was void and darkness, then The One Who Lives Above awoke and brought forth light.' There are many, many others. The ancient Greeks believed that the dark, silent abyss from which all things came into existence had a name, Chaos. Over and over I found that everything comes from nothing and to nothing it shall return."

Before he can continue I holler down at him, "Kyle! What are you talking about?"

"Another. Listen to me. Another. Plato spoke of passageways leading to the realms of the afterlife where there are spirits. The Tibetan Book of Dead talks about leaving the body, being suspended in a foggy void."

Victor steps from behind me and motions to Smith and both of them grab Kyle's two arms and hoist him up and it is as if they are merely a distraction to him.

Before they can haul him off he says, "I tell you

only this, Gabriella. I have spent a lifetime in the Void. For you, out here, it was a number of days, but for me… a lifetime. Maybe more than a lifetime and I would like to say that, 'I saw the light' but more appropriately I can say I saw the darkness. Let me speak wisdom to you. Right here. Right now. A wisdom that will save you from much pain. Nothing is or nothing isn't unless you happen to believe it to be so. Remember your Shakespeare. He said as much and he knew it was truth. 'To be or not to be?' Remember? Gabriella, you are fighting against nothingness all the time by mentally creating a series of barriers to what is the real truth. No different than all of us. I did it too! But now I am free! We create these worthless shields that we place in front of our eyes that we call personality, history, feelings, ideas, and points of view. But they are all illusions!" My eyes fog over, somehow, and for some reason his words penetrate me.

Kyle continues, "Everything that you are or conceive of yourself as being is just an idea. It's an illusion! It's a hallucination! Yet there is still one truth—"

Victor jerks Kyle's arm and stiffly says, "All right, philosopher! That's enough! Let's go! You can talk all you want when we are done with you."

They hustle him off and put him in the back of their car. Victor nods at both Mom and me then sits himself in the passenger seat. Smith waves at my mom and mouths, "I'll call you," then gets in the car and drives away leaving the two of us standing there staring at tail lights.

Mom jerks me from my stupor. "Let's go home."

Chapter 9

New Girls

"Just do what I say and I'll take care of the rest. Leave it to me and you're in." Mercury's voice comes strained, filtered and shallow through the locker room entrance door and a few months ago I would have been embarrassed to be caught listening but not anymore. I wait for the voices to stop and I open the door in a full trot as if I *wasn't* just standing there with my hand on the door handle for seven or so minutes trying to figure out what the new girls are up to. Mercury is just stepping out of the room and glances back as I enter but continues to leave as if I am a long-dead victim of some gutter homicide. Sandstone and Greta are still in the room but neither of them acknowledges me verbally although Sandstone gives me a cautious little-girl wave and a half smile. After what I told her in the locker room last time I am surprised she even does that.

I change and head out to the practice field. It's been a few days since the Sacramento game, a few days since these new girls showed up and it feels like we all are falling back into the training grind without Elektra.

On the field, Mercury and Greta are whispering to each other, then, just as Donavan turns to watch them, they sprint down the course and up the warped wall. I guess the new girls are catching on to exactly what Donavan wants, at least what she wants to see, and it seems they have the uncanny ability to display it in dramatic fashion at the exact moment that she is watching them.

Just then I notice something. I can't believe what I see. Sebastian is back! I jog over to within shouting distance. "Hey Sebastian! How's it going?"

"Hey Gabriella. Good to see you." And it actually looks like he is telling the truth this time. He is seated on a small plastic chair behind a grayish folding table that doesn't look rated to carry the weight of all his monitoring equipment and screens, on a tiny strip of grass bordering the practice field.

I look back at the rest of the team briefly then dodge over to his monitoring station, "It's really good to see you back. I'm glad you got in. How'd you do it?"

"Eh, you know, location. Here in the Philadelphia area, this isn't such a great assignment. Don't get me wrong, you all are the best, but the other tech specs— they are too upwardly mobile and if you are going to be in the Philly area you want to be at the corporate office not running a monitor on a B-team. Hahaha." He chuckles.

"Never thought of it like that."

"NuGen's all about either the field or the research and this, right here, is not the best field position."

"Well, I'm glad you're back anyway."

"Hey, you know I love this. I get to watch my girl all day. What could be better than that?"

"Is she?"

"What? My girl? We'll see."

I whisper, "Remember what I said," and begin to walk off but before I can escape he says, "Hey by the way, I heard some crazy stuff went down between you and Kyle. Heard you lost it at his release?"

"Well—"

"You didn't tell anyone that I told you did you?"

"No."

"Okay, because you know Smith—" Sebastian leans back and smiles but I know this is serious for him. Corporate politics can be ruthless.

"Too well. He was over the other day again. You know he's dating my mom, right?"

"Oh yeah, I know all about that."

I take a few steps back and this warm emotion comes over me and all of a sudden it is like I have a friend again. "What do you know?"

"Just that they are dating. I heard that Smith knew your mom and dad a long time ago. Like twenty years ago or something?"

"Yeah, something like that."

Donavan blows her whistle so I say, "Hey I gotta run," and jog back onto the field.

At the practice court on the left, near the swinging ropes and warped wall, Mercury is talking to Greta and Sandstone, plotting probably, mumbling something that I can't hear, and on the right court, near the new obstacle stands Sidney, Max and Qi talking with each other, plotting probably, mumbling something that I can't hear and I am alone, in the middle, all alone, all alone. I jog over to the right practice court and start stretching then I overhear Sidney telling Max and Qi, "I can't stand these new girls. They're so fake! And they show up here from nowhere and they think they are going to run *us* off *our* field. We have to do something about them."

Max looks at her, eyes big, not saying anything. After I walk away, she mumbles something but I can't quite make it out. I am becoming too much of a snoop. I have got to stop this. I wish someone on the team would talk to me. Someone besides Sandstone anyway. I don't want the rest of the team turning against that poor girl.

"All right! Gather around!" Donavan bellows and Sandstone leaps up, giggles and sprints over to Donavan and quickly finds a spot on the grass in front of her. The rest of the team walks to Donavan except Mercury who sort of saunters over. "First a progress report on Elektra! She's coming along fine! Looks like two more weeks and she can practice!"

Donavan looks down at her screen for a few moments then says, "Next weekend's game is key! I don't have to tell you all that we want to win it so we can be guaranteed our birth in the playoffs! But there is another reason that I want to talk to you about that match up! As you all know it is Brazil and some of you might be interested in inflicting some damage on them after what happened last time we saw them. Others of you might have some concerns and I understand that! No one wants to be smashed off course by an enforcer and no one wants broken bones! I need all of you healthy for the rest of this season so we are going to play this match calm and cool. We are not going for revenge! We are not going for blood! Is that understood!" Donavan pauses and looks at each of us slowly, then turns to Max and Greta and says, "So we need some protection for our sprinters and I am going to rely on our enforcers to do it!" She looks at all of us again and bellows, "Understand! Enough breaks! Let's get out there!"

As we run, jump, swing, balance and leap it is becoming more and more evident that Greta is listening more and more to what Mercury has to say. Qi is right there too, playing both sides of the fence. As I loop past them Mercury whispers, "Don't worry about that one. She's not that fast and won't be long for this team after I'm done with her."

Qi quips a little too loud, probably so I can hear, "Bad genes. Her. She won't make it anyway. She no good."

After the short training session, I clean up and can't wait to get out of there and away from all the drama. High school isn't anywhere near this bad!

Chapter 10

The Diary

The next day I find myself trudging through the front office hallway past one office and then another and I can't help but look into the open doors as I pass. I wave at one guy in a white shirt—what's his name?—and then peek in on another as I tramp on but he doesn't look up from his screen. Then I tread past another office where I see a new girl with her back to me standing and talking to a guy at a desk and—No way!—she has a black spot on the back of her neck, right in the center, in between the top of her shirt line and the base of her pinned up hair. I can't help but stop and stare at it and the longer I stand there, moments turning into an eternity, the more the black spot on my own back tingles stronger and stronger, pulsing in an odd rhythm, over and over, pulse, pulse, pulse.

"Can I help you?" comes from behind the desk and the girl stops talking and turns to me.

"No, I... I'm good. I was just looking for someone."

"Who are you looking for?"

"Oh, Coach Donavan. I'll check her office. Thanks."

I hustle down the hall as fast as I can walk without jogging and the spell is broken; the black spot no longer tingles and I can't believe what I just saw.

As the team gathers before our last practice, before our match in Brazil, Donavan calls us into a circle for another one of her inspirational speeches.

"Gather round! This is our last practice before the long flight to Brazil tomorrow and thankfully the last training in this heat. I, for one, have had enough of it! But enough of that! Today is a recuperation day! We are going to focus a lot of time on balance and stretching and just try to stay loose! I don't want anyone too sore going into the big game!"

Donavan drones on and on and I can't help but lose focus on what she is saying after what I just saw. Could it be possible that girl was involved in Dr. Duggan's experiments? Maybe she took a trip through the Void? Maybe Kyle touched her? Can he do that to people outside of the Void? And Kyle and that crypto-babble he fed me at the police station—what was that all about?

When I saw him the first time I just thought he lost his mind in there but something the Void-man said to me keeps coming back into my mind. How exactly did it go? Something about a sparrow and a hawk and making a choice—a sacrifice. No, before that. There was something about one who is a friend who would destroy you, destroy me. I don't know why, but that line—I just can't stop thinking about it. Something like? Something like—how did it go?

Then, suddenly, it bursts into my mind:

There is one who is a friend who would destroy you. You watch whom he follows and who follows him. He is not what he seems but you are not deceived. No, not deceived by the bouncing numbers or the shaded letters or the shaking digits or the random dots.

He will chase you and chase you but you will hide very well, and it is your ability to hide that will allow you to hide your deepest of secrets.

Woah. That was weird. Could he have been talking about Kyle?

"Gabriella? Gabriella! Are you in there?" Donovan questions.

"Oh… Yeah. Sure."

"Figures," Qi mumbles.

"Drop it!" Donovan's ears are unusually sensitive, Qi should know better than to mumble anything in front of her; Donovan hates that kind of stuff. She always said it was divisive to a team. "Gabriella, pay attention!"

"Sure, Coach."

Donovan explains a bunch more stuff that we already know, barking it out like a bulldog guarding a prized bone. She heads off and the girls ready themselves at their lockers and Mercury says to no one in particular, "She talks to us like we're kids."

Max and Sidney look over at her but don't take the bait.

Sandstone says, "How should she treat us?"

"Maybe you're used to that. Coming from a high school team. But I'm not a kid anymore."

"Oh. Yeah." Sandstone says pensively.

Donovan pops her head out her doorway and says, "Let's go! What's taking so long?"

Mercury says, "I'm ready to go, Coach!" I can't help looking up through my eyelids.

The training session is uneventful, we shower and get ready to leave. Heading into the parking garage I suddenly remember that I was supposed to get my own ride home tonight. Mom is out with Smith. I volunteered to take the bus—just another consequence of my little "incident" with Kyle and losing my license. I can't keep making mom suffer for my mistakes. But Sebastian is right over there. Maybe?

"Sebastian, where ya headed?"

"For a bite. Then home. Why? Need a ride?"

"I was going to take the bus. Yeah, if you don't mind."

"It's a little out of my way but I can suffer a little —for a friend."

I smile back at his smirk then open the door to his sweet vanilla-sky colored BMW 328. It is a sweet hardtop convertible and looks really sweet and oh, did I mention, it's sweet?

We head out of the parking garage and onto the highway with the top down and the music on a little too loud and Sebastian quizzes, "So what do you think of the new girls?"

"Sandstone seems nice. She won't last long though."

"I know what you mean. She's fast but those other girls are going to rip her apart."

"Too bad. I kind of like her. Now Greta on the other hand. She's a contender. Tough. Good work ethic. Professional. A lot of experience too. Just don't know if she is going to fit what the team wants."

"True. You can be the best enforcer in the world but if the team is not looking for an enforcer then you have no job. What about the other one? Mercury?"

"Hard to tell, that one. Not sure exactly what her game is."

"I'd keep my eye on her."

"Yeah?"

"She's a manipulator. Sneaky too. I think she's trying to build her own little mini-tribe. I've been watching them. Greta is with her but only as far as it benefits her. Sandstone, on the other hand, Mercury's trying to wrap her around her finger. Hard to tell if she's taking the bait. If she's listening to Mercury, it will be to her own detriment. She doesn't seem to have a clue. Maybe you should talk to her."

"Uhh… Don't know how involved I want to get in that. I mean this isn't high school, this is, well—this is supposed to be like—real life. I mean I know I'm still in high school and *even I* know that it shouldn't be like that."

"You'd be surprised how childish adults can be, Gabriella. I feel like I'm still in high school all the time and I never even went to high school."

Sebastian takes the exit ramp off the turnpike and jumps onto 295 South. The two lane highway is mostly empty.

"Let me ask you a question," I say.

"Go ahead."

"You were asking about Mercury? What I thought about her?"

"Yeah?"

"Well, we have been studying sociocultural motivations in school. I got this nutty, ultra-animated teacher named Mr. Dunberry and a few weeks back he was teaching us about survival of the fittest. Some crazy stuff about the origin of sports. Came from bored warriors waiting to kill each other. At least some of the sports anyway."

"What's this got to do with Mercury?"

"Oh, it's something else he was saying. Mr. Dunberry. This whole idea of the rat race. You know, getting ahead. Like western culture is full of people in this giant struggle to increase their consumption or something like that. Like people buy stuff just to be seen buying it. Like those giant gas guzzling SUVs. Nobody really needs the ones with all the bling-bling-bling, and they cost like twice as much, but they buy them because they want people to know it. They want to be seen."

"You're talking about conspicuous consumption."

"Yeah, yeah. That's it. That's what Dunberry called it too."

"It's been around forever. That's nothing new."

"Well, yeah, but I just don't get it. This whole rat race thing. I mean what exactly are we getting ahead of? Dunberry said, 'Even if you win the rat race, you're still a rat,' and—I don't know—it's like this whole idea of materialism is out of control and—we can't take it with us anyway."

"Err… You're starting to sound like a Marxist and what's this got to do with Mercury again?"

"Well, nothing about her in particular, but—she's the rat."

"What?"

"The rat race, you know. She'll do anything to get ahead. She'd step on my head to get to the bigs if she knew it would work."

"Gabriella, half the planet thinks that way."

"Yeah, yeah, I know. But, I don't know—it's just —"

"Gabriella's having an existential moment, huh?"

"I guess. Whatever that means."

"It means you're wondering about your existence, the meaning of life, the universe and how did those Reese's peanut butter cups *really* come into being. I mean did someone *really* trip and drop his chocolate bar into someone else's jar of peanut butter?"

"Something like that." I smile and look over at him. It is suddenly so great to have someone to talk to about nothing in particular. "I was thinking about something else."

"Yeah?"

"Something Kyle said."

Sebastian shifts in his chair. "What'd he say?"

"Nothing about you."

"Oh… Yeah. What'd he say?"

I answer, "Well, back to that materialism stuff."

"That again."

"He said we all come from dust and we all return to dust and he's right you know. I think sometimes that all this competing and getting ahead—it's really meaningless."

"Sure. Of course. We're all born and we all die but in the meantime—" Sebastian mashes the accelerator hard. "In the meantime it's nice to be able to have a really fast, fast car! Yeah!"

I giggle and wrap my hair in my hands to stop it from flying as I raise my arms and say, "Yeah! Yeah! I guess you're right!" But in my heart it's all still there. Life is pain. Life is struggle. And struggle for what? To get ahead? To get ahead of whom? We are all headed to the same place. Back to the dust. Back to nothing. Back to the Void, Kyle would say. What are we racing for anyway? No, no, no. No! NO! Kyle! Get out of my head!

Sebastian offers to take me to a drive-through fast-food place even though he knows I can't eat fast-food. In reality, I completely wouldn't mind a Gordita right now but unfortunately I have to refuse gracefully. I love those things. Gordita translates to "Little Fat Girl" which I guess says it all and I know there is no way I can handle all those calories. Especially right before bed.

We pull into my driveway, I get out and just as Sebastian pulls out of my driveway Smith pulls in and I can hear Mom giggling loudly and something about that bothers me.

I wave to Sebastian as he drives off and I say to them, "Hey, you two. Had a good time?"

"Hahaha." Mom appears a bit tipsy as she howls loudly through her open window and gathers her shoes off the floor. "Gabby, it was sooo nice! I wish you could have been there."

Smith quickly runs around to the other side of the car and opens the door for Mom.

"Hey, Gabby. Sorry to bring your mom back so late but it was a long meal."

"No problem. Glad you had a good time."

Mom says animatedly, shaking her hands in the air, "It was like the best! Everyone in the place was dressed to the nines. We had four waiters just for our table alone! Can you believe that?! Four! And it was a seven course meal, right Smith?"

"Seven or eight. I lost count."

Mom continues, "And get this! In between every course this guy with a meticulously shaved head wearing the nicest tuxedo comes out and cleans our tablecloth off with a little metal scraper tool. He sweeps up all the crumbs! Cool right?"

"I *guess*. How many crumbs did you make?"

Smith chuckles, "Not many. Tell her about dessert. That was funny."

Mom throws her hands up. "Gabriella! Listen to this one! So they wheel out this dessert tray with about fifty different desserts. Think of all the best desserts you can think of and pile them up all on one mega-dessert cart and that's what this was."

"Okay." I was just fantasizing about a Gordita at Taco Bell and she wants me to think about fifty desserts? I know Mom's lost it.

"It was absolutely the hardest decision because

they all looked sooo good and it took me sooo long to pick. We were even discussing all the pros and cons of my choice in front of the guy, you know, the guy with the shaved head, wearing this beautiful tuxedo, and I know he had to be getting frustrated waiting there for us. So, anyway, I pick one. Then the guy slices the tiniest sliver and I am like, 'No way is he giving me that tiny piece.' And I thought, 'Maybe the guy is mad because I took too long to pick. But still. That's not nice.' "

Smith smiles and picks up the story, "So I begin to order. I was just going to order the same thing and give your mom my piece since hers was so small but the waiter holds his hand up at us with a stiff upper lip like we just broke protocol and we both were completely confused."

"What happened?"

"The waiter pointed at your mom and said, 'Would madam like anymore?' "

They both bust out laughing and I say, "Oh, so you could have as many different slivers as you wanted?"

"Hahaha. Yeee-ah!" Mom laughs loudly and I wonder when the neighbors are going to come out.

"Guess I had to be there." I turn toward the door and punch in our code to unlock it saying, "Got a big day tomorrow. Heading up."

"Hey Gabriella, one thing before you go."

"Sure, what's up Smith?"

"I just wanted to tell you something about the other day." Oh boy. Here comes.

"Sorry about that. Did I make you look bad in front of your boss?"

"It's not that. It's just your mom and I here—I like to think we got something special."

Mom giggles. "We did tonight. Hahaha."

"Hold on, honey. This is serious. I feel responsible, you know, for Kyle and you two. I mean, I gave your mom his information and, you know, I didn't know all his history. I just knew that he worked for NuGen and, you know, not that he... he was lying about his past. And then what happened later, you know, him chasing you and all, that made me feel terrible."

Mom grabs Smith's arm as if it is a lifeline holding her from sinking in a swirling ocean and says, "Oh Smith, it wasn't your fault."

"Anyway. I don't think we will be seeing much of him."

"Oh no?" I reply.

Smith continues, "Of course Victor was going to fire him but he quit before he could—at the debrief. Kept babbling something about the nothingness being the absolute and this world being an illusion and that nothing was real, except what's in our minds. He's lost it. Got Victor really angry. It's a shame, all that money NuGen poured into him."

I say, "He was in there a long time."

"Almost a month." Smith doesn't know about the Void. Time moves on a whole different scale in there. A minute out here is like a couple hours in there, maybe longer, maybe days, who knows? A month? It could be like a year in there, maybe a couple years. A couple years in the pitch black. Yeah, he had to have lost it.

"Thanks, Smith." I say as I place my hand on the door handle.

"Okay, I'm off." Smith gives Mom a little nibble and it makes me shudder.

I hold the door open for Mom and we both go in. Mom is in the 'I'm stuck on a cloud and never coming down' mood.

"Oh what a wonderful night Gabby! I didn't want it to end."

"Sounded nice."

"Nice? Nice? Oh yes it was oohhhh sooo niiiice!!!" and she giggles as she makes fun of her favorite phrase.

"Okay Mom." I kiss her cheek. "I'm going up."

She stops me halfway up the first staircase with, "Gabby?"

"Yeah?"

"Kyle really hates NuGen now. Smith said it was like—what's the word? Disdain? Yeah, that's it, disdain. If you bump into him, Kyle I mean, don't listen to him. And—probably better to just stay away from him."

"Okay, Mom."

I slink up the stairs and slide under the covers and tonight there is so much to think about, so much to ponder but I don't want to think about anything, just sleep. I used to try to sleep on the long plane flights but with a big game coming there is no way I can bank on that. I need to get as much sleep as I can, when I can, to make sure I am well rested. And with so much on the line for the team and with the three new girls chomping on our heels any mistake right now could prove to be fatal.

I quickly fall asleep, thankfully, but awaken with a start and looking at the clock see that it is 3:00 AM. Three AM, three AM, why is it always three AM? I lie on my pillow, eyes open, looking over at my alarm clock and the bright moonlight shining in from the open window and down at the nightstand and the two books I am trying to get through for school, *The Great Gatsby* and *Mrs. Dalloway*. I don't know where they get their book choices in UNA but the stories are boring. Don't get me wrong; I love the writing. I mean who wouldn't? The sentences in Gatsby are so scrumptious, like living in a linguistic candy-land full of lollipop trees, cotton candy fields and happy unicorns. But the stories —booooring. At least to me, anyway. And that bit about the best thing a woman could be—something about being a 'beautiful little fool'? No, I can never forgive Fitzgerald for that one. In Venezuela it was *One Hundred Years of Solitude* for me. Now there's a book to read.

It is obvious at this point that I am not going to get back to sleep any time soon. The clock rolls to 3:20 AM and that night, out in the woods, comes to mind. Did it happen? Or was it a dream? In either case, the weird poem is stuck in my head. "Weird. Yeah, weird," I hear myself saying and all of a sudden I find myself downstairs with my hand on the rear handle door. Gabriella, where are you going?

I feel a little tug at my heart and I know right then that I was heading out to the woods. How can I be sleep walking if I am awake? I turn the knob as my mind continually oscillates between deciding whether to go back to bed and *not* fall asleep, laying there, staring at the ceiling, or opening the door and seeing how far down the rabbit hole Gabriella can fall without going completely insane.

I open the door, slowly, quietly, trying to not wake up Mom, and step out onto the back patio and try to shake the feeling that I have done this all before.

I slowly scamper across the wet grass, dew caressing my ankles and quickly dampening my shoes as my eyes dart at the neighbor's yards on the left and right, feeling completely insecure and completely paranoid.

I duck into the woods, less cautious this time than last, if last time actually happened, and head to the clearing as if I know exactly where I am going. I don't need a blue light to follow. I am not looking to smell his weird clove perfume. I just want to get this over with and get back to bed. I will head to the clearing, if it is even really there, make sure there are no weird Void-man blue lights or aliens there, then head back in. I leap the fallen tree, quickly cross the small opening, duck between the two too-close trees and step out into the clearing. And there he is. And I am completely shocked to see him. The Void-man. Even though some part of me thought it was a distinct possibility that the Void-man would actually be standing there, waiting for me, I can't help but be surprised beyond belief. I mean, that was just a dream last time, wasn't it?

Shaking, twitching, goose-bumps suddenly all over my arms, neck and back, I step slowly up to the Void-man, a vision of my father long before I was born, young and full of vitality, with the slightest of blue glows. The scent of jasmine is suddenly unbearably strong.

"I... I... I... Dad?"

He stares at my face unflinching, giving no indication that he heard or understood me or even that I am even there, standing just in front of him. Whether or not he can perceive that I am here, whether or not he is here, in front of me or that any of this is real, I have to say something. "Listen... I don't know what you are doing out here in the woods behind my house. I don't know much for that matter. I don't know who you are or why you saved my life. I don't know how you touched me and healed my leg. Or why you would do that. I would love to think that you are my... my father—the ghost of my father that is—but I don't know anything. You could be an alien that sucked my brain and are just showing me what I want to see until you destroy the planet for all I know. I just… I just wish you would give me some answers. And before—last week—was that real? Because if it was, then those are not exactly the types of answers that I am looking for. Some cryptic poem? I don't even know if that was good poetry or not but I have no idea what you were talking about. I mean how am I supposed to understand that stuff? Frozen spirits thawing into hawks and sparrows?"

I stare up into his face expecting him to say something but he stares back at me, no, through me—it's more like he is staring through me than anything, like I am not even there and he is looking in my general direction. I turn, slowly to see what he is looking at but I don't want to take my eyes off him in case he tries one of his disappearing acts so I keep him in my peripheral vision. There is nothing behind me so I snap my head back and plead, "Hey! You in there? Are you going to say anything?"

His stare is unflinching, unblinking, so without knowing what else to do, I continue, "Hawks, sparrows and choices. Everyone makes choices every day! We all try to do the right thing—with the amount of information we have anyway. I just don't get it. So please. Please—" My voice grows unexpectedly desperate and I say, "Please just talk to me!"

He holds his glowing hand up and I instantly stop and stare at him because I can't believe I actually got a reaction out of him. His reverberating voice penetrates me as he speaks, "Your father has a diary. It is still in your house."

He then points toward the path that I came into the woods on, the path that will lead back to my house. My eyes follow his finger then when I look back he is gone and I instantly mentally kick myself for taking my eyes off of him.

I gingerly step through the woods, my heart rate still fast but finally slowing a little and as the briars and prickers scrape my legs I am reminded that, no, I am in no way asleep. This is real!

I stop and nearly cry but I don't know why.

Chapter 11

Busted

Why did you go into the woods! You have to fly to Brazil in the morning! In—like—six hours!

I stomp back to the rear of the house, confused, upset, freaking out and not knowing what to think. If he really is my dad then he would know that he had a diary but how would he know that it is in our house? And if he had a diary then why would he tell me to read it instead of just telling me what's in it? He wrote it, right?

I climb the rear steps to the back patio and slide off my shoes. I should just go back to bed and forget this ever happened. Try to get some sleep for tomorrow's trip.

"Yeah right," I huff out loud. "Looks like it's going to be a long, long night and a long, long day. Maybe I can sleep on the plane anyway."

I squeeze open the door softly and slowly and tiptoe into the house.

"Where! Were! You!" Mom bellows.

"Mom?"

"Don't look at me like that! Gabriella!" Mom looks really mad.

"Mom? You're up? Why are you up?"

"Me! What were you doing out?"

I lie, "I was just... on the back porch. I mean... in the back yard. There, just right there."

She barks, "Gabriella! I understand you are a teenage girl but never, and I mean never, would I have thought that I would have caught you like *this*, sneaking in the house at three o'clock in the morning! Now you better start talking and talking fast!"

"Mom. I can explain—" Panic is in my voice and my brain is completely locked up because no way can I explain.

"Explain! Explain! You better start saying something because my anger is about to explode!" Mom inches forward, spittle on her lips and I don't know how she is holding herself back from grabbing me.

"Did Dad have a diary?"

"What?!" Mom takes a few steps closer and I don't know if the Mid-Easterner in her is about to boil over first or the South American, either way this is not going to be good. "Gabriella! Don't you try to change subjects with me! I want to know the name of the boy you were out with right now! I am going to call his parents! Out with it! Out with it! Right! Nooooooooow!" Her face is flushed red and I can see the pulse of her heartbeat throbbing in the little vein, suddenly raised up and fat, on the side of her temple. She is really, really mad.

"Mom! Mom! Calm down!" I pause momentarily and say slowly, "There's no boy—"

"What? Listen to me! I don't care how old you are or that you think that you are something because you run over there with your little friends! You still live under my roof and this is my house! You are my daughter and I! Will! Not! Have! You! Out! like—like—like some, uhh, like, one of those—you know what they are! I'm not going to have you out there like one of *those* girls!" She turns away for a moment and it's almost as if she is more mad at herself than mad at me.

I walk up to her and try to give her a hug but she pulls away.

"Stop it!"

"Okay mom, you win." I slink down onto a dining room chair and tell her about my dreams, slowly at first, looking up at her with each increasingly bizarre revelation, her protesting and thinking that this is some kind of obtuse midnight boyfriend cover up. I tell her about the Void-man, about how I think he healed my leg, about how he saved me when Velocity tried to hurt me again in the off-season match in Spain. I tell her faster now, more animated, more excitedly, like I am so happy to be finally getting all of this off my chest to someone. I tell her about how he saved me from Kyle in the Void, all of it, all of it, all of it, pouring out now in a rapid fire, semi-automatic, gang land, drive-by spray down. I tell her everything—well… everything except his cryptic poem —no need to let things get too wild and crazy now. Then I pause, hold my breath for what feels like a tremendously long minute, and then blurt out the biggest bombshell of them all, "And he looks like Dad."

Her head is bobbing, listening to my tale, somewhat weary-eyed, seeing as it is the middle of the night, weary-eyed no matter how fantastic it all is; her head is bobbing along, yes, it is, bobbing along, up until that exact moment.

"Enough!" She towers over me then grabs her breath like she is about to say something deadly serious. "Okay, I get it. You don't want to tell me about the boy. And maybe I can believe that you think you saw some things and I still can't explain how your leg got healed— although I still think that maybe you just heal extraordinarily fast. I know you said it happened when you were in Archibald's crazy contraption. But this! No! I won't have it! You can't *come in here, in the middle of the night,* and start telling *stories* about your father, my husband, who gave his life—" Mom bursts into tears and turns her back away from me. *"I didn't raise you to disrespect his memory like that!"*

I leap up and loosely put my arms around her from behind.

She continues to cry as I wrap my arms around her. She feels so much smaller than me. Frail. Weak. And I love her so much right now. I feel like I want to protect her, hold her, love on her for all she has sacrificed for me. And Dad, I wish I could love on her for him too. I know what he did. He was trying to protect us. A world-class scientist hiding in a crappy, low rent clothing store that was barely hanging on, barely able to make our bills, barely able to put food on the table. I can imagine the thoughts that went though his head each night, up late, everyone else snoring in their beds, him staring at the crumpled papers and struggling to make the numbers add up, figuring out what he would give up next to keep his daughter in school. And Mom was right there with him. She would do anything for us. She would do anything for me.

"Mom?"

She rocks back and forth with me for a few seconds as her sobbing begins to slow and she chokes out, "Yes?"

"He looked so beautiful. Handsome. It wasn't the dad I knew—for some reason. He was young. He was so young. Maybe a few years older than me."

"Yeah?"

"Yeah… I mean, I'm not saying it was him."

"Tell me more." she softly shudders and shakes my arms off her body and turns towards me. *"Tell me again* what he looked like?"

"Tall—taller than I remembered. Handsome. Yes,

very handsome." I almost giggle and I can't believe I am describing how good-looking my dad is to my mom! "Mom, you know what he looked like. It was Dad. Just a younger Dad."

"I know, I know, Mija. Just tell me." She finds a spot on the edge of the steps and sits down.

"Oh, all right." I lose myself in my memory of him. "Okay, let me get his face in my mind." I exhale again and close my eyes, "Uhh, okay. He was tall, yes, taller than me. Taller than I remember him being—by a few inches anyway. He had good skin, great skin actually, the lightest of browns, like a creamy almond but it somehow had depth to it, like you want to dive in and swim in it. And his eyes, a soft brown with hints of hazel."

"Oohhh, I remember those—"

"His strong, square jaw—he looked so confident —commanding—like he was in charge—but not in a militant sort of way. No, his eyes would never let him look like that. Commanding yet with a soft and caring looking, like he's in charge but you absolutely want him to be because you know he has your best interest at heart. I just wanted to trust him to the ends of the world."

"That was him."

"But no. Mom. I don't know. I don't know if it's really him."

"Well I still don't know if I believe that you really saw him. But let's say you did. For a minute. Why? Why would you say that?"

"His voice, Mom. It wasn't his voice. It sounded— weird. Alien. Like there were two of them in there. I don't know, Mom. I just don't know."

She stands up and looks at her watch. "My, my,

Mija. Look at the time. My alarm should be going off any minute. I have to get ready for work."

She turns to climb the stairs and I stop her with, "Mom?"

"Yes, Gabriella?"

"Did Dad have a diary?"

She pauses, looks down at the floor and then back up at me. "Is that what he said?"

"Yes. And he said it was in the house."

"Hmm." She looks down again then over at the living room bookcase. "No. No, I don't think so." She walks over to the bookcase and stands in front of it. "No. Well, maybe he did have a diary, but if he did then no way is it here. We left Venezuela with just backpacks remember? And then left Brazil with barely more than that. Everything in this house is either rented or came from the discount store. Your father's diary—no. If he had one then it's not in this house. You must have dreamt wrong." She chuckles and heads up the stairs then says, loudly from her room, "I am going to let you slide on this today—at least until I decide what to do about it—but don't think about sneaking out again."

I check my watch and yawn. I really need some sleep. At the bookcase I check through all the books. There are only about twenty and most of them I bought anyway. No one buys books anymore. Everything's been digital since before I was born. Mom isn't a big reader either. All my favorites are here from *Ender's Game* to the *Earthsea* series, *Girl in Landscape* of course, along with a few books Mom found for me, self-help books about mean girls and how to survive high school in the hostile social environment that is UNA. No, Dad's diary is not in this house.

Mom comes back down the stairs and says, "You

know, Gabby, I had one of the most wonderful evenings last night, out with Smith, a wonderful, Cinderella night, and one of the worst night's of my life, finding you sneaking into the house." She says it casually, keeping her eyes on me and I am relieved that her rage looks to be cooling off.

"I'm sorry, Mom. I know I shouldn't have snuck out. I should have woke you and—I don't know—gone together? I just didn't think there was any way that you would let me go into the woods in the middle of the night."

"You're right there."

"So. Let me ask you this."

"Go ahead."

"If Dad had a diary, where would it be?"

"Umm, I guess it would be in the house in Venezuela which means that it would be lost. Lost with all the other stuff we lost."

"Venezuela. Yeah. The house in Venezuela. That makes sense."

I quickly change and grab my bag then head off to the car. Mom and I drive towards the airport so she can drop me off before she leaves for work.

It is a quick ride to Philadelphia International and I should absolutely be focusing on my race in Brazil but all I can think about is my father's diary and why would the Void-man (I still am not convinced he is my dad) tell me about it if it is lost?

Mom interrupts my train of thought. "You know Smith and I had a little conversation about Kyle last night."

"Oh really? What did he have to say?"

"He took me back for a minute. Said, 'Kyle was right.' Then when I asked him what he was talking about, he said something about 'Kyle was right about our perceptions being illusions' because our eyes trick us all the time. He said that he has seen many experiments where what we think we see and what the instruments show are two different things." She pauses for a few seconds and lowers the music on the screen. "Of course I knew that already. Your father used to say things like that all the time. Scientists all think alike, I guess. If it's something they cannot measure then it doesn't exist. Empiricists! Huh!"

"What does that mean?"

"My goodness, Gabby. What are they teaching you in that school?"

"I don't know. What does it mean?"

"Empiricists are people that believe that if something cannot be measured then it doesn't exist. Basically," she explains.

"I guess that makes sense."

"It makes sense until you think about all that you lose."

"Like what?"

Mom says, "For them—this is a generalization now —not everyone thinks the same way, of course. But for them, the most strictest cases anyway, they don't think that there is any world outside of the material world."

"So there is no—what?"

"No thought. No spirit. No self." She looks over at me for a moment and smiles a half smile. "There is no Gabriella. The pile of flesh that we all label as Gabriella is merely a collection of cells that happen to work together for the mutual success of the organism. There is no 'you.' You have no *mind*, no *thought*; there is no *you*. What we consider as *you* is merely a collection of responses from neurons in that fleshy brain in your head, responses that were conditioned by years of stimuli. You have no thoughts. What we think of as thoughts are merely the effects, the results that is, of prior causes, of previous stimuli."

"Smith thinks that?"

"I don't think he goes that far. But still—he *is* a scientist. He doesn't take too quickly to theories that cannot be proven. All theories must be tested with experiments. And he doesn't trust what anyone says that they *saw*. That's for sure."

"And Dad? What did he think?"

"Much like Smith." She pauses for a moment then continues, "You remember the peanut butter experiment, don't you?"

"Hahaha. How could I forget? I was like five?"

"Five or six."

"Yeah. All I said to Dad was, 'This peanut butter is the best!' and I remember I was holding the sandwich in my hand, one of the first that you let me make by myself, and the peanut butter was dripping down my arm. Remember? And Dad says, all serious and scientific-like, 'Oh, we'll see about that.' "

Mom chuckles.

I continue, "The next day, Dad, without warning, shows up with ten different brands of peanut butter, labels off the jars of course, and makes ten different sandwiches for *each of us*. I loved it and you couldn't believe it. 'The only way we can know which is the best,' he said, 'is to run an experiment.' That was the absolute greatest!"

"Yeah. Those were good times." Mom has an almost smile but her voice sounds suddenly sad and distant.

We pull onto the access ramp for departures of

Philadelphia International, coast up to the drop off and I get out with my bag. I give Mom a big hug and whisper, "I love you," in her ear and then I am off to the terminal and she is off to work.

I pass through the automatic doors, my small carry-on luggage in tow, sweeping my eyes around the baggage and ticketing sections looking for the rest of the team when my eyes land on a young man wearing fashionably tight jeans and a semi-transparent shirt, good-looking, really good-looking, staring at me. My heart starts racing the moment I see it: a small semi-round black spot with tiny tendrils sweeping away from the center on his left forearm. He is across from me, on the other side of the space, and even though I don't see the rest of the team, I involuntarily start walking quickly to the left, my eyes glued to the floor in front of me, hoping that he is not still looking at me and completely lost to what all of this means. He has a black spot! I near the main entrance doors and glance back at him, somehow dreading what I already know I will see; he is still staring at me, propped up against the wall like he is part of it.

"Gabriella! Over here!" Donavan bellows.

I turn and almost trip over my own feet as I scramble towards the team congregating near the security checkpoint. They are all there; Sidney, Cyndi, Max, Qi and Nomi; the new girls, Mercury, Greta and Sandstone; the team doctor, coaches, trainers and Sebastian; and even the pro team runners, some of whom I remember from last season; Jena, Mercury and Dart. I am somewhat surprised to see our pro team runners until I remember that this is a duel match; both the pro and semipro teams will travel together and will both compete; our team first and the pro team the following day. I don't know why I forgot that. Too much Void-man distractions on my mind, I guess, and I know I have to stop that. I have to focus on competing. The team is counting on me.

I join with the others and Donavan says that we are waiting for a few more of the pro runners and then we will leave. I slide over to Mercury, Jena and Dart to say 'Hi'. At the beginning of last year's season we ran together, when I first joined the team, before I was hurt, and before they moved up to the pros. Now they are like movie stars to some people, the fast and the famous, and they definitely look it: custom, designer clothes, beautiful hair and their shoes, my goodness, those shoes—to die for.

"Hey Jena. Hey Dart. Mercury, how's it going?"

"Hey, err, Gab— Gabriella, right?" Jena replies.

"That's me! We ran together for a short while last year."

"Yeah, yeah, yeah, I totally remember you, Gabriella. Your name just slipped my mind too," adds Dart. "You are that all-natural girl. I remember the *SI* issue. And then one of the Brazilian girls broke your leg."

"Velocity Jones. You've raced her, right? Got to watch her. She likes to break girls."

Mercury chimes in, "Oh, we've seen her a few times since then. Actually she's part of the reason we moved up to the pros."

"Oh yeah. I seem to remember that. When I was out last year Velocity moved up to the pros and took out some of the Liberty's girls, right? Then you all got the call?"

"That and one of the girls got pregnant and retired." Dart says.

"I'd just watch out for her that's all. She has two underlings with her. One of them is named Carilla. Velocity pulls those two around by the nose and the three of them work together."

Jena answers, "Oh don't worry. Us three work together too. That's why we're all still in the game. If you don't have someone watching your back it's not long before your leg is broken or you have a cracked skull. Either way you're out of the game—hasta la bye bye and see ya later, sucka. Like Donavan used to always tell us, you're gone."

And that's me. All alone out there. Sooner or later someone's going to take me out and I'm going to be stale, dry toast.

"Hey Mercury, you heard we got another Mercury?"

"Yeah," she replies, looking over toward our new Mercury.

After a few moments of uncomfortable silence, I say, "Okay. Good seeing you three and good luck out there."

Later the rest of the girls show up. With them is the new staff girl that I spied through the doorway about a week ago, the girl with the black spot on the back of her neck. Her name, I found out, is Allison. Her hair is down but I know it's there, the black spot. I know it's there not because I remember what she looks like but because as soon as she steps near me the black spot on my back starts tingling and as soon as it does she turns toward me with a queer, questioning look on her face.

I have a black spot. She has a black spot and that guy with too-tight jeans has a black spot. What's going on here? Now I'm seeing black spots everywhere?

All of us start to move through the security check

point, the large lot of us snaking through the long winding line in order for the bored guards to check our passes and each time the black-spot girl—her name is Allison, I know, but I can't stop thinking of her as black-spot girl—and I cross paths my black spot begins to tingle and the more that this happens the more that she watches me out of the corner of her eyes. I can't wait to get out of this line. After our third pass, I come to the end of a row, turn and see the young guy I saw before, leaning against a planter with a palm tree erupting out of it, noodling his sunglasses, as if he is a fashion model selling his ultra-tight jeans, watching me but pretending that he is not watching me. My heart rate speeds up but not as much as before because I know he can't do anything to me; I am surrounded by my team; there are security guards everywhere; he can't get me. I keep scooting forward, every few minutes, our team like one long awkward centipede and just as I come up parallel with black-spot-girl Allison I notice her wiggling her fingers in an odd pattern at someone behind me. I quickly flash my eyes back and see that ultra-tight jeans guy is wiggling his fingers back at her and once he sees me, he stuffs his finger wiggling hand in his pocket and casually moseys off. I pass through security and the guard who checks my papers is very thorough, overly thorough, insanely thorough, probably because I am shaking, twitching and looking around too much, but he eventually lets me through and it is not until we are at our gate that I start to calm down.

We board the team's plane, the front office staff in first class, the pro athletes in the first twenty rows and us farm-teamers in the back. It is going to be a twelve-hour flight so most of the girls brought pillows but of course I forgot mine so I grab a window seat near the back corner so I can wedge my head against the cold wall—nice sleeping this is going to be.

After we take off and the stewards and stewardesses go through all the boring safety stuff, the plane grows quiet and all the main lights go out so everyone can rest. Of course I can't sleep with my head bouncing off the ice-cold wall so I form my body as comfortable as possible which isn't really comfortable at all and think about all the crazy stuff that has been happening recently, all the crazy stuff that I shouldn't be wasting a thought on, all the crazy stuff that has absolutely nothing to do with my race tomorrow.

I still don't understand why the Void-man, if he is my dad, doesn't talk to me, doesn't tell me anything I can understand, doesn't answer any of my questions, at least answer them in any way that I can understand. He said that my dad had a diary. If he is my dad, my dead dad's spirit anyway, then just tell me what's in it! He must not be my dad! But how can he look like him? And why does he know so much about me? And why is he helping me anyway?

I wish I could sleep! A sharp pain enters my neck as the plane hits a small patch of turbulence so I reposition again.

Diary! Diary! Diary! I sure wish I had that thing right now! I wonder what's in it? I wonder why the Void-man wants me to have it? I mean, what does he care? Mom is right though; I think that it would still be in Venezuela, in our old house, lost somewhere. I know when we fled to Brazil, I heard later on from Mom, that she had someone from the family, one of Dad's cousins named Issa, come and sell the building. They told everyone that we all had died, tried to cover our tracks for the escape. Weird. Now we are in UNA and Smith knows who we really are and it's like it's no big deal. I still can't wrap my brain around that one.

Issa's not a very common name, at least in Venezuela. I never heard anyone named that in Los Teques. I wonder if I could track him down? I wonder if he has the diary?

Turning around, trying to get into a more comfortable position I spy the girl with the black spot on her neck—Allison—looking over at me from across the plane and she quickly looks away. I need to find out more about her. She got that spot from somewhere and it can only be one of two places: from Kyle or from the Void.

As much as I hate to open up old wounds, I am going to have to contact Michael. I really need to talk to him anyway. I need to at least try to make friends with him. If this girl was associated with Dr. Duggan's project then Michael would know. And what about the guy in the airport? Weird. It almost looked like he was following me. And those two with their fingers—almost as if it was some kind of sign language. All I know is that when I am around that girl I start to feel funny, almost the same way I feel when I am around Kyle. Clearly this black spot is affecting me and not in a way that I like. If I can get back on Michael's good side maybe he can help me to figure out how to get rid of this thing?

Just as drowsiness begins to permeate my brain something starts wafting across my semi-unconsciousness. "Do not be deceived... Do not be deceived... Do not be deceived... the bouncing numbers... the shaded letters... the shaking digits... the random dots."

I sit up straight.

What! The shaking digits! The shaking digits! They

were shaking their fingers! The Void-man—he was trying to tell me something—in his poem—it was some kind of warning. He was warning me to not be deceived by the shaking digits! It all makes sense now! No. Actually nothing makes sense. Ohh, I just wish I had that diary! Maybe then I could figure out what's going on!

Chapter 12

Brazil

We grab our bags from the overhead compartments, slowly snake through the exit isles, say 'thank you' to the stewards and stewardesses, step off the plane into the long crooked tunnel, and exit into the terminal and the bright flashing lights, the reporters and the screaming fans, fifty or so of them who happened to be at the airport traveling themselves. There will be many, many more once we leave the airport. Welcome to Brazil and Ultraball insanity. Several security guards form a circle around the team to give us a large enough birth to deboard. The front office staff, trainer and coaches along with us farm-teamers all continue to walk to the baggage claim and ground transport area as the fans typically are only interested in autographs from a handful of the pro team girls. Right now, I am so glad that the men travel in a separate plane.

Most of us only have carry-ons since we are to be here only a few days but the trainers always have extra equipment so we have to pick that up from the baggage claim. By the time their stuff is out the pro girls have shown up, signed more autographs and then we all board the team bus for the hotel where there will be more fans and more autographs to sign.

Sandstone sits next to me on the bus and as we pass through street after street full of people and traffic, horns honking aggressively, pedestrians weaving in and out of vehicle traffic as if they belong there and cars ignoring them as if they were carrion birds hovering over road kill. The mountains in the distance are covered with dirty, shiny metal objects.

"Wow! I can't believe I am here! This is my first time out of the country and I am in Brazil! This is so cool; this is so cool; this is *so* cool!" Her eyes look over at me for a reaction but I give her none. "Look at all the people. They are everywhere! It's so much more congested than New York. And all the fancy buses—why do they paint them like that? And look at that! That blue car just bumped into that other car— Ohhh, look at that! He kept on going! I guess they are just like that here? And those mountains—I love the mountains. They are covered with little shack houses? People actually live there? In those—shacks? Hey, Gabriella, you used to live here, right? Did we pass your neighborhood yet? Did you live around here? Huh?"

Looking at the mountains and the shanties, it all floods back. There's something awful in the commonness of it all—urban decay—lost hope—to know that people who once had dreams and aspirations are now broken, that human beings are living in despair, a despair so comfortable that they don't realize that they are even in it, that they have given up, that they *know* they have no future—and that is the worst part of all, the *knowledge* that they can't do anything about it. It's flooding back into me, the hopelessness of poverty, and I want no part of it because I know exactly what it feels like. I am not a tourist; this was once my life.

"I lived in Rio. It's south of here. On the ocean."

"Ohhh, on the ocean. Nice. I love the ocean. Did you love the ocean? Did you go swimming much? It's a big city too? Like this? Was it like this, huh? Did it have mountains like that with all those shacks? Do a lot of people live there?"

"I guess most of Brazil has mountains. Yeah, we had areas like that."

Sandstone says, "Poor people live there, huh? That's so sad. You know, that people have to live like that. In UNA the poor at least have apartments and screens to watch."

"Except the homeless," I say.

"Oh, yeah. I forgot about them."

"Everyone does."

The bus pulls up to our hotel and another group of waiting fans, some holding signs, begins to cheer. One of the front office staff exits the bus first and tells the fans how the autograph signing will be handled as the rest of the team gathers their stuff and exits the bus. The pro team girls exit last to minimize the ruckus and as they do, the loud and sudden howl of the crowd hits my ears through the hotel lobby doors, the hotel staff look up at us and smile, and it is now that I realize that I am not jealous of the pro girls at all. For once it feels so good to be ignored and just be left alone to my thoughts and my hotel room and my bed.

We are all issued room keys. Sandstone is paired with me as Donavan astutely observes that she is the only one who can currently tolerate me and we head up to our room and some precious relaxation time. Tomorrow's our big game. We need to sleep.

In my hotel room, I call John Murray. I don't know why. I have no reason to. Maybe being in Brazil reminds me of him.

"Hey Gabriella. How are you? In Brazil, right?"

"Yeah. Just wanted to say, 'Hi.' " I say.

"Hope you do well tomorrow."

"Me too. Don't really know what's gonna happen."

His voice is somber. "No one ever does. That's why people watch. It's unpredictability that people like. If everyone already knew who was going to win not so many people would pay attention."

"Makes sense," I reply.

"So, obviously I can't tell you what to do—"

"I know. You work for NuGen and you can only help NuGeners. No problem."

He pauses then says, "So—yeah—I can't remind you about what I told you before either."

My voice tenses. "What's that?"

His voice lowers to a near whisper. "Ahh, I can't remind you that you sometimes slow down before obstacles. Actually a lot of the girls do that. I can't tell you that you should try to speed up there."

"Oh, I remember that."

"And slingshotting. I can't tell you about that either. The São Paulo course has no obstacles on its curves. I can't tell you to try to speed up out of the curves. Try to use your momentum to slingshot out of them. I can't tell you about that."

I say slowly, "Cool idea. Is there anything else you *can't* tell me."

"No. That's about all that I can't tell you."

I say, "Surprised Donavan isn't telling me these things."

"She's a different kind of coach."

"I guess."

"We complemented each other really well. Too bad we don't work together anymore." He sounds detached from the statement and it bothers me.

"I know. Too bad. Listen, I gotta go. Gotta get some sleep. Thanks for everything."

"No problem, Gabby."

Just as I hang up, my screen rings.

"Hello?"

"Err, Gabriella, hope you don't mind me calling."

"Who is this?" I ask.

"It's Antonio. Err, I was hoping you would have recognized my voice."

"Antonio. How'd you get this number?"

Bashfully, he says, "Spike. He got it for me."

"Spike? He's a sneaky one I heard."

"Hahaha. Yeah. Listen, I just wanted to tell you good luck for tomorrow. I'll be watching you run."

"Oh, really?"

His voice has an attractive growl to it. "Yeah, I always watch you run."

"I'll try to get some points for you then," I tease.

"Okay. You didn't mind me calling did you?"

"No. And Antonio..."

"Yeah?"

"I knew it was your voice."

"Cool."

I click off. Lying in my bed I say to Sandstone, "It's late. We got a big day tomorrow. I'm going to sleep."

"Sure." Sandstone turns out the lights but I can still see the outline of her body by the filtered moonlight streaming in through the window shades.

"Gabriella?" Sandstone whispers softly a few minutes later.

"What's up?"

"Are you asleep yet?" she asks.

"Yes... No. What?"

"Can I ask you something?"

"I guess."

"You're from Brazil, right? But when you played

them, they targeted you. I looked at the footage. They went after you when they really should have gone after Sidney," Sandstone says.

"Yeah."

"And now, the rest of the team—they don't like you either."

"Your point is?" I ask.

"I didn't mean it like that. I mean… It's just that you don't seem so bad to me. When they broke your leg—how did that happen? Do you remember? Or did you bump your head too? Or the pain killers—don't they make you forget too? You don't have to tell me if you don't want to."

"Can't sleep, huh?"

"I'm too excited. I still don't know if they are going to race me tomorrow. And Brazil. They are so—physical."

"Ahh… Okay. I can tell you a little but pretty soon I need to get some sleep," I say.

"Cool."

"Three girls on the Brazilian team, they're not there anymore, one named Velocity, the other two followed her around and—it's not important—Velocity, she hates me," I explain.

"Why?"

"Good question. I think it was because I'm not modified."

"So what?"

"Sandstone, you're going to see that everything here is not what it seems. Just keep your eyes open. You'll see. Anyway, Velocity and her two goons set me up, trapped me, boxed me in and then smashed me down to the field, breaking my leg. I didn't know what was happening, what they were up to and why they were surrounding me. I wasn't the fastest. I shouldn't be their target, I thought. Then it happened, it was too late and I was tumbling, falling, out of control, I couldn't stop it and I thought for the briefest of moments, 'Oh no. This is gonna hurt,' then a POP! and a CRUNCH! and all of a sudden everything was silent and dark and black and I couldn't understand and I tried to talk but I couldn't."

"Oh my God."

"Yeah, I know. So, Donavan was screaming and I couldn't seem to form any words then I saw Sebastian and the team doctor through my watery, blurry eyes. I closed and opened my eyes, it felt like for just a moment, and when I opened them I was in the hospital, most of the team around me, and I was so pumped up full of painkillers that I can barely remember anything—except one thing—Max was crying. I am sure of that much."

"Max. She's really got a giant heart trapped in that giant body, doesn't she?"

"Yes, she does. Later I found out—and this is gonna sound weird—I found out I would never compete again. At least that's what the white coats said. The team doctor and Donavan and some of the front room staff were there too. They all looked at the floor for a few moments then left the room. I heard them through the wall talking about whom they were going to get to replace me and it all felt so final. My life was over before it even began. I couldn't stop thinking about what was going to happen next. I was just so sad and angry at the same time. I wasn't really mad at Velocity, I don't know why, just mad at myself. I kept thinking that I could have stayed in Brazil."

"Brazil." Sandstone says dreamily like it is some kind of beach-front paradise.

"Brazil. It was totally the worst. Living in a sheet

metal shack on the side of a mountain; dirt floors, no running water, no electricity, but I had friends and life was simple." I can't tell her why we were there. I can't tell her that I thought we were trapped there, hiding from anyone who was wearing anything even resembling a blue-black suit, NuGen goons who might be hunting for us. At least that's what I thought at the time.

"So you lived like that? I didn't know."

"No one does. I don't know why I'm telling you anyway."

"I won't say anything! I promise!"

"Sometimes I think it doesn't matter anymore. Sometimes I think that nothing matters anymore. But don't tell anyone, just the same."

"So you hated it? It looked really bad to me."

I reply, "It was. Sometimes. I mean we were dirt poor but there were good things too."

"Like what?"

"I remember." I pause as it comes back to me. "I remember people peeling green beans sitting out in the open, friendly people, not having much but always willing to share. I remember sitting out in the sun, sharing bananas and guava. I remember a hammock in the cool night air. I remember being hungry and a neighbor killing a chicken to feed Mom and me. I remember waking to the sound of roosters, just outside our door. I remember children playing with whatever they could find, flutes carved from sugarcane, hanging iguanas from their ears, cardboard, anything really. It was a simple time."

"Oh."

"Anyway, it was a wild ride at first. Getting 'discovered,' coming to United North America to play Ultraball, even if it was just on a B-grade farm team, even if the pay was only marginal and even if I had to learn a new language—well, forget about the language, the culture is completely different in Philly and I still haven't gotten that down—it was a lot to swallow but it still seemed like a God-send at the time, but after my leg was broken and I thought I would never walk again—that was too hard."

"So I guess that explains why those girls wanted to take you out. You are not modified and they don't like that? I guess there are a few nuts out there, right? But why do the girls on our team give you the cold shoulder? Why did you tell me to stay away from you? I don't care if you're not modified. Why should I care?"

"Do you really want to know?"

"Yeah, I think so. I know you told me to stay away but at least I think I should know why," she says.

"Okay. I'll tell you but when I'm done I'm going to go to sleep and you can join the others in hating me too."

"I would never do that."

I exhale in the dark, me staring at the ceiling, knowing I shouldn't tell her anything, but knowing that I need to tell someone, just to let it out. "We'll see. Do you remember the cute guy on our practice field? The new guy with the fold-up table?"

"Yeah? The NuGen monitoring guy? Him?"

"His name is Sebastian. He's actually returning to us. He used to have a workstation set up on our practice field all the time and did 'bot monitoring of the NuGen athletes. You know their sales pitch, right?"

She says, "They inject nanobots that flood an athlete's body in order to monitor all of their discreet cellular performance measures down to the muscle fiber level. At least that's how they describe it."

"Right. All I know is they run internal tests on an athlete, look at a lot of squiggly lines, point at one and tell a girl to run faster. Anyway, he's a nice guy. And he used to date Cyndi."

Sandstone gasps. "I didn't know."

"And his partner, another guy who worked for NuGen, named Kyle, he used to be there on the field too."

"Yeah?"

"And he was my boyfriend."

"Ohh, this sounds like it's about to get juicy."

"Not really. Sebastian and Kyle were both assigned by NuGen to the Philadelphia Freedom in order to increase the performance of the NuGen athletes on the team. Kyle and I—here it is—got engaged."

"You're, like, what? Seventeen? We're the same age, right? And you were engaged? No way!"

"Way. So anyway, I am not sponsored by NuGen but for some reason that I could not understand at the time, NuGen extended the offer to me. I don't know if it was because Kyle, my fiancé, pulled some strings. I don't know why but hey, who wouldn't take a free offer from one of the best to help you improve?"

"I know I would."

"So I did it. Sebastian was a great help and he sincerely seemed interested in helping me become stronger, faster, more agile and more intelligent about my training and performance. Of course with two girls on the team dating two guys in the near vicinity, there was some distractions. Then something bad happened. Cyndi was attacked."

She sits up on her bed. "Attacked? I never heard anything about this!"

"It was on the news. I don't think they emphasized

the 'attacked' part much. NuGen and the team didn't like the bad publicity, I'm sure. Said something more like, 'out for surgery,' I think."

"Wow."

I stare at the ceiling, refusing to look at her. "Well —here it goes—it was Kyle, my future husband who did it. And when Cyndi was attacked and most of the team suspected some kind of lover's quarrel, they all thought that it was Sebastian. Hey, even I thought that he did it. No way did I suspect Kyle."

"This is deep."

"So when I found out, I panicked. I didn't know what to do. I didn't let Cyndi know that it was really Kyle as soon as I found out. I didn't let her know that it wasn't Sebastian. I was going to. I was. Really. I just didn't know how to do it."

"Oh. That was a mistake. For sure."

"I know. In the end, Kyle and Sebastian had this major fight, full of fists and broken glass and everything, and Donavan banned Kyle and Sebastian from our facilities."

"Oh… So you didn't tell her. Even then."

"I know. I wanted to. I was going to. I can't blame them for cutting me off. I totally screwed up everything. I trusted Kyle too much or maybe for too long and I ruined my relationship with Cyndi and Sidney because I didn't trust them enough. I never made many friends when we moved here from Brazil, Cyndi and Sidney were all I really had, the only ones who could seem to relate to balancing this crazy Ultraball lifestyle with trying to be a normal teenager. I really miss them and I wish there was some way I could make it up to them, somehow get them back, somehow make everything like it used to be, but that looks impossible right now.

Anyway, I really can't believe Sebastian is back and although I have my suspicions about his past I am really glad to see him right now."

"I saw you two talking. I guess he forgives you."

"I hope so. Anyway, even though I knew Donavan couldn't keep NuGen and their nanobot monitoring off the practice field for long, them being our biggest sponsor, I am still surprised that Sebastian of all people actually made it back when Donavan swore that neither Kyle nor Sebastian would *ever* step foot on her field."

"No one wants people on the team fighting."

"My guts are spilled. Now you know everything. Good enough? I'm going to sleep."

"Sure. G'night. And Gabby?"

"What?"

"I don't hate you. You made a mistake, that's all."

Chapter 13

The Match

"All right! Listen up! Mercury! You're in today! Warm up and get ready! Greta and Cassandra, you're sitting. Don't suit up. And the rest of you! You know what to do! I want all seven of you out there warming up! Don't let them know who's running first half or how many! I better not see anyone slacking! What are you all doing still standing there? Move it!"

The rest of the girls all hustle out to the field and I don't know if Sandstone looks dejected or relieved. I turn to her and whisper, "Don't worry. You'll get your chance."

Just as I pass Donavan I say, "Coach? Can I speak with you privately?"

She frowns, turns and walks into a tiny office and says, "Make it quick."

Closing the door behind me I say, "Coach? I know I have no right to ask this—"

"Then don't!"

"I know, I know, but… It's just that—"

"Okay! Out with it!"

"I don't know if you were planning on running me first or second half but I really would like to run first—"

"Really! Well guess what! I'm the coach and I don't take requests. Gabriella, you *know* better. I can't believe you are in here doing this!"

"I'm sorry, Coach. It's just that… I have family and friends here and—"

"Stop! Stop! Stop! Stop right there! Not another word! I don't want to hear it!" She's not hollering but she is getting agitated so she shoos me out. "Out! Out! Out!"

I open the door and hustle out to the field and immediately jump into my warm-up run, about two and a half even-paced miles around the track followed by a quick half mile sprint. I try to avert my eyes from Qi who is glaring at me, clearly disapproving of me talking to Donavan privately, clearly assuming that I was asking for some kind of special treatment. I know because that's what I would have thought too. Max, Sidney and Cyndi are ignoring me, intentionally, as always. The others are just focusing on their pre-race rituals so I follow their lead and try to focus my mind on the exact movements of my body. We follow the warm-up run with striders then move on to the practice obstacles and then Donavan comes out with her screen and we all gather around her. The stands are still filling up, the field team is just finishing their warm ups and start time is getting real close.

"Gather round! We're running four first half, just like we practiced! I want Sidney, Mercury, Maxine and… Gabriella, ready in five."

A small fish leaps in my chest when she says my name and Qi immediately turns her gaze directly at me but I ignore her.

Donavan continues, "Sidney, I might run you in second half too but I need three points out of you now! Save some energy if you can but don't save anything if you have to use it to grab the prize. Let me know how you're feeling at the half. Max, you know your role! I'm counting on you! Mercury! Show me what you got out there! I don't have to tell you how important this race is to your career here with us! Gabriella, I don't want to see any of this sacrifice baloney today! Score some points will ya! And all of you, the techs are telling me that our little experiment in running with the stadium heat turned up should show us some performance gains today so if what they say is true, and I ain't saying it is, I expect to see some fast times today! That's all I gotta say! What are you all doing still standing there? Move it!"

Antonio and Spike are warming up near us. Spike gives Antonio an elbow to the ribs and Antonio looks my way and smiles. I would wave if it wouldn't get Donavan barking so all I do is smile back.

The Brazilians send out three muscular sprinters, about Sidney's size, and I feel small and fragile next to them as we jostle for position at the start line, the Brazilian fans cheering, chanting and howling already, hundreds of samba drums in full rhythm and an occasional air-horn blasting. The gun fires, the entire stadium crowd screams, the field teams kick out the blue and green balls and us girls jump into a full open-field sprint to the first obstacle.

Run, run, run! I torque up to a full speed sprint. It isn't long before I can't hear the crowd anymore I am so focused on every movement. Run, run, run, swing, leap, jump, run. Sidney and Mercury are quickly in front and two of the Brazilians are about ten yards back from them. Mercury is far too close to Sidney and I hope that they don't get taken out. That would be a disaster. What is she doing! Trying to pass her?

The rope swings are in front of me and I always slow for them since the ropes are usually in motion and missing them and falling into the water below is an instant disqualification. I force myself to not slow down, like John Murray said, and it takes the entire force of my will to do it as the creeping dread of falling into the water blankets my mind. I speed up, leap and my forearm hits the rope. I pull my arm back in a panic and barely grab the rope and continue my swing, swing, swing, from rope to rope to rope, trying to not think about what would have happened had I fell, trying to keep my focus on what comes next, every fiber of my mind in the moment, in the now, in the right now, now, now. Max is hanging back waiting to pounce and as I pass her I smile quickly. I can see indecision on her face. The last Brazilian is just behind me and Max lets her pass.

John Murray's voice is in my head. All the things that he couldn't tell me are repeating over and over and I am suddenly so aware of each time that I slow down, just like he said I would. Going into a curve I accelerate as hard as I can and try to—what did he call it?—slingshot out of the curve. The warped wall is one of my favorites and I am glad they have it here. The Brazilian fans cheer for me as I easily fly up it, grab the top ledge and hoist myself over in one swift graceful move. I am sure the news reports are claiming me as a Brazilian, even though I only lived here for a very short time. But they don't know that. No one keeps track of the poor people in the favelas.

I catch up to the two Brazilian girls, there is only one lap left and suddenly I am not exactly sure what to do. We are all close, too close, so very, very close, Sidney, Mercury, the two Brazilian girls and me. It is a recipe for disaster. If I try to pass them, one of them will surely try to tackle at least two of us. If I stay back then I don't score. What should I do?

We single file across the hanging balance beam, narrowly hanging on by the tips of our fingers. The foremost Brazilian girl is kicking her legs at Mercury with each swing, trying to hit her 'accidentally' and knock her off. After the beam we accelerate into the barrels and we hit another curve and I know it is now or never. I take the curve wide and accelerate hard, trying to slingshot as hard as I can to the point where I almost feel my legs getting too far out in front of me. I pass the two Brazilians for just a moment but the faster one speeds up and is almost parallel with me. I come up on Mercury, just to her right and the Brazilian dives towards us and gets a hand on Mercury's heel. I leap forward and vault over Mercury's tumbling body, roll and flip back into a full gallop, then yell up to Sidney, "We need to separate! Speed up or let me pass!"

She quickly glances back at me and the other Brazilian. Eying our widening gap she lets me pass. Max steps out onto the course just after we pass and opens her arms wide to take out the second Brazilian. Just as I cross the finish a twisted mix of exhilaration and relief rushes into my chest and a booming cacophony of sound floods into my ears: drums, cheers, horns and squeals. It is the first time I score three points and it suddenly feels so good.

I don't know why Sidney let me pass her. She gave those three points to me. Why? Because I just made Mercury fall?

I trot off the field and Sandstone is bouncing in the air, cheering, "Epic! Epic! Epic!"

As I reach the benches, Mercury screams, towel held to her bloodied cheek, "What was that! Gabriella! You screwed up! You got too close to me and I got tackled!"

"I—"

"Nothing to say! Right!" She points the bloody towel at me. "This blood should be on your face! Not mine!"

Donavan turns and barks, "That's enough! Mercury! Sit down!"

I walk over to Coach who is alternately staring at her screen and at the field game as she mutters to herself. "Coach? My stomach doesn't feel so good. I'm gonna go talk to doc and then lay down. You weren't planning on running me second half were you?"

"No. Good job out there. Go get yourself checked out."

"Thanks. And oh by the way, after the game I am going to go out with that family I told you about."

"Ahh... Okay, but check out with the handlers first. That's not my call. And make sure to be back at the hotel by lights out."

I hold my stomach and walk past the team, not looking at any of them, then down to the lockers, change my clothes, grab my bags, head out the back door and hail a cab for the airport, all the while thinking that I can't believe that I am doing this. I can't believe that I am sneaking out to try to find my Dad's diary.

In Venezuela.

Chapter 14

Escape to Venezuela

I am lucky enough to catch a flight to Caracas. The whole time in the air I calculate and recalculate the flight time there, the flight time back, how much time I'll have in Venezuela and how I'm going to get back in time to not get into too much trouble. Time, time, time, I wish I had more time!

There is obviously no way that I can make it back before lights out. The flight to Venezuela will take over four hours. I am going to have to try to bluff the front office girl. Call her in a few hours and tell her that I am spending the night with my family. If I can make it back by tomorrow night then maybe I won't get into too much trouble. But even that is a tight schedule. Total travel time with taxis and all, maybe ten hours. That gives me maybe fifteen hours to find the book. Twenty tops. And that's if I don't sleep at all except on the planes. And I hate sleeping on planes. And how can I sleep? I'm too worried about what Donavan's going to say. And too worried about trying to find the book.

Then, right there, on the plane, the loneliness comes hard and fast; the isolation rises up and grabs my throat. It leaps onto me like it belongs here; an old, worn, comfortable sweater. It is my true condition now. I am ignored, suppressed and unwanted; a pest, a disease. I am alone, here, doing something that, when found out, will make me more alone. It is all my fault. I have exiled myself from anyone who has ever cared about me. Now

I will make it worse. But I don't have a choice. Do I? I must take a risk. A metaphysical risk. A risk that all the insanity is real.

The flight is uneventful. I exit the plane, cross the tarmac and head toward the taxi area. There's not many people in the airport at this time of evening so it jars me when I see two young guys wearing blue-black suits. I would know those suits anywhere and from a mile away; they are NuGen guys. We lock eyes for a moment then I turn and jog down to the street and grab a taxi in the front of the taxi line. He drives me into Los Teques, my old home town, and it looks so different; more congested, more decayed than I remember it. I have him drop me off about a block away from our old store so I can walk the rest of the way up the hill.

"<Thanks. Here you go.>" I say in Spanish, passing some money to the cab driver as he pulls up to the intersection and I exit. Whipping out my screen I call the number I have for Issa, one of my Dad's cousins that for some odd reason I have never met. It rings and rings and rings and he doesn't answer.

Maybe it's too late? Now what?

I stroll up the curved street, toward our old store and I can't believe how bad it's gotten here. So many stores are boarded up or look run-down. There is graffiti on the side wall and it's not even good graffiti. You know it's bad when your graffiti is of such low quality that the good scrawlers won't even waste their time with the neighborhood because it's so raunchy. The front window to the appliance place is broken and the giant cracks in the glass are held together with strips of gray duct tape.

I reach the front of our old store and a constant stream of people seem to be going up and down the staircase on the side of the building.

Just then it starts tingling, the black spot, and I can't help but look around.

Every time it has tingled in the past I was in close proximity to someone who had a spot, someone else who had something to do with the Void. But how is that possible here? There must be another reason.

Across the street, standing in front of the liquor store, brown bags in hand, are three young guys. One of them is louder than the others and just as our eyes meet he motions and they start to cross the street towards me. I can see the bulges in their shirts, just above their waistlines; they all have knives. I turn on my heel and walk back in the direction I came, towards the bus stop, back down the hill, and where the taxi dropped me off but it is long, long gone. I pull out my screen as I walk and frantically dial Issa's number again. Pick up! Pick up! Pick up! I glance back at them and they are clearly following me.

"<Ayyee, Mommy! Where ya going?>" one of them hoots and I know I need to be somewhere else.

I could run. Yes, I could run. I don't think they could catch me. But where would I go?

"<Ayyee! My love! You don't have to go! We just want to talk!>"

Yes. Yes, as a matter of fact, I have to run. I glance back once more and see them in the light, under the corner street lamp, and they look dingy and gross. Even though it is the last thing I want to do I immediately turn and fall into a sprint. It is the last thing I want to do because I know that here only victims run. Eyes everywhere are suddenly on me; I can feel them. I duck to the left at the corner and fly, full speed, dodging pedestrians, quickly dart across the street, avoiding oncoming traffic as if it were standing still, horns blaring, driver's fists waving, landing on the sidewalk pavement and slide to the right at the next corner running directly into a couple of young men, me bowling over one of them, us tumbling to the ground.

"<Hey! Hey! Watch it! Watch it!>"

I bound to my feet and look back to see if the three are still following, me pressing my back up against the wall and whispering loudly in Spanish, "<Sorry! Sorry! My fault! My fault!>"

"<Hey! Hey! Watch out! Where you going?! Wait a minute! You're Gabriella!>"

Oh no! An Ultraball fan? How is that possible? "<You know me?>" I say, sliding down the wall, trying to position myself for a sprint if needed, if the three round the corner.

"<Know you? It's me! Tony Motorola!>"

It's Tony Motorola! We grew up together. Kind of. His father owned the store down the street so we saw each other sometimes; we had a few classes together; we had a similar story, children of store owners. Foreigners. But he always seemed lecherous to me, even as a kid.

"<Tony? Wow! I haven't seen you in—>"

He brushes some dust off my shoulder and his two friends give us some space. "<Yeah. Since... you died? Right? That's what they told us. That you died. Some freak car accident? Now you're here, in the flesh. Imagine that!>"

"<Yeah. Well it's real good seeing you again. I have to be going—>"

"<Woah. There a problem?>" Tony looks back in the direction from where I came and sees the three standing on the opposite side of the street eying me.

"<Those three?>" Tony asks.

I nod.

Tony yells over to them, "<Eyyy, Coco! Get your own meat pie! This one's with me!>"

The leader howls, "<Ayy, Tony! Who ya think you are? I had her first!>"

"<She's an old friend! Beat it!>"

He grabs my hand and tugs and I don't like it but I follow him. The three stagger off.

"<So, Tony Motorola, what have you been up to? Working in your father's store?>"

We turn down the street and retrace my escape route.

"<Yeah. What else?>" he says.

"<By the way, thanks. And... by the way, I'm not your meat pie.>"

"<Ha ha ha. Sorry. It's just an expression. It doesn't mean anything.>"

I say, looking around at the decay, "<The old neighborhood. I don't remember it like this.>"

"<That's because it wasn't like this.>"

"<I wasn't sure if my memory was that bad, but yeah, it looks run-down.>"

"<I know. Look at this,>" he says as he points at the cracked front window to his father's appliance store. "<This would have never happened five years ago. Is that how long it's been? Five years since you died? Since they told us you died?>"

"<Not quite. More like four, I think.>"

"<You know I was heartbroken.>" He grabs his chest with both hands and leans back, then smiles at his own performance.

"<Oh yeah?>" One thing hasn't changed in all these years. Tony is still cute, although I didn't recognize him at first, but now I don't see how I mistook him. No, it's him All right; the cute boyish smile. It's just covered by a layer of muscle and manliness that wasn't there so many years ago. But I am sure he is still a skirt-chaser.

"<Yeah. I had a crush on you for years, but I never told you, never let you know. When I heard the news I was kicking myself for months, like it would have made a difference. You being dead and all.>"

"<Yeah, me being dead,>" I repeat.

"<But here you are!>"

"<Hey Tony, by the way, what happened to my house? Who bought it?>"

"<Some guy. The guy who told everyone that you were dead came and sold it. Quick too. He didn't care either. Sold it cheap and fast and that's when it started.>"

"<When what started?>"

"<He sold off the building to some clown from Caracas who is never around and never responds to any of the complaints from the neighborhood. So, yeah. This clown who bought the building, he goes and rents out all the rooms of your house, individually. Like there's a guy up there who rents your bedroom.>"

"<What?>"

"< Yeah, he rented it out to a bunch of scum-sucking troublemakers. You know the type. Criminals, street gangers, drug dealers, all kinds of scum.>"

"<No way,>" I say wondering how I am ever going to find my father's diary now.

"<Believe it. And the women. Oh no, don't get me started on them.>"

"<So. The neighborhood went down because—>"

"<Don't blame yourself. You were dead, remember. It's just what happens, I guess. So anyway, what happened to you? Where did you go?>"

"<It's a long story and I don't have that much

time. Basically we moved to Brazil. I'm in a real rush though. Wish I could stay and talk. I need to track down my father's cousin, the one who sold the house, to see what he did with our stuff.>"

"<Your stuff? Most of it they left in the building and some of it got put out on the curb. What exactly are you looking for?>"

"<I was looking for something, something we left behind, something my dad left behind.>"

He points at my old house. "<You want to go check it out?>"

"<What? What do you mean? Go up there?>"

"<Yeah. I'll go with you.>"

That's what I came here for, but no way was expecting this. I don't know what I was expecting actually. But not this.

I wrap my arm in his and say, "<Okay, I guess.>"

We cross the street and mill into the pack of them, grungy, dirty people, people who smell of urine, people with strong body odor, and I squeeze Tony's arm tighter.

Tony wades through, me in tow, and makes nice with the group. "<Guapo, how's it going? Maria, cleaning up tonight? Chulo, saw your pop the other day. He looked good.>"

We push through and head straight up the cement stairs poured into the side of the hill following an old guy with scraggly white hair wearing a torn jean jacket, his arm tight around a beautiful young woman who could be his daughter, but certainly not the way he is holding her. He pauses halfway up the stairs, grabs the metal pipe that is posing as a handrail and retches over the side.

The woman pushes back away from him and yelps, "<Eeww! I'm not kissing you now!>"

He mumbles, "<It's only a little vomit.>"

Tony pulls me up the stairs and we squeeze past them, me hoping none of his splatter gets on my shoes. We scale the steps and enter the center courtyard of the house and I am astonished at what I see. It is the end of the warm season in South America, past the longest day of the year, and it's not quite dark yet. The sky still shows a tinge of the daylight color of the sky and I remember how it used to shine through the avocado trees, a slight shade of blue. I remember the air, mild and fragrant. The scent of cut grass mixed with flowers, the scent of crops and farming and well-wrought hard work. We used to stand at the rear of the patio, Dad and I, leaning on the veranda overlooking the back of the village. Our house is near the top of the hill and the view was magnificent. Yes, we used to stand there and look across the olive groves, cattle grazing the countryside, the small single-story homes in the distance, people sitting on porches or beneath shade trees and the church with the steeple. On Sundays, if I sat quietly, I could just make out the music, the choir and the people singing praises, faintly wafting on the breeze. But now all I see is refuse and destruction. Rolled up diapers, dirty papers, rags and all form of things that humans have used up, destroyed, broken and discarded litter the floor, strewn here and there. About twenty people in various states of intoxication stand, sit or lay on the open floor. Several of the doors, the doors that were once our bedrooms, Dad's, Mom's and mine, are hanging open and random people walk in and out of them as if it is some kind of public space.

Tony says, "<Where do you want to look first?>"

"<Look! Are you kidding me? What's going on here?>"

"<I told you already. Now you see it with your own eyes.>"

I question, "<But... why are the doors open?>"

"<C'mon. I'll show you.>"

He tugs my arm and we head towards an open door, the doorway to my old bedroom, and I am terrified at what I might find in there, terrified of why he might be pulling me in there.

We walk into the room, me trying to step over dirty and torn clothing strewn on the floor. A single incandescent bulb hangs from a wire that has been pulled from the wall where my ceiling fan used to be. Where my metal-tube-framed trundle bed was lies a dirty mattress on the floor. No sheets, a bundled single blanket covers its foot, dirty. We round the corner to the small L-shaped room and sitting behind a desk, my old, "little-princess" desk, is an old, fat man wearing a wife-beater shirt, leaning back on the hind legs of a wooden chair, his left foot on the desk, my desk, rocking slowly back and forth.

"<Hey Paco, what's low?>" Tony says.

"<Nothing. You know,>" the fat man says.

"<No customers today?>"

"<In and out. Slow,>" the fat man replies.

"<Yeah? Competition?>" Tony asks.

"<Maybe. My product's good.>"

"<So they say,>" Tony says.

"<What ya buying?>"

The conversation is too surreal and I can't believe I am here, in my old bedroom, right now, listening to two men talk about buying and selling things that I am quite sure are illegal in most of the known, civilized world, as if they are at a donut counter.

"<Nothing. My girl here, this was her old

house.>"

"<Oh yeah? Before my time.>"

"<This was her old bedroom. Right, Gabriella?>" Tony turns to me and smiles but right now, in the dim light, it looks more like a grin.

How would he know that? How would he know that this exact room was my bedroom? And what is he trying to pull? Not knowing what to say, I spit out, "<Oh. Hi. Yes. My name is Gabriella.>"

The fat man looks at me, an open smile on his face, then laughs hard, through his belly, as if Sidney just told one of her gassers in the locker room. I have no idea how to respond so I quickly stow my arm at my side.

I place one foot behind Tony's leg, just in case I need to run out of the room, and say, "<I was... I was hoping that you might help me? Help me find something that we left behind?>"

The fat man slams his chair down and puts a large, open hand on the desk. "<You see what you see?>" He motions at the room, the bed, and the broken and lost things strewn on the floor. "<Tell me what you want. Everything is for sale.>" He pauses for a moment, then looks over at Tony and adds with a hiss, "<Everything.>"

I don't want to think about what he really means by that last word.

I stammer, "<A b-b-book. I am looking for a book. Err, I don't see it here. Okay, thank you. Bye bye.>"

I quickly walk out the room, step just past the doorway and press my back into the wall. It feels safer, having the wall on my back.

Tony steps out, turns to me and chuckles.

"<Comedian, that Paco. Did he scare you?>"

"<It's not funny.>"

"<I think it is. Hahaha. Sorry. Let's look in another room.>" He smiles again as if something is hilarious, as if this is the most fun he has had in a long, long while.

"<No thanks. I really don't think it's here. I mean... look at this place.>"

"<A book, huh? Not a lot of readers here. Maybe you're right,>" Tony replies, scratching his head.

I dial Issa on my screen again and still no answer. I leave a message this time.

Tony says, "<Hey! You know I just realized. Your father's old desk. My dad grabbed that when they put it out on the curb. Maybe it's in there?>"

"<Worth a try, I guess.>" Anything to get me out of this freak show.

Chapter 15

Buzzing Spots

We head down the steps, avoiding people shuffling up, and cross the street. My black spot is buzzing again, suddenly, so I look around as we walk, then we enter Motorola Appliances and the buzzing stops.

Someone or something is outside. Is my black spot trying to warn me?

Tony says some words to a few of the employees then we exit out the back of the store and take the stairs up to his home on the second floor.

We enter an open-air courtyard similar to the one we just left at my old house except this one is clean and well kept although simply furnished. Tony tugs me toward a doorway and twists the handle. We enter and he quickly closes the door behind me.

"<Here we are,>" he says.

"<Tony? Where's the desk?>"

"<I thought we could... you know.>"

"<Is this your bedroom? Tony. No. I don't know what you're thinking.>"

"<Ahh... You know. For old times' sake.>"

"<There were no old times.>" I reach for the door handle and he grabs my hand and I feel like things are about to become violent.

"<Tony, do you want to know what really happened? When I left? What really happened to me?>"

He backs up a little and says, "<Yeah, sure.>"

"<I play Ultraball.>"

"<Hahaha. You? Right!>"

"<Grab your screen. Look me up.>"

"<You're serious?>"

"<I'll show you.>" I pull up the team's page on my screen and show him the team roster.

"<That's... you? It looks like you. But the name's different.>"

"<It's me. So don't make me smash you. I could do it. I could.>"

"<Yeah? Okay, I was just kidding anyway. Let me show you that desk.>"

We exit the room and the way Tony moves is as if he has lost interest and wants to get rid of me as soon as possible. I couldn't agree more. His father has a small room where he apparently does the record keeping for the business. Under the clutter of picture frames, papers and used Styrofoam containers is my father's old desk. I start rifling through the drawers and Tony says, "<Hey! Wait a minute!>"

"<Don't worry. It will all go back,>" I say as I continue to rapidly inspect every crevice.

"<What's this book for anyway?>" Tony says.

"<Ahh... Something my father left me. Just memories, you know.>"

"<Memories?>"

"<Yeah, my father died in that car accident. But not Mom and me. We lived. And we left.>"

"<Oh,>" Tony says but he still seems uninterested in anything but my legs.

I dial Issa's number again and still no answer but for some reason I feel like I am missing something.

I didn't find it. It's not here. But where next? It's getting late and I feel like giving up. But then what? Forget this ever happened? I am already in trouble. To go back now would be to go back with nothing. But what do I do now?

Looking at the front of the desk an old memory of my father flashes in my mind. He used to sit at that desk for hours, running through the numbers, the sales figures and the orders. My father had a screen of course, but he always used a pencil and he always had mountains of loose leaf papers on this desk. But there was a book, a little blue book, that was there too. I never thought about it. Actually, I never thought about much of the stuff on his desk or in his office. Not until now. I remember once walking in on him, I was maybe nine or ten years old, and he was stuffing the little blue book behind the desk. That was a weird place to keep a book, I thought at the time.

I pull on the desk, sliding it across the hard wood, trying to not cause any scratches on the floor.

"<Hey, what are you doing?>" Tony says.

I squeeze my body between the wall and the desk, sit on the floor and push the desk away using my feet then stand up and look at the back of the desk. Tony walks around and stands next to me. I run my finger along the edge of the wooden seam. My finger feels a small raised bump so I slap the desk hard.

"<Hey, stop that!>" Tony says.

I look up at him then back at the desk and hit it again.

"<Hey! That's enough!>" Tony grabs my hand.

"<Okay, I'm done,>" I say and stand facing him.

"<Sorry you didn't find it,>" he says as he turns to leave.

As soon as his back is turned I kick the side of the desk as hard as I can and the back pops open and the little blue book falls out. I quickly retrieve it and tuck it under my arm. I got it! I got it!

"<Hey! What's that? Let me see that? What do you have there?>" Tony reaches for it.

"<I got what I came for. My Dad's book. I won't bother you anymore.>"

"<Wait a minute now. Let me see that. You are taking that from my father's desk. Maybe it's his. Give me that book,>" Tony demands.

"<You're not serious, are you?>" And from the look on his face, he absolutely is serious.

I push him hard on the chest with both arms and run out of the room, across the open courtyard and down the steps. He is following me close yelling, "<Hey! Hey! Hey! Stop! Wait!>"

But I'm not stopping. I'm not waiting. I'm running. As soon as I push through the appliance store exit doors and dump out onto the street my black spot rises quickly and begins a full on tingling-buzzing sensation. I dodge street people, careening down the hill as the fast fading sun leaves us. People are looking at me, lots of people, because I'm running, and—I know— that's a bad thing to do here.

I duck down a street to the left and Tony's yells are becoming more distant and another block later they stop altogether so I stop running, start walking and look back to see where he is. He's gone.

Taxi. Taxi. Taxi. A taxi right now would be nice.

An older gentleman with a long wooden pole in his hand steps out of the doorway just in front of me and uses the pole to pull down the metal accordion to protect the store front. I pass another store and another and just as I reach a small bakery the black spot goes into full alarm and it—feels—so—good! An exotic tingling massage all over my neck and radiating down my back. Whoever is causing it, is close, real, real close.

I duck into the next alcove, an apartment entrance, and pull out my screen, pretending that I am on it. I see a woman and a man in the bakery and the woman motions to the man and they exit the bakery and start looking around, pointing at people across the street. I am behind them by less than five feet and I hope they do not turn around. The woman—oh no!—She has a black spot!

Please don't turn around! Please don't turn around!

Just then, one of the apartment entrance doors opens in the tiny alcove and I yank the door open and push myself in.

"<Hey! Hey!>" the young girl who opened the door yelps.

"<Shhh! Shhh! Please! Please! Shhh!>"

The girl turns and runs up the steps. "<Mama! Mama! Mama! A girl! At the door!>"

I run behind her up the steps and enter their kitchen and quickly say, "<I'm sorry! I'm sorry! Please! Can I hide here? Just for a few moments? Please? Please? Please?>"

The girl's mother has a wooden spoon in her hand and she looks down at the knife on her counter then back up at me.

I say, "<I'm sorry. I didn't mean to barge into your home. I 'm just trying to hide from some people. Just for a moment and then I will leave. Please?>"

She pauses, staring at me, and then says, "<You can stay a few minutes then you have to go.>"

I walk to the window, looking down onto the street, but the woman with the black spot is nowhere to be seen. I call Issa again on my screen but still, no answer. Then I look up the number for a taxi service, call them and ask for a dispatch. While I am waiting for the cab, I thumb through my father's little blue book but nothing looks significant. Numbers, dates, quantities; it looks like a sales and ordering ledger from the clothing store we used to own. It is clearly my dad's though. It is in his hand writing.

The cab arrives so I turn, say thank you and apologize again. Neither the mother or daughter respond so I quickly head down the stairs, pop open the door and head toward the taxi cab parked on the curb a few feet up the street. As I place my hand on the door handle a distinct voice rings out behind me, a voice as clear as a one of those Sunday afternoon church bells, a voice speaking English in a dialect I am quite familiar with, a voice with a South Philadelphia slide. "There she is! Get her!"

I fling the door open, leap into the back of the cab and slap the back of the chair, saying, "<Airport! Airport! Go! Go! *Go!*>"

As the cabbie quickly pulls away, I smack the door-lock down and peek out the window to see two men in blue-black suits arriving just a moment too late.

I exhale and let my tension all-out. That was close, too close. NuGen dogs! Somehow they knew I was here. But how?

In the safety of the cab, knowing that I am now on my journey back to Brazil, I gaze at the buildings of my old neighborhood. I can almost recognize them. A few of the buildings are the same but most are painted and decorated differently as businesses have changed hands. Funny how things change.

And the lady with the black spot. What was she doing here? She must have followed me?

I massage my black spot noticing that it is not

raised. I am safe. I am safe.

Looking out the window, I am puzzled as to why we are not on the highway yet.

"<Driver? You understand I want to go to the airport, right?>"

He doesn't answer.

"<Excuse me? Sir?>"

He glances back at me and smiles and it's as he turns his head that I notice a very small black spot on his neck.

No. No. No. This can't be. Not here. That must be a mole. Am I seeing them everywhere? Am I going crazy?

He passes another entrance ramp for the highway and continues to burrow deeper into the city. I don't know where he plans on taking me but it is not to the airport and I have to get out of this cab. I grab hold of the door handle and softly unlock the door, staring out the window, eyes ablaze, looking for an opportune moment to exit. He glances back at me quickly, too quick for me to get a good look at his face, and he speeds up suddenly, flying through an intersection without stopping, leaving honking and screeching cars in his wake.

My hand squeezes the handle harder and I begin to sweat. Up ahead is a small underpass. It's now or never. The cab slows slightly, but not much, as it bounds over a speed bump just in front of the underpass and I fling open the door and dive out, trying unsuccessfully to land on my feet, tumbling, tumbling, tumbling onto the hard pavement. I am scratched, scraped, hurt and bleeding but there is no time. I quickly roll to my feet, dodge back down the road about fifty feet. The cab is in reverse now and speeding towards me. I leap over a railing and run down the hill towards the road below. As I reach it, I look up and see the driver out of his cab, stepping over the railing to follow me.

Run! Gabby, run! I speed through street after darkening street, taking turns at random, left, right, right, left, left and I know I am lost but I can't think about that right now. I have to hide. His foot falls are more distant now.

Hide! I look back and he is no longer in sight. I take another turn, duck down an alleyway and slide my body into an icky pile of rubbish, covering myself with trash and try to breathe shallowly, silently, trying to force my heart rate to slow. Fear wraps me in its long cloak and I know that if he walks down this alley he will find me. There is no exit. I'm trapped.

I wait. And wait. And wait. Lying there, trying to ignore the pain of scrapes and bruises, trying to not think about what happens if some of this rot and decay rubs into my open wounds, I wait. I hear footsteps near the alley entrance but am not positioned to look. I can't move, can't take a chance or revealing my location. The sound dissipates so I wait. And wait. And wait. Two late night partiers go by then I wait. And wait.

A noise and footsteps at the alley entrance throw me into full alarm. Someone's coming down the alley! My mind reels, gauging my odds of escape. The steps become louder and I do not know if I am imagining that they are getting closer or if it is just the fear.

"<Hey!>" a man hisses loudly.

Paralyzed, I don't move. I don't even breathe.

"<Hey! He's gone! Come with me. We will hide you.>"

I move the dirty cloth from my face and see a ragged-looking older man looking down at me. I push up from the trash heap, not as easily as I thought as my injuries have stiffened my arms and legs. He reaches down and grabs my arm so I flinch.

"<Let me help you,>" He says defensively.

I struggle to walk next to him, cautiously, my hip in tremendous pain, then throw my arm over his shoulder and we hobble off. When I finally sit down on the chair in his room, a woman looks at me nervously and I begin to cry.

His young daughter walks across the room and up to me then strokes my arm, perhaps imitating something she has seen her parents do before.

The woman brings me a wet rag so I clean my face then wipe my scrapes. The woman and the man step into another room and I cannot understand her words but her tone is enough. The woman does not want me here.

When they return, I say, "<Thank you for helping me but I cannot bother you further.>"

The man raises his hand and says, "<You are in my protection now. It is our way.>"

"<I really just need to go to the airport. Do you know how far it is?>"

"<It is too far to walk. And you cannot... No, not on these streets. Not at this time.>"

I look down at the young girl who has not left my side and not stopped staring at me. I stroke her young head and look back at the man.

"<You've taken a risk bringing me here. I must go.>"

"<Manuel, my friend, he runs a cab. It is very late, but I will call him. Maybe he will answer me.>"

When the cab arrives, I thank them quickly and run as best I can to the cab and dive in as if I am a wildebeest traversing a stream of crocodiles but there is no motion on the dark street.

"<Please, to the airport. Please don't wait. Please, just go.>"

He drives me to the airport but we do not talk. A cab driver hears too many secrets and sometimes they know better than to ask.

I pay him double his fare and enter the airport.

I book a ticket and wait for my flight by the floor-to-ceiling windows and look out at the rising sun masking the city in silhouette. Then it hits me. A part of me feels dismay at the thought that I am here, in this city. It seems impossible now, that I am even here, but once it seemed impossible that I would ever leave this place. I left Venezuela the first time on equally short notice, an equally frantic escape, taking the clothes I was wearing and not much else, a few items thrown hurriedly into a backpack. We had just left a Brazilian restaurant. I can still remember the taste of seafood.

Nothing is certain. Where will I be tomorrow? I cannot say. I cannot say what will happen or what will become of me.

Chapter 16

Caught

"Gabriella, this is out of my hands." Coach says it soft and low and that is why I know she's serious. If she screamed like she always does, I could handle it, but this —no, I'm in big trouble.

I wait in the small room as she leaves. I try to distract myself, looking at the floor tiles and cinder block walls, anything to keep my mind from wandering to what comes next.

Donavan returns with Lyttle, Jerry and a few others of the front office staff. Allison is there too, the black-spot girl, but she stays near the back of the pack.

Lyttle keys his screen and I hear mom's voice. "Hello Mrs. Conceição? This is Mr. Lyttle from your daughter's team. We are here at the hotel and we wanted you in on an interview with your daughter. Some things have happened here so please listen in. Okay?"

"What? What's going on? Is Gabby All right?"

"Yes, Mrs. Conceição, your daughter is fine. We are just investigating some events that happened and need to interview your daughter. Since she is only seventeen, we would like you in on this conversation. We felt it was really too important to wait until we returned to Philadelphia."

"I'm fine, Mom," I say.

"Okay," Mom replies but there is nervousness in her voice.

Lyttle turns to me and two of the others begin

scribbling notes on their screen.

He says, "Gabriella, it will be much quicker and easier if you answer all our questions truthfully. We just want the truth here. Understand that your status on this team hangs in the balance and lying will only make things worse."

"Tell the truth, Gabby!" Mom's voice rings out.

"Sure," I reply, looking at Lyttle.

"After your run yesterday—good job, by the way—you told Coach Donavan that you had stomach pains and that you were going to see Doctor Androsani." His eyes look over at Androsani and back to me.

"That's right," I say.

"But you never went to see him?"

"Correct," I reply.

"And you told Donavan that you were going to go out with some of your local family here?"

"I did say that."

"But you never checked out with anyone. So what happened? Where did you go? Why didn't you go to see the doctor?"

"The truth is—"

"Gabby, tell the truth! You know I always taught you to tell the truth!" Mom's voice squeaks out again.

"The truth is... that I lied. My stomach didn't hurt. I just wanted to get out of sitting through the second half of the game. I'm sorry. I shouldn't have done that."

Donavan says, "We had no idea where you were. Gabriella, you put me in quite a spot."

"Coach, I'm so sorry."

Lyttle heaves his big frame as if moving his appendages requires major amounts of effort and rests one leg on a wooden chair, then continues, "Then what? Did you actually go visit this family? Are they available to speak to your whereabouts?"

Nervousness creeps across my skin. Whereabouts? Allison is right there and my spot is buzzing lightly. With her in the room, I am suddenly battling to keep my emotions in check. "I called and called and called and no one answered. I did run into an old friend and go to his house though."

"Really? And where was that?"

Oh boy. Here it comes. "Los Teques."

"What?" Mom bellows.

"Mom? I—"

Lyttle interrupts, "Calm down. We checked the airport. We know you left the country."

I really want to say something but no words are in my mouth.

"We know you flew to Venezuela, stayed there through the night and flew back in the morning. I see some cuts and bruises there on your arms so I am guessing the reunion with your old boyfriend didn't go so well," Jerry says.

Mom barks, "Gabriella, I can't believe this! You flew to see who? You went to visit some boy? Who? I want to know right now!"

Lyttle stands and moves his hands, "Mrs. Conceição, please. You can ask those sorts of questions a bit later, okay? Please, for right now, we'd like to stay on topic."

What other questions could they have? They know everything—everything that the team should care about anyway.

Lyttle turns his head back toward me. "Let's continue. So, Gabriella. We are displeased that you chose to lie to your coach about the stomach pain and going to visit your family. Well, you didn't lie about visiting your family but you should have actually said that they were in Venezuela. That—although not technically lying—was misleading. You know we would not have allowed that. You are only seventeen and this team... You know we don't need that kind of publicity."

"I'm sorry."

Jerry looks over at Androsani and says, "You can leave. Nothing else here for you."

After the door closes, Jerry continues, "Let's move on. After you left Coach Donavan and before you went to the airport, what did you do? Where did you go?"

"What do you mean?" I ask.

"Exactly what I said. What did you do in the time between when you spoke with Coach and you arrived at the airport?"

I reply, "Nothing. I went straight to the airport."

Lyttle adds, "But your flight didn't leave until a few hours later. What did you do with all that time?"

"Nothing. Sat at the airport and waited. Why?" I question.

Lyttle's eyes rest on Donavan and he nods.

Donavan says, "At the half, after I gave out the assignments, I went looking for you and Androsani said you hadn't been there. I was worried, but I figured you just wanted to get going with your family. That made me upset, but okay, I understand. Then after the second half we returned to the locker room to find almost all the lockers ripped open and all the girls' stuff out on the floor. Even the office where I had my things, my notes, team strategies—"

I gasp. "What? Someone tore through the locker room and... you think it was me?"

Donavan looks at me more softly. "I'm having a hard time with this. Gabriella, just be honest with me.

Did you do this?"

Lyttle and Jerry and the rest of them stare.

I reply calmly, meeting her gaze, "I didn't do this. I know I lied to you about sneaking out but I had nothing to do with this. I was at the airport. I am telling the truth."

Mom chirps, "My daughter would never do anything like that."

Lyttle looks at the ceiling then says, "Gabriella, you are walking a knife's edge right now. I mean after what happened with Kyle I thought we were clear. I thought you understood our position here and where you stood. I mean, I really thought you wouldn't do anything like this." Lyttle exhales and looks at the ceiling. "Let me level with you. If it were up to me we wouldn't even be having this conversation. You'd have been kicked off the team the moment you boarded that plane. But apparently the owner is having second thoughts. I have to think that the only thing preventing me from booting you off this team right now is those three points you scored yesterday. And you better keep performing because she has a tendency to change her mind pretty quick, if you know what I mean."

"Thank you, Mr. Lyttle. Thank you for not kicking me off the team."

He continues, "Please, don't thank me. I'm really not happy about this. Anyway, so what we are going to do is give you an escort." He waves at the back of the room and Allison steps forward. "Have you met Allison here? She's in clerical. She graciously volunteered to keep an eye on you when we are out of town. From now on you will go nowhere without either the rest of the team or Allison. Got that? Nowhere without her, okay?"

"I understand."

Chapter 17

A New Father

Just don't look at them. Don't return their stares, I tell myself all the while hating the fact that I feel like I deserve to be ostracized.

But I didn't do it. They have to know that.

I hustle off the plane, eyes on the ground, trying to not look guilty and trying to not make eye contact—impossible to do both. Mom and Smith pick me up from the airport so I climb into the backseat and the tirade starts immediately.

Mom bellows at me from the front seat as she drives, "What were you thinking? I can't believe you did this! And back to Los Teques, no less! You don't know that place like I do. Do you know what could have happened to you? Aren't you going to say something?"

"I don't know what to say."

"Well, you can start by explaining yourself. And don't try to tell me you went looking for your father's diary because that's pretty thin."

Smith looks back at me and says, "Is that what you did?"

Mom yelps, "Smith, stay out of this. Gabriella, start talking. Now!"

"I know you don't want to hear this but that's exactly what I did. I went to try to find Dad's diary. That's it."

Mom snarls, "You're kidding, right? Do I have to get you checked out? Do I have to take you to see someone? You had one stupid dream and you risk everything for it? You had me worried to death! And you do that without talking to anyone? You just hop on a plane and fly to a different country? For what? For a dream? I'm sorry. I can't believe you did this."

The car is quiet because I have nothing to say, nothing that would make my situation better anyway. How can I explain how I feel without sounding crazy?

"Did you find it?" Smith says casually.

"Yeah," I say and I don't know why I am even responding to him.

Mom says, "You're kidding, right? You're trying to say that your father actually had a diary, a diary that I knew nothing about, and that you went to Venezuela, on a whim, and found this mysterious diary? Are you dreaming things up again?"

"It's right here." I pull out the blue book and Smith quickly turns around in his chair.

"Can I see it?" Smith says, trying to hide his eagerness. I pass it to him.

He thumbs through page after page as if he is looking for something specific. "This doesn't look like any diary I've ever seen. There are no entries. It's just... invoices. Sales records. This isn't a diary. It's some kind of record keeping book. It is your father's handwriting though. Here you go."

I tuck it back in my bag as Smith looks at me dubiously, as if he is wondering if he's missing something.

"Why do you think that that book is your father's diary?" he asks.

"I don't know. It's something of his. Something he had. Maybe it's not his diary. I just miss him. That's all."

Mom exhales softly but doesn't say anything.

We arrive at our home and there is an odd feeling in the air. Depression? Sadness? I don't know what it is but I don't like it. I feel like I need to do something so I make tea for Mom and Smith without saying a word.

Mom says, "Gabby, I don't know what we are going to do about this."

"Why? What do we need to do?"

"You can't keep doing things like this. Things like this are going to catch up with you. You're not a little kid anymore. I think I am going to take you to see someone. I understand you miss your father. I miss him too. But he's gone. He doesn't show up in the middle of the night and call you out into the woods. He doesn't tell you to sneak off to Venezuela to find his old, dusty record book. He wouldn't do that. You understand that, right?"

"It won't happen again. Please don't take me to a head shrinker."

Smith blurts out, "Too bad."

"What?" Mom says.

"Oh, I was just thinking out loud. Sorry."

"And what were you thinking?" mom says, glaring.

Smith blushes. "I was just thinking that it's too bad that Gabriella didn't really find her father's diary. You know if she did it might have really helped me, you know, with my work. Victor's really pushing me lately. He's only going to live so much longer. He's a lot older than he looks and he really wants this one... Sorry, I was being selfish for a moment there."

Mom looks at him like she's disappointed then snarls, "Don't talk to me about Victor Chavez right now. I don't want to hear that name."

Smith says, trying to dig himself out of the hole, "Sometimes I think Jonathan may have cracked it. And if I could just put those last few pieces together."

"See, Mom. Didn't I tell you?"

"Gabby, It's not like that," Mom says and I know that she is upset that I am forcing the conversation away from what I did.

"It's not like what?" Smith asks.

Mom says, "Go ahead. Tell him. Tell him your crazy conspiracy theory. We might as well get this out in the open right now before you fly off to some other country looking for more clues to this dream too."

"Mom!"

"Go ahead. Tell him."

I look at Smith, trying to not turn red, and say, "Here it is. I don't like the fact that you are dating my mom and at the same time you are interested in my father's research. For me it is just a little too easy to think that the only reason you are interested in Mom is to get some of Dad's secrets somehow."

Smith laughs. "That's rich. Well now that you put it that way, it does kind of make sense. Of course, you don't have all the facts so I can see why you might think that. Is that all or are there other conspiracies lurking in there?"

I stare at him and hate him for laughing.

Mom says, hands on her hips, "Go ahead, Gabby. Tell him the other thing."

"What other thing, Mom?"

"Being forgetful are we? I'll say it then. Smith, Gabby here thinks that you have been stealing pieces of her DNA. Lip prints off of cups, strands of hair, anything you can get your hands on so that you can run experiments on her. That's crazy, right?"

Smith's smile quickly fades which brings a troubled look to Mom's face.

"You wouldn't do that. Would you?" Mom asks

but she suddenly doesn't sound so sure.

"Elia, Gabriella, have a seat. I need to tell you both something."

We both sit and he says, "It is true that I gathered some data without your permission."

"I knew it!" I quickly stand.

Smith motions with his hands, "Hold on, hold on. Let me say that I'm sorry for that; I shouldn't have done that. And Kyle. Yes, I had him gather some information too. Your blood sample at practice. It was mainly used for exactly what it was supposed to be used for, performance measurement. But he also fed me a little bit of information and it was helpful. Well, initially confusing, but in the end, helpful."

"Mom, see? I told you. It's just like I said. Smith, what kind of crazy experiments were you running on my blood? Tell us."

Smith paces around the room then says, "At first I couldn't understand it. I ran it again and again and again and it just didn't make sense. I needed another sample. I needed more data. But it just kept coming back the same, over and over, again and again. Finally I had to admit it. The numbers don't lie."

Mom stands and says, "Smith, now what in the world are you talking about?"

Smith looks down at my mom. "Elia, tell me about your pregnancy."

"Why?"

"Just humor me for a minute."

"Don't tell me you really think that Gabriella is modified? Because if that's what you are going to say, you're wrong. We made Gabby the old-fashioned—"

Smith interrupts her, "I don't mean to damage the memory of your late husband or your pregnancy or anything like that but we have to face facts—"

Mom steps back. "No! It's not true! Jonathan would never—"

Smith adds, "There's more."

Mom backs away from the table. She looks like she is really getting upset. But me, I want to know. I really want to know. "Go ahead," I say.

"As near as I can figure—I don't have all the facts obviously—but as near as I can figure, Gabriella, before you were born your mother here got sick so she was admitted to the hospital. Your parents were trying to get pregnant anyway so it was a perfect opportunity for your father to artificially inseminate, you know, he cooked up some DNA and then, when your mother was in the hospital, he injected it and nine months later—"

"Enough! Smith! Enough!" Mom barks.

I contend, "No, Mom. Please, I want to hear the rest. I want you to hear all of this too."

Smith looks at my mom and then back at me then continues, "So I never suspected to be honest. Not until you started playing Ultraball. And how well you ran. Of course I was suspicious then. So I grabbed a few items, hairs, yes, several times, hairs. You may have seen me once but I got hairs off your brush a few times also. It was sneaky but I couldn't put the data together. I just had to be certain."

I look at my mom. "See, Mom. It's just like I said."

Mom says, "Oh, Smith. I think you should just go."

Smith doesn't leave, he just keeps right on talking. "Please, hear me out. Just give me one more minute. Let me say what I have to say and then I will leave if you still want me to."

Smith pauses for a moment, looking at the floor,

gathering his breath, then looks up and me and says, "The numbers don't lie. It's all there. In black and white and A and C and T and G. Jonathan is not your biological father. I am."

The room is silent for a few seconds as we all digest what Smith just said. Even Smith has a somewhat shocked look on his face as if he still can't believe it himself.

"Smith! No! You can't mean that!" I yell, horrified.

He says slowly, "Wait, let me finish."

"Finish! I'd say you're done here!" I storm off towards the stairs.

Mom's face is expressionless, in a state of shock. "Gabriella, wait," she mumbles softly.

I scream, "Wait! For what? To hear more of his lies?"

Smith says, "Gabriella, Jonathan is still your father. I can never take his place. I would never dare try to. And even if I would have tried to raise you, I couldn't have done a better job. He's your real father. All I'm saying—"

"You've already said too much!" I bark. I'm hurt, hurt because I don't want to believe it, hurt because I know there is a sliver of a possibility that it is true, hurt at considering that my father would even do this to me. I know my father was a scientist. An experimenter. A tinkerer. I know who he was and the way he did things, even in the clothing store. I wouldn't put it past him at all. Strange. Unbelievable. Yes, it is. But this is something that I could see him doing. And thinking about it hurts.

"Okay, I will go now. I have more to say but it can wait for another time." Smith starts walking to the door slowly, as if he is waiting for one of us to stop him. Mom is staring at him and completely at a loss for words. I want him to go. I don't want to even think about the possibility that Smith, who was up to just a few minutes ago my arch-enemy, at least in my mind, is now my biological father and that maybe he wants to somehow assume some type of fatherly role in my life. No! I can't accept that!

Smith leaves and for once Mom is silent. I walk over to the stairs intent on heading up to my bedroom but Mom is still standing there, staring blankly at the floor. She attempts to move out of my way, looks up and then our eyes meet. I grab her hard and hug her. I hug her long and hard and I can't help but cry. I miss my Dad so much and I just can't handle this.

Chapter 18

A New Vector

"When are you going to stop fumbling through that book?" Mom says as she drives me to practice.

"I don't know. Something about it is hypnotic. I feel like I'm missing something."

"Missing what? It's just a ledger, a record book. What's there to miss? I got that it's in your father's hand writing and I got that you miss him, but Gabby, it's just a record book."

"I know, but here, right here, this name. Durand. It keeps appearing over and over and in the weirdest places. It's over here under a sale and over here under a purchase. The more I look at the columns the more it sticks out. Did you know someone named Durand? Was he one of your clothing suppliers?"

"Durand? That *is* weird. No one we dealt with in Venezuela was named Durand that I remember and I did all the ordering, not your father."

"So what could it mean?" I question.

"Back in the old country, there was a Durand. Another researcher who sometimes came over the house. I think he did genetics also. Have to ask Smith about—"

I interrupt, "Mom! No!"

"Wha—Why?"

"Please, Mom, don't pull Smith into this, okay?"

"Okay, I guess. I won't call him for now anyway. Just don't do anything loopy, okay?"

"You don't have to say it like that, you know. But I promise. I'll be good."

I stare at the book for a good long while and the more I look at the lines the more that I am certain that it is written in a code and that perhaps the code is for me. I remember the puzzles that Dad constantly played with: lists of strings of squiggly lines using the special characters of Physics and Genetics. Each symbol had a verbal equivalent, not a letter but a sound, and written out they looked like they would create some kind of formulae that might make sense, but were in fact utter nonsense, until the code was deciphered, of course. Dad seemed to take great pleasure in decoding these messages. I even caught him writing a few but I never knew to whom they went or where they came from. Everything was so secretive with him. Once when I was very young, I asked him to teach me how to read them and he pulled me up on his lap and read one to me. I found the story very funny, I recall. He said it was from a friend. It was the only time I bothered him about them.

Mom drops me off and I have about fifteen minutes before practice so I call Dr. Duggan on my screen. "Hey Dr. D, how's it going?"

"Busy, my dear. Quite busy. What can I do for you?"

"Well, a few things. First I wanted to apologize to you again—"

He replies calmly, "No matter, Gabriella. It was all my fault. I shouldn't have been so reckless with you."

"Thanks, Dr. D. It's been on my mind a lot, you know, that I ruined your life's work, and I feel so bad."

"Oh. Right. Well, let us say that when one door closes a window tends to open."

"You are back at it?"

"No, err, not really. I can't say exactly, but my research has taken a different approach, that's all." He is clearly hiding something.

I reply, "Good. I'm glad. That makes me feel better. Oh, the other thing I wanted to say, to ask you really. Did you know a Dr. Durand?"

"Durand? My my, now there's a name I haven't heard in quite some time. Yes. Impetuous man, he was. Intelligent though. What of him?"

"Just came across his name and thought he might have known my father."

Duggan replies, "Know him? They worked together quite a bit, I think. Of course, he knew him. Smith could tell you more though. I'm a physicist, remember? I didn't know all the geneticists that well. There were so many of them."

"Right."

He whispers, "But one thing—"

"What's that?"

He continues, "From what I remember, Durand kind of lost it and I would recommend that you don't try to track him down. I think you should stay away from him actually. Durand, he's not so savory and I don't think he could bring you anymore resolution concerning your father."

"Thanks, Dr. D, I'll keep that in mind. There *is* one other thing I wanted to ask you."

"I only have a few minutes."

"Me too. We're about to start practice. I wanted to ask how Michael's been. Have you heard from him?"

He replies, "I talk to him almost every day. He's fine. Good. He's burying himself in his work as always. He has a new girlfriend too. Shenanigans, maybe I shouldn't have said that."

My voice is suddenly hollow. "It's okay. Anyone I know?"

"Maybe. There was a girl that ran the lab in Portugal. Maybe you remember her? Maryann?"

I try not to sound agitated. "Her? Are you serious? I thought they hated each other."

"Oh, I don't know about that. They're together now. Well, I have to go."

The connection terminates and my loss of Michael suddenly feels so final. The idea that I would somehow win him back now has been summarily flushed down a urine-stained toilet.

I enter the locker room, quickly attend to my pre-practice ritual, not talking to anyone, even Sandstone, and go to the field. Practice goes well and we even have a small audience. Antonio and Spike are in the stands watching us run. I start to become self conscious of my movements because every time I look up at them Antonio is staring at me. I know he's in to me, obviously, but I don't know if I want to add the courtship, flirting, yes-no-I-don't-know drama that is the dating scene to my already racked brain. I can't seem to focus enough on either school work or Ultraball, what with the mystery of my father's record book-slash-diary, the front office ready to eject me from the team for my escapades in Venezuela, the rest of the girls ready to sacrifice me up to the enforcers for their lockers being ripped apart and my heart still stinging from the loss of Michael. But still, the way his eyes warm my body sure feels good.

After practice, on the drive home, Mom asks, "Gabby, would it be okay, do you think—" Mom stops mid-sentence.

"What?"

"I want to invite Smith to the house." It's been

over a week since we've seen Smith and he has enough sense to not call. But I knew this day was coming and there is no reason to avoid it.

"Okay," I reply but I have no idea how I really feel. Confused.

Smith comes over and we talk about this and that, Ultraball and science and running faster, good meals and nice restaurants and the traffic in Philadelphia, everything but the elephant in the room. Then Mom looks at Smith and he nods and says, "So Gabriella, I was wondering what you thought about the things that Kyle told you?"

"*What* that he told me?" I say defensively.

He answers, "All that stuff about the nothingness. You're not buying into that are you?"

"I don't know. Mom said you scientists don't believe in anything except a material world either."

"Hmm, not exactly," He replies.

"Well, what is it exactly?"

"Do you believe in a *self?* Is there a Gabriella besides your flesh?"

"Of course," I say, but I am distracted. I still can't believe Smith might be my biological father.

Smith asks as mom watches him, "Where? Where is it?"

"I don't know. In my brain. In my heart. Somewhere."

"Gabriella, listen to me. What we call *Gabriella* is really just a combination of many organs. In some ways you are a single, solid mass of flesh; in others, a collection of organs and subsystems. Different parts of your body act independently and autonomously of the whole. It doesn't all happen in the brain, or even the heart for that matter. Consciousness and control and purpose is an illusion. Kyle had that much right."

Mom interrupts, "So you think we are all just a collection of cells?"

Smith replies, "I used to think that."

"And now?" Mom asks.

Smith continues, "Now I am older. Now I only speak about what I have experienced and what I know. I used to deny that certain things existed because they seemed illogical and I had not experienced them."

Not really caring where this is all going, I say, "So what's your point?"

Smith says, "I just don't want to see your mind getting poisoned with all his notions about the Void and nothingness and all that. If you run into him, he's probably going to spout whole rivers of 'nothing exists' and 'all is an illusion' and I would hate to see you swallow that."

Mom quizzes, "And what do you *really* think, Smith?"

Smith looks at her and says, "I think life is a struggle. Life is a huge competition and there are winners and losers. The weak get eliminated. We only exist through a ruthless, merciless, unforgiving struggle."

I add, thinking of what Mr. Dunberry said in 5th period history class, "Survival of the fittest."

Smith eases back into his chair. "Yes, but of course there is more to it than that."

"What else?" I say.

Smith waves his hand in the air. "The old ideas painted a world where the strong killed the weak and that was that. The model didn't take into account that the weak don't always go softly into the good night. The weak sometimes adapt. It is like the cold war from a century ago. An arms race."

I reply, "I remember that. Each side keeps designing bigger and better guns."

"Kind of like that. Anyway, I want to see the best survive. I want to see you advance, Gabriella. I don't want to see you dragged down by Kyle's philosophical fantasies."

Mom stands and interrupts, "Does anyone want some cookies?"

I am glad Smith is opening up to me about some things. Must be Mom's influence. But there is still a great white elephant in the room swinging his trunk to and fro and no one wants to acknowledge that it is there so I hit it lightly with a stick. "So Smith, tell me. What is it that you and my father were working on? What was it that he figured out that you couldn't crack for all these years?"

He casts a wary eye at me. "I can't tell you intimate details but I can paint some broad strokes." He exhales and leans back in his chair. "NuGen still owns that research, you know. We had several projects going on simultaneously. One involved being able to modify DNA without leaving any traces. An untraceable modification. It's actually been called the holy grail of genetics. Many labs out there are working on that one. We never got that far with it. Another project involved longevity, extending human life span. Of course, that's where the money is. A company that can provide such a finite resource, life itself, time, they would become immensely rich."

Mom says from the kitchen, "I thought that was done already. I mean, it's in all the commercials."

Smith replies, "True, in one aspect that is true. What those companies can offer is to clean an unborn child's DNA. Basically they take the sperm and the egg and remove all the precursors for diseases, at least the ones we know about anyway, which, in a way, extends life. Statistically the majority of people die within ten years of a major illness. If you don't get sick then you live longer, right?"

"Well, what else is there?" I ask.

"There's a lot more we could do. Your body is composed of cells. Millions of them in fact and every one of these cells have a lifespan. They die. But they also divide and reproduce."

"Sure," I reply.

"When they divide there are enzymes that come into the cell and copy the cell's DNA—and what we know is the cells telomeres become shorter."

"Tele-what?"

Smith says, "Telomeres. Every cell has chromosomes—that's where your DNA is stored, right?"

"Yes, everyone knows that."

Smith continues, "On the ends of each chromosome is a chunk of material called a telomere. It's like a tail that hangs off the end of the chromosome, got it?"

"I'm with you."

"So because of the way this cell replication takes place, in the chromosome copying process the enzymes can't copy all the way to the end. So what happens is a tiny portion of the telomere is lost."

I say, "What do you mean lost?"

"It isn't copied. And so the telomere is there as kind of a throw away piece. It's okay to lose it because there isn't any DNA on it."

"Oh, so that's good."

"Yes, it is. But as division after division occurs, the telomeres become shorter and shorter and eventually run out. Then as cells continue to divide, DNA material on the very end is lost each time which tends to lead to aging and diseases." Smith smiles.

I add, thinking out loud, "So the telomeres are kind of like a clock for our cells. Each time your cells divide, the telomeres lose just a little bit of their length and when they are gone is when aging sets in. We become old and then we die."

Smith says, "Effectively. So all genetic work, for the most part, has been performed on unborn children because that is the easiest way for us to work since, obviously, we are only working on one cell at that point. Once a person is born they have millions and millions of cells and to change the DNA in all of the cells would be a nightmare. But if we could... Yes, if we could somehow lengthen the telomeres of an adult, make them much, much longer, we could extend life."

Mom says from the kitchen, "But scientists have tried gene therapy, right?"

"Of course," Smith replies.

"And?" I say.

"So far the work has only been on adults with diseases, diseases that had a genetic cause and where gene therapy was thought to be the answer. Unfortunately, the results have been unpredictable as yet. In several cases people with life threatening genetic diseases were cured. That was great. In a few other cases, patients who had a non-life threatening genetic disorders died from a treatment that was considered very safe and innocuous. We just don't know enough right now and there is a moratorium on giving adults any type of gene treatment."

"So then that kills it," Mom says.

"Except..." Smith says.

"Except?" I say.

Smith's voice is almost a whisper. "Except that there are people, old people mostly, old people who are filthy rich and are staring death in the face who are willing to pretty much pay anything and try anything for another crack at life."

Mom steps in from the kitchen and says, "You're not—"

Smith cuts her off. "Absolutely not. Your father didn't either. We would never provide an untested treatment. But we were working on some things. Your father, he made some progress, I think, that he didn't share with me and, I don't know, it was lost. I would sure like to find it."

"So how would something like that work?" Mom says. "You just said that you would have to change all the cells and that it would be nearly impossible. I understand how you change a zygote—that makes sense to me—it's only one cell. How would you treat an adult?"

Smith exhales again. "In a single cell approach, what we are doing now, is basically a DNA bullet. At least you can think of it that way. We fire the changes into the cell and if all goes well we allow the cell to continue to divide and nine months later we have a child, there you go. For an adult that's not possible. What your father proposed as a vector was a virus."

"A virus?" I say.

"Yes, a modified virus, a virus constructed for each individual, tailor made. We would inject it in a syringe and it would begin to multiply and spread throughout the body, revising the DNA sequences of every cell that it came upon, lengthening telomeres, resetting the genetic clock, so to speak. Of course we would expect the subject to become sick, deathly ill actually, fevers, chills, muscle pain, joint pain, weakness and, well, the entire body would be pretty much wrecked. It would be tremendously painful. Imagine the worst influenza multiplied with double pneumonia and added to dramatic arthritis and you may be almost there."

Mom asks, "How long would something like that last?"

Smith says casually, "For the virus to run its course? Maybe two weeks. Maybe six. If the subject survived the ordeal then we would really have something to study."

"Wow. And you never tried it?" I say.

"Hahaha. I already told you that." But something tells me that he most certainly has.

"I guess my dad really was some kind of a genius."

"He was. Losing him hurt me more than you could ever know."

Mom and I don't respond. It is a wound that is too deep. And with Smith still working for NuGen, it is a wound better left unopened.

Chapter 19

A Dip of the Toe

"So I don't want any fooling around, okay?" she says.

"Sure. No problem, Allison." She has an odd look on her face whenever she is around me and she can't keep her hand off of her black spot, stroking it, touching it and I know exactly what she is feeling. I don't let on that I have one too, of course, but it is only a matter of time before she finds out.

"All right then. Don't get me wrong, Gabriella—"

"What?"

She continues, "I want you to have a good time in Europe too. I am looking forward to this trip myself. When I volunteered to watch you, I was kind of thinking of my career here and a lot less about what fun I might miss so, I think, we could do some things together if you want. Maybe go out for some sightseeing? We'll see."

"Sure, that sounds like fun."

The entire team has been looking forward to this trip, two weeks in Europe, eight matches total between both the pro and farm teams with tons of autograph signing and exposure for the team mixed in. Of course, there will still be plenty of time for museums, art, restaurants and fun; all kinds of stuff. I'm not a big fan of having a baby sitter, but maybe I could turn this thing to my advantage—work it so that I can do more than I would normally be able to do since I have Allison with me. Just have to see how much of an adventurer she is.

Waiting for practice to start, I quickly dial Michael. He answers, "Hello? Gabriella?"

"Hey, Michael. Didn't know if you were going to answer."

"Oh, why's that?"

I respond slowly, "After all the drama. And I heard you have a girlfriend and I know how that goes."

"You heard that? From who?" He sounds defensive.

"From Duggan."

"I've dated a few times. But nothing steady at the moment. I'm keeping my options open."

Staring at him through the screen, I realize how hungry I've been for the simple sight of him, unreasonably hungry. His face is intelligent and cheerful; In his eyes there's a darkness, not an opacity but a depth, almost like the black powder of volcanic ash, soft and inviting. I'm ashamed of the pleasure I'm taking in looking at him so I quickly look away as if he can somehow read my mind by looking at my eyes. "Right, so the reason I called—"

"Yeah, what's up?" he replies eagerly.

"You're good with puzzles. I thought you might be able to help me."

"You? You're doing puzzles?"

I smile and say, "No, not really. I have something that I think might have a hidden message in it. But if you help me you can't tell anyone. Can I trust you?"

"You have to ask?"

Suddenly my voice melts and I can't control it, "No, Michael, I don't have to ask. I know I don't have to ask. I trusted you once with my life and I would do it again. I just want to make sure you know that this is *really* important to me and I don't want anyone to know. That's all."

"You know I'm in. What do you have?"

I compose myself and say, "It's a record keeping book. On paper and all. Kind of like an old ledger. My father's actually. But it's kind of weird. Things don't line up. Like maybe it has clues in it. I already found one myself. A name. Durand. But I think there may be other things. I think he left it for me. I don't know, it could be nothing too. I just want to make sure. Do you think you could take a look at it?"

"Sure. It sounds like fun. Gabby's father's secret message from the grave. You know I'm in. Hey. Hmm. Durand? If it's who I think it is, I met him."

"Really?"

"Odd bird, that one. Came to tour the lab once. Dr. Duggan authorized him. Said he was an old friend. Didn't stay long," Michael says.

"That's got to be him. Is there any way I can contact him?"

"Maybe. If I come up with anything I'll send it to you."

Paranoia sweeps over me so I whisper, "Just be careful with what you figure out. Don't let anyone know you're working on it. And don't let anyone see you with it."

He says, "You're worrying me now. What are you afraid of? What do you think is in it?"

"Maybe some notes on his research. Probably nothing I could understand anyway but—"

Michael's brow furrows, "But what?"

"It might tell me whether or not he played around with my DNA. It might tell me... tell me whether or not he is my *real* father, err, I mean my biological father."

He asks, "Deep. Why would you think that he's

not?"

"It's a long story. Of course he will always be my father. Words on a page can't change that, but if there was some kind of DNA trickery, I'd like to know."

"Wow. So you think you might be modified and you think that your father didn't use his own DNA? No one will know. I promise."

My voice bounces back to normal. "Hey, by the way, you know we are starting our European tour, right?"

"Sure do. I already got tickets," he replies.

I dip my toe in the water to see how warm it is. "I wouldn't mind seeing you if I can get out."

"That might be nice."

Suddenly I feel warm all over. "Might be?"

"Yeah." He smiles.

*****

We have an uneventful practice and it seems lately that we are not training to face a specific type of team as we will be facing so many in such a short period of time. The trainers have been telling us about various players and strategies of the European teams but it all seems to blur together for me. I just can't wait to get on the plane and get over there. The waiting is killing me.

After practice, Mom picks me up and she is uncharacteristically silent. I could be okay with a little silence, especially after being rocked by Smith's bombshell the other day but I have been learning that it is better to get things out into the open than to let them fester.

"Mom? What's bothering you?"

She blinks as if her mind was somewhere far away. "Ah, I don't know how to say this—"

I turn towards her in my chair and I am nervous about what she is going to say. "Just say it."

"I had forgotten. But what Smith said, the other day, it all came flooding back." She pauses and glances over at me then back to the road in front of her.

"Tell me," I mouth the words but suddenly I don't really want to know.

She doesn't look at me. "Before you were born, we were trying to get pregnant for some time and it just wasn't happening. Jonathan brought papers home from the in vitro clinic but I laughed it off. I had totally forgotten about it until just the other day. And then, later on, I got sick. And when I was in the hospital, I was so out of it. You know those pain killers make you forget everything. I just can't be sure."

"So, you think—"

She exhales softly and says, "I don't know what to think. I just don't know anymore."

The road noise is loud in my ears as I let it soak in. I have to admit it, at least entertain the thought, no matter how much I don't want to, that Smith may very well be my biological father.

Chapter 20

Chelsea

The air is hostile, seeing as we just disassembled the home team, and the fans' reaction surprises me. Our Philadelphia fans are enthusiastic, even vulgar sometimes, but I was never afraid that they might storm the field with violence in mind. That is how I feel now in Chelsea.

"Okay, lets go! Everyone off the field! Now!" Donavan barks and she doesn't have to say it twice. The team hustles off the field and down to the safety of the locker rooms. As we run to the tunnel, a large wave of fans are pressing against the security gates, bending them. They look to be ready to break through. I am scared.

We run down the tunnel, through the halls and into our unmarked room. Several security guards stand in front of our door and lock us in.

After changing, I approach Allison, trying to shake off what just happened. "What's going on?"

"What do you mean?" she replies.

"Are we going out?"

"Oh, uh, I am tonight. But you are too young to go where I'm going. You are going to have to stay in the hotel. Sorry." She rubs her neck briskly.

I don't try to hide my disappointment but it's not her fault and I can't blame her.

At the hotel everyone goes out to celebrate the team's qualifying for the playoffs, everyone but me and there is no way I am going to risk sneaking out again. I spend the evening on my screen trying to track down someone named Durand who might have had something to do with genetics. It is amazing how many people have the same last name. There must be hundreds of thousands of Durands on the planet. I narrow my search to Durands that have doctor in their name which narrows the field considerably.

I begin calling the numbers and all of them either do not know what I am talking about or do not answer the phone. The disappointment of hitting dead-end after dead-end smacks me.

A few hours later Michael sends me a number that he thinks might be Durand's. It is one of the same numbers that I already tried. Just then my screen rings.

"Hello?" I say, staring at a man I called earlier.

"Yes? Gabriella?"

"Speaking."

"You called me previously. This is Dr. Durand."

"Oh, really? We spoke?" I know that we did but I am humoring him.

He says, "Yes, I told you I, ah, didn't know what you were talking about at the time. I needed a moment to verify who you were first. Listen, I only have a few moments here. This line isn't secure. I will call you back."

He abruptly hangs up. Moments later my screen rings again.

"Hello?"

Durand looks around quickly as if he might be being watched which is very strange as it looks like he is in his living room on the screen. "As I was saying, I needed to verify who you were. Jonathan's daughter. Very nice. I checked out some of your game footage. You have his eyes. Call you back." The line goes dead then quickly rings.

"Hello?" He is on a different screen this time.

Durand continues, "So what were you trying to reach me for? To ask about your father, I presume?"

"Yes."

He whispers, "I can tell you some things. But not here. Not now. They may be listening. I will be in touch." The call ends and I don't know what to think. Duggan said he was off and now I know why.

Later, I take photos of every page of my dad's record book and send the first few pages to Michael. I have to remind myself that I can trust him but at the same time I can't help being paranoid. I know it's just a record book but my dad might have died for this.

Staring at the empty hotel room I realize how alone I am and wonder why I am doing this to myself. Mom wants me to quit the team and be a "normal" teenager and right now that sounds appetizing. It would be a lot safer that's for sure. But then I would have never met Michael. And Cyndi and Sidney. Even though they hate me now. And now this oddball Durand. At least he is going to tell me some things. Who knows how reliable he will be.

The screen rings and I reach for it thinking that it's Durand again.

"G, Antonio over here. Heard you weren't going out?"

"Hey, Antonio. Yeah, I'm in lock-down mode. Came all the way across the Atlantic to stare at these four walls."

He smiles and says, "I'm down in the lobby if you want to come hang out."

I can hear Spike yelling in the background, "A, let's go."

Funny how these two call everyone by their first initial.

I reply, "That sounds good but I wouldn't want to hold you up."

He points his screen at Spike, who is across the hall, and says, "What? That knucklehead? Who wants to hang out with him?"

"I'll be right down." I quickly dress, throwing on my white blouse that drapes down off my body in all the right places and a simple black skirt. I scamper through the halls and over to the hotel lobby. there is a restaurant and bar so we sit together and munch snacks but neither of us can eat much and especially not the salty-sugary concoctions that they push here.

"So, you passed up a night out with Spike and the boys to sit in the lobby with me?" I say.

He tilts his head and says, "It's obvious that I like you. I thought there might be a spark. Giving up one night with Spike isn't much of a price to pay to find out, is it?"

"They say all you Ultraballers are forward. I guess you're no different, huh?"

"When you live your life five minutes at a time you tend to not want to waste any opportunities." He smiles.

"I guess, never thought of it like that."

"It's the same with you, isn't it? Every time you step out onto the track could be your last. Today you're a hero, tomorrow you're a goat—"

I say, almost under my breath, "I'm always a goat —"

He grabs my wrist softly, "You are most definitely not a goat."

I look away and wonder what exactly I am doing here. I don't say anything so he pulls his hand away and asks, "So you had some drama before? With that performance monitor guy?"

"Yeah," I say, not sure if I really want to talk about that.

For a man who exudes confidence on the field, he seems flustered by my silence, "I guess you don't want to talk about it? We can talk about something else."

I look at his face and see that he is really trying so I let him in. "I guess you ought to know. It's not like it's a big secret. I was engaged to be married to him, Kyle. It was an arranged marriage; I didn't really know him that well—"

He interrupts me. "An arranged marriage? People still do that?"

"In my country there are still indigenous people living in the forest, hunting monkeys and wearing loincloths. So I guess it shouldn't be surprising that some old-world practices are still around. I heard someone say once that 'The future is now, it's just not evenly distributed.' That makes sense, right?" I am momentarily shocked that I am quoting something Michael once told me.

"True. Brazil, right?"

"Yeah, Brazil," I say, but it was Venezuela I was thinking of.

He is silent for a moment and I think he is wondering if I am going to change the subject. I have to admit it is awful tempting. I continue, "So I was engaged. Weird because I am totally not looking to get married."

"Me neither." He smiles, seemingly happy that we have something besides Ultraball in common.

"It happened. He was a weirdo. I regret it, but hey, who can change the past?"

"I've had a few bad ones too."

"I bet you have a lot of groupies."

He sits back in his chair. "You don't know the half of it." A panicked look in his eye, he quickly says, "A girl in every city? That's Spike, not me. I don't mind the attention and, of course, we are expected to be nice to the fans, but I don't want any groupies." Then he awkwardly says, "I'm single."

"Uh huh," I say with a half-smile.

"No, I'm serious!" he says, then laughs. "Honestly, I'm not like the rest of them."

"We'll see."

"Will we?" he touches the back of my hand with two of his fingers lightly, subtly, and it makes my hairs stand on end. "I won't hurt you," he says, suddenly serious.

We continue talking about this and that, nothing really, but maybe everything, dancing the dance of the modern courtship ritual. We don't say much but communicate everything in a nod of the head, a slight tilt of the shoulder, intonation, pitch and tone, my voice teasing, wavering between interest and disinterest, coaxing his ego, trying to find out his motivation and commitment, his voice chasing and baiting, luring me like a fish to a fly-hook. It is then that I overhear Allison, a few tables away, on her screen, whispering.

The human brain's ability to focus in on one conversation in a room full of talking heads still amazes me. As Antonio and I speak, I simultaneously try to hear what Allison is saying.

She whispers, "Right. There is no evil, there's nothing bad; there's no good. I got it. Right... all human ideas."

My brow creases and I realize that Antonio is staring at me. "Something wrong?" he says.

"No. I... Sorry, you were saying?"

"If something's bothering you then that's okay. I don't mean to be too pushy on a first date."

"A date? Is that what this is?" I say quickly.

"Well, yeah, kind of, I guess." he blushes and it feels out of character for him. I think this hulk of bulging muscle really likes me.

Allison whispers, "We are made up of nothing. Yes, yes, got it. There is no self. We are whatever we decide we are. Certainly."

"What's up, G? Something *is* bothering you. Is it something I said?" Antonio says.

I reply, "Don't look but over there. Hey, I told you not to look. Allison, she's supposed to be my *babysitter* and she told me that she was going out, but there she is."

"So."

I snicker, "*So,* she ditched me."

"That's good, right? Then we can spend some time."

I say, "Yeah, it's been fun. Listen, I have to get some rest. See you again?"

He gets that hungry look on his face and replies, "Yes, definitely."

I stand and he stands with me and looks like he wants to give me a peck but I don't acknowledge it and retreat to the exit, then pause at the tourist stand and look at some pamphlets. I have no interest in them; I just want to hear what Allison is saying.

She mutters, "Oh, it was so great. It changed everything. I've heard of people going to church and having these life changing experiences and I always thought it was so fake but now, now that I've had one myself, I know what it's like."

I put down one flyer and pick up another. She continues, "Right, not too excited. Yes, I know. I just... right, I know."

I unconsciously glance back at her and she is staring at me, then says, "I have to go. Talk to you soon."

She stands and walks over to me. "Hey Gabriella, how's it going?" As she approaches my black spot buzzes.

"Good. Just heading up."

She says, "Me too. Sorry, you couldn't come with me today. You wouldn't have enjoyed it anyway."

"No problem. I understand."

Chapter 21

The Letter

We head off the field for the half time break. As we walk Sandstone says, "Hey, did you hear?"

"No, what?"

She answers, "One of the French girls is missing. She didn't show up to the stadium and they say she's been missing for some time. Called out sick a few weeks ago but now her family says they don't know where she is. The police checked her apartment and it looks like it's been empty for a long time. They're looking all over for her."

"I hope she's okay," I say but don't continue the conversation as my mind is elsewhere.

The crowd dies down as we exit the field for the half. It feels good to be winning. It also feels good to have watched Antonio play so well. His eyes never drifted over to mine though. That disappoints me. In the locker area, my screen rings so I grab it while I stretch.

I look at the face on the screen and say, "Hi, Dr. Durand. How goes it?"

"Fine. Can we talk?"

"Sure."

"I mean, is anyone listening? Can anyone hear this conversation?"

I tuck my head in my locker and whisper, "How's that? I think we're good."

"Err... ah, I'm at the stadium. Second floor east, by the stand that sells croissants. Can you meet me?"

"Now? I don't think so."

"I'll call you right back." He quickly hangs up before I can respond, then just as I pull my head out from my locker the screen rings again. He appears to have moved to the men's bathroom. Gross.

He says, "Sorry, have to make it quick. You never know."

"Right," I say, but I really don't. I finally met someone who is more paranoid than I am and it makes me feel all the more ridiculous. What with the way I had been suspecting Smith of stealing my DNA for some evil plot and thinking there was some kind of sinister NuGen design that exterminated my father. True, they chased him. True, he wrecked his car and died. I can't forgive them for that, but I don't think they wanted to kill him. There is no conspiracy.

He continues, "So uh, yes, I, uh, knew your father. Hmm, you sure do look like him. Having a different last name doesn't help your story though. Well, um, you know I have to be careful."

What I really want to know is about my father's research but no way can I blurt that out. This guy is too squirrelly. "I miss him so much. After we left the Mideast —I was just a baby, of course—after my parents fled, they found themselves in Venezuela. That's where I grew up."

He looks around in the men's room stall and it looks like he might be standing on the toilet. "Yes, I remember the day well."

"So my parents never told me much about what happened before. I kind of grew up living a lie. It is only recently that I am finding out that my father did what he did. I only knew him as a shop owner."

"I see. So you, ah, just wanted to, ah, know more

about your father?" He pulls on his collar to loosen it's grip on his neck.

"Yes—well, more than that. But that too, yes."

"And, ah, what else?"

I gather my breath, fully expecting him to hang up after I say it. "Well, I am the only girl in the game who isn't modified. Don't you think that's odd? I would really like to know if he did anything."

"I suppose that makes sense. Innocent enough, anyway." He coughs a little and looks around at the walls of the stall, then says, "And your mother and, ah, Smith, yes, Smith. What is his role in all of this?"

He has done his homework, I see. I guess I might as well tell him something to put his mind at ease. "Smith? He still works for NuGen and he's dating my mom. But I don't trust him. I think he's after my father's research and that's the only reason he comes around. I suspect he may be trying to seduce my mother to get some information from her but, as far as I know, she doesn't know anything. Neither do I."

"Let me call you back," he says quickly and my screen goes dark. I fully expect to never hear from him again. Too bad, I thought he might be able to help. I pull my head out of my locker and look about. The rest of the girls are preparing to head up to the field.

Allison and Donavan are talking, so I walk up to them and ask, "Coach, I have a headache. Could I stay here for a bit? Could Allison stay and watch me?"

The way Coach looks at me, I know she wants to bark but something stops her. "Yeah, sure. Allison, can you handle this?"

She nods.

I don't have a headache at all, but I feel off. Maybe just a bit depressed. That's too strong a word—sad, that's it. I miss my father and talking to Durand is reminding me of some things I had long forgotten: the way Dad used to push me on the swing that hung from the avocado tree, the way he used to laugh at Mom's jokes, even though they weren't very funny, how hard he worked and how much he loved us. I just miss him right now.

The screen rings and it jars me. I answer it, "Hello?"

Allison looks over at me then goes back to looking at her fingernails.

"Me again. We good?" I can't believe he called me back.

"No," I say because Allison is there. She is on the other side of the room but without the ruckus of the rest of the team, I think she can hear our conversation clearly.

"I see." he says.

I plug in my ear-piece so that she can only hear half the conversation then I glance back at her. She stands, nods and steps into coaches office. I completely don't know why she would do that.

"I can talk now," I say softly.

"Are you sure?" he mumbles.

"Yes, I'm alone."

"Your father, he was a good man. Dedicated. Loved your mother terribly. You were his pride and joy. Your baby pictures were all over the lab. I used to complain about them sometimes. Hahaha, they were magneted to most of the cabinets." He pauses and grows somber, "He was working on some cutting edge stuff. Research. I don't know how much I can tell you about that though. The problem, for us scientists, is the company paying the bills doesn't always tell us the whole story. You know that don't you?"

"What do you mean?" I say.

"Think about it this way. Say you're a big company who has a great idea that will make buckets of money. But you just don't know exactly how to do it. You need someone to help you figure out the process but you don't want to give away your idea either. Of course you can hire some genius professors at the best universities to help you. You give them research grant money to figure out the solution to the problem but—now here's the rub—you don't want them slipping any details of the idea out to your competitors, even accidentally."

"That makes sense."

"So what do you do?" He asks.

"I have no idea," I say.

"Hmm, Jonathan's daughter? Are you sure? Okay then, here is what you do. You cut the problem up into tiny little pieces. You take the one big question and divide it into twenty or more little questions then you parcel out some of these questions to individual researchers with individual research grants. You have to do it in such a way that even if someone knew all the areas of study that you are contracting out, they couldn't discover what you were really after. That is the big problem here. What your father was really working on— I mean what he was *really* working on—no one knows. I mean even he wouldn't have known. He only had a tiny jigsaw piece and he probably didn't know where it fit into NuGen's puzzle."

I switch my position to stretch my other leg and say, "I understand. But do you think it would have been possible for him to alter my DNA? Before I was born?"

"How old are you? Twenty? Twenty-one? That was cutting edge stuff back then."

"I'm seventeen," I say.

"Seventeen years ago," He rubs his chin and shifts his body weight on the toilet. "Certainly he could have done it. But *would* he have done something like that? That is the real question and I think that is one only you can answer. What does your heart tell you?"

I look at the open doorway that leads to coach's office and wonder if Allison could possibly be listening. I really have no idea who this guy is. His number came from Michael, who probably got it from Duggan, so I am pretty sure he really is who he says he is, but that doesn't mean I can trust him. "What you say is true, but, there's more—"

He interrupts me, "Hold that thought. Call you back."

I stand and ready myself to return to the field. Even though I am not running in the second half, the fans like to see us sitting on the bench. It lets them know that we are not hurt. The screen rings again and I answer it.

"So you were saying," he says. He is now back out in the food court, tucked in the corner near a garbage can. For someone who is trying to be inconspicuous, he really stands out.

I decide that I am not ready to mention anything about the diary. "Nothing. I may have some other details to share with you, but it's probably nothing."

"Very well," he says but he doesn't look at all disappointed.

"By the way, did you know someone named Victor Chavez?" I ask.

"Of course. We all did. He was liaison for all NuGen research at that time. Greasy man. I didn't like him."

"He's here."

He panics. "Where? There? With you right now? He's there?"

"No, no, no. Calm down. I didn't mean he was with me right now. I meant that I saw him. He's in Philadelphia. I met him some days ago for the first time."

"I see. I have to go. Jonathan was a good friend and, what happened to him, it wasn't right. Let me know if I can help you with anything. I will be in touch."

"Thank you," I say.

"And Gabriella, one more thing, remember this always. You can't trust anyone. No matter what they say, no matter what they tell you. Victor. Smith. Hey, even me—it's a hard thing to say—but don't even trust me. This world is full of liars and monsters. Don't trust anyone. Please, for Jonathan's sake, don't trust anyone." The screen goes blank before I can respond.

I feel like I should return to the field but I can't seem to motivate myself. Just ten more minutes, I tell myself and I start scribbling on my screen. Before I realize what I am doing I see that I am writing a letter.

Dear Dad,

I miss you something terrible. Words wouldn't be enough to explain how much I really, really miss you. I understand you were trying to protect us and maybe— maybe you were embarrassed? I still can't understand why you had to leave if you were planning on giving them the information. Why did you have to hide it from us? I don't understand so many things.

If the man in the Void has anything to do with you —I think he does—I hope he does—then why would he tell me to retrieve your diary? Did I get the right book? If that is the secret you were hiding, then why didn't you just give it to them instead of trying to lead them on some goose chase. You would still be alive!

Dad, I know it was your life's work, but was it worth dying for? Was it worth leaving Mom and me alone?

Smith says he is my biological father and maybe that's true. I still don't really trust him. I wish you were here to tell me what's going on. I know Smith was your friend and you worked together but I can't get past the fact that he works for NuGen.

Now I've met the oddest oddball, another old friend of yours and I totally don't know why I am even bothering with him. It would be so nice if I could just talk to you instead of trying to pull clues out of your old crazy friends. If you could just tell me. You are the only one I can trust. I wish you were here.

I close my screen, poke my head into the office and call Allison who is leaning back in Coach's chair, "You want to go up?"

"If you want," she replies.

We head up to the field and the game is just ending. I grab a spot on the bench next to Sandstone who says, "Hey, look over there. What's the commotion?"

Everyone is standing at the French team's bench. One lady is hollering, shaking her hands in the air and crying. A few of the girls are trying to console her. The rest of the team is standing and staring.

"I think that's the missing girl's mother," Sandstone says. "It looks just like her."

Suddenly the hairs on the back of my neck stand at attention. "No, I don't think it is."

We both stand along with the rest of our team and

edge a bit closer. We want to see what is happening but not come too close and invade their space. We are still in a competition after all.

"It's her," I say. "I think it's her."

"How is that possible? She looks... I don't remember her looking like that. I mean I never saw her in person, only on the screen, but she looks so different. Older." Sandstone says.

"Somehow she's aged."

We can barely overhear parts of the conversations from their bench and they are yelling in French so it is difficult to make out.

"What'd she just say? You speak Spanish. Can you understand any of that?" Sandstone asks.

"Shhhh, let me listen. I think she said it's been going on for a few months. She was.. Something about trying to... hide it? Woke up this morning... Oh my God. A clump of her hair fell out... on the pillow, yeah, pillow, I think she said. She couldn't hide it anymore. She's been aging. Fast. Too fast."

Chapter 22

Blank

We bank hard and fast on the cobble stone streets, me trying to stay near the drainage ruts on the side since the stones there are usually longer and smoother. We have a few days off before our next meet but there is no rest for the weary; we have to run our morning maintenance run.

It is beautiful here. The old village streets wind, dip and turn among stucco buildings with clay tile roofs. I wouldn't want to run anywhere else. I really love Spain. And it's not just because I know Michael is here and that I might be able to see him tomorrow.

Roosters caw in the distance just barely over the heave of my breath. The air is crisp and light. Sandstone and I are running next to each other and we let the others drift ahead of us; we are just putting in miles and there is no need to race. I usually hate maintenance runs because they seem to have no purpose to me. Back in UNA they always felt like drudgery; putting in miles just for the sake of putting in miles; running with no goal in mind besides just running; I hated it. But here, surrounded by this view, It's great. Sandstone and I can't keep ourselves from smiling.

After our run, we return to the hotel, shower and clean up. Allison calls and asks me if I want to go out for a walk-about. You know I do. The center of the village supposedly has a quaint row of shops, eateries and bodegas that she wants to check out.

We meet in the lobby and ask the guy at the front desk to call us a taxi. Mercury and Spike are standing there and mumble some words to each other, then Mercury says, "We are going into town too. Can we share the ride?"

Allison agrees but I wish she didn't because the cars are very small here. We jam into the cab, Spike in front and us three girls wedged into the backseat, and the driver speeds off through the winding hills. He slows way down as we enter the village and it slugs us forward. There are hardly any cars and the center courtyard and roadway of the town is most filled with pedestrians. There are no sidewalks which strikes me odd until I realize what it is. Allison looks perplexed so I say, "Shared space."

"What's that?" she says as we exit the taxi.

"In UNA the roads are for cars and the sidewalks are for people. Here it's not like that. They share." Allison rubs the back of her neck. I wonder if she has put it together that being close to me makes it tingle.

"And how do they stop the cars from running people over?" she says.

Spike and Mercury quickly wander off so Allison and I walk down the open road, looking at this and that, trinkets hanging from roadside carts that are not actually on the roadside since there is no division. She keeps glancing back, wondering if a car is going to zip around the corner and take us out but no one else seems to have such a concern.

"They don't stop them, per se. In UNA, there is nothing to stop a car from jumping the curb and running you over there either. There is nothing to stop a car from running a red light. The drivers just don't do that. Here it is the same thing. Drivers know that when they come into a village that they have to drive very slowly and give the right-of-way to pedestrians who are most certainly going to be in the streets."

Stopping at a stand that sells hand-made jewelry, I say, "Hey, check this out." I really like the earrings that depict little runners.

"You would wear that?" Allison says.

"Sure. Why not? When I'm racing, anyway."

"Ask her how much for these," she says as she points at a dull, black pair that look to be carved from some kind of rock.

"<How much?>" I ask the attendant in Spanish and as I do, I realize why Allison was eager to bring me; she needed a translator. But I'm okay with that.

Allison asks me to ask the attendant a few more question about several of the earrings but she eventually goes back to her first pair, the black ones, and buys them without haggling, clearly paying too much. I know she can afford it and the poor woman at the stall probably needs the bonus, so I don't say anything. I wonder if it is Kyle's Void-speak brain-washing that drew her to those black earrings. No, it's just a coincidence. Mom said I am always putting things together that don't jell and here I go again.

We walk for a while then stop at a tapas place and grab some food. I can't eat as much as Allison can, but it is nice to watch her enjoy it and I like the different smells around me.

Allison stops eating to rub her neck. I know she is going to find out about my spot eventually so I casually say, "You rub that tattoo a lot. Does it bother you?"

Suddenly conscious of what she's doing, she quickly stows her hand under the table and says, "Oh. That. Yeah. Kind of a botch job."

Playing along, I say, "Were you allergic to the ink?"

"I don't know. It bothers me once in a while."

I see Spike and Mercury across from us, standing on a terraced section, and when Mercury's eyes meet mine she quickly looks away.

"I don't like tattoos," I say, "not that I don't respect the art, I just don't like marks on my skin. Even scratches. It's one of the things that I don't like about Ultraball. Everyone who plays for any length of time seems to be covered in battle scars."

"I know what you mean. I don't like tattoos either. This is something different; It's kind of like a birth mark."

"Oh, you were born with that?"

"You could say that," she says then smiles at her own ingenuity.

We finish off our scraps and a street magician-slash-juggler comes by and takes advantage of the captive audience. While we watch him I try to push the bile out of my throat. A birthmark! Is that what this is? Have I somehow been initiated into some weird Void-relationship with everyone who has gone through? Have I been claimed? I know it is affecting me; it was like I couldn't control myself when I was around Kyle. And now, around Allison, it's not as strong, but I can feel it. We are linked somehow. Whenever we are around each other, our black spots go into overdrive. What does it mean?

The magician isn't very good so we clean up and move out allowing others to take our chairs and enjoy the show. We walk down the hill a bit. As I stop to check out some cute little hats, I notice Spike and Mercury about fifty feet behind us. When I look back at her she yanks his arm and they step into a shop. I have no idea why they would be following us. That must have been another coincidence. I have to stop thinking everyone is out to get me.

I ask the attendant about the hats and she tells me that they are not for adults. They are for babies. They are handmade and they wear them for christening. A buzzing, tingling erupts from my black spot and I squint my eyes. What now? I turn around to see a disoriented Allison rubbing her neck and across the street stands Maryann. The girl who stole Michael from me. Stop it, Gabby. She didn't steal him. You left him for Kyle. What did you expect him to do? I can't believe Maryann is here. Who am I going to see next? Michael?

Then there he is. Michael steps out of the bodega and Maryann and he turn and walk away. They don't see me. Thank God. And suddenly our little jaunt out to the village to see a little corner of Spanish civilization has taken a turn towards the surreal. As they walk away the buzzing of my black spot decreases and I ask Allison if she is All right.

"Yeah, weird though."

"What?" I say.

"Oh, just felt weird for a moment, that's all. Reminded me of something."

We continue down the row and I try to tease out some more information from her. "Remind you of what?"

"Someone. A friend. No one you know."

I know she is lying now because I know she is talking about Kyle so I decide I am going to really screw with her head. "Makes you wonder, all of this, doesn't it?"

"What do you mean?" she asks as she stops walking.

I raise my hands up and point at all of the shops and shoppers. "All of these material things. They don't last. They have no enduring value. Why do we chase after them? In the end they are all worthless."

Allison's eyes grow wide for a moment and I know I struck a nerve. She cautiously says, "Gabriella, I didn't know you felt this way."

I turn my head away. "I've been just thinking a lot lately, you know, about life and things. And I have come to the conclusion that, you know, we live in this world and we have to deal with this world around us but we don't have to like it."

"You sound like someone I know right now."

I know I am laying it on too think so I pull back. "Oh, it was just a thought."

"No, no, I know what you mean. I feel it too."

"What do you feel?" I say, maybe too eagerly.

She crinkles her forehead as she looks up at the sky then replies, "What has value—true value I mean—are things that are eternal. We have been brainwashed, from when we were babies, I think, to run and jump—no offense—like rats. It's that old rat race idea."

"Oh, I know that one."

She continues, "I just want to keep myself pure, clean, you know, blank."

"Blank?" I question.

I can see the look on her face and it is as if she thinks she said too much. "Well, pure and holy. Yeah, holy. That's what I meant."

I try to steer her back. "No, I think I know what you are saying. Blank is a better word. Like your mind has nothing in it." Then I go for it and hope I am not pushing too far. "In the beginning there was nothing and to nothing we return. All ends in nothingness."

She looks at me in a sort of puzzled kind of way so I change the subject as I step into another shop, "Are Spike and Mercury riding back with us?"

"I can't be bothered with those two," she says and I know the spell is broken, "It's bad enough I have to babysit you."

"Hey, tell the truth. You wanted me around so you could have me translate." I chuckle.

"Well, that was an added bonus," she says.

The back of the shop leads into an inner courtyard with a mixture of store entrances and vendor pushcarts. Mercury and Spike are there and I overhear her say, "Where is she? Did you see where she went?" They must be talking about someone else. They can't be looking for me. Not them too. Gabby, you are becoming like that nut, Durand. Do you think everyone is out to get you? It's not like that. That's not reality.

I step nearer to the exit and look at them through a picture postcard rack. They are clearly looking around for someone.

Allison tugs my sleeve and tries to see what I am looking at, so I turn and say, "You ready?"

We walk out and enjoy the rest of the afternoon then, just as the sun begins its long crawl toward the horizon and the shop keepers start to roll up their welcome mats, we grab a taxi back to the hotel. Spike and Mercury are not with us. I can't keep from smiling, even with all the little weird things that happened it sure was an enjoyable afternoon. It almost makes up for the fact that I am trapped in the hotel for the remainder of the day.

At night, Sandstone and I share stories of what we both did and she seems so happy that playing Ultraball gave her this free trip to Europe. She tells me that unfortunately she might have to quit soon as she plans on attending the University of Pennsylvania in September.

"Everyone from Chestnut Hill Academy goes to U Penn," she says, "Everyone. It's just what we do."

I wish I had a college opportunity but for me I have to run. It's all I have right now. Still it was a great day and I don't want to think about anything else. Just soak it up, sleep well and be rested for tomorrow. Tomorrow the pro team races and we need to be there for them for support. The fans and reporters expect us to flex our muscles and have on our cheery faces. Once again I have to become something I am not. I have to put on the actor's mask and be who they want me to be. The team thinks I am one thing; the fans another. Mom wants me to be something else entirely. If I knew what I really wanted, I guess I could ignore them but for now all I can do is keep playing the actress.

Sometimes I wish I was still that little girl in the corner clothing store who sold shoes. Even though that life was all a lie, I still miss it. It was easy. It was simple. It was innocent and uncomplicated. I wish my life was simple again.

Chapter 23

Sidney

Sweat drips from my skin as we line up for our second half run. Antonio catches a pass near us and quickly throws the ball but fails to acknowledge me even though I know he could. I jealously think it is because Mercury and Sydney are standing next to me. I can't help wonder if he's really into me or just playing. All of the rest of the men on the team seem to be that type: users, players, gamers. It's what they do; none of them can be trusted.

It's terribly hot here and we can all feel it; this isn't going to be a very fast race. I press Antonio from my mind as the gun fires and we spring into a full gallop.

The girls grunt as we swing, run and jump. Up the warped wall and across the water leap, cascading round the course, we go. The Spanish girls have the home field advantage and even though the course is slightly altered from match to match, placing some of the obstacles in different locations or occasionally adding a new one, they still have the rhythm and feel of the track in their bones.

Two quick Spanish girls are in front, followed closely by Sydney, then me, then Mercury. The third Spanish girl is an enforcer and is waiting to pounce back near the crossing. We are taking the major obstacle slow as it is tricky and none of us want to fall into the water and become disqualified. Sydney reaches it and starts across. When I reach the obstacle entrance, I am forced to pause for a few moments for her to clear it. We have to take it single file and the few seconds that I have to wait feel like an eternity. She leaps off and I leap on. It is a series of three rotating wheels suspended vertically in the air. They look like big Xs and earlier, waiting back on the bench, we started calling them the X blades. We have to leap, grab onto the first one with one hand, try to use our momentum to swing forward as it rotates then leap and grab the next and then the next. The gap between them is too large to hold two at the same time, at least for me since I am not of amazonian proportions like some of the girls. If my timing is off by a hair, I will fall.

I make it across, land, then fall into a run. Glancing back I see from the look on Mercury's face that she thinks I took too long. By the time we loop around again Sydney is close to the second Spanish girl and I am close to Sydney and Mercury has caught me. We are all in a bundle but not close enough to try to pass each other so again we have to single file across the three X blades. It's frustrating because it makes it nearly impossible to advance past anyone as it takes too long to get across the obstacle and then catch the person in front. Sydney leaps off and is pushing hard and fast, trying to catch the Spanish girl. I quickly leap onto the first blade, then the second and as I grab it, I hear the metallic squeak of the blade behind me and I know Mercury didn't wait. I can't stop now. If I do she will crash into me and we will both fall. I leap at the last hand hold but it is out of position. I wish she wasn't there. I'm not ready. My forearm hits the bar and I barely slide my hand into position without falling. I pause for a moment, allowing my body to swing back, attempting to propel my body forward and toward the track landing pad, then Mercury yelps, "Move!" as she crashes into me. I grunt as I hang on for dear life.

Mercury bounces off of my back and falls into the pool and must leave the course. I swing my legs back and fling my body forward, landing on the ground, then run, trying to catch up to the other runners. Just as I reach peak acceleration on the curve, Sydney is pushed off course by the lone Spanish enforcer. She was unable to dodge her. I finish third and am the only scoring runner for our side.

As I exit the course, I wipe the grime from my forehead with a towel and watch the men dodge, leap and throw. Antonio is swapped out with another player and as he jogs past me to the men's bench he ignores me as if I am a roadside vender selling stale, soggy watermelon.

A soaked Mercury bounds off the bench as I reach it and barks, "What's your malfunction? You made me fall! Again!" The heat of her breath is on my face and I can sense that she had onions for breakfast.

I look at Donavan for help but she doesn't so much as turn her head.

My black spot starts to buzz but I mentally quench it. I can't erupt here. Not right now. I don't respond to Mercury and quickly step around her and grab the only open spot on the bench; unfortunately I am forced to sit next to Sydney. I hope she can tolerate me being so close.

Mercury follows, standing in front of me, legs spread wide in an aggressive stance. "What? Nothing to say? If we weren't on the same team I would grind you to powder right now!"

"Beat it," Sydney says. I turn to look at her and can't believe my ears.

"You got nothing to say. This isn't about you," Mercury snaps then quickly returns her eyes to their target; my beet red face.

Now the fans are watching us and I know I must be careful. No telling if a camera is trained on us right now. This could be all over the screen in minutes. I try to defuse the situation even though I feel like it was completely her fault. "Hey Mercury, it was a comedy of errors. You went in too soon and I couldn't keep my momentum going. Sorry I knocked you down. I didn't do it on purpose."

"Comedy? Comedy? Yeah, you're a joke. That's all I know."

I stare up at her and wait. No way am I going to be the first one to lose it here. Although my black spot really wants me to. I don't want to be kicked off the team. I can't afford another screw up right now.

Sydney glares at her and repeats, "Beat it. You had your say, now move along newbie."

After Mercury realizes that she can't goad me into a fight she retires to the far end of the bench to sulk. Sydney leans over slightly toward me without turning her attention away from the field and whispers, "Sandy Stone told me what you said," then pulls away.

I don't know what to say but I feel like dirt is in my eye so I quietly wipe it before I tear. Is Sydney going to let me back in?

After the match, the team retires to the hotel. Sandstone and I go out to the rear patio. There's a few hotel guests there but it's not crowded. It's such a good evening, good for everyone but Mercury, but I can't be bothered about that right now. The setting sun is still shining and the crowd on the back patio of the hotel are cordial. One of the benefits of being on the farm team is that we can still mingle with the so-called "normal" people without the team body guards and having to worry too much about swarming fans. Sandstone is with me, soaking up the rays, and we are both stretching lightly and talking about how today's match went.

She says, "You were great. I was cheering for you the whole time. Too bad about Mercury though. She should have waited. I would. I would have waited. She should have known better than that. And Sidney too. Too bad for her. I hated to see her get pushed out." Sandstone's mile-a-minute style of talking is set to maximum volume at the moment. Maybe it's because she actually got to sign an autograph for a little girl. She was beaming the whole time.

"Being the fastest certainly puts a bulls-eye on your back," I reply as I switch my stretch to my other leg.

"I'm just waiting for my shot. I hope Donavan lets me run soon. I am so ready to fly. I would have preferred to do it here though. Now I'll have to run back in UNA."

"Why's that?" I question.

"Here in Europe, there wouldn't have been as much pressure on me to perform because my friends and family wouldn't have been in the stands." She smiles back at me as if it is something that I couldn't understand.

"But they would be watching on screen wouldn't they?"

"It's not the— Hey! Hey, Sidney tough luck today, huh?"

Sidney and Cyndi step out of the hotel onto the patio and Cyndi pauses when she sees me sitting there. Clearly she didn't know I was out here and clearly she wouldn't have come if she did. Sidney speaks as if the fans are listening and the cameras are rolling, "You win some, you lose some. I am just trying to add value to the team and do my part to help the Freedom win matches."

A few of the hotel guests nod their heads and return to their conversations. The small girl who previously got our autographs runs up to Cyndi just as she is about to turn around and says, "<Autograph! Autograph!>" in a heavy accent but no one has to translate to know what she wants.

She pauses, signs the girl's screen, turns to Sidney and says, "I changed my mind. I think I'm heading up."

Sidney looks at me for a moment, then says, "I'll be right behind you."

Cyndi leaves and Sidney grabs a spot on the far side of the patio. A few of the adult fans ask her some questions in broken English so she tries to answer them. She signs a few screens and then they leave her alone. Of all of us, she is the most popular because she is expected to move up to the pro team soon. Sandstone is mesmerized by the way they treat her and for once she is silent. I would love to walk up to Sidney right now and completely pour my heart out to her but with the other hotel guests sitting around I am glued to my chair.

My thoughts are interrupted by the ring of my screen. "Excuse me Sandstone, I have to get this," I say as I stand and walk around the corner of the building to a more secluded spot. It's Durand.

"Hello, Dr. Durand. Did you see the match?" I start with a little small talk as I look around to make sure no one is listening.

"Yes, wonderful work. Glad you put up some points. Are you able to, ahh, talk right now?"

"I think so. Let me put in my ear-piece. There. How's that?"

"Better. Just be careful what you say," Durand replies as he glances around then clears his throat.

"So what's up? did you think of anything else?" I say trying to be as vague as possible in case someone is listening.

"I was thinking about what you told me last time. About whether or not your father may have tampered with your DNA. I was piecing it together and, well this is all supposition on my part, but I was piecing it together and I figured that with Smith dating your mother you could have had him test your DNA and you would know right away if you were modified. So I am assuming that you did that and that it came back clean?"

"Yes."

He continues, "So I was wondering why would you care, to be honest with you. I mean it would be really something if Jonathan cracked that egg. It is something that they still haven't figured out how to do and for him to have done it so many years ago—well yeah, that would really be something. But whether or not you are modified makes no difference really. At least it shouldn't. Or is there something else you are not telling me?" I can see the puzzled look on his face and I know I have to give him something.

"Hold on a minute," I say as I walk to an even more secluded spot. "Okay, Dr. Durand, it seems to me that you are the paranoid type—"

He adds without the least hint of a smile, "That goes without saying."

"So I don't want to make you more nervous than you already are."

He says, "I don't think that is possible. Go on."

"As you already know, our entire family was in hiding in Venezuela because, I don't know, my father thought we needed to, I guess. Smith says that he stole his own research and that it was NuGen's property. I would really love to know why my father didn't feel safe out in the open but for whatever reason that's where we were. Then one day, two NuGen goons show up and chase my father. He crashes his car and now he's dead."

He answers, "Yes, I know. Again, I am so sorry for you. Jonathan was a good man. He didn't deserve that."

"So now here we are in UNA, me and my mom, like nothing ever happened and my mom is dating Smith, who she thinks is just peachy. I don't trust him and I still have this feeling in the pit of my stomach when he is around."

"Smith, I hate to say this, is not that bad of a guy. We disagreed on a lot of things but he's predictable. It's just the science with him. He just has to know, that's all."

I squirm at the thought.

He continues, "Is there anything else?"

I exhale then say, "Yeah, there's a lot more, but—"

"I understand. I wouldn't trust me either. You don't know me. Don't feel obligated to tell me anything."

"It's not that," I say but I am lying because that is exactly it. I think Durand is something of a kook and I want to really tell him as little as possible. "On more than one occasion I have felt like there have been NuGen people following me around. It seems to be too often for it to be a coincidence."

"That all?" he says and it surprises me that my statement didn't set off Captain Paranoid's alarm bells.

"No, there's more. I caught Smith stealing some of my DNA, several times in fact, and he claims that when he tested it, it showed that I was his biological daughter."

"Well now, that thickens the plot, I'd say." He rubs his chin as he says, "Would Jonathan do *that*? Hard to swallow, that one. Maybe—"

"Maybe what?"

He looks at me an says, "If I were Jonathan and I tested my own DNA and found some major defect, precursors that we hadn't figured out how to adjust out, something incurable, yeah, maybe I would have considered not using my own genetic material. Hmm, that'd be a tough one. And to not tell you, too? Wow. And your mom didn't know either?"

"She said she didn't and, yeah, by her reaction I don't think she did."

He asks, "So that's a curve ball. True. But what are you really searching for here? If you don't like Smith, you don't have to let him into your life. I mean I am not here to tell you how to live your life but I guess I am still trying to understand why you reached out to me and what you think I can do for you. How did you find me by the way?"

"My father had a diary," I finally say it and my eyes are glued to his face for any hint of a reaction. A momentary flicker of excitement, a smile, a look of surprise, anything to tell me that he may have some form of ulterior motive.

He doesn't flinch. "And my name was in it?"

"Yes, well, sort of. It's written in some form of code. I deciphered your name. That's about it so far."

"I see. And what do you think this diary *is*?" He seems a little nervous, as if the realization that his name being in my father's diary may have somehow exposed him to some unseen danger.

"I'm not so sure. Clearly it contains a coded message. I would like to think that it's a message to me. But maybe it contains his lost research. I don't know. If he wanted to tell me something, you know, a last message from beyond the grave, I sure would like to know. You were my first clue. That's all."

"Well, I am sorry that I couldn't help you more. Your first lead has led to a dead-end of sorts."

He looks like he is ready to hang up so I say, "Do you think you could look at it, some of it, I mean, if I sent you a few pages?"

"Gabriella, what did I tell you about trusting people? Is this what you are doing with my information? I hope you haven't told anyone that you have spoken to me or that you have my contact information. Smith? Victor? I am really trying to stay anonymous and I would prefer to not have Victor Chavez knowing my whereabouts."

"No, I would never. I just thought you might be able to help me. There aren't many people I can trust—not saying I trust you either—Could you just look at a few pages, please?"

"Send them over to me and I'll look them over. No guarantees though. And please, try to be more discreet." He closes the connection and I walk back over to the patio. Sidney and Sandstone are chumming it up and the other hotel guests have dissipated so I sneak over to them.

Sidney says to Sandstone, "I have three little brothers, Jonathan, Scott and George and none of them are normal. The youngest, little Georgie, he just creeps me out. The kid, he's just weird, and I can never tell if he is serious, what he's thinking, or what. It's like I don't know how to take this kid and he's only four years old."

"Oh yeah?" Sandstone says.

"The other night—you tell me what you think—the other night I wake up in the middle of the night and roll over and he's standing there, over my bed, staring down at me. The lights are off. It's dark in the room and he's just standing there looking down at me with his blank-stare, creepy-face. He's just four years-old, mind you. I'm like, 'Georgie? What do you want?' my voice all shaking. He doesn't say a word, turns on his heel and walks out."

Sandstone's completely on the fish-hook. "You're kidding right?"

Sidney smiles and says, "So whenever he wants something I just let him have it. You want to watch your stupid cartoons when I'm right in the middle of watching the Ultraball championship? Sure, go ahead. I just don't want my body to be found folded up, stuffed in a trash-bag, at the bottom of a dumpster somewhere because I didn't let you watch your stupid show. Yeah, he's creepy like that."

Sandstone shakes her head in disbelief so I say, "Sandstone, Sidney likes to tell jokes."

I stand in front of them and wait for Sidney to look up at me. Sandstone looks up at my face and then over at Sidney then says, "I'll let you two alone."

"No, don't go," I say. "I won't be long."

"Who says I'm going to sit here and listen to you?" Sidney adds.

"Sidney? Please? Just this once. Listen to what I have to say and if you still want to cut me off then I'll respect that. Please, just let me tell my side of the story?"

Sandstone pushes back in her chair and now I am sorry that I asked her to stay.

The night is quiet and a small bird flutters in a tree. Sidney says, "I'm listening."

"I don't know where to begin. So, I guess I should start with I was wrong. I shouldn't have lied."

"That's obvious," Sidney replies.

"Well, one thing I want you to know is that I didn't know it was Kyle, at least in the beginning. I was as confused as the rest of you as to who hurt Cyndi. It wasn't until the night that Kyle and Sebastian fought, the night they were kicked off of the practice field, that I found out. I should have said something then. I had the chance but I didn't. I don't know why. I think I didn't know how to do it? Maybe? Kyle and I were engaged and when I found out what he had done I knew I could never marry him but I felt trapped. Us being engaged linked us together in my mind and I thought no one would believe me that I didn't know. I was just trying to buy time, to figure it all out, to figure out what I should do."

There is acid on Sidney's tongue. "What you should have done was open your mouth for once."

"I know that now. It tore me apart that he did that to her. Thinking about it, I still can't believe it. And do you know he blamed me? He said it was all my fault because I was asking too many questions."

"What are you talking about?" Sidney asks.

"NuGen. I wanted to know more about what they were doing. There was a lot of drama that I don't want to drag you through, but Kyle wouldn't tell me much, at least I didn't feel comfortable asking him outright, and Cyndi seemed to be able to pull information out of Sebastian." Sidney's brow furrows so I say defensively, "She volunteered to find out from him."

"I didn't know anything about this," she says.

"So when Kyle found out that Sebastian was giving information to Cyndi to give to me, he beat her up. So, yeah, in the end it was all my fault. If I hadn't asked Cyndi to spy for me then she wouldn't have gotten attacked and she wouldn't have been in the hospital. I wanted to tell you both that it was Kyle but I think something inside of me felt guilty. I still do. I didn't know how to handle it."

Sidney exhales, looks around the space then says, "Is that all?"

I reply, "I guess I am not asking you to forgive me. I don't feel like I have the right to ask that. I just wanted you to understand my point of view, to know what I was going through and to know this: to know that you and Cyndi were all I really had as far as friends here in this country."

I turn to walk away then stop when Sidney says, "It can never be the same. You know that, don't you?"

Her words pummel me softly, slowly. There is a far-off singing in my ears and I do not know where it is coming from and I realize that it is not birds or someone's screen but the noise of me stopping myself from crying.

"I know," I say and place my hand on the door handle, turn it slowly and step through the doorway. I wanted it to come out differently but it's over. It's all over now.

In the hotel lobby I see Allison and Coach Donavan and several of the team doctors and front office staff in a semi-circle discussing what appears to be some sort of match strategy which seems odd to me since it will be a week before our next match. We are only waiting for the pro team to compete tomorrow and then we will travel home. As I pass through the lobby the meeting ends and Allison jogs up to me. "Hey, did you hear?"

"No, what?" I respond, shaking myself away from Sidney's words. My heart is still beating fast.

"That French girl that didn't show at the match a few days ago and then showed up a hot mess?"

"What about her? Is she All right?" I stop walking

and look at her.

Allison says in a morbid voice, "She is most definitely not All right. They don't know what's wrong with her but she's aging rapidly. You almost wouldn't recognize her. She looks twenty years older."

"Some kind of disease?" I say.

"Here. Look." She pulls out her screen and swipes over to the news feed. A before and after picture are on the screen.

"Wow. I remember her now. We raced once before. And that's her?" I say, pointing at the older woman in the photograph. "When was that taken?"

"This morning," Allison says. "Apparently she freaked out and went into hiding. Weird, right? I would have gotten my legs moving towards a hospital pronto if I was her."

"Yeah, right. She looks older in that picture than when we saw her a few days ago. And they're saying that's twenty year's older? She doesn't look like she's in her forties. Where'd they come up with that number?"

Allison replies, "That's what I thought. Her skin's mottled and she looks a little sick, like maybe she has the flu, but other than that, she doesn't look *that* bad. But they checked her DNA and it was the DNA of a forty year old. That's what they said."

"They can do that? How do they know?" I ask.

"Her telomeres. They were chomped right off. You know what those are?"

"Yes, I do. I'm still in school, remember. I guess she can't run anymore?" I can't stop my arms from shaking. "Telomeres, telomeres, telomeres," is ringing in my ears.

"That's why she didn't show up to the meet. Her joints are roasted."

"Yeah, listen Allison, I need to turn in. Bad news about the girl there."

I ride the elevator up to the fifth floor and slink into my room. My mind is blank. I don't know what to think. A few minutes later Sandstone shows up but we don't talk. I change into my pajamas and slide under the covers and turn out the light.

Is that what's going to happen to all the modified girls? If I am really one of them, is that what is going to happen to me?

Chapter 24

GRN

"It's good to see you, even though it isn't under the best circumstances," Michael says as he leans back into his chair and stares up at the sky.

I can't read him. No, not at all. "I know. I'm glad you came. Sorry, it feels so high school." We are sitting out on the hotel patio and luckily we are all alone. Having him meet me here was the only way I could see him. At least that's what I told him, since there was no way I was asking Allison to escort me out on a date. No way.

"I understand. No problem. The team has rules. Next year things will be different."

"I can't wait to turn eighteen," I say. My voice is hollow. I am sitting next to him in the same chair Sidney sat in just twenty-four hours ago, an eternity ago, but I am still stinging from the encounter.

"So, I think I got something," he says as he sits upright and turns toward me.

For a moment I am not sure exactly what he is talking about. "Oh? Really? The diary?"

Michael smirks, then says, "Yeah, took a while though. Almost gave up, I did, but I was thinking of your pretty smile and how you were going to flash it at me when I told you."

I give him a big, toothy grin but for some reason I have to labor to create it, as if my face muscles feel really tired right now and would rather hang down despondently.

"I was just kidding."

My brow furrows, as I tease, "You didn't want to see me smile?"

"Oh. No, I meant I was kidding about almost giving up."

I smile again. "So what did you come up with?"

He speaks slowly, as if he is trying to choose his words cautiously. "Well, the first thing I can say is that it is definitely not just a sales ledger. There's something else."

"I thought so," I say eagerly.

"There seems to be certain patterns that keep cropping up. And another thing, the first letters, did you look at the first letters?"

Puzzled, I answer, "No, what do you mean?"

"Here look at this." Michael pulls a sheet of paper out of his pocket that has a single page of my father's diary printed out on it. There are scribble lines and notes all over it. "If you look at the first word on every line, I mean the first letter of the first word on every line. There? See that?"

I spell out the letters, "G—R—N—A—P—R—R. Okay, that means nothing to me."

"Me neither. I'm a physicist, remember? But I got this friend—"

"You didn't?" I say as I push away in my chair.

"Calm down, I only asked this friend—he's a microbiology guy—if those letters meant anything to him."

"And?"

"And they did." Michael is grinning and for some reason it irritates me.

"And now you're torturing me?" I scoot closer to

him. "Tell me then?"

"Do you know anything about cell differentiation?"

"A little. All our cells start out the same—stem cells I think they are called—in fact, all the information for every cell starts out in the one first cell and as the cells divide, something tells each cell what to be, like, what it's function will be, what body part it will become. Right? Something like that. That's about all I know."

Michael says, "I didn't pay much attention in Biology class either. I did some research and it turns out that our cells are like little bags of chemicals and that part of the differentiation process is internal to the cell but there is another part that comes from the surrounding cells."

"Okay, so it sounds like this has something to do with my father's research?"

"Maybe. So these cells communicate with each other, using chemicals of course, and form a sort of a neural network. That network is called a gene regulatory network or G—R—N for short. The letters in the diary, I think they mean something."

"I am not sure I understand what this has to do with—"

"Stay with me," Michael says. "So the cells communicate with each other through chemicals, right?"

"Right," I say and nod my head, trying to not feel lost.

"But the cell that is sending the communication, he just sends it, he just releases these proteins and pushes them outside of his cell wall and moves on to doing what other things a cell does."

"And then what?"

"So all these cells are pushing out proteins and

some of those proteins are being absorbed by the surrounding cells and these proteins cause the cells to do things. For one, they alter the cells behavior. That much everyone already knew but they also do something else."

"I'm listening," I say but I am still a little disappointed that Michael didn't find a message in the diary coded directly to me, some little love note from my father to his little girl.

"They actually go into the cell and sometimes turn certain genes on or off. Do you understand that? They can actually tell a cell to turn into something else, to alter the composition of the cell."

"Yeah, so it helps the cell decide what it is going to be."

"More than that. It can happen in an adult too. That's the key. I think your father found something; I was thinking maybe a way to rebuild, to regenerate cells with a refreshed, embryonic DNA, maybe using some form of released protein. See, it's in the network. Not only can the protein communicate the order for the cell to change, it can communicate for the receiving cell to release identical proteins and pass the message along— that's where the gene network part comes in."

My brow furrows again as I think of Smith and how he had my father's diary right in his hands. "Hmm, that would explain some things, I guess."

"Yes, I think so. I think he was working on this network and maybe figuring out how to control it. See the messages can be pretty complex and full of AND, OR and NOT logic—well NANDs would work better really, it would make sense to be all NANDs—and that is how one single message could be propagated through an entire organism and refresh it." Michael is talking to himself at this point, lost in his thoughts. I am staring at him, waiting for him to finish when he says, "And another thing, this other series of letters kept cropping up too. G—E—R—G—E—N. and I couldn't figure those out until I put it all together. "

"What do they mean?" I say.

"This is just a guess, but I think it stands for geriatric-genesis. You know? Ger Gen? I don't know. That one is just a guess." He sits back in his chair and smiles wide. but I am not satisfied.

"And that's it?"

"What do you mean, 'that's it?' " He looks a little shocked and unsure if I am joking.

I lower my voice. "I just thought there might be something in there about me."

His expression is pained. "Oh right. Sorry Gabby, that's all I found so far."

"At least it's something. At least I know there's something in there. What do you think it means?"

"I think your father may have found something. Unsure of how far he got, of course. It could have been all untried and theoretical or it could have been something that he already knew worked, but it sure looked like he was working on some sort of life extension, to my blind eyes anyway. Exciting stuff."

I lean back in my chair again and am suddenly paranoid but I am not sure why. "Who was this guy you spoke to anyway? This friend of yours?"

"No one important. Just an old friend from the university. I didn't tell him anything about you."

"Oh. Okay." I turn to him and grab his hand. "I don't want to sound too skittish but you know how important this is to me, right?"

"I know, Gabby. I promised, remember?"

I can't let go of his hand just yet as touching it

suddenly floods my mind with images of a beach in Portugal and the two of us diving into crashing waves, laughing, hugging, smiling and rolling onto the sand. It was a different time. "I miss you," I blurt out and then am sorry for saying it.

He looks away and doesn't respond so I say, "Sorry, I shouldn't have said that. I know you're really with Maryann."

He tugs his hand lightly but leaves it under mine. "No, that's not it. I told you we weren't anything to each other."

I pull my hand off of his so I don't force him to pull it away. "Why's that?"

"I don't know. She's different. I probably shouldn't tell you this—"

"What?" I say.

"No. It's nothing."

"Hey, you brought it up. Tell me."

His face turns red with embarrassment and regret. "The experiments. We're still doing them," he whispers.

"What? How? You lost your funding."

Michael looks at me and his face is sour. He clearly doesn't want to talk about it.

"Michael, I won't go raiding Dr. D. I promise. Just tell me."

"Ahhh, it's these people that Maryann knows. Kyle too. He's involved—although I have never seen him in person, only through the screen. Some of the old techs too. I don't know where their money comes from. They are funding the project."

I am astonished. "What? That makes no sense. Why?"

"I have no idea. They are kind of secretive. I asked Maryann out on a date. Well, a few dates. I was trying to get into her head, trying to figure this out, but she's smart, you know."

"I know," I say.

"We are definitely not together. Get that out of your head. I was curious, that's all."

"So you didn't find out what they're trying to do?" I ask.

"I didn't hear much when I was out with her. I overheard a few phone calls. Seems like real shadowy stuff. It's almost as if it's a religion with them."

"What do you think they're after? Dr. D was trying to make a new mode of travel. A transportation machine for quickly moving goods and people across the planet. That can't be what they want." And I already know where this is going but I still can't believe it.

"I think it's the Void experience. It's like they worship it, as much as I can tell. It's like a drug for them. They go in and stay for hours."

"And Dr. D is okay with that?" I ask.

He says, "They gave him the money for his research and signed off on it all. They gave it to him with no strings attached. His research and all. Just so long as they can run their space-cadet, Void-worshiping zombies through."

"And you see them? You know who they are?"

Michael looks like the conversation is tiring him. "I have no idea who most of them are. It's not like I have a name list. It's a nuisance, really. Dr. D and I are trying to do research but we have to keep running these people through. I just try to ignore them. Can we talk about something else?"

I pause. "Yeah, sure. But one last thing. The marks. Do they have black marks on their skin, like a birth mark or an odd tattoo?" My black spot suddenly begins to buzz as if it knows that I am talking about it.

He starts speaking slowly, as if his mind is elsewhere. "Now that you mention it, yeah, they did. I didn't think anything of it. They all had the black marks."

Chapter 25

Millennia

I fall into the mud and can't seem to pull myself free so I yell at it. My voice comes out awkward and cawing and it frightens me. Then another voice behind me says, "Look." It is my father's voice.

I roll over in the mud, suddenly not caring that my bottom is sinking in and is getting wet. There he stands, over me, shining and bright, and I am pierced through with joy. "I have something for you," I say but I don't know where it is.

I look down and my nightgown that I thought I was wearing has somehow been replaced with my jacket so I reach in my pocket and pull out the letter, the letter that I wrote him, the letter that I wrote my father. I hold it out to him but he only stares at me. We are most certainly in the woods behind my home but there are no shadows here. He is so bright right now.

Since he will not take it, I unfold the page and begin to read the words out-loud to him, my eyes slowly tearing. When I finish, I look full on his face, expectantly, and it is blank, steady and expressionless. It does not affect him and it's as if he knew what the words were before he heard them. I am more than disappointed.

He opens his mouth and mumbles something that I cannot quite make out, then I hear him say, "You will fight for it as a small sparrow, a sparrow that will become a mighty hawk."

The breath is ripped from my throat as I realize

that it is what he said before and I realize that perhaps he is saying my future is set in stone. I can't change it. It wasn't a poem; it was a prophecy.

Then he adds, "You must speak the words of your destiny. They are who you are and until you embrace them, you will not become. It is the becoming that is important."

My eyes creep open as the plane shakes and I am in no way surprised that it was a dream. Sitting there, staring at the back of the seat in front of me, I wonder what he meant but somehow it makes me feel doomed and I can't help but want to change it. How can he know the future? Or is it just a warning? I hope it is. Is there nothing I can do to alter what he said? Or was it just another stupid dream?

The plane lands and it feels great to have my feet back on UNA soil. We grab our bags and head to the bus which drops us off at the practice building. Mom is waiting for me so I trudge off to her car dragging my small luggage behind me.

As she drives, she asks about Europe and soaks up every detail, but her tone strikes me peculiar. She asks questions as if she has been to those places before, or at least ones like them, and it reveals, once again, that mom and dad had a completely different life before I was born, a life that I know nothing about.

I tell her about the races and the markets and the people but not about Durand. I don't want her to know about that yet but it bothers me to not tell her, especially since keeping secrets tends to get me into big trouble. I don't say anything about black spots or what I learned from Michael about Dr. Duggan and the machine. I will tell her everything, eventually, just not now. I can't right now. Right now I don't want to think. I just need to feel normal again. I need to go home, put on my shoes and run. I need to feel the wind in my hair and think about nothing. Not Michael, not Durand, not Duggan. No one. Just blank out my mind and think about nothing.

"Nothing," I unconsciously whisper out loud.

"What's that, Gabby?" mom says.

"Oh, nothing. I said nothing." An eerie feeling crawls on my skin as if I am covered by a million gnats and I wonder if thinking about 'nothing' is such a good idea after all. It's the kind of thing that Kyle would say. What am I becoming?

Mom steers the car into the driveway and we go inside. "I am going to go for a run," I say.

"So soon? You just got back."

"I won't be long."

Mom replies, "Because Smith is coming over. I'm making dinner."

"Mom, I don't know if I'm up to seeing him."

"Gabby, no matter what he says, he's not your father. Whether or not you have his DNA in you, and I am not saying he does, Jonathan raised you. He's the man I loved and the man that was your father. Smith's just a guy. Okay?"

"Thanks, Mom." But that has nothing to do with why I don't want to see him. I need time to focus. I need time to make sure I can fool him, to make sure that I don't accidentally give away some clue as to what I know about what's in my father's diary. I can't risk me letting some seemingly innocuous little detail slip out and him becoming more curious than he already is.

I change and go out for a slow run and try to think about absolutely nothing. I find it impossible. Every time I think that I am thinking about nothing I find myself thinking about something. Michael and his soft brown eyes. His lithe body. His British accent. I squeeze him out of my mind and again try to think about nothing but too soon other thoughts invade my head. Durand and how he didn't flinch when I told him about my father's diary. Should I find that suspicious? And why he keeps telling me that I shouldn't trust him. Is he trying to tell me something? I can't do this. How can anyone think about nothing? It doesn't make sense. None of Kyle's mumbo-jumbo does. I don't see how Maryann and the rest of them are buying into it. And still going through the machine too? And Duggan? How can he, a scientist, be a part of it? Nothing. Nothing. Nothing. I just need to relax and not think about anything.

I run slowly, focusing on my breathing and my footsteps, taking an all-too-familiar path, one I've run thousands of times and slowly lose myself to the run. Left, right, breathe, left, right, breathe; the run takes over and all things fall away as I become the run. Left, right, breathe; nothing is important, nothing but fluid, silky, continuous motion, my body drifting hypnotically across the landscape as a disembodied spirit. I am the run; I flow, I go. Nothing is important and, really, nothing is. Left, right, breathe; pumping my arms and legs, sliding on satin sheets, I glide. I am the run.

I complete just under ten miles, shake my mind awake, then slow to a walk for the last block and stop. I realize that I did it, somehow. My mind blanked to nothing but I don't know how I did it. It just happened.

Smith's car is in my driveway. I mentally prepare myself, quickly go inside, exchange some niceties, telling Mom and Smith that I am not very hungry and to not wait for me to eat. I scamper up the stairs, shower, then enter my room.

My screen is ringing when I walk in and I barely

hear it since my head is wrapped in a towel. I dive onto the bed and answer it. It's Antonio and I'm not sure if I want to speak to him. I've still got Michael on my mind.

I swipe the screen and he says, "Hey G, A here. What's hot?"

"Nothing. You?"

"Just needed to refill. I've been yearning to feast my eyes on you," he says.

"Really? It doesn't feel like it on the field."

He frowns. "Well with Bustoff. And Donavan. You know the rules. I can't—"

"It's fine. Really. I understand. It just feels like you only want to see me when no one is around. Are you going to come knocking on my window next?" He would have to climb to the second floor. Love to see that one.

"G, it's not like that," he defends.

"I gotta go," I say and it makes me sound angry when I'm actually not all that mad at him. I just have another call. I hang up on Antonio and swipe the other call in. It's Durand.

I whisper, "Hiya, I'm alone in my room. We can talk."

"I looked over some of the, err, data, that you sent and, err, there appears to be some abnormalities. As you suspected." He seems more jittery than before and is clearly trying to cloak his words. Why is he so nervous? He must have really found something.

"Oh, cool. I think I may have seen something wrong in the data too," I say, not sure of how to reply without some mystery person who may be listening on his side figuring it out.

He pauses then looks at me intently and says, "That's great. Real nifty." He drawls on the first letters of each word and I immediately recognize them from what Michael told me. Great—Real—Nifty. G—R—N. Durand saw it too. I try to not let my face light up too much. I nod.

"We need to talk more on this," he says. "Go outside somewhere, a park or something, and give me a call back." He terminates the connection and I realize that he was not nervous of someone listening on his side, but on mine. He didn't like the idea of me speaking to him from my room. A chill runs down my back. My room can't be bugged. Can it? Gabby, don't let that nut Durand get you paranoid too.

I dress and hop down the stairs. Smith and Mom are eating. I try to sound bubbly. "Hey, Smith. How's it going? Mom, I'm going out with a few friends. Be back in a jiff."

"Where are you going?"

"Just out to the park," I say too quickly. Trying to change the subject, I blurt out, "I'll be back in about an hour. Smith, will you still be here? I wanted to ask you something."

Smith says, "Sure—"

"See ya then." I dodge out before mom can stop me and head for the park a few blocks away. As soon as I am there, I call Durand.

When he answers, I duck behind a tree and sit down. "Hey Durand, I'm at the park. Can we talk now?"

"Yes. I believe so. No one is around you, right?"

I look around. "A few people but they are on the other side of the field, by the duck pond. No one here."

"Good," he says. "So, you noticed the letters too? G—R—N?"

"Yes, but they mean nothing to me. I noticed that they seem to repeat though," I lie. "Does it mean anything to you?"

He scratches his neck slowly. "Yes, of course. But in this application, I mean, what we were working on so many years ago, it is certainly a different direction. We were working with virus vectors. This, no, this is something totally novel. I am surprised to find it and I don't see how Jonathan could have been working on it without Smith knowing. And me, it has me really puzzled."

I lean against the tree and say, "But what is it? Were you able to piece any other clues in there together?"

"Oh yes, there's a lot there. There's an entire network formula. I am still deciphering the code and of course you only gave me a few pages, so there is a lot missing. I have many questions. But alas, it is no longer my line of work, you might say. I know you were looking for some sort of message to you personally. That, my dear, I did not find."

"I kind of thought so."

"Anyway, I wanted to speak to you away from any prying ears. I wanted to warn you."

"Warn me?" I say.

He clears his throat. "Yes. I think you should destroy that book. I know it is hard to hear, it being one of the only things you have of your father's. It is in his own handwriting and all and, I understand, really I do. But for your own safety, it should be destroyed."

"So you are not interested in it? I thought you were working on this kind of stuff too?"

Durand blows his air our slowly and replies, "I was. Like your father. Like Smith. It was my passion, then, back there, so long ago. But people change."

"How so?" I am really surprised that he doesn't

want the other pages. He is nothing like Smith.

"Back at the university we thought we had it all figured out. You know we would sit there, your father, Smith and I, and talk about evolution and the advent of the Australopithicus and Homo habilus, and of course Homo sapiens sapiens, and grandly, our coming perfection. We were ushering in the dawn of a new man, a super man, we told each other and smiled broadly. Hahaha, what fools we were. We threw around millennia like they were play toys. All was due to random mutation we told ourselves and now we would control mutation. What took thousands of centuries using randomness would take tens of years under our guiding hands. It all seemed so simple." He stops talking and looks down.

I ask, "And now you think? What? That my dad shouldn't have been doing these things? I mean if you three didn't, someone else would, right?"

"It all boils down to this, Gabriella: the question. I think your father came to it too, in the end, before he fled. We never spoke of it, but I knew. I could see it in his eyes. It was the question."

"What question?" I say.

He looks at me sort of surprised, as if it was obvious. "Where did we come from? What started life? That, my dear, is the question. That is what stopped me. That, I think, is what stopped your father." Durand looks down again, lost in his thoughts and begins to ramble. "Life simply consists of a set of characteristics, we knew this clearly—metabolism, reproduction and the like. Life undergoes evolution, of course. The body is merely a collection of discreet processes, a collection of autonomous and semi-autonomous processes—we call it life, sure. Under the microscope it seems quite random. It is soup. But deep down I knew that there was more than that, that the sum was more than the total of the parts."

"I don't know where you are going with this," I say.

He continues as if he did not hear me. "And of course there is always Schrödinger. I couldn't keep him out of my mind. Dead for over a hundred years and I couldn't keep his voice out of my head. Hahaha."

"Schrödinger?" I say.

Durand looks up. "Sorry, I was carrying on, wasn't I?"

"Who was Schrödinger? Someone else who knew my father? No, my father wasn't that old—"

"No, my dear. An old dead physicist. No, a philosopher. A great man, anyway. He had a cat. Maybe you heard of it?"

"I don't think so," I say.

" 'Most physical laws on a large scale are due to chaos on a small scale,' he said. Chaos on a small scale tends to produce order on a large scale. An elementary concept, but it defies true understanding. Order out of chaos. We say we understand this, but do we really? At a deep level? It shook me. Cells have order, you see. DNA is information. It is data. And mathematically, there is not enough time to create a single cell—even a very simple cell, mind you—through a truly random mechanism. This has been proven—"

I reply, "It sounds like you are talking about—"

He interrupts me, "No, oh no. I am no religious fanatic. Neither was your father. We are scientists. Your father was. There must be some explanation; there always is. I believe in evolution but it's just that it's clearly not caused by a single factor. There are instigating factors that are causing specific cellular actions. There is something, somewhere in the cell, that is somehow making choices that are—here it is—not random. There is some kind of informed decision making going on in the evolutionary process. Oh, what a bold statement. If any of my colleagues heard me say that, they would label me a heretic. But... but it stopped me. I mean, who am I to say that my design decisions would be better than evolution's? We were tampering with things that we didn't truly understand. I... I had to stop."

"I see," I say, unsure of how to reply.

He ponders my face for a moment then says, "I will let you go, daughter of Jonathan. I suggest you destroy the book as soon as you can. Otherwise it will bring you nothing but pain." The screen goes dark before I can respond so I close it, pull myself up from the ground and begin walking home slowly.

I am troubled at Durand's words and not exactly sure how to take them. I am still a little surprised at his request. When I was back in my room and he hinted that he had found something, I expected him to ask for the remainder of the book so that he might gain the rest of the work. But to ask me to destroy it? Durand's a neurotic-paranoid but his heart is in the right place. I think I can really trust him.

Michael, on the other hand, is another story. I can trust him, sure, but he spoke to some stranger at the university and Maryann is just too close. I don't think I should give him anymore information from my father's book.

I turn the corner and stop; my house is a block away. I try to sort my thoughts. And destroying the book? Maybe, but not yet. I need to think about that more. It is safe with me for now, anyway. No one really knows what's in it anyway. Only Michael and Durand.

I enter the house and Smith and Mom are being

cozy on the couch.

"Hey all," I say as I head toward the stair case.

"What was it you wanted to ask me?" Smith says.

"Oh, yeah, I forgot about that. Just something that you said the other day. We can talk more another day. It's nothing."

Mom says, "Tomorrow would be good. Smith is taking us on a picnic at the park. You used to love picnics."

"Yeah, when I was five," I say.

"It'll be fun." Mom says as Smith looks at her and then back at me.

He's trying, I think. "Okay, sure. Tomorrow then. But I have to do some things in the morning. What time?"

"In the afternoon. Does that work for you?" Smith says.

"Sure," I respond and scale the steps.

In my room I whip out my screen and start searching some terms. Everything that both Michael and Durand told me is quickly melding into one big pot of soup in my brain. Soup. Like cellular soup. I start with gene regulatory network since it is something that they both mentioned. I am quickly thrust into a flurry of long multi-lettered acronyms like RBICS1A, GBSSI and APRR, letters that all appear in my father's diary. There is much discussion about how the networks function and terms like 'transcription factor' and 'stochastic and Gaussian models' are everywhere. It is over my head but I at least glean that this is in line with what my father was working on.

After a few hours, my head begins to throb so I set the screen down and roll over on the bed to stare at a blank ceiling. I still don't know what to do with the diary.

It would be easy enough to destroy it, of course. Is that why I was supposed to retrieve it? I don't think so. Maybe there is something else in there. The man from the Void—huh, the man from my dreams—he seems to know the future—at least his bizarre prophecies—if that's what they are—point in that direction. If he knows the future and he wanted me to retrieve this book then I must need it for some reason. I can't destroy it. No, not yet. I need to speak with him. I need to take him my father's diary. And not just in my dreams.

I dial Allison's screen. She answers, "Hey, Gabriella. Didn't expect to hear from you at this time. What's up?"

"I need you to do something for me," I say softly.

"Okay but can't this wait until practice?"

I whisper, "This isn't about the team. It's something else."

She looks at me oddly and says, "Are you in some kind of trouble?"

"Not at all. I just need you to give someone a message. Kyle. I need you to tell Kyle and his friends that I want to go through. Tell him I'm ready. Tell him I want to go into the Void."

"I, err, I don't know what you are—"

"Allison, you know exactly what I'm talking about. I'm done pretending. Just give him the message, okay?"

"Okay," she says sheepishly.

"And one other thing."

"What?" she says.

"I need you to take me. Can you pick me up tomorrow morning? I don't have a license, remember?"

She still looks shaken. "If Kyle says so, then I will be there."

Chapter 26

Black and White

"Mom, I'm off."

"Okay, just don't forget about the picnic," she calls out from the kitchen as I dart out the door.

I hop into Allison's car. She watches me, eyes wide, and caresses her black spot knowingly. Without saying a word, I pull my hair back and turn my head to the right so she can see mine. I look back at her, expressionless. She nods then pulls the car out onto the roadway. There is nothing to say; I am one of them now.

It feels like such a long drive to Princeton, much longer than the fifty or so minutes that it actually takes. We drive in silence and I am lost in my thoughts of what I will say to Kyle, what I will say to Duggan, what he will say to me, how I am going to convince him, them both really, to let me go through, and then, oh then, what I am going to say to the Void-man. Allison startles me when she places her hand upon mine as she drives and it tingles brightly. I don't move my hand, although it is my first impulse, but only look at her. Her eyes glance at me without turning her head and she smiles briefly and then removes her hand.

"You have it too," she says plainly. Her voice is dull and expressionless.

"What?" I ask.

"I couldn't understand why it tingled when I was near you. It's so obvious now. I don't know how I could have missed it. We are Void compatible." She speaks in a monotone.

I reach my hand up to her arm and hold it just millimeters from her skin. Nothing happens. I stow my hand and say, "How did you do that? What do you mean?"

"There is so much I could say, but I do not know much. I am just a learner. Kyle will explain all." Her blank, emotionless voice wears on me. It does not sound like the Allison I know and I feel that somehow this is the real one and the other was a façade.

"C'mon, you can tell me something. You're not going to sit here in silence for the next half hour in this traffic, are you?"

Allison looks over at me briefly. "I'm not really supposed to but I guess it can't hurt. Some people can connect with each other. That's about all I know. Not everyone can do it and I am not sure what exactly it means to be able to connect. It's just that there is some form of connection; that's all I know. I know that when certain people are close to each other, if you pay attention to it, listen for it, you can feel it. Do you want to try?"

"Sure."

"Do what you were doing before," she says.

I place my hand a short distance from the skin of her arm as she drives. "Like this?" I ask.

"Now close your eyes and focus. Try to connect."

I think about the tingle but nothing happens. I try to connect, to somehow connect to her but nothing happens. I feel very silly. "I'm not feeling anything," I say.

The car is silent for a few moments then she says, "That's because you are concentrating on the feeling. Don't do that. Don't look for it. Feelings are an illusion. Feelings do not exist."

I sit there, eyes closed, holding my hand mid-air, feeling like a fool. "But I don't feel... I mean, I don't, nothing is happening."

She says slowly, softly, "Do not try to feel. Do not try to perceive. Step beyond your role as a perceiver, merge everything into the flux. Go into the stillness." She exhales long and slow. It's as if she is trying to reach me from her side; I know that now. "The world will collapse. There is no time, no space, no viewer, no viewing, no object to view, nothing. Let it come. It is there."

Shallow waves waft over me and the air around me grows slowly thicker. It feels smoky. I want to open my eyes but I don't as I know the spell will be broken. Something about what she said makes sense, even though it doesn't, really. I do not try to understand the words, but I try to do them, to become still and nothing and void.

"That's it, Gabriella, follow my voice. Follow me. When you stop all thought, the battle will be won. Everything will be still and peaceful and right and perfect. You will come to see the eternal voidness of all things. You will see that nothing is, that *only* nothing is. Follow me there."

Small sparkles erupt between us; I pop my eyes open just long enough to see them disappear and the spell is broken.

"We're here. Let's go," Allison says as she parks the car in front of the large white building, Princeton's Plasma Physics Laboratory. Before I can say a word she is out of the car and heading up the building's steps.

I scale the large stone steps, trying to shake away goose-flesh, open the door and enter. Several people who appear to be university students lurk in the vestibule, their mouths forming flat lines. They stare at me as I try to push toward the winding staircase and I have the distinct feeling that they were waiting for my arrival. Others stand on the stairs and their eyes and bodies turn and follow me as I pass them. At the top of the landing that overlooks the atrium stands Kyle. He is wearing a black shirt and black pants that look somewhat stylish and form fitting. Allison is now next to him.

"Welcome, Gabriella," he says coldly.

"Hi, Kyle. I wasn't sure if you would actually be here."

"How could I miss this. My former fiancée? The one who opened my eyes to the true nature of things? I would be remiss to not escort you myself." It is as if he is speaking to the crowd surrounding us.

"So what is this all about anyway, Kyle? What are you trying to accomplish here?" My voice doesn't sound like theirs. It has emotion and it stands in stark contrast. I feel like an outsider.

"Can I see it?" he says.

"What?" I say then immediately realize what he wants. I hold my hair up and turn my back toward him. He steps closer to inspect it. "It is where you were strangling me, remember?" I can't help it; resentment drips from my voice and all of a sudden I am no longer concerned about hiding it. "Where you touched me. In the Void. You were trying to kill me. That's how I got it, remember?"

He steps back so I drop my hair and glare at him. I didn't want to be confrontational. I need to go through the machine. I need them right now but I just can't stop myself. Allison too. I glare at her too. She should know. They all should know who Kyle really is. He is not some prophet. He's just a nut-case. I turn and look at them all, glaring. But all of their faces are blank and expressionless. Don't they know? Didn't they hear what I just said?

Kyle explains, "The person you refer to is long dead. In fact he never existed, at least in the form that you think of. I answer to the label of Kyle as it is convenient for the worldlings of this place. You, Gabriella, are not of this world and once you begin to realize this, you will have taken the first step toward realization. I am here to help you."

I try to calm myself. I just need to get through this. I need them to let me go through the machine. "I'm sorry. I didn't mean to become emotional." I look around at them again, then continue calmly, "But you didn't answer my question. What are you trying to accomplish?"

Allison looks at Kyle who nods, then she says, "Complete liberation and insight into ultimate reality."

I look at her through my eyelids.

Kyle adds, "What Allison says is correct and true and perfect and right, but we are not trying to do it."

A few of the students behind me mumble, "That's right."

Kyle continues as if he is teaching a Sunday school lesson, "The moment you say 'I am doing this', you have become self-conscious and then are not *living* in the action but are *doing* the action. I say 'you' only that you might understand as, of course, there is no 'you'. Do you understand these things?"

"I have no idea what you are talking about," I say.

"It will become clearer in time," Kyle consoles. "Think on it this way. Let us say that you are doing some *thing*, some action, whatever it may be. You might perceive yourself performing the action and live in the idea that 'I am.' The result is, of course, that the work is tainted. You must forget yourself completely, lose yourself completely. Remember this. All great work is produced at moments when the creators are completely lost in the creation, when they forget themselves completely and are free of self-consciousness. Whether they realize it or not, it is because they have reached out and touched their true state."

I remember how I fell into a sort of trance when I was running the other day. Goose-flesh crawls over me when the realization strikes; I think I know what Kyle is talking about.

Those below have slowly scaled the step and are standing around me nodding their heads. The experience is surreal. I don't say anything so Kyle motions his hand at the doorway and says, "Shall we then?"

Allison opens the door and Kyle and I follow her in. The others stay outside and I suddenly feel trapped as if those outside might prevent me from leaving.

"Standing by for return," a student says at the monitoring station at the far end of the room. Others call out statuses as Dr. Duggan, standing near us, looks down at squiggly lines on his screen.

"Yes, fine, go on. Bring them back through," Duggan says to no one in particular.

The operators flip switches and pushes buttons then the large metal ring shakes. A neon-blue translucent light erupts in the center of it as a strong wind blows. I know what comes next so I crook my arm around a support pole. Kyle and Allison grab one on the rear wall. A large rectangular frame bursts through the light and glides out of the center of the ring and into the room, sliding on metal tracks, coming to a complete stop some feet away from me. The old chair that I used to sit on when it was called the transport chair module—that goofy name that they called it—has been replaced by something that looks more like a small, frameless bus. There are six chairs on the metal platform set in a two by three pattern and bolted down hard and fast. Four young people unbuckle themselves, stand and slowly climb down from the platform. They all squint as if they are staring at the sun; long exposure to the black of the Void has given them mole eyes.

"Come, come," Kyle says. "How was it? Progress made?"

One of the women says, "Yes, I did not want to return. A week there, I perceive. I was truly becoming."

"That's good," he replies then leans toward me and whispers. "There is no 'I'. She only speaks this way to aid conventional understanding."

I would love to reply with a salty "whatever" at this point but I need these people to let me into the Void so I can speak to the Void-man, so I keep my mouth shut and nod. I already said too much out in the hallway.

After the machine is shut down and appears stable, Dr. Duggan, blushing and red, steps over to me and says, "So you see what has become of me? Do not judge me. I have my reasons for this."

"I understand more than you know," I say but here is not the place to elaborate.

"Very well then. I understand that you are going through? I must protest, of course."

"Really? Why?" I reply.

"Well, I, shenanigans, does your mother know you are here?"

"Dr. Duggan, please. I will only be making a quick trip in and out. I cannot explain at the moment, but it is something I need to do. Please don't contact my mother.

Please?"

He looks over at Kyle who is staring back at him, then places his eyes back on me. "Shenanigans. Well, if you will be quick. You can make the trip in and stay long enough for the boarding then carry on through. That should give you twenty minutes or so. Good enough?"

"I think so. Thank you Dr. D," I say and reach my hand up to touch his forearm in a sign of appreciation. I am so glad that I don't feel a tingle when I touch him. He's not one of them.

Kyle opens the entrance door and says, "Let's go. Next group up." Five of the twenty-somethings step into the room and one of them seems suddenly apprehensive and it strikes me odd. They walk the rail and climb onto the platform, sit in chairs and strap themselves in. The nervous one can't seem to get her seat-belt on right. I follow them, sit down in the last row and strap myself in. I pull my welding goggles from my pocket and put them on.

The young man sitting next to me says, "What do you need those for?" but I ignore him.

Kyle claps his hands together three times and barks, "Everyone ready? Let's get this thing going."

Dr. Duggan says, "Yes, shall we then." He strokes his screen obsessively.

Kyle pops up to my left and says in my ear, "I am so glad you decided to come, Gabby. Really I am."

As the machine begins to whir, I dread what comes next: the pain, the mind numbing pain, the feeling of being ripped in two as we cross the threshold of the Void. The hum accelerates and brightens then the bright blue light blinds me. I clench my eyes down tight. I can feel the platform shuddering and rolling toward the entrance, faster, faster, sucked toward it. Suddenly my mind freezes as a spike of ice stabs my consciousness and all is still and silent and numb. Pain.

Then it's gone. I slowly unsqueeze my closed eyes as I fumble with my welding goggles. I am surrounded by a pitch black darkness; I tilt the goggles up and there is no light.

"Stand. Quickly. Hold the hands of the worldlings," a woman in front barks.

I try to stand but stumble and strange hands are on my body, supporting me. How can they see? A gnawing grinds me deep in my chest. It feels like an insatiable hunger but is not in the pit of my stomach but higher up, in the center of my chest. It is a sort of longing for something that is not there. A loss of something that can never be regained and the knowledge of that loss is painful. I don't know what I lost; I have no idea, but something is missing and it hurts dreadfully. I swing my head to and fro, looking for it, looking for what is missing, looking for something to fill the hole in my chest, looking for light. Yes, that's it. That's what is missing here. It's light and suddenly I. Must. Have. It.

I push away at the hands, trying to break free, trying to run, to run anywhere, to get away from this gnawing emptiness.

"What's she doing?" I hear one voice say but I don't know where it is coming from. The voice is around me, close, but my mind has lost all spatial perception. There are no echoes here. All sounds are immediately extinguished.

"It's a panic attack. Grab her. Hold her down," another says.

Hands grab at me so I push and pull and swing. Someone grabs my hair and yanks it so I kick at where the person should be but I hit nothing.

I scream, "Aarggh! Let. Me. Go!"

An appendage—I cannot tell if it is an elbow or a knee—strikes the middle of my back and I tumble to the ground. Someone lands on top of me, hard, knocking the wind from my lungs. I can't breathe; I am blind; I am dying; I am lost in the emptiness and my fight is dwindling quickly.

A voice close to me speaks, "Calm yourselves. Gabriella, stop. Please stop. Breathe for a moment and let it seep in. You will be fine. This happened to many of us the first time."

I would fight them off if I could. If I could see them, but I cannot so I lie still hoping that the oaf on my chest might move soon. When he or she or whoever it is gets up, I finally can breathe so I gasp for air and try to not sound like I am crying even though it is obvious that I am. I wipe the tears from my cheeks and say, "I'm fine. I'm sorry. Can I sit up?"

They release me, all except one of them who has a strangle-hold on my wrist. I twist into a crouching position and push myself up slowly, more slowly than I normally would so they don't attack me again. Black still surrounds me but I can feel their breath and their eyes on me. They are close.

A voice announces, "Worldlings, all of you, now we begin. Embrace the darkness. It may be hard for some of you at first but that will pass. Remember, this is your true state of being. You are merely returning to the primal state, to the void, to the nothingness. In time you will realize that this is reality and the 'so called' world from which you came is only an illusion."

I try to shake my hand free from the grip of my handler but he only tightens it. I know it is a man now. I can tell by the width of his palm; his hand is too big for it to be one of the women.

It is quiet and deathly still. I know I shouldn't speak but I do anyway. "Whoever's in charge here, excuse me? A word, please?"

The voice says, "You are interrupting."

"I'm sorry," I say. "It's just—"

"What? What is so important right now? You are squandering, worldling," answers the voice.

"Nothing."

The voice replies, "That's right. Nothing is important. Nothing is very, very important and you need to grab hold of that fact. All of you, do you see? A worldling has had her first realization."

"Could this person release my wrist? I think it would help me to concentrate on the voidness of things," I say, trying to drop in a few of their phrases.

The black is quiet for some moments then the voice says, "Release her."

The hand opens from my wrist and I am blinded by bright, white light pouring in at me from every direction and every angle. It feels so good. It is warm and radiant and where I was empty I now feel as if something is filling me, making me whole. I fall to the ground, clutching my hands to my face, quickly dragging my welding goggles down over my eyes then slowly open them a sliver. I can see! Well, I can see white anyway. It takes time for my eyes to adapt to the light. Once they do I stand and look about. None of the others are here. I am in the Void, my Void, the place I know, endless white, low lying misty clouds and all.

I am happy; the empty, gnawing need for light is gone and I feel normal. No, it's better than that. I feel much better than normal. I feel full of life and light, as if I could do anything right now. All is merely a matter of will and desire.

About fifty meters in either direction are the entrance and exit portals. I can see them. One leads to Portugal and the other to Dr. Duggan's lab. The minibus contraption sits next to me but no one is here. Somehow I popped over to this side. Sort of like Kyle did.

I don't know where they went or where I was. I don't want to waste time thinking about it because I know I don't have much time. I have to find him. "Dad? Where are you?"

I walk around the cart, calling out, "Hello? Please. I don't have much time. Please come out now. Void-man? Whoever you are."

He's not here.

The cart tilts slightly and I realize that they are boarding it. I can't see them; I can't hear them but they are preparing for their return trip. I have to hurry. I pull the diary out from the inner pocket in my jacket. "I have your diary. I brought it to you like you asked."

Silence.

"It wasn't easy to get, you know." The transport sled moves more. "I don't have much time! Please!"

Then I am mad. "Do you know what I went through to bring you this? And now you don't have the decency to show up? And you know it wasn't where you told me it would be! It wasn't in my house! It wasn't in our old house either! It's lucky I found it, you know! You sent me on a wild goose cha—"

The white shudders before me and I fall silent as he appears. The Void-man is just in front of me as if he was there all the time. My arm moves involuntarily and I stare at it as it extends from my body, holding the diary out toward him, wondering what my arm is doing.

Jasmine. Jasmine is swirling all around me.

He looks down at it briefly and for the smallest of moments an expression crosses his face and I see my father there, then, just as soon as it came, he goes back to being a mannequin of him.

"Did you see?" he says.

I mentally force my arm to retrace its path and hang listlessly at my side. "See? Do you mean the code for your research, I mean my father's research? The funny letters that keep reappearing. Yes, I saw that."

"Good," he says but the look on his face says he was referring to something else.

"But what am I supposed to do with it? Am I supposed to destroy it? Should I, I don't know, give it to Smith?" My train of thought is broken by the movement of the cart. I really don't have much time. They will be making the return trip in moments. When he does not answer, I continue, "And the athletes that are aging? What about them? Is there something in your diary that can help them? And what about me? Is that going to happen to me?"

He exhales as if my questions are tiring him somehow. "All these things seem important. They do. They seemed important to me once, also."

"To you?" I shiver. He suddenly sounds like Dad.

He closes his mouth with a snap and looks at me hard. "Your physical condition is not who you are. It is not who anyone is. It is not your true state of being. You must recite. You must become."

His words remind me of something Kyle said and if the Void-man calls me a worldling I think I might throw up. Before I can question deeper, the cart begins to drive away so I turn and run toward it, grabbing one of the handrails and flinging myself up into a chair. As I land, I fall onto someone's lap who was not there a split second ago and everything blinks out as darkness envelopes my sight. The light that was inside of me slowly seeps from my body and is extinguished.

"Hey!" the voice of the person I'm sitting on squeals.

I try to stand and move in the dark but before I can reposition myself, we are through the gate and back in Dr. Duggan's lab, the transport sled crashing down onto the metal rails and screeching to a stop.

"Sorry," I say as I step off the cart. Several of the other passengers are scowling at me. I leap off enthusiastically and then, realizing that I shouldn't show emotion, wipe the smile from my face.

"Report?" Kyle says.

A taller woman speaks as she helps the others step down off the cart. Her voice is cold and calculating. I recognize it as the voice of the woman in charge inside the blackness. "We had an incident but besides that, everything was as to be expected." I don't like her tone.

Kyle stares at her and then me. He turns to Dr. Duggan and says, "Doctor, she's all yours for a while." He addresses us, "V, Gabriella, come with me. Let us talk." The way he says it feels like a command more than a request.

"I really need to be going," I say even though I know my words are futile and wasted. I am trapped here until Kyle allows me to leave.

The girl who spoke, the tall one, is apparently the 'V' that he spoke to as she walks over to Kyle and stands next to him. They are both looking at me. He extends his hand to me, palm open and says, "Come."

I take the offer of his hand and he tucks my arm in his as if we belong to each other and walks us out into the hallway, down the steps and back behind the building. The young people look at us as we walk by. There is longing in their eyes as if they would love to be me right now and be so close to Kyle. Oddly, even the men have the look. It is not amorous or adoring; it is something different. Awe.

When we are sufficiently far away, Kyle says, "Tell me, V."

The tall woman named V answers, "Your girl here had a freak out. Sorry I wasn't really expecting it from her. You told me that she's voided before. I wasn't prepared." Her tone is familiar and accusational which seems odd considering the near worship that the others give to Kyle.

"That surprises me," Kyle says unphased.

V continues, "Then, I don't know what exactly happened. She... disappeared."

"What do you mean 'she disappeared?' " Kyle's brow creases as he looks at her then at me and then back at her.

"I can't explain it. Maybe she can," she says as she shrugs her shoulders.

He looks at me blankly and I am uncomfortable. My mind is a just turned off lottery machine, full of ping pong balls that are falling to its base, lying idle. I don't know what to say. "Kyle, you know what happened. You did it before too."

Kyle ponders my words for a long moment. "V, you can go back now. I need to speak to Gabriella privately."

She obeys without comment.

"So you went over there, did you? I thought something like that might have happened."

My mind feels a bit scrambled from the trip through. "Why do you call her V?" I ask.

He looks at me, head cocked. "Her? She is becoming. It is only a symbolic gesture. As a person frees themselves of this world, we shorten his or her name. It is a meaningless thing to do but it helps people to recognize their accomplishments and progress. She is 'V'. Only a single letter left, you see. Now about what happened to you, tell me how it happened."

"I'm not sure. I panicked when we got there. No one told me I would be blinded and feel that way—"

"It is better to not confuse people with preconceived expectations of experience. Everyone must find their own way."

"Fine. So I freaked a bit. Sorry. Then they held me down and I couldn't breathe and that quite made me angry. Once they let me up and let me go, I disappeared, like she said. When the cart started moving I hopped on and we left. That's about it, I guess."

Kyle looks down at the ground as if he is calculating. "Tell no one of these things. Tell no one where you went."

He turns on his heel so I follow after him and say, "Kyle, where do you think I went?"

"There are quantum dimensional planes of existence. They are all around us and exist simultaneously. The machine, the wonderful machine, allows us to travel between them."

"Okay, I guess, but where was I?"

"I don't know," he says as he holds the door open for me.

Something just doesn't seem right. "But wait a minute here, Kyle. I thought you said that the Void was the true reality and where we are now is an illusion?"

He smiles at me oddly then holds the door open for me, saying, "Is it? I cannot show you reality, only tell you that it is and hope that you find it. Everyone must have their own personal realization."

We scale the steps and enter Dr. Duggan's lab. Kyle seems distracted as he says, "That is it for today. We will leave the good doctor to his experiments. Those who can attend, we will start back up in the morning."

Most of the black spot people are not sad. They are not disappointed; they show no emotion at all. All except the newer ones, this is the only way I can determine who is new to this; they still show emotion. They slowly file out of the room.

I walk over to Dr. Duggan to say goodbye but before I can speak he says, "I could not lose my life's work, my dear. You understand that, don't you? And these people are not so bad, are they? It's not like I'm Mengele or Himmler working for Hitler on some twisted Nazi experiment, right?" He finishes every sentence with a question and I am not so sure if I am supposed to answer or only listen. "They are looking for something spiritual, it seems to me, and what's wrong with that? The American Indians smoked some form of cactus, I forgot what it was called. Peyote? Lots of people do things to touch the limits of consciousness that others think are crazy. Who am I to judge?"

I reach my hand to his shoulder. "I understand Dr. Duggan" is the only response I can muster then I walk out. Allison is waiting for me outside so I sit in the passenger seat without a word.

The car is silent for the entire ride back to my house. Normally that would make me feel uncomfortable but right now I have too much to think about. I wish I had more time in there. I wish I could have gotten more out of the Void-man. He didn't seem interested in the diary. What do I do with it now?

And what did he mean by recite? Recite what? Something from the diary? Maybe he was talking about his poem, his prophecy. I'm not going to recite that, that's for sure. It's in my head, somehow. Somehow it penetrated me. I have always had the hardest time memorizing things in class but this I can't seem to forget, even if I wanted to. I begin to decode it, line by line.

I think about a line and it comes to me: You find a partner in the place that you least expect it, in the lowest of lows, but it brings you to the highest of highs.

I would like to think this is talking about Michael. But maybe it is Antonio. Or maybe someone that I haven't met yet.

I focus on another: There is a one who is a friend who would destroy you. You watch whom he follows and who follows him. He is not what he seems. But you are not deceived. No, not be deceived by the bouncing numbers or the shading letters or the shaking digits or the random dots.

This has to be about Kyle, it just has to. But he was never really my friend. A boyfriend? Maybe. I go to the next line: He will chase you and chase you but you will hide very well, and it is your ability to hide which will allow you to hide your deepest of secrets.

I don't know what secrets I am hiding. I have my father's diary but other than that, what do I have to hide? And my father's diary is not really my secret, it's his. I don't know what this is talking about.

In this time of trouble, you will look deep. You will think hard. You will look down deeply and you will find strength within yourself.

Well, this is true. I've certainly been thinking about a lot of things. Hopefully I do find some strength. That would be cool.

You will fight for it as a small sparrow, a sparrow that will become a mighty hawk. Above all and in the end, things cannot be as you would like and a supreme sacrifice you may have to make. A choice, a choice, a choice. It is yours to decide.

This is the part that I totally don't like. I have no intention of making some kind of supreme sacrifice, that's for sure.

I shake myself away from my thoughts and look over at Allison. The silent drone of the road doesn't seem to bother her either. She seems content. She steers the car into the driveway and waits for me to exit the car. Just before I close the door she says, "Not a word of this to anyone, right?"

"Sure," I say and close the door. I walk slowly toward my home and try to push the morning's events out of my mind and quickly fashion a cover story in case Mom or Smith has questions. I have to be normal. Completely normal.

Chapter 27

Picnic

"She's here. Smith, let's go," Mom says in a giggly voice.

The three of us walk the few blocks to the park, my mom draped on one of Smith's arms and a picnic basket on his other. I walk next to them and try to insert myself as much as I can into their conversations but they are meaningless and all I can muster is one or two words at a time.

"What a beautiful day," Smith says.

"Yes," I quickly say.

"Oh, I've rarely come to this park." Mom says. "Gabriella, you run past it don't you?"

"Sure," I reply. The words are difficult for me for some reason. My mind is elsewhere. "I run... here."

"How about over there?" Smith points to an open space near a few trees. Teenagers from my high school are playing Frisbee-Golf nearby.

"Oh yes. What do you think, Gabby?" Mom says.

"F—fine." I have to clear my head. They are going to think something is wrong if I keep this up.

Mom looks at me funny but doesn't say anything. Hopefully she only thinks I am uncomfortable being around Smith in this type of family setting. Right now that is the furthest thing from my mind. Smith spreads out an old blanket on the ground and begins setting out the condiments. I help him and try to engage myself.

Without looking at me, he says, "So you wanted to

ask me something the other day, Gabby. What was it?"

"Oh nothing. I—I was just thinking about the implications of my father's work. I know you said he left without completing it."

"Okay..." Smith looks at my mom but before she can switch the subject, I say, "I mean, I was just wondering, not trying to start a fight or dig up old wounds or anything like that."

"Yeah. Okay. I guess," Smith says.

My mind is mostly clear now. I continue, "So I was thinking. You all were working on life extension, right? And if we extended everyone's life then we would quickly burn out the planet's resources. So, I was thinking that would be a terrible idea."

Mom scoops out helpings of three bean salad into foam bowls for all of us as Smith constructs a sandwich. He says, "Not everyone would have it, of course. It would be expensive. Only those who could afford it would get it."

"So only the rich can live longer. Figures. Wouldn't there be rioting in the streets? I don't see the poor standing for that."

Smith stops cutting lettuce and looks at me oddly. "They are not rioting now."

"Why would they?" Mom asks.

"The rich have the best health-care and the poor don't riot. The rich have the best cars, homes, jobs, pretty much everything. The poor, they work hard; they hope to one day be rich, to have those things; they dream and play the lottery. When they feel their work is worthless, they lose hope and sometimes drown themselves in despair, but no, they do not riot. They never riot." He looks down and completes his pastrami creation. "Are you going to eat?" he says.

For some reason I feel comfortable talking to Smith. "Sure," I say. "But it doesn't seem, I don't know, fair? I mean to have one group of people live ten years longer than another—maybe that doesn't seem so bad. But one-hundred years longer? Or one-thousand? It's just not right."

"Mustard? Mayo?" he says.

"Mustard. No mayo," I say. "Mustard has almost no calories."

"Gabby hates mayo," mom says as if it is something Smith should learn.

"That too," I add.

Smith says, "The entire world is a series of unequal distributions. Military, financial, health care, green spaces, technology, you name it. All of it. There are some few people or groups that have access and others that do not. I would imagine that it will be that way forever. There are people that are dreaming of a future that already exists somewhere else for someone else. This is the fact of life on this planet. It is impossible to make everything equal."

"I suppose," I say as I pick up my sandwich. It is not something I can argue about but still I don't like it.

Smith leans back and stretches his back. "Of course it will not only be the rich. The scientists and engineers who come up with these things will have access to it also. People like your father, people like me." Smith looks over at my mom as if he is reminding her of a prior conversation. "And their families, of course."

We are all silent for a time as we eat. The weather is wonderful; the birds chirp to each other, the trees sway lightly in the breeze, the sound of children playing twinkles around us; it is a slice of neighborhood, idyllic paradise. I wipe my mouth after a bite and smile as an idea pops in my head. A strange feeling washes over me, a feeling I haven't had in a long, long time. I say, "Seems very selfish though."

"Selfish?" Smith says as if the thought surprises him.

I am smiling to myself because I am reminded of the game my father and I used to play. "But maybe everyone is selfish. Don't you think?" I say.

He ponders me, so I continue, "In some way we are all just satisfying some selfish desire."

"No," he says slowly, his brow still locked in a mild furrow, "Lot's of people do things to help others—"

I cut him off, "Yes, yes. Of course they do. But why do they do it?"

Mom says, "Oh, I remember this one."

Smith's brow furrow deepens enough that I could jab seeds down in it and mixed with his body heat and a little sweat it might soon sprout. "I guess because it feels good to help others? I don't know. It's the right thing to do?"

I pounce excitedly, "Exactly my point! Maybe you go shopping because buying things for yourself makes you feel good inside. You are pleasing yourself. That's selfish. Maybe you don't spend that money, but stuff it in your mattress. Why? Because having that money makes you feel better than spending it. Again, pleasing yourself. Again, selfish. How about if you spend your entire evening volunteering at a soup kitchen, feeding the poor and destitute, making beds at the homeless shelter, and mopping floors at the church. Are you selfish? I say yes! It makes you feel good inside to do these things. You are only doing them to please yourself. You are doing them because it stimulates pleasure sensors in your brain. Once again, being selfish." I smile at him, looking for a rebuttal because, of course, I didn't believe any of it. It's all just my opening run at mental jousting and I suddenly remember, in a rush, how much I enjoy it.

Smith looks back at me astonished and not sure how to reply.

I was just repeating one of the many old, philosophical arguments that Dad and I would go through on the slow days at the clothing store in Venezuela. One day he would take one side of an argument and I the other. Another day we would switch sides. What we truly believed wasn't the point, it was about exploring every angle and being able to argue your chosen side effectively, cornering your opponent, tripping them up with their own words while carefully measuring your own. Mostly dad toyed with me, smiling, laughing, enjoying my feeble attempts. But at the end I did win a few and it made him so happy to lose and at first I couldn't understand why. My heart twinges and I think, Yes—that was at the end, right before I lost him.

Looking confused, Smith says, "Okay, I guess. Want me to make you another sandwich?" Disappointment washes over me and I can't help but look away. He didn't understand a thing I said. He doesn't know the game. Smith is not my father. He never will be.

"No. No thanks," I say as I look away. "I think I want to go over to the pond. I want to see how many ducks are on the little island."

"Don't be too long, Gabby," Mom says.

I rise and stroll toward the water. Parents are watching their small children play in the sand area and there are a few teenagers with fishing poles looking for a catch. The fish and wildlife department adds fish to the pond from the hatchery so people can angle, I seem to remember. After fifteen minutes or so I return and announce, "About twenty ducks."

Mom looks over at Smith who then says, "Gabby, your mother filled me in to what just happened and I guess I don't know what to say."

"It's nothing. Don't worry about it," I reply.

"That's generous of you," he answers then pauses for a moment. "Let me tell you, this is really difficult for me and to be honest, it wasn't my choice—"

Mom interrupts, "You don't have to, Smith."

He replies, "I know I don't but I want to. Gabby, let me tell you a little about myself."

He looks at me as if he is waiting for permission, so I say, "Go ahead."

He starts slowly, pensively, as if he is remembering and I know what he is saying is not rehearsed. "All my life, all I was ever interested in was science. My research. Your father and I are about the same age—the age he would be, I mean—and I remember the conversations. He would ask me, 'Don't you want to get married? Don't you want a family?' And I thought about it and decided that it would slow me down. I'm being honest here. He met your mother, got married and had you, but me? No, I didn't want that life. I chose to stay single and I was fine with that. This was my life and I wanted to spend it in the lab. So when I found out about you—"

"I understand, Smith," I say trying to allow him to not become too emotional. He is clearly uncomfortable.

"No, it's okay. What I want to say is that it wasn't my choice to be your biological father, Jonathan took that from me, but I am fine with it. Now. As the years have passed, I saw what he had and what I was missing. I just thought it was too late for me, that's all. But now that this has happened, I want to try. I want to try to do it. To become some semblance of a father, if that were possible. If you will let me?"

I don't know what to say so I keep quiet and look away but then feel rude for not answering. "I'm not all happy unicorns over the idea but maybe. We'll see."

"Fine. Good," Mom says. "Whew. Glad that's over. Now who's ready for dessert?"

Chapter 28

Three More

We pack up the picnic and head for home. It is the twilight of a long day. I am not exactly sure how to treat Smith at the moment so I don't say anything. They hold hands and for some reason it does not bother me much.

We reach home and mom invites him in for a late tea. She really wants him and she wants me to accept him, I realize. I am a bigger part of her equation than I thought. I decide right then that Smith may be here to stay, whether I like the idea or not; so I may as well get used to it. I would like to go up to my room, but it is not what I think mom wants right now. She doesn't want Smith to stay for her, it's for me. She wants to know that I wasn't going through the motions; she wants to know that I am going to accept him, that she has the green light to move forward. It is written all over her face.

I lean on the handrail at the base of the staircase and address Smith, trying to make more small talk but not sure what to talk about. "You said the other day that my father was working on a virus? Aren't viruses contagious?"

"They can be," he replies. "Huh, you think like him. That was one of the things he was worried about."

"Oh, really?" I am just making conversation for mom's sake.

"Sure, the virus idea was a good one. I thought it would work. But of course the problem was complexity. The virus would have to be tailor made for each and every individual, and then how would we test it to see if it worked before administering it?"

"So what would you do?" Mom says from the kitchen.

"Actually, we did some very preliminary tests. Like all labs, we experimented with small animals, rodents mostly. It never got past that stage. It seemed promising at first, even with the high mortality rate. But then there was a problem."

"What was it?" I say.

"Viruses mutate," Smith replies.

"Oh, right."

"There was one mouse though—I'll never forget him—Jeremy we called him. His code id was J3R, so one of the techs started calling him Jeremy. I discouraged this, of course. Never become attached to a test subject that will most certainly die was the rule. But I will never forget him."

"Why's that, Smith?" My mom calls out.

"He was one of the first. We administered the virus and he went into a coma, like all the rest. It didn't look good for him, seizures, bouts of cold, clamminess followed by burning hot skin, especially in the extremities, vomiting, bleeding from the mouth and eyes, you name it. Then, when all the rest died, he shook it off. I came in that morning and there he was, staring up at me, jumping around, running on his wheel, he was a young mouse again."

"So it worked then?" I ask.

"Yes. Victor was very excited, of course. The little guy didn't age like the rest. He outlived his great grandchildren. But we couldn't repeat it. Jeremy, that was his name."

Mom exits the kitchen, drying her hands with a

towel. "Maybe in the future, Smith. Someone will figure out what went wrong with the others."

"I suppose. No one is working with viruses anymore. I'm looking into gene regulatory networks now. It's a novel idea. It's showing promise. It's something we have only come up with very, very recently." He doesn't look at me while he says it and I am glad that he doesn't because I cannot stop my face from contorting. Is he spying on me? Was Durand right to not want to talk in my room?

"I don't know what that is, Smith. Can we talk about something else? I hate to say it, but I find people talking about work to be so boring. You work so much, do you have to talk about it when you're not there?" Mom says with a chuckle.

Smith laughs, "I know, I can be obsessed sometimes. Ahh, the life of a scientist. Anyway, it's getting late and I must be going," Smith adds.

"So soon?" Mom pouts.

"I have an experiment running at the lab that I have to check on. We're round the clock now. Hired in a bunch of techs. Haven't seen the lab this busy in ages. It feels almost like the old days." Smith says as he stands.

"Don't tell me. It's Victor again," mom says.

"His deadlines are a bit arbitrary, true. But I'm onto something. It's not totally his fault."

"I didn't like him twenty years ago and I don't like him now. Some people never change. Selfish, obsessive man," mom mutters.

"He's dying," Smith says.

Mom purses her lips.

"I'm heading up to my room. Got an early start tomorrow," I say as I scale the steps, my back towards them.

"Good night, Gabby," mom says.

"Good night," Smith says cheerily.

I quickly change into my pajamas and slide under the covers, propping my screen up on my belly to check the Ultraball statistics before I nod off to sleep. One headline jolts me. "More Ultraballers Contract Aging Disease." I pop out of bed and jog down the stairs. "Are you seeing this?" I bark out.

Smith is still at the door with Mom in his arms. When Mom and Smith turn their heads toward me, both with a confused look, I add, "Turn on the screen! Quick!"

Mom flips it on.

"The Ultraball channel," I say.

The news feed shows a camera person following hospital staff. When they reach a door, the doctor turns and says, "You are not permitted here."

The announcer is describing the toll, "Two more came forward just this morning. One of them, Agnes Rivera, another NuGen athlete, was thought to be on maternity leave for almost two months. Our report says that she is not actually pregnant but went into hiding when the aging started."

"Not another one," Smith says.

The announcer continues, "Here she is here; the picture is from a match about five months ago." A picture of the woman appears on the screen. "And now one from this morning." Another picture runs onto the screen adjacent to the first.

"It's like the French girl. Smith, what's going on?" Mom says but Smith is silent.

The screen pans back to the hospital entrance and a reporter on the scene says, "Late breaking news. We have from a source inside the hospital that another girl has been found. That makes a total of four counting the runner from France. This last one was found dead in her apartment. Initial reports say that they thought it was an elderly woman and the neighbors did not recognize who she was. Our sources say that she aged rapidly and authorities have taken her here for an autopsy, to this hospital, where the other two NuGen runners are being treated."

"That's U Penn," Smith mutters.

University of Pennsylvania medical center is not far from Smith's lab and the NuGen home office.

"I have to go," Smith says as he stands quickly. Mom walks him back to the door and gives him a quick peck on the cheek. My eyes are glued to the screen. Mom returns and looks at me long.

"Mom? Is this going to happen to me?"

She grabs hold of me and pulls my body in tight. "I don't know, Gabby. I don't know."

As she holds me, the black spot tingles and anger wells up inside me, anger at being modified, anger at not being in control, but I push it away.

We watch the screen for what seems like hours and after watching the same footage several times we both decide to shut it off. It feels too morbid and there is no new information. I drag myself up the steps reluctantly, knowing that I will not sleep well tonight. Mom follows me up.

After a long night of staring at the ceiling, the light peeks through the curtains and mom enters my room, asking, "Why aren't you up yet? School?"

"Not today, Mom. I can't."

Surprisingly, she acquiesces. She leaves for work and I finally fall asleep for a few hours then rise, roll out of bed and stare at veins developing on my feet from too much running. I don't want to grow old. After a half hour or so of sulking, I change into my workout clothes and go out for a slow run around the park. Maybe it will help me not think about it.

I run down the block, make a left turn down Wingate Drive, the turn that I always make, and speed up just past the soccer fields. A few teenagers are kicking some balls into a goal there. They stop and stare at me as I go by. Oddly, my black spot buzzes. A couple blocks later I tuck right to avoid running past my high school. I doubt any of the teachers would see me but why take the chance? Another right and I am at the park and sprint onto the dirt path. I round the first corner and slow by the duck pond, trying to avoid the little presents they leave on the path. Just ahead, near a cluster of elms, a man steps out. I cautiously slow.

What's this now?

I steer wide of him then come to a stop when I realize that it's Kyle. There are a few others waiting by the trees. How did they know I would come here? I'm supposed to be in school.

"What's up, Kyle?" I say.

"Thought you might want to talk. Funny bumping into you here."

"Yeah, funny," I say.

He smiles back at me which is very uncharacteristic of the man with no emotions.

We walk together on the path and as he passes his group he shakes his fingers at them and they do not follow us. I am sweating; he is wearing a suit. The sun is hot.

We are quiet for a time so I blurt out, "I don't know what you want me to say."

"Something concerns you. I can tell. I want to help

you, to help you realize, to help you recognize the true nature of things."

I sneer, "I bet you do. You are just so concerned for me out of the goodness of your dear, little heart."

He pauses, then replies, "Good? A subjective judgment of a material world. There is no *good*." He pauses as if he is pondering the sound of his own voice, then adds, "There is no good; there is no bad. There is no such thing as sin. The root of all evil is ignorance and false views. It sounds odd, does it not?"

"Most of what you say sounds odd, Kyle."

"How could there be good or bad if all is an illusion?"

"I can't believe I'm having this conversation. Listen Kyle, I think you're a nut-job. I used you, get it? I only needed to go through the Void so I let you think what you wanted to think. That's it."

He doesn't flinch at my words. "You think I did not perceive these things? Of course, I knew this. 'I was aware,' I should say."

I keep walking, considering falling into a run and wondering if he would be able to keep up with me or if he would even try.

"Let us speak of something else. I do not want to continue to make you angry," he says.

I lay into him heavy and deep, "Again, I don't know what you want me to say. I think I've said everything I need to say to you. You attacked me once. You attacked Cyndi—put her in the hospital. And me, chasing me into the Void; I think you would have killed me if it weren't for... Anyway, you come back and now you think you are some kind of holy-man. You have these followers, more power to you, but I'm not buying it. You're using Duggan for his machine, tricking people into thinking that you've found something. You're a charlatan. It's all lies."

Kyle walks for a while, expressionless, and I wonder if I went too far but I totally don't care right now.

"Truth," he says. "Truth *is*. You are grabbing at truth and that is good. It is realization. The man I was did those things. Truth. Before my realization, I was selfish." He brushes the back of his hand against mine as he walks and chills run down my spine. "Perhaps I am wrong about all that I have seen—I must admit that— but I know this: the only thing we can do is see. Realize. Listen to me Gabriella, you may arrive at a mountain along a path, but the mountain is not the result of the path, the mountain simply *is*."

His voice grows gravely in an attractive, sexy yet secretive way but beneath the voice there is something tugging at me to trust him, something comforting and soothing, something hypnotic.

He continues, "You may see light, but the light is not the result of your eyesight. The light simply *is*. Me, I have seen something. All I am doing is pointing the eyes of others, letting them see, helping them to realize. I don't tell them what to see or put preconceived notions in their heads; I only point their eyes, nothing more."

I want to say something, to protest, to resist. I open my mouth but no sound comes out. I feel as though it might be nice to just listen to his words. Yes, just continue to walk and listen. No! I have to control myself! But the reverberating, buzzing sensation pulsating through my body has me now, drawing me, pulling me. I am a ship with neither anchor nor rudder nor oar, drifting where the wind and sea might take me. Where I venture, I know not.

He touches my hand again and turns his head toward me. "This idea is frightening to the uninitiated worldling. To see the world as it really is. Terrifying, really. When I saw it, I cried. I understand your resistance."

The buzzing of my black spot has spread throughout my entire body. I let out one final resistant, desperate yell but it no longer make sense, "Kyle, you talk too much!"

"Talk? It's not talk. It's not reason. It's realization. I touched emptiness; I held it."

He grows quiet and pensive. There's a heavy silence into which I fall, carelessly, inconsequentially, falling, falling, into the deep, the dark, the Void. I feel lost to it.

We near the elms where I first met him and my whole world feels twisted. My voice is merely a breath, a whisper. I say, "Goodbye, Kyle," and turn from him as I speak. As I turn I glimpse some part of his face changing drastically, folding dark and black and bronze; a nightmare, then it's gone. I refuse to turn back to look at it again for fear that it may be there staring back at me. That must have been my imagination.

I jump into a hurried run for I don't know what else to do; everything feels foreign, even my own body. As I turn the corner I allow myself to look back at the cluster of trees. Kyle and his people are gone. I do not understand what is happening to me. I am confused.

I continue to run but suddenly feel like I can't breathe. Realization. I'm having a realization, that's for sure. Somehow Kyle can touch me, something deep inside of me—I don't know how—through the black spot. Stupid black spot! I hate that thing! I slow to a walk and try to suppress tears but find it difficult. I have to stay away from him. I can't let that happen again. I don't want to be one of them. I am losing control.

The tears come; I can't stop them. It's all happening too fast. Any day I may start aging dramatically, who knows? Other modified girls are dying. And now this. I can't even trust myself. I can't control myself around them. I wish they would just leave me alone.

Just.

Leave.

Me.

Alone!

I turn back down the street that leads toward my house and slow to a walk. My face is wet but I refuse to wipe it.

A voice behind me resounds, "Gabriella." It is the Void-man; I would know that voice anywhere. I turn my head and there he is, floating beside me.

"You need comfort," he says and places his arm over my shoulder.

A dark gray car passes by but it is clear that the driver does not see him. A calm slowly seeps into me. I shudder, wipe my wet cheeks and look at him.

As we walk a peace eases into me more and more; it is the same feeling I felt there, in the Void, the white Void, with him. I don't know what to say so I ask him a question, the first meaningless question that pops into my confused and twisted head, "Why, why does Kyle go to one... dimension and I another? Why do I see you and the others—"

"And you think I know these answers?"

"Why wouldn't you? You're there. You must be able to explain something," I demand softly, still somewhat incoherent.

"Imagine you were an alien, an alien child who somehow found himself lost and alone on this planet, how would you explain to humans where you came from if you had no idea yourself?"

"I suppose," I say but somehow I don't believe him. He has to know. He just won't tell me. "So you can't tell me anything." My mind is starting to clear.

He pulls his arm from my shoulder as he says, "This is not what is important. What is important is becoming. That is the key. Remember what I told you. Recite."

Flustered, I say, "Recite? I don't know what that means. Can you at least tell me what is happening to me? Why do I have this black spot? Why can Kyle have such an... influence on me?"

"The black spot? It is merely a mark, a pointer, an indication. It is an outward sign of something that is inside of you, inside all humans, really. All humans have light and dark in them and must war within themselves to fight for the light. Kyle pulled it out of you. He brought it to the surface. It was there all the time."

"Kyle said there is no good."

"I know what he said. He's wrong. Test your heart."

I look up at him and ask him for what feels like the hundredth time, "Are you my father?"

"I once was," he says as if it was so long ago. His final words fade away with him and he is gone like he came. A car horn blares behind me and I duck to the curb. Somehow I wandered into the roadway.

"Stupid kid!" the driver yells as he speeds by.

"Dad? Dad? He *is* my Dad," I say in disbelief looking around for him even though I know he is gone and I will not find him. I walk the last block back home in a state of dulled shock. Even though I really thought he was my father the entire time, to hear him say it out-loud like that changes everything. Is he telling the truth? He has to be. He just has to.

The subdued, reverberating pull of Kyle's touch is still there, roiling my internals, gurgling, but it is fading. It is almost gone. Now that I can think about what happened, I know I must do something. I have to stop this. I have to stop Kyle and his people from following me around and popping out from behind trees to mess with my mind. I have to talk to Duggan and persuade him to shut down the experiments. And if he won't, I have to somehow—I don't know—make it so no one can ever go through again. Can I do that? I have to do something. This has to stop.

Chapter 29

Duggan's Pickle

"Get it together! Act like a playoff team!" Donavan barks while we sprint.

Antonio and Spike are in the stands again, alone, and Antonio is being overly vocal, "You got this, G!"

At the break, Sandstone says to me, "The man's got it bad."

"I know! I wish he would stop." I don't know why I told him to be more obvious. I wish I hadn't said that. "I wouldn't mind the attention but he's doing it in the wrong place and at the wrong time. Did you see that vein on coach's forehead? She's ready to pop."

Antonio yells, "Hey G! I'm up here, see?"

Just then Coach howls, "Gabriella! Get over here!"

I hustle over to her, saying, "What's up, Coach?"

"If you don't get rid of your boyfriend up there then I will and it won't be pretty."

"Uhh, he's not my boyfriend, but, uhh, I'll take care of it."

I run up into the stands and plop down next to Antonio and smile.

"Hey G," he says, smiling wide. "Did I overdo it?"

"You have to ask?" I reply.

"Let's go," Spike says. "I don't need to hear about this from Bustoff. You know he hates being yelled at by Donavan."

"Right. We're out. See you sometime?" Antonio says.

"Call me," I say squeezing his knee lightly. When I remove my hand, there is a sweaty hand print where my hand was.

"Hey, look what you did!" he says jokingly.

I hop up and run down the stairs. "I marked you, boy."

As I reach the field, Donavan waves me over. When I reach her, she looks up at the empty seats that Spike and Antonio were sitting in then stares at me as she says, "We're not going through this again, are we?"

"No Coach. I didn't tell them to come. Honest. I didn't invite them to our practice. I would never—"

She interrupts me, "Because you know fraternization isn't allowed—"

"Honest, Coach. We're not dating—"

She interrupts me again, "Listen, I don't care what you two do on the outside, but when you're on my field, you're mine. Got it?"

I jog back to the track and I can't wipe the smile from my face. It feels so good for someone to want me around. I so missed that feeling. I bound over to Sidney and line up next to her, grinning. "What're you doing next?"

She looks over at me then down at the dirt. "Eight by eight-hundreds. Then I'm done for today."

"You wouldn't mind if I paced you, would you?" I ask.

"I don't care."

We run the first three eight-hundreds in thirty seconds each and at that slow pace I know something's bothering her. "Why you leaving so soon? Something going on?" I probe.

She looks at me hard for a moment then her lip quivers momentarily. She looks away then says, "Cyndi."

"What?" I say loudly, suddenly realizing that Cyndi didn't come to practice. The four girls aging rapidly jumps into my mind.

"Shhh. Quiet. They'll hear you," Sidney say.

I look across the field and no one is looking at us. "What? So what? If you know something, shouldn't Donavan know? Did something happen to her?"

"I shouldn't have said anything. No, I spoke with her this morning. It's just a little problem. Just don't say anything. I don't know why I told you. Let's run. Breaks over," she says as she swipes her watch.

We complete the remainder of the runs in silence then Sidney leaves. I can't help but wonder if Cyndi is falling prey to the same aging disease that the others have. I wish I could go with Sidney to check on her. I want to be there, back in her life. But I know I can't have that right now.

After practice, I ask Allison to shuttle me to Princeton and call mom and tell her I have a ride home. She seems relieved to not to have to make the loop to pick me up. I cleanup and then Allison and I jump in her car. She smiles and waves to one of the office staff as we pull away. As we hit the highway the expression slowly melts from her face and she says, "Glad that's over. I don't know how much longer I can keep up the charade."

I don't answer her.

At Princeton, Dr. Duggan's lab is mostly deserted as it is getting late; only a few of the black spot people are there and the grad students at the controls look restless. Clearly, they've had a long day. Duggan ignores us when we enter. Allison and I move to the back of the room and wait near the poles for the module to return. A few minutes later the ring glows blue and the module bursts into the room and slows on the tracks. There are only two people occupying the seats.

"Last trip back," one of the grad students says. The others swipe their screens and push buttons in anticipation of the end of the shift.

"Begin shutdown," Duggan says then swipes his screen a few times, looks at a table of data and charts full of red squiggly lines then moves in our direction. "Hey you two. Here kind of late, aren't you?"

"Hi Dr. D, I just wanted to talk to you for a minute. When you're done," I say glancing around at the others and suddenly feeling uncomfortable.

"I see," he says, picking up on the hint that I want a private conversation. "And that's all?"

I nod.

"And you?" he says to Allison.

"I just gave her a ride. I'm always there for a sister of the Void," she says as if she is talking to me.

He turns away from us and helps the others with the shutdown procedure for a few minutes then says over his shoulder, "Allison, I can give Gabriella a ride home. I've wanted to visit her mother for some time anyway. You don't have to wait for her."

Allison looks at him with her mouth open, then over at the others. "Okay," she says, but I have the feeling that she doesn't like the idea of leaving me here.

After the last of the students leave, Dr. Duggan closes the door but doesn't remove his hand from the handle.

"So, Dr. D—"

"Shhh," he hisses.

We stand there quietly, me staring at Duggan, Duggan staring at his hand on the door handle, listening. After a few minutes, he flings the door open and pops his head out, then quickly closes it. "Okay, they're gone."

I am unnerved at his precaution. I take a few steps back and stand by the controls for the machine. I don't know how to begin.

I look up at him and he looks at me, then half-smiles. "A pickle, this? Ehh?"

"I don't know how to begin," I say, then stutter. "We have to do something."

He sets his screen down on his desk and replies, "Do we?"

I run my hand across the top of the workstation. I have never been this close to it and I have the feeling that it would be so easy to destroy it right now. It looks fragile. All I would have to do is start smashing it. But of course, they would just rebuild it.

I say, "Kyle's controlling these people. He's using them. I don't know what for but he's—I don't know—building an army—"

"Army? You exaggerate, my dear."

"You've seen them. You see the way they are around him. If he told them to jump on a sword, you know they would." I walk slowly around to the front of the console and my hands are there, just in front of the controls, within striking distance. It would be so easy.

"Charisma. Machine or no, you can't take that away from him," he says.

My fingers ease closer to the controls and I can't stop staring at them. Sweat emerges on the top of my hand. "So you're not worried about this? If this whole thing goes south, you're a part of it—"

Duggan slowly stands and moves toward me, his eyes squinting. "You don't get to be my age being a fool. I've contacted the authorities. They're monitoring his movements and associations." He moves toward me and the workstation. "But for now, he's funding me. I'd like to keep the relationship as is for as long as I can. At least until I can secure another sponsor. I am working on several grant proposals. Hey, what're doing there?"

"Nothing," I say as I pull my hands into my lap.

He blows out his wind then leans back. "Gabriella, let me show you something." He dials his screen and says some words to someone on the other end then swipes the picture up to the wall screen. It's Michael.

"Hey, Gabriella. Doc, it's really late. I was just heading out the door. What's going on?"

"I need you to run a solo from your end," he says as he pushes the transport module into position for another run into the Void.

"Sure, how long?" Michael's face disappears from the screen then pops back up from below.

"A quick in and out. One minute, Void time, should do." Duggan places himself on one of the chairs of the module and straps himself in then looks over at me and says, "What are you waiting for? Hurry up. Get up here."

I hop up onto the chair next to him and unconsciously check my breast pocket for my welding goggles even though I know they are not there.

"We're ready!" Duggan yells back to the screen.

I can't see what Michael is doing but he must have initiated the procedure because a low rumble shakes the room momentarily as the whir of coils surrounding the ring resonates briefly. Before I can catch my breath, the blue erupts out of the center of the ring and the cart swings forward, accelerating toward the electric light. Lightning fires through my body then we are there, in the Void and I am blinded by the bright, white light.

I feel Duggan's hand on my elbow. "Here, take

these," he says as he places something in my hand.

They are sunglasses. I put them on and open my eyes. "Not as good as my welding goggles," I say, squinting at him.

He unbuckles and stands, holding out both hands, "See? See?"

"Wait. You're here? In the white?" I can't believe it. Dr. Duggan went through the machine and instead of arriving in Kyle's black Void, the empty nothingness, he arrived in the same dimension that I did, full of low lying fluffy clouds and blinding white light.

I begin to unbuckle but before I can, he sits down and places his hand on mine, stopping me from leaving my chair, saying, "There's no time."

The module begins to move back towards the gate so I clench my hands down on the chair in front of me. The mind-numbing pain is over faster this time but it leaves behind a dull ache. As the module slows, he says, "Michael, that's all for today. Sorry for the late run. See you in the morning. And hey—"

"What?" Michael replies.

"Sleep in an hour. We'll start late."

"And what about Kyle?" Michael asks.

"This is still my lab," Duggan snorts then kills the connection. "You ready to go?" He asks me.

"Sure," I answer.

He grabs the door and swings it open quick and fast, like he did the last time, popping his head out into the hallway again. "Clear," he says to himself then walks out nonchalantly. I follow him to his car, rubbing my temple, trying to massage away the pain.

He pulls the car out onto the highway and before I can ask, he says, "I found it quite interesting that we were the only two who experienced something different.

It was an anomaly that needed to be accounted for. I kept an eye on it as we progressed. And then it happened. There were others."

"Others?" I ask.

"Yes, of course. String theory posits as many as twenty dimensions. If I am correct, we have found at least three. The question, naturally, is why do some people go to different places."

"Exactly."

"And although that is an interesting academic question, it was never my focus—not even on my radar, actually. I wanted to create a machine to move people and cargo quickly and efficiently across the globe, not do theoretical physics. But it was something I was aware of."

"But now Kyle—"

He cuts me off. "A distraction. That's all. Don't get too close to him. He's headed for a bad end, I suspect."

"Thanks, Dr. Duggan," I say as we pull into my driveway next to Smith's car. "You're stopping in, aren't you?"

"I suppose," he says but he looked like he was planning on driving away.

"Smith's car?" he says as we walk up to the door. I nod as I turn the door handle.

"Look who I brought home," I announce.

Smith pops up off of the couch and shakes Duggan's hand. Mom gives him a big hug and a peck on the check. Duggan says, "I haven't seen you two since... since the engagement?"

Mom looks at me then down at the ground briefly. Smith says, "Good job, bringing that one up, eh?"

"Oh. Right. Sorry," Duggan replies. "I didn't mean anything by it. I, ahh, brought Gabriella home. Just thought I'd stop in and say hello."

"No problem, Archibald," mom says. "Would you like some coffee? Tea?"

"That's very nice of you but no thanks. Don't want to be up all night."

"So how's the testing going? Heard you've secured a new financier?" Smith asks with a grin.

"Yes, thanks to your little trouble maker I am back at it." Duggan laughs. "But he's not so bad. I keep my distance. He keeps his. I should be free of him soon."

"Good luck with that. I think he may burrow in a little deeper than you want. And you should never expect sane behavior out of the insane anyway." Smith says.

Duggan asks, "And you? I see your handiwork all over the news."

"Not nice. Not nice. And in front of the ladies too."

Duggan looks over at mom and me. "Don't mind us. Old rivalries, you know."

Smith points at the screen. "I've been watching constantly. Can't turn it off. Seems like everyday they find a new one. Premature aging, didn't see that one coming."

Duggan scratches his head. "Almost feels like mean reversion."

"Not possible."

"I know. Hmm, late onset genetic disorders: Alzheimer's, schizophrenia. Any commonality? Clearly genomic replication failure. Have you found an environmental mutagen?" Duggan replies as we all look at the screen. Several crews of reporters are camped out in front of the hospital with caravans of support staff.

Smith replies without looking at Duggan, "We checked. No common environmental factors. It's an inappropriately activated gene, of course. We've already found it. Causes transcription errors. Obviously."

Duggan adds, "Dormant? A single gene?"

"Yes, a single gene is mutated but the mechanism seems to be regulated by several modifier genes. That's where the pattern gets complex." Smith slouches.

"Huh. And all at once like this. There has to be a common trigger," Duggan says.

"Not really." I jump into the conversation. "Some of the athletes disappeared. Some hid it. Some are aging faster than normal but not so dramatically like the ones showing up in the news. This may have been happening for some years."

"Gabriella's right," Smith says and again I feel like he knows much more than he can say.

"Smith? If Gabriella is modified, like you said, do you think, I mean what are the chances of—" mom asks shakily but cannot complete her sentence.

"Gabriella? Modified?" Duggan asks.

The three of us stare at Smith as he speaks. "I am close, really close. I hate to say this, but if only Jonathan were here. I really wish I had his notes. I'm close. We are, I think, close to meaningful progress. But yes, I, I don't know. I don't know if we can stop this. I don't know if Gabriella... I don't know who will—"

"So Gabriella's Modified?" Duggan asks, looking at me.

"Maybe. Yeah. I don't know. My dad might have done something." I look at mom and it's as if the worry on her face is transferring directly into me through her stilted, self-conscious stare. "It's just a theory," I say.

"I didn't know," Duggan says into the stillness of the room. "Woah, uncomfortable here. I guess I should be going."

"Archibald, sorry to be a downer. It's really is good

to see you. Please come by more often?" Mom says.

"Sure. Gabby, let me know if there's anything I can for do." Duggan exits and mom and I stand at the door and wave to him as he drives off.

I give mom's hand a squeeze and as I walk back into the living room Smith is standing in front of me as if he would like to hug me and I look up at his face. He says, awkwardly, "You're a smart young girl, Gabriella. You know that I know more than I can say. Company proprietary information and all that. Let's just say that Victor, your father and I were working on this a long time ago. We were a team. If we can crack the code, a big if, we may be able to stop this. Believe me, I have you in mind." He reaches up in a stiff and wooden motion and caresses my check. I don't flinch and his stroke feels forced. "Daughter," he creaks.

Chapter 30

Object Me

"Bleep! Bleep! Bleep!"

I roll over and smash the alarm clock off. Everyone uses the alarm on their screens nowadays but I don't. It's not that I'm nostalgic for these old things; I just like the fact that I can smash them; it gives me a tiny bit of satisfaction, a sweet revenge for waking me up so early. Mom hates it but she still buys me a new one every four months or so.

I rise and shower. I should be peppy and excited about today—we're having a photo and interview session before the playoffs begin—but I can't keep from questioning myself about last night. My hands were right there. I wanted to smash Duggan's machine, didn't I?

I let the water blast my face. I don't have to answer; I know I would have. And what does that make me? I really don't feel like myself anymore.

It's not my property; I had no right. And why? To stop Kyle? It's another one of Dad's old arguments: does the end justify the means? No matter which side I took in our little games, in my heart I always believed that it never did, regardless of the circumstances. But I was ready to do it, there in Duggan's lab, smash, mash, crash, destroying his machine in a blind fury.

I exit the shower and towel off, look at myself in the mirror and tell myself, "I'm not like them," but I don't know if I'm convinced. The black-spot people, they can do whatever it takes to lure people into their cult. Kyle said it himself, there's no good; there's no bad. Nothing is evil. He can do anything he wants as long as it furthers his goal of making everyone on the planet like him, a mindless, black-spot zombie.

"No! I'm not one of them. I didn't do it. My hands were there, sure. I thought about it. I know I could have done it, but I didn't. I made the choice; I didn't do it. I'm not one of them. I'm not."

Mom bangs on the door. "Everything All right in there?"

"Yes, Mom."

"Well hurry up, will you? I have an early appointment."

I open the door and go to my room, leaving the bathroom to her. Through the door I call out, "Mom? Are you coming to the photo shoot?"

"I don't think I can make it today. I'll catch it on the screen though." She pops her head into my room and adds, "You'll be fine. You have such a beautiful smile."

Mom drops me off at the stadium and zips off; she's late for work. I pass-code through the back entrance, pressing those thoughts out of my head and walk briskly down the hall and into the team locker room. The girls are putting on their new, clean uniforms and two makeup artists are painting faces. Another stylist is blow drying hair. The lights seem to be too bright and I feel like our locker room, our sanctuary, is being invaded. Sidney scampers over to me, grabs my forearm and pulls me aside. "Gabby, I'm sorry I didn't say anything. Sorry, I, I don't know. I just, I need your help —"

"What? What? What's going on? Is it Cyndi?"

"She's got the disease. She's aging. I don't know

what to do."

I grab her arms. "Why haven't you taken her in? To the hospital? NuGen, they can do something."

"Those butchers? It's all their fault. I don't trust them. She doesn't either. They just want more meat to experiment on. This isn't a game. It's her life—"

Before our conversation can continue, Donavan bellows, "Gabriella, Sidney, no time for chit chat. Get over here!" Lyttle and Jerry are standing next to Coach.

"We'll talk later," Sidney whispers. "You have to help me." She turns quickly, pats down her uniform and walks toward the group. I follow her.

Lyttle says, "Ladies, this is a big, big day for us. We really need you all to shine. They're calling us the Cinderella team, you know, and regardless if you like that title, the fans are eating it up. You know Philly loves to be an underdog and it would make a victory that much sweeter."

Jerry adds, "And with the Liberty being eliminated we are gaining a lot of attention from fans who didn't want their Ultraball season to be over. There's going to be a lot of new eyeballs on this team starting today so we really need you all to play it up."

Most of us girls don't like the objectification but we all know that there is almost nothing we can do about it. It's just a fact of the game. Men, the pigs that they are, love to look at girls wearing skin-tight outfits, running real fast and smashing each other into pits of mud during the lulls in the field game. We need to smile and look beautiful. It makes me squirm to think of it; the team is using our looks and our bodies to sell tickets and make money; they're prostituting us, in a way, and they want us to agree to it. Or else we're off the team.

Some of the girls hate it, Sidney and Cyndi do.

Max too. Others don't mind and a few actually love it. Me, I don't like it, but I know it's a part of the business, the ugly part, and there isn't much I can do about it. The only choice I have is to quit and I don't want to do that right now.

Donavan says, "As some of you may already know, one of the new girls, Mercury, has been let go. So if any questions arise concerning her," Donavan's eyes barrel down on me, "then politely refer to me or Lyttle. We'll handle it."

We file out of the locker room down a long hall and into the largest conference room in the building. The room is already full of reporters and as we enter the camera flashes commence. The front office staff is lined up against the far wall and they clap but the media does not join them. Lyttle steps forward and announces, "Introducing the Philadelphia Freedom!" then calls out each of our names. We each stand behind a chair, then all sit simultaneously. Jerry told us to do it this way as he thought it would make us look more like a team, more unified. We thought it was a stupid idea.

I'm nervous but I try to smile anyway. The cameras are all around us and I find it weird to hold a constant smile on my face. It feels so fake, so contrived, and I can't help but wonder if that's how it looks.

Donavan handily answers a few questions about how we are expected to perform in the next game then Sidney answers a question about moving up to the pros. The reporters all raise their hands and Lyttle points at a young female reporter from one of the fashion and entertainment channels who smiles cheekily then says, "Gabriella, you had some boyfriend problems in the past. Do you have any comments about your new relationship."

"What relationship?" I say defensively, then look over at Donavan for help.

"Oh, it's been all over the Ultraball channel for nearly two hours. Almost old news," the reporter chuckles. "I guess it was a secret? Your evening in EU with Antonio. There are photos of you two sitting together in the stands and at other times too. You two look great together. I'd like your comments."

I look at Donavan again then over at Lyttle who is pointing his big frame away from me and out towards the reporters. He's straining to keep his smile.

Several defensive angles quickly run through my mind; that it's my personal life; I don't want to talk about it; we're just friends; and on and on and on, but I know none of these deflections will work and the fact that I have taken so long to answer has already sealed it; the reporters smell blood.

"I thought this was going to be an interview about the team and our chances in the playoffs," I say. Heat is radiating off my neck and I don't really want to know what I look like right now.

Another entertainment reporter stands without being called on. "Yes, tell us. We need to know how this is going to affect the dynamic of the team. Coach Donavan, didn't you have fights here, on the practice field last year? Two of the male players were fighting over one of your players and they were both kicked off the team by Coach Bustoff? Was she the one? Weren't they fighting over Gabriella here?"

Another chimes in, "Sounds like a black widow to me."

Donavan blurts out, "Sit down!" then blushes and looks over at Lyttle.

"Err, we called this news conference to speak

about our playoff chances but, err, I suppose we can field other questions." Lyttle looks nervously at me. "Gabriella, could you please briefly explain and then we will move on?"

I can't believe this is happening to me. I hope Michael doesn't see this. I say, "Antonio and I are teammates. Fraternization between teammates is not allowed. Obviously, I would not break those rules." I try to smile but it feels awkward. They are all staring at me.

"Obviously," the young female reporter says slowly, drawing out the first two syllables.

A few cameras flash then Lyttle quickly points at one of the sports reporters who asks a question of Greta. Lyttle refrains from pointing at any of the entertainment reporters for the rest of the session and thankfully no one asks me another question.

One reporter does ask where Cyndi is though and Donavan quickly says that she is fine and will play in the next game. I wonder if she knows.

After the press conference ends, most of the reporters leave. We all exit the conference room for the practice field and the photographers and a smattering of remaining reporters follow us out. We pose for some of the shots and run and jump for others. While we are waiting for our team pictures Sandstone shows me the screen page of Antonio and I. We are at a table at the restaurant in EU and by the angle we look to be sitting quite close together, even though we really weren't. We are both laughing and smiling and the picture is zoomed in real close. She then swipes over to a picture of me from the interview. Only ten minutes ago and it is already on the first page of the gossip section. There is a huge caption under my face that reads, "Ob-vis!" The script underneath describes how team policy does not allow dating and "a girl like Gabriella would obviously not break the rules. Right?" The story goes on to describe me as a flirt who has probably dated the majority of the men on the team and that most of them have fought over me at one time or another. My blood is boiling and I feel betrayed.

Jerry walks up to us and says, "Ah, Gabriella, ah, the front office thinks that, ah, this might not be so bad for the team. Some controversy, you know, it sells tickets. The fans like spice. Might attract more of a female audience. We would like you to—"

"What?" I say a little too loud. "You would like me to *what* exactly?"

Several of the reporters quickly turn toward us.

Jerry reaches out toward my shoulder then thinks better of it and lets his hand drop to his side. "Just don't say anything. Let them run with the story. Don't acknowledge it; don't deny it. Just let it play out. It'll blow over in a few days anyway."

My lip is quivering. "Why should I?" I say, trying to squelch my anger.

"Okay look, you don't have to. Do whatever you want. I'm just the messenger." He storms off and he's lucky that I don't have laser beams in my eyes or his head would have been separated from his body by now.

"What are you going to do?" Sandstone asks timidly.

"I have bigger things to worry about right now."

Yet again, Gabriella, the actress, playing another role. I wish I could just be myself for once. I scratch my leg and step forward in line; I am the next to be photographed. Whoever I am, I am most certainly not who they think I am, that's for sure.

Just before Qi steps away from the colored

photographer's tarp, Sidney walks up to me and says, "Gabby, you look a mess." She combs my hair over my right shoulder with her fingers.

I hiss, "Did you see—"

"Shhh, calm down. Breathe. Right now you can only make things worse. You're going to have to ignore all that. Okay?"

"I know," I say. There is no exit. I just have to hold on, but I don't like it. A runner never likes the idea of being trapped.

"Look at me, okay? Just look at me. You got this. You can do this. Just walk up and be beautiful. I know you can do this," she says.

Qi leaves and the team photographer impatiently yells, "Next!" even though I am standing right there.

I walk to the screen and spin on my heel and try to ignore the bright lights. I try to look natural, normal, like nothing is wrong in the world of Gabriella Conceição, the super-athlete, super-flirt, super-sexy-teenager, super-everything-I-am-not. I hate that I am not only sales pitching a lie but also selling a lifestyle that I don't believe in. "How's this?" I say as I twist my hips slightly and open up my smile.

"That's fine," the photographer says as he stares down at his screen. "Twist a little more," he mumbles as he waves his left arm. I turn slowly, then he yells out, "Stop! That's it. Now push your chest out a smidgen." I want to throw up at the thought of what I am doing but instead I tilt my head slightly, inhale a breath then hold it, suck in my stomach, push out my chest and smile full and wide.

After Sidney finishes we both walk to the outer edge of the field and my stomach is twisting. Sidney is letting me back in, it feels like, but maybe it's only because she needs my help with Cyndi. Will she X me again when this is all over?

"So what's the plan?" I say.

"Follow me," she whispers then walks up to Jerry, Lyttle and Donavan and says, "Mr. Lyttle, I'm going to take care of that thing. Gabriella is coming with me."

"Sure, no problem."

I follow her out quickly, neither of us saying a word. We walk to her car and she floors it, squealing the tires. Sidney has always been a speed freak. She loves to do everything fast.

"I don't know what to do," she says calmly without looking at me.

"There must be something—" I begin to say but cannot finish the sentence.

We are quickly at Cyndi's apartment. Sidney opens the door without knocking and it jars me that it was left unlocked. All of the lights are out and a figure sits on the far living room chair cloaked in shadow.

Sidney stops in the middle of the room. "Cyndi, I brought Gabriella."

"I see that," she croaks. "You may as well turn on the light and get it over with."

Sidney waves her hand in front of the wall plate and the lights slowly brighten. Cyndi has a blanket draped over her legs, an older version of the Cyndi I knew, a frail and wilting copy of the lithe, bouncy girl who was once full of life. She is nearly bald and what little hair she has is all white. She is covered in wrinkles and her skin sags from her frame as if gravity grows somehow stronger and hungrier around her.

I gasp, "Cyndi, no."

She holds up her skinny arm to me in a feeble gesture. "It's true. It's me."

I jump forward and slide to my knees in front of her, grabbing her bony hand at first then plunging my head into her shoulder, uncontrollably. I grab her and hug her and try not to cry. She is so old, so frail. I feel like I am holding a twig. She places her arms around me, slowly, and says softly, "There, there. It's not the end of the world."

I can't believe that she is trying to console me when that is what I should be doing for her.

"I've made my peace with it," she continues. "No one lives forever."

"But we have to do something," I say then pull my bleary-eyed face away from the crook of her neck and stare at her close.

"Gabby, there's nothing they can do," Cyndi says slowly. "I'm an adult. It's all over." She looks away and huffs. "I'm going to donate my body so they can study it. I hope they can stop it for the next generation, but for me it's all over."

Then it happens. She cracks. Cyndi begins to cry hysterically and I can't look at her anymore because it is too painful so I bury my face in her shoulder, hiding my eyes behind her, hugging, hugging, hugging because I don't want to let go. I don't want to lose her again.

Sidney kneels next to me and strokes my back and Cyndi's arm. "We are going to have to tell them soon," she says.

"No. No, I don't *have* to do anything," Cyndi says but her voice is raspy and lacking the force of air. "I'm going to stay right here. They can all figure it out after I'm gone."

The room is quiet except for our sobbing. I slowly gain control of myself and pull my head away. Cyndi looks at me and says, "We've been talking, Sidney and I, and I decided that I didn't want to go out like this, I didn't want to lose the opportunity to tell you that I understand. About Kyle and Sebastian."

I reply, "Oh, Cyndi, I'm so sorry. You know I am. I just don't know what to say."

"Don't say anything." Cyndi heaves slightly and wipes her eyes.

Sidney places her hand on my shoulder. "Gabby, give Cyndi some room. She can't get upset. She's too weak. We need to keep her calm."

"Oh, oh sorry," I say as I stand and step back.

"Please, just sit with me," Cyndi says so Sidney and I sit down in the still and quiet room and stare at her.

I have no idea what to say so I blurt out, "I'm not who you think I am."

Both of them stare at me oddly then Sidney asks, "What are you saying?"

I exhale as I look over at Sidney, then Cyndi. "My father was a geneticist working for NuGen in the early years. Many of the genetic modification enhancements that NuGen offers were discovered in his lab, decades ago. Then something happened, I am not exactly sure what, but my father and my mother and baby-little-me fled the country, my father stealing all of his research, at least as much as hadn't been already turned over to NuGen and we hid in Venezuela."

I pause and Sidney says into the quiet of the room, "I thought you were from Brazil."

"That came later," I answer. "I can't believe I am telling you all this but," I pause and exhale again, "but you two are my best friends and I trust you, I trust you with my life."

Cyndi wheezes then says, "Gabby, you don't have to—"

"Yes. Yes, I do. So NuGen found us. I don't know how but they did. They chased my father and he died—"

"What?" Sidney exclaims, "Those dogs! They killed your father?"

"I don't know, maybe, yeah. They were chasing him. He crashed his car. I guess it was their fault."

"I'm so sorry for you," Cyndi says.

"There's more," I say. "And this is going to be a little difficult to hear. But I think Sebastian may have been one of them."

"I find that hard to believe," Cyndi says calmly. "Why would you say that?"

"Because I was there. I saw him. I don't know. Maybe I'm wrong." I look down at the ground and add, "Maybe I shouldn't have mentioned that part."

"Everyone has a right to believe what they want to believe," Cyndi says.

I continue, "So we changed our name and hid again, in Brazil, mom and I, but then Ultraball happened and here I am."

Sidney says, "But NuGen is so close. Do they know who you are?"

I reply, "They do, but they just wanted my father's research. At one time I thought they wanted me too, but no, now that he's gone, I'm not afraid of them."

"You didn't have to tell us, Gabby. You didn't have to say anything." Cyndi sleepily pushes back into the couch. She doesn't have much energy left.

"I did," I say. "I needed to tell you that so I could say this: I have it. I have his research and I think it may be able to save you."

"What are you talking about?" Sidney stands.

I stand and begin speaking faster, too fast I think, but I can't help myself, I want to help her so bad. "I'm not promising anything but this is exactly what Smith is working on and he told me that if he had my father's research that he could crack this problem and stop the aging. And I have it. I have my father's notes. Maybe he can save you, don't you think? Maybe? Isn't it worth a shot? I could give it to him. We could go to him. Together. Maybe he could use my father's notes to figure all this out. To save you."

They both stare at me so I ask, "What do you think?"

"I'm dying, Gabriella. Before, just before you came, the shadows were here. They were moving around me. It's not long before they will come for me, I can feel it. And I don't want to live my final hours being poked and prodded. I don't want them experimenting on me."

Sidney looks at me but I don't know what to say. She asks, "Do you think he could do something with just a blood sample?"

"We could ask," I say then we both simultaneously turn toward Cyndi. "I'll be with you the whole time."

I look at Sidney so she nods and says, "We both will."

"Come, hold my hands," Cyndi says.

We both kneel in front of her then she squeaks, "As long as you two are with me, I will go."

Chapter 31

Cyndi's Battle

We both wrap our arms around Cyndi's back and gingerly raise her to her feet. Cyndi stumble-steps a bit but can manage to walk with Sidney and me next to her, guiding her. We carry her down the apartment steps then walk her to the car and put her in the front passenger seat. I jump in the back.

As Sidney pulls out of the parking lot, I dial my screen, "Smith, this is Gabby. Are you at the hospital?"

"Yes, I'm kind of busy right now. What can I do for you?" he asks.

"It's Cyndi. She's got it. She's got the sickness. She's aging. I'm bringing her in."

"Cyndi? From your team? All right, fine. No problem. Call me when you're at admitting and I'll be right down." He closes the connection.

"I guess there's no turning back," Cyndi whispers but neither of us answers.

The car ride is long and quiet. We have nothing to say. Our friend is dying, right before our eyes, aging days in minutes, and our only option is to hold her and watch her expire while we throw a Hail-Mary pass to a company that we have all suddenly grown to hate, NuGen. Honestly I don't expect much from them but right now they're all we have. No exit. I know Smith has turned a corner. I know he is trying to act like my father but when he is in his official NuGen capacity something deep inside of me doesn't want to help him. It reminds me too much of my father's death and how it happened. But there is no way to help Cyndi without helping Smith. No exit.

I rub my hand on Cyndi's shoulder as I slowly grow numb to it all. Death. Dying. The fight seems so futile. We can't win. Dad's voice pops into my head and a million different angles and arguments rush through my brain. The old game. Kyle would say that physical life in this dimension is meaningless; the only true life is in the darkness of the Void, his Void, the dimension of nothingness. Why would a person want to extend life here if all that surrounds us is merely an illusion, he would say.

And the scientists that mom spoke of, and Mr. Dunberry, and Smith, yeah Smith, they say life is only a struggle to survive. Life is a constant, warring, bloody fight. Why would anyone want to extend that? It sounds so gory.

And the religious, they think that after we die we go to some kind of happy place, to heaven, to nirvana, to somewhere much better than here. I'd like to think that's where Dad is now. Yeah, I think I'd choose that one. But if the afterlife is so much better than this life, why are we fighting to stay here longer?

I exhale softly as it slowly seeps into my skin. I understand why Cyndi wanted to stay on that couch and just let it all go.

I pull my hand from her shoulder and lean back in the chair. We are pulling into the hospital parking lot and it is full of news vans with satellite dishes on their roofs.

I can't accept any of the arguments anymore. I don't want to argue; I want to live. I want Cyndi to live. I don't know what it is but it's there. There's something burning inside of us, inside all living creatures, that makes us want to live, to live more fully, yearning to live longer. We have to try. I have to try to save her.

"Visitor parking," I say. "Don't go to emergency. This is going to be bad enough."

Sidney nods and pulls into the lot. We exit and try to act like visitors. I help Cyndi out of the car and, in my mind, pretend she is my grandmother. We walk slowly, making a long arc through the parking lot and away from the news crews then one of them yells out, "That's Sydney Scott!"

A mad rush of reporters and cameramen run toward us. We try to quicken our steps but Cyndi cannot go much faster. Before we reach the entrance, they are in front of us, blocking our path.

A reporter sticks his microphone near Sidney's face barking, "Sidney, who are you here to visit? Woah, who's that you got there? Is that? It is! It's Cyndi Battle! She's aged." Waving at the camera, he yells, "Are you getting this? Cyndi Battle has the aging disease!" The reporter is excited, almost happy at Cyndi's illness.

We try to push through them and the hospital entrance doors slide open and a security guard steps out and hollers, "Don't block the entrance to the hospital, please!"

Most of the reporters peel away, giving us a small gang plank of a path into the building. Some are already turned to their cameras and calling in the report. "Breaking news. Another athlete is found with the aging disease..." Cameras are flashing and I can feel the heat of the high intensity lamps on my skin. The others pelt questions at us and it is all I can do to stop myself from lashing out at them. But I stop myself as I realize that this is not about me. I have to protect Cyndi.

We push into the hospital and the guard points to

his left. "Admitting, this way." He does not smile.

We turn a corner, then another, following the arrows and the signs, then finally we arrive at admitting. I call Smith as Sidney delicately slides Cyndi down onto a molded plastic chair.

Cyndi begins shivering immediately. "It's so cold in here," she says. I notice that a new set of wrinkles has appeared on her forehead.

Sidney wraps the blanket around Cyndi's legs and looks at me, saying, "What's taking him so long?"

Smith and a white coated man pop through two double doors and walk directly up to us. I run up to meet him and throw my arms around his neck without thinking and whisper in his ear, "I need your help." My voice sounds desperate and when I hear it, I realize that I really am. I'm desperate for a miracle. I don't want to lose her.

He grabs me quickly, just under my triceps and I pull my arms away. "I'll do my best," he says but worry is on his face. This is out of his control.

The lab-coat stands in front of Cyndi, saying, "Please extend your arm."

She looks up at me so I turn to Smith and he says, "The gene sequencing takes about half an hour. We'll take a sample now so we can start the process while you're being admitted."

I nod at Cyndi so she sticks out her arm and the white-coat sticks a large needle into her, piercing her fragile flesh. Smith and his assistant leave then we sit there and wait.

A screen in the corner is playing the scene of us entering the hospital, over and over, and several different newscasters are speculating on how much longer Cyndi has to live. They stop the footage, frame by frame, zooming onto different areas of her face and circle the wrinkles with a red screen pen.

"Could you turn that off?" Cyndi whispers.

A male nurse comes through the double doors and calls out, "Cyndi Battle?" We three stand so he adds, "Follow me, please."

The admittance procedure takes about half an hour, just like Smith said, but it feels like much longer. I can't stop looking at the time on my screen and morbidly over at Cyndi, looking for new signs of aging; wrinkles that weren't there moments before, the gradual but rapid thinning of her skin, and strands of hair falling out and drifting in the air-conditioning breeze. Sidney rolls her fingers on the counter incessantly and it is irritating all of us, even the white-coat who is processing her in. After he wraps a plastic bracelet around Cyndi's wrist, she is placed on a gurney by two hulking men who look like they could play Ultraball and they wheel her up to the third floor. As the two men push Cyndi through the halls they smile, nod and comment, sometimes freshly, to all of the nurses they pass, at least all of the pretty ones, and it irks me that they can do that while casually pushing a dying woman as if she is a shopping cart at the grocery store.

They drive her gurney up to the D wing entrance, the wing that NuGen and all of the aging patients currently occupy, and stop in front of two militant looking security guards holding heavy weapons. I've seen many security guards before; we have them at the stadium and the practice field; I've seen them at airports and rail stations all over the world; but I've never seen any like this. They look military, commando, brash, aggressive and short-fused.

One of them growls, "Pass code!"

The two gurney drivers laugh like all of this is some sort of sick, twisted joke then swipe their badges. The twin doors slide open and the guards step aside while the cart is pushed through. When Sidney and I try to walk in the other guard barks, "Wait! Pass code!"

We step back and I call Smith. He pops out and tells the guards that we are clear to come in. He takes us to Cyndi's room telling us that he will have to get us both id badges then leaves us.

Cyndi is in a two-bed room but the other bed is empty. Another nurse begins setting up Cyndi's IV drip. I step out of the room and walk down the hall, poking my head into each open doorway. The first two rooms are empty but in the third lies the French girl. I freeze when I see her. She looks so old that I don't know how I recognized her. She is nearly bald now, only stray wisps of hair emanate from her thin gray skin. She could be one-hundred and fifty years old, even two hundred, by the look of her. Skeletal.

"Gabby, over here," Smith calls out from behind me shaking me from a trance.

I turn toward his voice, he is walking away from me and waving his hand over his head to follow him into a room on the other side of the hall. I walk to it and enter. Inside are several lab-coats behind large screens covered with moving colored lines of data. Smith walks behind the row of them and says, "The sequencing is complete. It is as I suspected. She has the gene. A different trigger mechanism it appears—"

"Smith, stop," I say. "I don't care about how it's happening. I just want my friend back." I pull my father's diary out of my jacket pocket and place it in his hand.

"Your father's diary?" he says.

I pull out a stack of papers and hold it out to him,

saying, "The translation. What I have of it so far. It's his research." He reaches out, places his hands on the papers and pulls but I do not release them. He looks at me and I say, "Don't make me regret this." I let them go and return to Cyndi's room.

Time seems to slow to a crawl as we wait. None of us want to turn on the screen, that's for sure, so we talk about this and that, nothing really, keeping our subjects banal and innocuous, Sidney and I avoiding any mention of the future, or plans, or dreams, or aspirations. It is all very polite conversation, talking a great deal about nothing interesting or important. We smile at each other and try to hide our anxiety with lighthearted meaningless gossip. Slowly the gaps of dead space grow and the time we converse decreases and I find myself looking out the window more and more. Silence is overtaking us. Death is overrunning us. It feels inevitable.

My screen rings and for once I am thankful. It's Michael. I answer it without leaving the room because I don't have the mind or stomach to hide things anymore. "Hey Michael, how's it going?"

"Gabby, it's good to hear your voice. Been a few days. I was wondering if you were going to send me any more pages to look at."

"Oh. That," I say. "I appreciate your help. You don't know how much. I'm hoping that you gave us the first leg up. I decided to turn it over to Smith though. He has it all now."

"You did? I see. So you trust him now?" Michael asks innocently.

I pause for a few moments wondering how I can answer the question verbally and yet show all the subtleties that I am feeling. I decide that it is not possible. "He's my father. My biological father." I would like to say more, to say that I don't feel like I have a choice, that it's only to save Cyndi's life but I can't say any of those things right now. Sidney and Cyndi are listening.

"I understand," he says. "By the way, you've been on the screen lately. Over here in Portugal. I've seen you a few times. Is your friend Cyndi sick? I saw you at the hospital entrance."

"I'm with her now. We're still waiting on the doctors," I reply but I know what he really wants to find out: he wants to know about Antonio.

"I hope she feels better. Is there anything I can do?"

"No. I don't think so, Michael. Thanks for offering though. You're such a good friend," I reply then wish I hadn't used that word. Friend. The connotation draws an invisible line between us that can never be crossed and it is not what I feel for him.

"Friend," he mumbles. "I want to put my cards on the table. Can I? I know you are at the hospital but something has been really bugging me and I just need to —"

I interrupt him, "I know Michael and I don't know what to say. I'm sure you saw me in the interview and you probably know what they've been saying about me. It's not true. I mean the pictures don't lie, I did meet Antonio in the lobby restaurant at the hotel but I was restricted. I couldn't leave, remember?"

"So there's nothing?" he asks. "Because I just have to know. I can't keep living like this. Hoping that I am going to win you back. Sometimes I think—" he stops himself and looks at me.

"What? Sometimes you think *what?*" I ask.

"I don't believe that you dated everyone on the

team like they insinuate, but yeah, sometime I think you *are* a flirt. Maybe that's too strong a word, but, I don't know, I'm a scientist. I'm used to cold hard facts and analyzable data. I can't figure you out and it's messing with my head. Can't you just level with me?" Michael is breathing hard.

I look up at Sidney but she is trying to ignore the conversation by looking out the window as she holds Cyndi's hand. Cyndi is fast asleep.

I look at Michael and say, "Michael, you want the truth. That's not so much to ask but I guess my heart is all over the place right now. I don't know if I can give you the answer you want. Maybe if we—"

He cuts me off. "That's fine. Just tell me. Please?"

"Michael, I love you." I breathe out. "But is that enough? We live so far away from each other. We're on different continents and, right now, a long distance relationship... And then there's the lifestyle gap—"

"Lifestyle gap?" he repeats.

"You're a scientist. I'm an athlete. We're so different. You know algorithms. We're completely incompatible. Aren't we?"

"I hate to say it but I have thought about that. But does that matter? Does any of it matter?"

"I just, I can't think about this right now. Michael, I hate to keep making you feel like I am leading you on. I just can't commit. Not now. Not at this moment. I need the rest of my life to stop being so crazy so I can think things through. Is that too much to ask?"

"I don't know. Maybe," he says. "I have to go." His face is replaced by a blank screen as the connection closes.

I look back up at Sidney and she says, "If you're waiting for your life to settle down then you're going to be waiting too long. It's never going to happen. No one will wait for you that long. No one."

"I know," I reply but don't know what to do about it.

Smith bursts into the room and it jars Cyndi awake. "Amazing," he says, smiling. Two lab-coats follow him in carrying large screens under their arms.

"What? Did you find something?" I ask. Sidney and I both stand.

"No promises. You know I can make no promises but I think we may be able to generate something." He sits on the edge of Cyndi's bed. "What we would like to do is generate a serum, Cyndi. It will be custom formulated for your body chemistry, for your DNA. That's really what you're here for, right? It'll take a few hours to run the calculation and generate but then we would like to administer it. Aziz and Mark here, they are part of my staff and liaise here at U Penn Medical, they will help you through all the forms. If you give me verbal permission, I will start the process while they walk you through them."

"What forms?" Sidney asks.

"Consent and release mainly. Nondisclosure. A few others. Basically, you can't tell anyone what we did and, of course, Cyndi, it may kill you. But you already knew that, right? You have to release NuGen and the hospital from all responsibility."

"I'm dying anyway," she says.

"Okay then? Good?" Smith says and Cyndi nods. He starts for the door as Aziz and Mark turn their screens over and pull up the forms. Smith pops his head back in briefly and says, "Gabby, Sidney, you'll have to sign too. The nondisclosure. No information leaves this wing."

It takes a long time to sign all of the forms and near the end we all stop reading them as they are full of gibberish and gobbledygook. After the last form, the two fold up their screens and leave and we wait again. It is getting dark now. I call mom and give her the full situation and she is completely understanding. I knew she would be. I tell her that I plan on spending the night. She suggests that Sidney and I alternate which sounds like a good idea but neither of us wants to be the first to leave Cyndi so we both stay.

A few uneventful hours pass then Smith returns with Aziz who walks over and operates Cyndi's bed into a seated position. Sidney and I clear away from the bed. Smith shakes Cyndi awake lightly and says, "I'm going to inject it now. This is going to be a painful process. It's going to rack your body. I really hope you live through it." He waits until she nods again. I grab Sidney's hand as Smith sticks the needle into Cyndi's IV tube and squeezes the syringe of viscous orange liquid. We watch it flow down the tube and into her arm. She passes out.

He stands, turns to us and says, "Now we wait." Smith walks out while Aziz stays and monitors vital signs on his screen, logging a dataset every few minutes and building a long term graph. Mark wheels in another screen on a tripod and places it along the wall. Aziz puts the long term data on that screen and it is obvious to even Sidney and I that something drastic is happening. Cyndi's heart rate is slowing while her temperature is rising.

Aziz calls someone on his phone and two orderlies arrive with buckets of ice. When Cyndi's temperature line turns red they begin placing ice on her body. The bed becomes wet quickly.

The ice convulses her body but they can't stop,

they have to lower her body temperature. They pile it on as it melts until Cyndi's body shudders endlessly and foam begins spewing from her mouth. Sidney smashes one of them to the floor, screaming, "Stop it! You're killing her!"

I run to the other side of her bed and grab her scalding arm and a lump of her skin slides down, puddling in an unnatural clump in my hand. I release it and place my head near hers, trying not to touch her, and call her name softly in her ear, "Cyndi, Cyndi, Cyndi, Cyndi," sing-songing her name slowly, softly, luring her. I don't know why I am doing this but I don't know what else to do. For some reason I think that she has some sort of mental control over what is happening to her but that is probably ridiculous. But I can't stop; it's all I have.

"Cyndi, Cyndi, Cyndi," I call to her. Then it rises up in my throat, the panic; I can't stop it; I can't control it. Tears stream out of my eyes as my voice shrills, "Cyndi! You can't die! Not like this! Not like this!"

We brought her here. This is all my fault. I killed my friend.

She coughs and foam spews out of her mouth then she gasps grotesquely. Her body pulses in one final hard jerk then stops. I watch, my voice suddenly ripped from my throat, as her chest sinks low and her head falls limp, leaning to my side, her unseeing eyes pointed toward me, locked in a dead gaze.

I stand, relieved that the convulsions have stopped until I realize that she isn't breathing.

"Beeeeeeeeeeeeeep!" The long squeal of the monitor is in my ears, the sound that we all know and hate, the noise indicating that her heart has stopped beating.

"Move!" The orderlies scream as they push

furniture out of the way. A nurse runs with a machine on wheels with many cords and wires hanging from it. Another follows her in and rips open Cyndi's hospital gown. The first nurse flips on the machine, slaps the paddles down on her chest and yells, "Clear!" then sends a jolt into Cyndi's tiny frame.

I slump into the back corner of the room, unable to believe my eyes. Sidney stands nearby, expressionless. She has on her brave face but I know what's underneath.

"Clear!" rings out again and Cyndi's body contracts violently. The two nurses look at each other and one of them shakes his head.

Once more, the nurse screams, "Clear!" and another jolt is sent through her, yet still the monitor cries, her heart does not beat and I hold my breath and hope.

"Try it again!" Smith yells out from the hall as he walks in.

The nurse rubs the paddles together, spreading the gel evenly then shocks her. This time her heartbeat returns.

I slide my back down the wall and sit on the floor trying to not cry. Smith walks over to me and says, "Gabby, this is only the beginning. I'm glad you're here for your friend but if you can't hold it together, you should probably leave."

I look up at him and nod. Sidney comes over to me and helps me up, saying, "We did the right thing," but she sounds like she's asking not telling.

I turn to Smith and say, "I can do this. *We* can do this." But I am not so sure how much more of this I can take.

Chapter 32

Chrysalis

The next morning, mom enters the hospital room escorted by a nervous Smith.

"How's she doing?" she asks.

I walk to the entrance-way and whisper even though I know Cyndi is unconscious and can't hear me, "I don't know, Mom. I really hope she makes it."

"Hi Mrs. Conceição," Sidney says as she walks up to us. She gives Mom a big hug. "It's been so long."

"I know. Too long. You have to come over with Gabby. I'll make biscuits," Mom says.

"That sounds nice," Sidney answers.

"Listen, I'm on my way to work. Just stopped in to see if everything was fine. Here's a change of clothes for you, Gabby. Give me a call if anything changes." She looks at the bed with Cyndi on it then frowns. "Okay, call me later."

Smith walks mom out and I can tell he didn't want her here but didn't know how to refuse her. He looks exhausted. I think he has been sleeping here. About fifteen minutes later Smith comes back in. Victor Chavez is with him. He doesn't say anything but only looks at the screens, mumbles and groans.

Smith points at a few lines, saying, "Here, see here. It's farther than we've gotten before."

Victor looks and nods his head slowly but doesn't respond.

After he leaves, Sidney asks, "Who's the ancient

guy?"

"That's Smith's supervisor. His name is Victor. Victor Chavez," I say.

"He's really old. I guess he doesn't want to retire." She shrugs her shoulders. "Hey," she says looking at the time. "We need to call Donavan."

We call her on Sidney's screen and explain that we will be alternating our training. Donavan is none too happy about this since we have our first playoff game in less than two weeks but she's surprisingly understanding.

An uneventful couple of hours pass with the exception of nurses entering and leaving every thirty minutes or so to inject another dose of something into Cyndi's body. Statins, amphetamines, analgesics, antispasmodics, enzymatic stimulants and the like, an entire cocktail of drugs that makes me wonder how much of the pharmacy is *not* being pumped into Cyndi's body. Then suddenly Cyndi convulses, her arm swinging wide, smacking a small lamp off a nearby corner table, breaking it. Before we can reach her she sits up and sounds uncharacteristically lucid, "I feel disoriented, confused. I am... in the hospital, aren't I? Is this the treatment?"

Sidney speaks first, "It is. You're doing great. How are you feeling?"

If Cyndi is doing great then I would hate to see what not-great looks like. Her entire body is splotched by a raised bluish rash and where there's no rash, her skin is pale and jaundiced. In a few areas her skin is torn open, revealing large lesions of three to four inches, as raw as open wounds. The bed is covered in pockets of dark blood.

"I feel bloated. I think I need to pee. But I can't," she replies, her lips chapped to the point of cracking.

Aziz says as he runs out of the room, "The catheter. Those idiots. They forgot it? I'll be right back."

Cyndi doesn't stay awake long, even though she tries to. The orderly returns with a long rubber tube and inserts it as Cyndi moans unconsciously.

A few more hours pass and I try to distract myself by thinking of something else, Ultraball, the playoffs, the Void-man, my father that is, Michael or even Kyle, but none of it seems very important right now. All I can do is stare at her body in sick fascination as gradually the small pockets of yellow, jaundiced skin are completely replaced by bluish bumps. She looks alien, reptilian, cold-blooded.

"At least she hasn't had a seizure in a while," Sidney says.

"That's something." My reply sounds almost rude even though I don't mean it that way. I'm really, really tired.

Toward evening, Mom picks me up and I go home to sleep in my bed. I didn't want to leave but I can't drop all of my commitments. And I need to get away for awhile; I need to feel like there's another reality besides what's happening in that hospital room on the third floor of D wing. I console myself by thinking that one of us will be there in case Cyndi wakes up. I just hope she doesn't die when I'm not there. I don't sleep well and my dreams are filled with insects, lizards and crawling things. In the morning, I go to class then off to practice then back to the hospital. When I arrive Sidney leaves so she can train and get some sleep in a real bed. It is wearing us down quickly.

After Sidney walks out, I step closer to Cyndi's bed and am shocked by what she has transformed into. The bluish bumps have grown larger and darkened. Her eyes are yellowish and open, blinking occasionally, as her head looks at the wall behind her, moving side to side, a lizard looking for prey. She no longer looks human.

"Is she conscious?" I say out loud.

Mark looks back from his screen briefly. "You can try to talk to her. Maybe she will respond. But don't expect much."

I move closer to her bed, but not too close. I am afraid of her now. "Cyndi? Do you want to talk?"

She ignores my voice as she sways her head back and forth, licking her black lips.

"Cyndi?"

Just as I am about to turn my back, she hisses, "Shadows."

"Yes, Cyndi. I'm here."

"The shadows. They crawl up and down the wall. They're here for me. They're waiting."

I look at the walls and see nothing. They are completely white, in fact. "There's nothing there. I don't see them."

"Like lizards, crawling up and down the wall. They're there. And there. And there. Lizards. Look." Her arm swings up quickly and she points but I see nothing. She croaks loudly, "I'll die soon. They're here for me." She promptly closes her eyes and drifts back to sleep.

Mark says, "See? I told you. She's senseless. Incoherent. It's a waste of time talking to her but knock yourself out."

Another day goes by and Sidney and I swap out two more times. It's becoming routine but I don't know how much longer we can do this.

During the night I am awakened by voices. I open my eyes to see Smith speaking with Aziz who is monitoring the screen. "What? Something?" I ask.

Smith looks at me and back at the screen. "She appears to be stabilizing. No promises, remember. She's not out of the woods." He walks out of the room so I scoot to the end of the bed and ask Aziz to show me. He points at the lines and says something about metabolic ratio and enzyme activity but I don't understand enough to ask a follow up question so I lay back down, roll to my side and watch Cyndi breathe. Most of the exterior three or so layers of her bumpy, bluish skin has sloughed off revealing pinkish baby-like skin underneath, sensitive and raw, although there are still rough, dark patches here and there, especially on her head, hands and feet.

While I watch, two nurses come in, one wearing a backpack vacuum, and they attempt to clean Cyndi's bed. One vacuums up large mounds of dander, her dead skin, hair and extraneous shedding while the other brushes the sheets steering the piles toward the hose. Once they have most of it, they roll her to the left, change half the sheet, then roll her to the right and change the rest. Mark barks at them to stop when a slight peak in one of Cyndi's numbers appears while they move her. They stop and wait for the numbers to settle out, finish cleaning then exit as they came, almost as if all of this is somehow normal.

The next morning Sidney comes in and I prepare to leave. We talk about our schedules and how we are going to alternate over the next few days.

"The team's been really nice about this," she says. "Everyone's real supportive." Sidney sounds like she's fishing.

"I haven't told them what she looks like," I say somberly.

"Good. Me neither."

"I'm going," I say. "Just let me say bye to Cyndi and then I guess I'll see you tonight." I walk to Cyndi's bed to say bye to her, a ritual I adopted early on. Somehow I think if she dies when I am gone that this would make it just a little bit easier.

"Okay Cyndi, Sidney's here. I'm leaving. I'll see you in a few hours."

Her hand clasps my wrist and it alarms me.

"Cyndi?" I want to pull her scaly hand away. Black fingernails pierce my skin. I call her name again, "Cyndi?" but her grip only tightens then her eyes pop open.

I feel like she may break my wrist; her hand is clenched tight. "Cyndi! You're breaking my wrist!"

She slowly releases her grip and begins coughing violently. Mark smashes the red alarm button and two orderlies run in and quickly set her up straight. Bluish goo drips from her mouth as she coughs, spewing viscous fluid, thick as maple syrup. One of the attendants flips a switch and positions a small suction hose in her mouth while the other braces her head.

She eventually stops coughing then they lower her back to her bed. When the orderly pulls his hands from Cyndi's frame a large chunk of bumpy blue flesh pulls away from her skull revealing a bald head below, covered in fine, blond hair. They look at each other and begin prying the rest of it off, a thick, scaly, skull mask.

"The hands and feet," Sidney says.

They quickly peel those also and I can't believe my eyes, a young Cyndi Battle is lying on the bed in front of me, fresh and restored, with the skin and hair of a just-born babe. I grab Sidney's hand and squeeze. I know I can't leave now.

I stay for a few more hours and stare at her in

fascination at the transformation. I am looking right at her and still can't believe it; I can't comprehend it. I can't keep myself from smiling. It's working. Smith did it.

Sidney is cautiously optimistic but she refuses to celebrate just yet. I won't either but I can't stop myself from smiling. Cyndi is still unconscious.

Around noon I decide to leave so I ask Smith to drop me off since Mom is at work. "so what happens next?" I ask just before I exit his car.

"I wish I knew," he says. "We've never made it this far."

The next morning, I flip on the screen as I prepare for school and am stunned to see Cyndi walking around in her room, shot from a distance through her hospital room window. The video is grainy but Cyndi can be seen clearly. I curse myself for leaving the blinds open.

The reporter says, "As you can see in this clip. Cyndi Battle, the latest athlete to contract the aging disease, is walking in her room. And as you can see, she appears to be cured."

Another reporter injects, "It's just amazing. NuGen does it again. She looks younger than she did a few years ago."

The first reporter continues, "Lost all her hair but besides that it appears that she's back to normal. The Freedom and Coach Donavan have to be excited about that. Not sure if she'll be ready for their first playoff game though."

Another announcer interrupts, "Ultraball? Who cares about Ultraball? Think about what this means for life extension. If they can do this for her, maybe they can do this for other older people. And zoom in there, yeah, right there. Look at her skin! Maybe they could do that to my skin."

The first reporter laughs. "A modern medical miracle and you want a skin treatment?"

"Well, why not?" the news-woman answers.

"Mom! We have to get over to the hospital!" I yell.

"What about class?" she calls out from upstairs.

"No! Cyndi's awake."

Mom drops me off at the hospital and I can't make my way to the D wing fast enough. I burst into the room and there she is, sitting on the end of her bed, nibbling on a few items from a cafeteria food tray.

"Cyndi?" I cry out as I run up to her.

"Gabby, slow down," Sidney says as she holds out her hand to me.

I walk up to Cyndi and stand in front of her. She gingerly tries to stand.

"Oh no, don't get up," I say, placing my hand on her shoulder.

"I want to," she wheezes.

Sidney and I help her to stand then Cyndi grabs both my hands and squeezes them. She softly breathes, "Thank you," then hugs me. I help her to sit back down.

"I can't talk... well," she heaves. "I don't have... my air back... yet."

I'm so excited. "It's fine, Cyndi. I'm just so happy. You look like your old self. Not your old self, your other self, like you're supposed to look, I mean. I just can't believe this. Oh my God, this is just so great." I look over at Sidney and am about to cry.

Sidney smiles. "Gabby, you did good."

Later that afternoon Sidney leaves and I spend the rest of the day watching Cyndi sleep; she sleeps mostly and is still really tired. During the few hours that she is awake she tries to eat and I tell her about what is happening on the team and all of the playoff preps that are going on. She is not quite time-synched yet to a daytime-nighttime routine so she ends up being awake in the middle of the night, so I get up with her and we converse, although I do almost all of the talking.

In the morning, I am awakened by noises again. I've overslept. Day and night are blending together for me now. I stand and tiptoe to the doorway and listen.

Victor demands, "It's my life. I'm ready. You see it's working—"

"Let's wait for it to run it's course. It's too early. We need more tests," Smith argues.

"Wait? I've been waiting for twenty years for this. No. Run the course. I'm taking my injection. I'm taking it today," Victor says as he walks away.

Smith walks into the room and I place my hand on the bathroom doorknob as if I wasn't standing there listening.

Smith asks, "Gabby, how are you feeling?"

"Cyndi is improving? Right? I mean look at her. It's a miracle. You did it, Smith."

"Right. Yeah. I meant you. How are you holding up?" Smith asks.

"I can handle it. At least I have hope now. I know we're not home free but yeah, I'm doing real good right now." I smile wide.

He steps in and closes the door. "How much did you hear?"

"Some. I guess Victor wants Cyndi's treatment?" I say.

"It's the only thing that can save him, but—"

"But you don't want to do it?" I ask.

"If I give it to him and he dies what do you think will happen to me? What do you think would happen to the project?"

"But Cyndi? And all the sign offs? Won't they protect you?" I quiz.

"A little different situation there. Victor doesn't have the gene defect. He was never modified by NuGen. There's nothing technically wrong with him. He's just old. There's a big difference between treating a disease with an experimental treatment and giving a perfectly healthy person an unapproved therapy."

"I see," I say. "So what are you going to do?"

"I'm going to give it to him and hope he lives. If he doesn't, I'll deny everything. We all will," Smith walks out of the room leaving the door open. I understand his message—he's telling me to forget I heard anything.

During the times that Cyndi sleeps I find myself drawn to her doorway to look out at the hall and the hustle and bustle of the white-coat staff as they prepare the room across the hall for Victor's treatment.

When Sidney arrives, I am at the doorway, watching. She asks, "What's going on over there?"

"Remember the old guy? Smith's boss? They're giving him the treatment." I know I probably shouldn't tell her but she's going to find out soon enough anyway. He's right across the hall.

Her nose flairs slightly as she pushes past me, into the room. "They can do that?"

I turn and follow her in. "Don't tell anyone. I don't think they are supposed to. We're not supposed to know anything."

Just then, screams emanate from across the hall so Sidney and I go to the doorway to look. Two orderlies run into the room.

I can distinctly hear Smith's voice echoing out of Victor's room. "Hold him down! Strap his wrists!"

A few minutes later the two orderlies exit,

sweating, and Smith steps out rubbing his neck.

I ask from across the hall, "What happened?"

He replies, "Not what we expected but with only one data point I suppose we were being careless. He didn't react as calmly as your friend Cyndi, shall we say."

Cyndi pokes me from behind with her finger and says, "I want to go out."

Smith barks, "What are you doing out of bed?"

"How long have... I been locked up in this room? I need some... fresh air. I want to go out," Cyndi wheezes softly.

Smith slowly looks at Sidney and me and replies, "Your two friends can take you down the hall if you'd like. There's a visitor's lobby in the unrestricted section. You can have a few people meet you there, but only a few. I don't need you being stressed out right now. Make sure you take Mark or Aziz with you. And you can't take off your telemetry so you're going to have to push that pole around wherever you go." He smirks, then adds, "Be careful. Oh, and NO MEDIA. You're not ready for that stress yet."

Sidney calls Coach and tells her that she can send a few people to visit Cyndi. She comes, along with Lyttle, Jerry, Antonio, Max and Sandstone. Aziz only lets three in at a time so Donavan, Jerry and Lyttle are first but they don't stay long. Next is Max, Antonio and Sandstone. I am not sure why Sandstone came since she has never met Cyndi but she gives me a big hug when she sees me and shakes Cyndi's hand then she leaves. Max sits next to Cyndi, Antonio with me.

"I missed you, G," he growls. "You know I'm into you, right? Hey Sid, you know that, right? I'm into little G here."

"Yeah, kind of obvious," Sidney replies.

Antonio motions with his hands, "Just so everyone knows because, you know, I don't want anyone to think anything else."

"Will you stop that already?" I say and hit his arm.

"What? You told me I was, like, hiding it or something, so I'm just making sure that everyone knows —"

"We know already," Max barks then smiles.

We all laugh. Even Cyndi. Then her laugh turns into a cough attack, one that doesn't seem to want to stop. We stop laughing then, one by one, stop smiling then we all stand nervously as Aziz tries to calm her down. She coughs hard and a splotch of red blood splats on the floor in front of us.

"That's it! Back to the room," Aziz orders.

Sidney grabs one of Cyndi's arms and leads her out. I push her IV and telemetry poles.

Antonio follows us, saying, "G, Can I help? Let me help. I can do something."

We reach the security door and one officer swipes his badge to let us through. We have been here so long that all of them know us now. When Antonio tries to follow us in they stop him.

"What? What's going on?" he says. "I'm with them."

"You have to have an id badge," I yell back at him as the security doors close and I duck into Cyndi's room.

I position Cyndi's poles as Sidney sets her on her bed. As Cyndi reclines her coughing slows then stops. Aziz monitors her vitals, holding his breath, then lets his air out long and slow. "That was close," he says.

Just then I hear screaming out in the hall but ignore it. Victor must be having a tough time.

After I see that Cyndi has calmed I say to Sidney,

"I'm going to go say bye to Antonio and Max."

She nods and waves me away.

As I reach Cyndi's doorway I realize that the screaming I heard was not Victor Chavez just across the hall but something entirely different. There are sounds of scuffling just outside of the security doors. At first I think it is Antonio, but that can't be right. Shadows move quickly across the frosted glass and then someone smashes into the doors pushing them inward. A gun shot is fired. I step back in fear.

The security officer's gun? What is going on?

Then another shot reports. Then another. As I stand there, gripping Cyndi's door handle in fear, muscles tense, ready to run, ready to do something but not knowing what, not understanding, not knowing what to think, blood slowly seeps into our space from underneath the security doors.

Chapter 33

Bleep-Bleep-Bloop

Sidney runs up to me, saying, "What *was* that?" Then stops and gasps before I can answer. She sees the blood. "Oh my God. Did someone just get shot?"

We look at each other then she adds, "The security guards?"

Smith and a few of the orderlies come out of their rooms. Smith barks, "What's going on here?" then, seeing the blood, yells as he points at one of them, "You! Sound the alarm!"

The orderly turns and runs.

The characteristic bleep-bleep-bloop emanates from the other side of the security door in a dull, thick silence as everyone catches their breath, wondering in sick curiosity at what will be on the other side. The door slides open, one of them sticking on the fallen body of a guard. The other guard is lying in an unnatural, broken position, a few feet from the first. Standing in the pool of blood, pass code in hand, is Kyle with the most peculiar expression on his face. Behind him is a phalanx of twenty-somethings, most of them dressed in black, several I recognize from Duggan's lab as Kyle's followers, others wearing blue-black suits, the typical outfit of a NuGen field technician.

They walk in, calmly, routinely, not a one having an expression on his or her face.

"All right, you know what to do," Kyle orders as several of them fan out into the various rooms. Two close the security doors and begin piling furniture in front of them while two others hold the semi-automatic rifles that they retrieved from the fallen guards outside. They train their guns down the hall and pan them back and forth looking for anything that might make a sudden movement.

Kyle announces, "Everyone. Come out of your rooms. Up against the walls, please. Do what we say and no one will be hurt. We'll be gone soon enough. We ask your cooperation. This is a NuGen matter and does not concern you. Yes, all of you. That's right, up against the walls."

The orderlies, nurses, and NuGen lab technicians exit their rooms and stand against the walls of the hallway. Two of the women are crying. Sidney and I come out of our room and stand on either side of Cyndi's doorway trying to block the view inside. Aziz and Cyndi are still in there. The stress of this alone could kill Cyndi, I think.

Smith leans against the wall then shakes his head and pushes himself off of the wall, walking toward them fearlessly, "Kyle? Have you lost your mind? Did you kill those men out there?"

Kyle ignores him and one of the men holding a gun points it at Smith as he walks up.

Smith barks, "What do you think you are doing? This is a hospital! We save people here, remember? Not kill them!"

Kyle replies, "What is death to one who has never existed?"

Smith throws his hands in the air. "What? Are you serious? You just killed two people!"

Kyle waves his hand as at a fly in front of him, then says, "I will have time to engage in detailed discourse with you at another time. Perhaps when we are all together, when we are all one, in the Void."

The man with his gun trained on Smith waves it at him, pointing for him to go away. Clearly he would have no problem shooting him. Smith retreats to his position on the wall and stands there.

One of the black spot people exits a far room yelling, "Not in here," as he goes to the next room.

Kyle nods.

Sounds of furniture being overturned and things thrown around come out of each room being searched.

"Kyle?" I say, but it does not sound like my voice. It sounds fearful and cowardly and I feel as though I am just a little girl. "What are you after? We will give it to you. Please just don't hurt anyone."

Kyle rotates his body toward me and replies, "Would you? I thought you might. You still feel it, don't you? The pull. In the end you will be one of us. It is unavoidable, you know."

I feel my black spot buzzing but it only makes me angry now. The last thing I want to be is like him. Murderer!

"Just tell us!" I yell and am shocked at hearing the harshness of my own voice. "What do you want?"

Several of the black spot people are exiting and entering rooms, each calling out, "Not in this one!" Others remove equipment and place it in front of Kyle. There are not many rooms left to search now; they will be entering Cyndi's soon.

Kyle says, "You know what I want. I want the serum. I want the research. I want all of it: data, notes, detailed drawings, whatever you have."

"But Kyle, why?" I ask.

"So I can destroy them," he answers.

At that word, Smith launches himself off the wall toward the closest assailant, attempting to grab his neck. The young man quickly elbows him a few times then punches him down to the ground. Smith groans loudly from the floor as two of the female nurses go to him. He cries out, "Why, Kyle? Why? We're saving lives."

Another enters Victor's room then yells, "Hey, there's someone in here."

Kyle says calmly, "Well, get him out here," then turns to Smith and explains, "This life is nothing but an illusion. It is merely a distraction from true reality, the ultimate reality. Don't you realize that I'm just trying to save you? I'm just trying to open your eyes?"

One of the woman attending to Smith spits, "My eyes are open. You're a jerk!"

The man in Victor's room comes back out, saying, "You need to see this."

Kyle follows him in.

Others begin wheeling screens, equipment, material and boxes out into the center of the hallway and dumping it in a pile. One of them squeezes out a full can of lighter fluid on the pile.

Kyle comes out of Victor's room and asks Smith, "Victor Chavez?"

"Yes," Smith replies.

"Can you give the treatment to anyone else based on his tissue or blood?" Kyle asks.

"No. I wish," Smith says. "Each person has to have an individual treatment, synthesized from his or her own sequence. It's all custom, tailor-made, so to speak."

"Well then, I won't have to shoot him," Kyle answers.

The man holding a gun closest to me says, "Do you think that wise?"

Kyle's eyes gaze at him.

The gun-man justifies his comment, "I mean, what's the difference, right? None of this is real anyway, right?" He pauses then continues, "We are in one big illusion right now, right?"

Kyle turns from him, ignoring his statement, then says, "Is that all of the rooms? Is this all of the materials?"

One of the black spot women replies, "All except that room there. The room that the resistant one is standing next to." She is pointing at Cyndi's room. Am I the resistant one?

"No Kyle," I say, stepping away from the wall. "You can't go in there. Cyndi's in there. She's very sick. The stress, the trauma, we have to keep her calm."

"Move out of the way!" the closest gunman barks, pushing at me with the butt of his gun.

"Hey! Watch it!" I say, still blocking his path.

I don't move, in fact I try block the room more completely, standing in front of it and spreading out my arms.

"Kyle?" I call out but before I can understand what is happening, something dull and hard hits the back of my head and I see the ground rushing up toward my face. It doesn't hurt. In fact, I don't feel anything at all. And all I can see is black.

For a few moments I think I must have somehow been transported into the Void, Kyle's black land of nothingness. But that would be impossible. Then I think I must be dead.

I feel something moving near my head and I open my eyes to see a large boot inches from my nose, stepping away from me and into Cyndi's room. Aziz spins from his monitoring station and jumps in front of

Cyndi. His face is panicked and desperate and I realize, in a fog, that he is moving too suddenly. The man has a gun, you idiot! Don't startle him!

His motions slow and I cannot understand why. Slowly, slowly, Aziz falls back slowly, his mouth open and gaping, falling back in an awkward dance, Cyndi reaching up, blocking herself, trying to grab at Aziz' arm as he plods toward her, both of them moving slowly, as if they were both somehow stuck to fly paper struggling to move.

Aziz' face contorts, frantically, but slowly, coated in syrup, reaching for his gut as red spills forth, trying to hold it, trying to squeeze it all back in as if a hand could even do such a thing, as if a useless human finger could plug the hole of a bullet and staunch internal bleeding.

I don't fear. I am not afraid. The scene and it's meaning still haven't registered. There isn't enough time for that. Aziz slowly falls to the ground and that is when I see it, that is when all of the pain comes rushing in, that is when I can suddenly see and feel and hear and I realize what all of this means.

Cyndi screams as loud as her fragile lungs allow her as she clutches her side, blood spurting from beneath her hospital gown, falling to the floor atop Aziz in a clump of tangled flesh, then she is silent and all is still and unmoving and dead.

Chapter 34

The Lone Gunman

"You killed her," I try to say but my voice has been ripped from my throat and all that comes out is an unintelligible rasp. I stand.

Someone throws a lit match on the pile of screens, equipment and material and I can feel the heat on my body as I look at page after page of my father's diary burn. It is torn and strewn amongst the other material, burning, the yellowed pages turning brown then black then disappearing and I cannot bring myself to try to move, I cannot bring myself to try to save them.

My head is throbbing fiercely now.

Cold splashes my face as the sprinkler system turns on, all of the lights go out and an alarm sounds.

Kyle's people stand around the blaze, their faces blank yet their postures revealing a sense of pride and accomplishment.

Kyle, mesmerized by the flames, a smirk on his face, taps the side of his leg with his hand, it twitching in what almost looks like a code.

"Now You've done it! You've destroyed everything!" Smith cries out, shaking Kyle from his stupor.

"Let's move! Now!" Kyle orders, ignoring Smith's cries. His people assemble behind him, much as in the way they entered. they begin moving the furniture and various items away from the double doors but before Kyle can run his pass code to open them a bleep-bleep-bloop rings out and the doors open, revealing a team of police officers wearing helmets, bullet proof vests and shock gear.

I struggle to my feet, placing my hand on my head, trying to not touch the rapidly rising, sensitive lump on the back of my skull.

"Freeze!" the lead officer yells. "Put your guns down!"

The array of officers point their guns at Kyle's people while the two black-spot gunmen point their guns at the officers, one holding his gun steady while the other nervously swings his around, apparently not sure where he wants to point it first.

Water streaming down from the sprinkler system has me soaked to the bone and I begin to shiver uncontrollably.

The lead officer orders again, "Put your guns down! Now!" but he appears somewhat unsure this time. The situation is rapidly deteriorating into a Mexican standoff and those never go well.

"I surrender," Kyle says unexpectedly, holding his hands up.

The rest of his team also holds up their hands, all of them except the two men with guns. Then one of them nervously places his gun on the floor and kicks it toward the nearest officer who quickly retrieves it.

"That's good. That's smart. You're doing good. Now you too, young man. Just put your gun down," the lead officer says. "Put your guns down and this will all be over and no one will get hurt."

The remaining gunman says, "Kyle, ah, what are you doing?"

"I'm surrendering. I've done nothing wrong," he says calmly.

The black-spot gunman asks, "But, I don't understand. How will we make it to the Void, to the machine, if we're in jail—"

Kyle answers as he stares at the police officers, "You killed all of those people, not me."

The black spot people standing behind Kyle all say in unison, "He killed all of those people, not Kyle. Not us."

The other officers train their guns on the one remaining gunman, several of them tilting their heads slightly and taking aim through their gun sites. The black spot people begin to side step away from him, moving closer to the far wall.

"Lay down your gun, son," the officer in front says, motioning with his hand. "Just lay down your gun. No one has to get hurt here. Not even you. Just lay it down and everything will be all right."

"what? No!" the gunman says, backing up. "This is not what was supposed to happen. This wasn't how it was supposed to go down." He moves back another step and bumps into the wall then slides back along it and into me. He quickly spins, grabs my arm and twists my body, placing it in front of him then points the gun at my head.

My head is pounding and everything happening around me seems surreal and dream-like. My mind is drifting in a cloud.

"I'm getting out of here, see? I going back to the Void. And no one is going to stop me. I'll not be trapped in this fantasy land," the black-spot gunman hisses.

"You don't want to do that, son," the officer says. "You're just making things worse for yourself."

"No! You don't understand! None of this is real. Can't you see that?" he spits as water streams down his face.

The lead officer looks at the one next to him and says to the gunman, "Sure, whatever you say. None of this is real." He holsters his pistol, holds out his empty palms to him and adds, "Now I'm here to help you. I'll take you wherever you want to go. Clear a path for him, boys."

The fog is slowly clearing from my mind although my head hurts tremendously. But still I feel quite strange; somehow I can agree with the man pressing the gun barrel into the crease of my back; none of this feels real.

The officers step to either side, clearing a narrow path between them. The gunman grabs my arm, shoves his rifle deeper into my back and pushes me forward. "Take me to the Void," he sneers.

"All right, we can take you wherever you want to go. You just can't hurt that girl there. Understand? That's the deal? you can't hurt her," the officer says calmly.

The gunman does not reply but only pushes me forward again and again, the cold, wet barrel of his gun gouging my flesh, deeply, painfully.

It hurts but all I can think about is Cyndi and her dying and how she died and I am trying to understand why did we do it all, what for and why. All my effort was wasted and spent and lost.

"Move!" the gunman barks and shoves me forward again, me stagger-stepping just in front of him, nearly falling. He grabs my arm tight and yanks me back, growling into my right ear, "Don't do that again! You stay close!"

I step forward slowly as he pushes me, his breath in my ear, clenching me tight, his body brushing against mine in an uncomfortable slow-dance, us walking between the columns of officers staring at us when just ahead and to the left, hidden behind the bodies of officers, I spy Antonio and Max, squatted down low. I wink slowly, intentionally, at Antonio and he winks back. We have to try something.

The gunman pushes me again and I place one foot in front of my other, tripping myself and try to fall down but his hand is still on my arm, holding me, preventing my body from falling completely to the ground. The barrel of his gun never leaves my back. I am splayed out in front of him partially up and partially on the floor when Antonio screams, leaps up and rushes the gunman, diving at him. The gunman quickly raises his gun, swinging it toward Antonio, firing off several shots as Antonio, airborne, tackles him, knocking his gun away in a fierce Ultraball-style maneuver.

The officers quickly pounce on the gunman, twisting him around, holding his hands behind his back and cuffing him.

Kyle steps forward, hands still raised, saying, "Fine work, officers."

The black-spot people repeat, "Fine work."

The lead officer barks, "Take him away!" pointing at the gunman. Then he turns to Kyle and says, "You! All of you! Get out here and line up against that wall!"

I scramble from the floor and go to Antonio, him holding his leg. One of the bullets struck home. "Antonio! You fool," I say as I slide down next to him.

Smith yells, "Attend to the wounded! There's two in that room! Move!"

I wave at Smith. "Antonio's been shot! Smith? Smith? Over here!"

A nurse runs up to us, placing a large gauze over his wound. Looking at me she says, "Here, put direct pressure right here." She looks at me, waiting to see if I understand. As soon as my hand is on the wound, pressing down, she jumps up and runs down the hall, barking, "I need gurneys to emergency! Now!"

"I can't believe you did that," I say to Antonio.

He reaches up and strokes my hair. "Anything for you, little G."

"Watch it," I say, twisting my head away. "I got hit on the head."

The officers have the black-spot people all turn toward the wall and put their hands behind their backs. Then, one by one, they secure their hands tight with large, plastic tie-wraps.

"Okay, move 'em out," one officer says.

They single-file out of the building, escorted by the officers. Kyle is the last one to go and just before it's his turn to walk, I yell to him, "Why Kyle? Why?"

He turns his head toward me as he begins to walk out, saying, "Extending life in this plane of existence would deter the advent of the new reality that I was sent to usher in."

"Sent?" I question.

Kyle smiles, "I was sent. I did it because *he* told me to."

My brow furrows. "Who told you?"

"Why the man in the Void, of course." Kyle disappears behind the corner of the wall. I would love to jump up and follow him, to find out what he is talking about, but I can't leave Antonio.

Several orderlies rush up to us as Smith directs traffic. "There! In that room there. There's two in there. Be careful with the girl! She's delicate. She just had a procedure."

Four orderlies run past us with gurneys and begin retrieving Aziz and Cyndi. Another set stop in front of us and lower the gurney to a few inches off of the floor.

"I got this," Antonio says and hops himself up onto the gurney using his one good leg. He lies back and the orderlies raise the gurney up to table height then wheel him away.

I begin to follow them then Smith yells at me, "Gabby, stop! you too. You've got a nasty head injury. Wait for your cart. They'll take you down."

A few moments later a gurney arrives for me so I place my body on it and watch the lights go by as they wheel me down the halls.

Chapter 35

Another Idea

Sometime between when I leave D wing and arrive at the emergency ward, I pass out. When I awaken, Sydney is standing next to my bed.

"What? What happened?" I ask.

Sidney frowns then replies, "You got conked on the head pretty good. How much do you remember?"

"Everything up until when they were wheeling me down the hall." I don't know how else to say it, so I just blurt it out, "How's Cyndi?"

"She's... alive," Sidney says, then lightly squeezes my hand. "She's been shot. Aziz too. It's touch and go with him but Cyndi, they said she's going to make it."

"That's good," I say. "And Antonio?"

"That boy? Just a flesh wound. They wrapped it and he's already been discharged. I wanted to smack him the way he was playing it up for the cameras outside."

"Well, he did stop that guy. Took a bullet for me too."

"That he did. You, on the other hand, have a concussion," Sidney smiles. "You took quite a blow to your little noggin."

"I know. It still hurts."

Mom and Smith enter my room, Smith saying, "How's she doing? Oh, she's awake. Good. Good."

Mom says, "How're you feeling, my brave girl?"

"I've been better. My head hurts but I'll be fine."

Smith places his hand on my knee through the

sheets. "Oh no. You're not going anywhere. You're staying right here and getting some rest."

"I will, Smith. No problem. Oh and about—"

"My research? Don't worry about it. We didn't lose much. Only some of the most recent real-time data. We have backups. Although we did lose your father's diary. His notes. We didn't have it all translated. That's a big setback."

"So you will continue?" I ask, stinging about the thought of my father's diary being lost.

"I have to find a cure," Smith says as he looks over at my mother and back at me. He adds, "Victor's dead."

"Oh, I'm so sorry, Smith," I say.

He replies smoothly, "He was an old man. No one can live forever." He looks slowly at both Sidney and me and adds, "He died of old age."

I nod back at him understanding exactly what he means. I say, "He died of old age."

Sidney briefly glances at me then repeats, "He died of old age."

They don't stay long and after they leave, I ask, "Can anyone go to Cyndi's room?"

Sidney replies, "I don't see why not. She's just down the hall." And before I can ask her to help me up, she lowers my bed-rail and pushes the button to raise the back of my bed. "Let's go for a visit," she says.

I stand and wobble slightly, then gain my footing. Someone has taken my clothes off and dressed me in a hospital gown and socks that have rubber grips on the bottom. I wonder who it was but don't want to ask. "Is my butt showing?"

Sidney looks at my backside and answers, "No, you're fine." I follow her down the hall, then we make a left, then down past a few more doors then we enter a room.

We walk up to Cyndi, her lying on the bed. She looks so small on it.

"Hi, Gabby," she says and just hearing her voice nearly makes me burst into tears.

I reach up and grasp her frail hand and give it a tiny squeeze. I don't know exactly where our relationship stands right now. "How are you feeling?"

"The doctors did a great job. Pulled out one bullet. Want to see it? I told them to save it for me." She holds up a long thin piece of metal then places it in my hand.

"Pulled it out of my small intestine. They got it pretty quick. I didn't go septic. I should be fine." She looks down then adds, "For a little while anyway."

Sidney leans up against her bed and touches Cyndi's shoulder.

I say, "What do you mean *for a little while?*"

Cyndi pushes back in her bed. "Listen. I appreciate what you two have done for me. Really, I do. And Gabby, I can't thank you enough. For everything. Really. I mean, you helped me see something, I think, that I was missing. But now. It's just—"

"What? It's just what? What's going on?" I say.

"The treatment. It didn't work. I'm aging again." Cyndi reaches up and quickly wipes her eye.

"What?" I say. "What are you saying?"

Cyndi pulls back the sleeves on her hospital gown, exposing her arms. They are covered with large dark splotches. Her skin appears young and lively in some places and in others, haggard and worn. "It's moving quicker than before. So far. But they don't know if it will accelerate even more, you know, like bacteria in a dish."

An old math question from school pops into my head. If bacteria doubles every day and fills a dish on day twenty-nine, how big was it on day twenty-eight? We might not have her with us for too much longer, I realize.

"But Smith... and the treatment?" I say. "He can try again. It was stopped by Kyle and his people. He can do it right this time—"

She interrupts me, "No, Gabby. I'll not go through that again."

Sidney is noticeably quiet. I think she may have already known.

"So you're just going to lay down and *what?*" I can barely bring myself to say it out loud. "Die? You're going to give up? You're going to just lay down and die?"

"Gabby, it's not like that," Sidney says.

"You agree with her?" I say pushing myself away, wobbling slightly then bracing myself again on the edge of her bed.

Sidney looks at me and says something that it appears she has put a lot of thought into, "No one can make another person live if they don't want to."

I stare at them and the room is suddenly quiet. "I have another idea."

"What's that?" Sidney says, clearly not wanting to lose our friend either.

"Take us to Duggan's lab. Take us there right now and I'll show you."

"No, Gabby. No. That's it," Cyndi says. "I'm just going to stay right here."

"Gabby, how do you think you are going to get out of the hospital?" Sidney asks.

"Cyndi, please? Just put on your clothes? Please? Sidney, we're going to just walk out. That's it. We're going to get dressed and walk right out," I say but I have no idea if this is going to work or even if it is a very good idea but it is all that I have. I've given up too much, sacrificed for too long to just lay down and let it all happen without putting up a fight.

Sidney supports me briefly as we walk out of Cyndi's room without another word. We walk back to my room silently, me not making eye contact with any of the hospital staff for fear that my eyes might betray me. I enter my room and Sidney follows me in and closes the door behind us. She is my accomplice now. I quickly change my clothes, turn to her and say, "What do you think?" sliding the plastic hospital wrist badge up under the sleeve of my shirt.

"I think this isn't going to work. I think we're going to get caught. And... and I think Cyndi won't leave."

"Let's go," I say stepping past her and opening the door. We walk back to Cyndi's room, Sidney holding my hand, us pretending to be really close friends, like girls do in Venezuela, when really she is doing it to prevent me from staggering, stumbling or doing anything that might draw attention to us.

We reach Cyndi's door, she steps out, fully dressed and says, "Okay, let's go." Her face is showing a few wrinkles now. She's aged years in minutes.

"All right. Follow me," Sidney says, wide eyed.

The three of us walk down the hall, me suddenly self conscious of my every motion. Am I walking too fast or too slow? Did that nurse just look at me too long? Did she recognize me? Should we talk or is being silent okay? We walk by a set of doctors so I nod to them and casually say to Sidney, "So that was a nice visit. I'm glad he's doing so well."

Sidney replies, "Yes. We're so lucky to have him here, in this hospital. They're the best."

We make it out of the emergency ward, exiting through the back corridors that lead to the rest of the hospital.

We would have most certainly been caught if we walked out of the emergency entrance, I think.

We snake through the hospital going down hall after hall, slowly finding our way to the main entrance, where all of the visitors enter. We near the entrance doors, seemingly free, when the guard says, "Visitors badges?"

We stop and I say, "Excuse me?"

"Your visitors badges," he replies. "You have to turn them back in when you leave. Will you be returning shortly?"

"Oh, yes. We'll be right back," Sidney quickly blurts out. We turn and walk out the door and make our way to Sidney's car.

The three of us sit down, Cyndi in front and me in the back. Sidney starts the car and steers it onto the highway. Cyndi says in disbelief, "That worked?"

"I know. I can't believe it was that easy," I say.

"So what happens next?" Sidney asks.

I don't know how exactly to answer seeing as I haven't thought this out exactly. I know the Void-man did something to me, my father that is. Maybe he can touch Cyndi too? It's just such a crazy idea that I don't want to say it out loud. "Can you call Duggan? On your screen? I need to let him know that we are coming."

Cyndi pulls up my directory on Sidney's screen and scrolls down to his name. Her hand looks weathered and old. "This one?" she says.

"Yes," I say so she taps the button and dials his number. When he answers I tell him, "Dr. Duggan, sorry for the short notice. I need a favor."

"My dear Gabriella, what are you doing out of the hospital? I saw everything on the screen. Terrible business."

"Yes, I'm fine. I should be there in ten minutes."

Duggan says, "I have to say I didn't foresee this one coming. I wish I had taken your advice. Kyle really lost it. Now what do you need from me?"

"I'm bringing Sidney and Cyndi with me," I say leaning forward poking my head between the two front seats so that he can clearly see me. "We need to make a Void trip. I need to take them through with me. It's kind of hard to explain."

"Shenanigans. Everyone always has other plans for my research. Okay, listen, I owe you one. I do." Duggan shakes his head then says, "I'll do this just this one last time. But make it quick."

The screen goes dark so I lean back in my chair and hope that they don't ask me any more questions, hope that Sidney keeps driving us there. I keep my eyes trained on her hands and I notice her slowing the car down. I look up at the rear view mirror and her eyes in it and then I nod slowly. She pauses, then nods back, then presses the gas pedal.

We arrive at Dr. Duggan's lab, I exit the car and try to dash out to the front door but then nearly fall down as a short burst of dizziness grabs me close.

Sidney gets out, walks around the car to Cyndi's side and opens her door. I think she may need more convincing so I come back to the car.

"I'm sorry," Cyndi says. "I'm just so weak." She aged a decade, maybe two, on the drive.

We have to get her into the machine soon.

Sidney and I help Cyndi out of the car, each of us holding one of her arms then Sidney asks the question that is on all three of our minds, "What's going to happen, Gabby?"

"We're going in. We're going into the Void. Time slows in there. It will give us time to figure this out. It'll slow down Cyndi's aging." I don't say what is my heart's desire, that we find the Void-man and he touches her, like he did for me, that he somehow restores her youth, fixing her DNA, making her young again, that he somehow displays the same compassion for my friend that he did for me. I don't say that because I know it just sounds too crazy right now and I need them to keep following me.

We enter the building and scale the steps slowly as Cyndi is having a very difficult time with them. Even with Sidney and I on either side of her, we barely get her to the first landing. She is aging faster now.

"Gabby, I don't know if I can make it," she says.

"You can make it! You can do this!" I howl trying to convince myself as much as her. "We're so close." I look over at Sidney and say, "Let's carry her."

Without answering, we each firm up on Cyndi's arms and push her in the air. She squeals in pain.

She feels fragile and frail, as if the slightest of movements might break her bones now. She is degrading right before our eyes.

We reach the top floor, finally, I run over to Duggan's door and knock hard as Sidney walks Cyndi the rest of the way. Duggan opens the door and we three go in. "So your plan was to—oh my, what do we have here?" Duggan says, looking at the humped over pile of flesh that was once my friend, Cyndi Battle.

"We're, we're going to go in, the three of us, I don't know, we have to do something." My eyes plead with Duggan.

"Time dilation. yes, I understand," Duggan says. He turns to the large wall screen and addresses Michael, "Start the process, Michael. We've a set coming through." In my rush to get Cyndi here, I hadn't noticed Michael there on the screen, watching us.

Duggan slaps a few pairs of sunglasses in my hand and wheels out the transport module.

I say to Sidney and Cyndi, "We'll sit there. On those seats there. It's like an amusement park ride. See? Easy."

Cyndi is slowly shrinking before my eyes as the hump of her back grows and her head hangs down low. I cannot see her face for the scarf that she draped over her bald head covers it.

"It's too late," she wheezes then falls over.

Sidney and I quickly kneel next to her crumpled frame as Michael calls out procedure steps through the screen.

"Grab her!" I caw. "We have to get her into the machine!"

Sidney pulls back Cyndi's scarf to reveal a woman that looks to be hundreds of years old. Ancient. I do not recognize her.

A thick skinned, arthritic hand reaches up and grabs mine as the wizened face smiles. She exhales one last, final time.

"Nooooo!" I cry out.

"If you're

going, you need to get in the chairs now! I can't stop in the middle of the procedure! Get in the chairs!" Duggan yells as he positions himself behind the control station.

I tug on Cyndi's arm, refusing to believe that she's dead, refusing to believe that we came this close and still missed it.

"Help me!" I scream at Sidney.

She stares at me and answers, "She's gone, Gabby."

"No! She's not!" I defiantly yell. "I refuse to believe that! It's not too late!"

"Get in the chairs! Now!" Duggan yells as the wind in the room begins to pick up.

"Let go, Gabby," Sidney says as she places her hand on my arm. "She's dead. You have to let go."

I slowly release my grip on Cyndi's arm then stand.

Sidney motions at the ring and says, "C'mon. I'll go with you."

We run toward the transport module but I don't know why. My mind is numb. Cyndi is dead. What's the point?

I follow Sidney in a dull stupor, unable to grasp what has just happened, unable to protest the futility of going into the Void, now, without Cyndi. We each take a seat.

Duggan barks, "Initiate!" then mashes a large button on the console in front of him.

I quickly buckle my seat belt as the neon blue erupts in front of us pouring out of the center of the ring, sucking us forward, us bracing ourselves against the metal hand rails, the module accelerating toward the bright light then breaching it.

I clench my eyes down hard and fast as I am briefly ripped in two, separated, divided, two different people at once, then reassembled in the Void.

The module slows, then stops.

I slide on a pair of Duggan's sunglasses then hand a pair to Sidney. We open our eyes but still need to squint to see.

"Where are we?" Sidney asks.

I do not answer but only unbuckle and step from the module. She follows me and stands next to me. I wipe my dripping eyes. I don't know why I am here. I can't believe Cyndi is dead. I can't acknowledge that we missed it by only moments.

"What are we standing on?" she asks. Then looking about, adds, "I can't see where this place ends. It looks like it goes on forever."

A group of slow moving clouds comes upon us and Sidney waves her hands into them then wipes her cheek. "There's no moisture," she says. "Strange clouds." When I don't respond Sidney comes closer to me and looks at my face then wipes it. "It's going to be All right. Maybe not today, but eventually. I loved her too, Gabby."

In the distance I see a figure walking toward us. I know who it is, I know who it has to be, the Void-man, the one who could have saved Cyndi, had we gotten her here fast enough. I feel like a failure and my heart is torn.

We watch him as he approaches, the smell of lilac suddenly swirling around us, his shadow growing larger, more defined, becoming more and more clear the closer he comes.

Sidney asks, "Who is that? Is that who I think it is?"

"He's my father," I whisper.

Just as he becomes close enough to make out his features another shadow appears in the distance, walking toward us. I hold my breath as the figure closes in on us.

Then a new smell mixes with the lilac. It's jasmine and it is much stronger, fresher, almost too strong; it's overpowering. I stare at the two approaching, squinting my eyes hard, trying to make out the face of the smaller one and when I can hold it no longer, I breathe out, "Cyndi?"

I turn to Sidney and yelp, "It's Cyndi! It's Cyndi!" and we both run toward her, meeting her halfway.

We both try to touch her, grabbing at her arms, but then stop, holding our hands open and at bay when she says, "Hello." It is not her voice, it is not her intonation or even how she would have addressed us. Her voice echoes oddly. Like my father. She's changed.

"Cyndi?" I cry. "Cyndi, it's you, isn't it?"

The white figure looks at me slowly, somberly, then over at Sidney. She pauses then replies, "I once was."

"I'm sorry I failed you," I say. "I'm sorry we were too late."

Cyndi replies, her voice reverberating, "You did not fail. On the contrary."

I look up at the Void-man, my father, and frown, perplexed, disappointed. He never communicated to me properly. He gave me a poem—I thought it was a prophecy—and none of it came true. I thought it was a warning but it warned me of nothing that I didn't already know about. It was no help. In the end it didn't help me at all.

Then, as I stare up at him, his words come back to me like shock-waves, "Recite..." and, "You must become..." and, "It is the becoming that is important..." His words wash over me again and again and suddenly a realization strikes me. His poem wasn't about me, it was about him. He was speaking about himself. It was his own story.

He was the one who found his partner in the lowest of places, I think. My mother, in the Mideast, a poor village girl. And she was the one who helped him to strive for great heights.

A friend betrayed him. Smith. The old Smith. He's a different person now though.

The poem comes back to me. He was not what he seemed but he was not deceived. No, not deceived by the bouncing numbers or the shaded letters or the shaking digits or the random dots.

My father was not deceived. No he wasn't. He fled to Venezuela before they could get their hands on him. And they chased him, NuGen did. But he hide his deepest secrets. They didn't find them. No, not until I gave them his diary.

Above all and in the end, things cannot be as you would like and a supreme sacrifice you will have to make. A choice, a choice, a choice. It is yours to decide.

He made the sacrifice. He died for us. Maybe he didn't mean to, but he died trying to hide us. It was his choice. A choice I wish he didn't make, but in the end it was his choice.

I look up into his eyes and there he is. The Void-man really is my father—was my father. It's him, there, in front of me. I can seen him now, in his eyes. It's my dad. He was reciting his story, his life. He was giving me an example.

A mini-tremor hits me again, deep inside, "Recite..."

I squeeze Sidney's hand then release it and address the Void-man, "I am the runner who leaps over barrels, swings on ropes and runs up warped walls. I hid once, then twice then revealed myself openly."

I clear my throat, realizing that something is not quite right. I'm not doing it exactly right. I continue, trying to find the sweet spot as I speak, "I did things to hurt my friends, not on purpose, but because I lacked confidence in myself. But I learned, and I grew, and that won't happen again. Because.."

I pause, suddenly knowing, realizing what he really

meant by *becoming*, then speak more assertively, "I am *not* that person anymore. I am Gabriella. I am the one who runs. I am the one who deciphers codes and figures out mysteries and retrieves diaries, in spite of the risk or the danger."

I glance over at Sidney and add, "I am the one who fights for her friends, regardless of what anyone tells me to do."

I turn my face back toward the Void-man and say, "And like my father before me, a small sparrow that has turned into a mighty hawk. At least, I aspire to be..."

I feel something odd and scratching on the back of my neck so I reach my hand up to it and realize, without having to look at it, without actually seeing it, that the black spot is disappearing. I feel the skin tightening; it's shrinking rapidly. I feel it pop then I know. The black spot is gone.

I look at the three of them, one by one, then add, "I don't know how it all ends. I don't. I can't speak about the end or choices or supreme sacrifices. But I know who I am. I know it now. I am Gabriella."

Cyndi looks over at the Void-man and he says to us, "You will not need us anymore." He smiles briefly and adds, "You are going to be fine."

Before Sidney or I can say or ask or do anything, they turn and walk away, their steps seemingly covering immense amounts of distance, them quickly disappearing into the white.

We watch them disappear then stare at the white spot where they were for a long time. Sidney reaches down and grabs my hand, gives it a slow squeeze then says, "Let's go home."

Chapter 36

I Know Who I am

The chair module slows to a stop and looking at Dr. Duggan's face I realize that we were only gone a few seconds in his time. Cyndi's body still lies crumpled on the floor.

"I took the liberty of calling the authorities," he says. "They're sending an ambulance and I am sure the police will be here soon also."

Sidney and I sit on the track waiting for them. A few minutes later, the paramedics come and take Cyndi's body away, then the University and Princeton police arrive. Sidney, Duggan and I answer questions for some time, then they release us.

Sidney takes me back to the hospital and we intend to just walk in the main entrance but Smith and mom are waiting for us there. I walk up to them defiantly, intending to justify myself, but mom throws her arms around my neck before I can speak.

"Archibald called. He told me everything. Gabby, I'm so sorry for you," she says.

I stroke her back and try to console her. I feel emotionless and I know it really hasn't hit me yet.

After I am checked back into the hospital and safely in my bed, the three of them leave me alone to rest.

I try to sleep but cannot for something is ringing in my ear and I know what I want now. I know who I am. At least I think I do. I replay the events in my mind.

I recited words to the man in the Void and it was like a revelation for me to say them. They were coming out of me and as I said them, it was as if I were hearing them for the first time myself.

I don't know what it all means and how these bizarre chain of events came to take place, but one thing I know: I am not going to be an actress on a stage pretending to be something I'm not. No, not anymore. I can't do that again. The fans, the coaches, Antonio and Michael, even Mom, they're all going to have to accept me for who I am. I'm Gabriella.

It may mean that I am let go from the team and if that happens, fine. Being an normal teenager in United North America can't be so bad.

I pick up my screen and dial Antonio. When he answers, I say, "Antonio, I need to tell you something."

"Sure G. Anything. What's up?"

"I really appreciate what you did. Taking a bullet for me and all. But I can't lead you on. I need to tell you that I'm in love with someone else. I thought it couldn't work between us and I was mixed up for a time, but now I know what I want. I really appreciate you and I just wanted to tell you up front."

"So, that's it? You're dumping me?"

"I'm afraid so."

"I understand. I guess," he says, but he looks confused.

I close the connection then sit my screen down and exhale long and hard. That was easier than I thought it would be.

I pick it back up and mash a button. When he answers, I say, "Hi Michael. I really need to talk to you."

We have a long conversation, negotiating how we are going to maintain a cross-continental romance, but I already know that he will try to pull some strings. I'm sure he can get Duggan to reassign him to Princeton. If so, that would be perfect.

After I hang up, I lay back and drift off to sleep with a smile on my face. Tomorrow will be a new day.

Reviews

If you have enjoyed this book, please be so kind as to provide a review of it on both amazon and goodreads and any other location that you may have purchased it from. This will serve the dual purpose of letting me know what you thought of it which will influence my future writing and also help expose the book to other potential readers. Thank you so much for your time.

Also, if you would like to give me direct personal feedback, you can message me on goodreads.

Acknowledgements

A huge thanks goes out to Tracy Boehmer who took the time to carefully proof, review and provide meaningful feedback to make this book that much better.

Questions for Teachers, Students or General Discussion

1) The two book series, at it's core, is a story about a girl who is trying to find herself. The first chapter of book one ends with her thinking, *Who am I, really?* after she realizes that her entire life up to that point was based upon a lie. At the end of book one, she is surrounded on a hospital bed by her friends and she still doesn't really know who she is but she looks at them and says that it is "good enough" to be surrounded by friends. In book two, several different ideas of what it means to *become* are contrasted by several of the different characters. Do you think, in the end, that Gabriella really knows who she is?

2) As in the question above, if a person is trying to determine who they are, should that determination be based upon his or her beliefs? Or his or her actions? Or a combination of both? If a person believes in good but does the opposite, can we say whether they are good or bad?

3) In Kyle's mind, there is no good or bad because they are all "subjective judgments of a material world," a material world which he believes does not even exist. So for him the only bad is the "lack of realization of the true nature of things." So, in his mind, what he did at the hospital was not evil. In fact he is most righteous because he is "opening eyes." What do you think of his

position?

4) Just before Cyndi dies, she thanks Gabriella for helping her to realize something that she was missing. What do you think that was?

5) Gabriella is made to feel like an object by the media establishment and her team in the *Object Me* chapter. She accepts this as a trade off for being on the team. Do you think that this is an acceptable and fair trade? Do you think that she could have taken another course of action or stance?

6) The curse from the title of the book refers to the ability of the black spot on Gabriella's neck to influence her emotions and, at times, her behavior. The Void-man says that it was something that was inside of her all along and that Kyle merely pulled it to the surface. Do you think that Gabriella's behavior and emotions will change once the spot is gone?

7) Durand quits his research because he does not think that his design decisions would be better than evolution's. Is this a valid reason? If you made his discovery, what would you have done differently?

8) Smith, it appears, probably had something to do with Gabriella's father's death, yet once he finds out that Gabriella is his biological daughter, his stance and manner seems to change. Do you think that he is being authentic? Can a person truly change? Should she accept him?

Also by James Cardona

Under the Shadow of Darkness
Apprentice Series Book 1
ISBN:978-0-9850284-8-0

A young adult fantasy romance drama series full of the kind of zombie-filled action that will keep you turning pages and up late at night. Perfect for middle schoolers and young adults who love magic, magicians, wizards, swords and sorcery. The book is full of drama and comedy, and is the prelude to an intense romance in the following books of the series.

Bel, a graduate from the Academy of Arts and Magic, takes the final vow of celibacy, sacrificing his love for Shireen in order to be an apprentice. After that traumatic experience, Bel attempts to start his new life under a wise-cracking wizard, but everything is not what it seems.

Grab hold of the book that readers describe as "the beginning of what looks to be one of those series you can't get enough of."

While being chosen as an apprentice is exciting for Bel, he is still hesitant. His new master is one of the most renowned wizards throughout the lands, but his two previous apprentices were killed under his watch. The mysteries surrounding each of their untimely departures from this world has left Bel skittish and insecure. And his mysterious dreams of a one-armed boy fervently warning him about something that he cannot decipher does nothing to calm his fears either.

Immediately young Bel and his magician master are thrust into an adventure when reality is torn open allowing the dead to spill out of the underworld. They must journey under the shadow of darkness to try to discover how the fabric of reality has been rent allowing the zombie horde to walk among the living. Who did it and why? Was it intentional? Can they defeat them? Can they close the rift? Can a teenager learning the ways of magic and an ancient sorcerer long past his prime stop the darkness, close the breach and save all reality?

One reader said, "I literally felt like I was journeying with the group into the darkness, remarkably to the point where it was practically tangible."

When zombie-like creatures start stalking the living, Bel and his magician master are faced with a twofold problem: how do you protect the living by finding the breach in reality, and how do you do find...well...anything when faced with an eternal darkness? With daylight no longer breaking through, they are forced along a dark, treacherous journey that tests the limits of their magic, an adventure leading them into the heart of danger, which may kill them all. And if they fail, all of reality may fall with them.

One reader said, "I really enjoyed the way he portrayed the ghouls. I found them both frightening and at times very humorous."

The book is full of swords and sorcery, but magic doesn't come easy for an apprentice. It requires resourcefulness and sacrifice for the source of all magic is the very light and life of all things.

Searching for the source of the tear in reality, magician's apprentice Bel and the wizard encounter the zombie horde time and time again. These creatures are the living dead and in constant search for human blood. Under the Shadow of Darkness is the sorcerer's and his apprentice's adventurous journey to find and attempt to close this breach so that the sun might return again, the dead will remain dead allowing the living to regain their lives once more.

Bel's epic saga is a hero's journey of a young apprentice who is thrust into a fantastic battle of good and evil, dark and light on his very first day with his magician master. His quest will take them through a dark land filled with zombie like creatures.

There's great detail explaining how magic works and the rules that surround it. It's hard not to compare teenage fantasy and magic with Harry Potter, but that is where the comparison ends. It's a different take on magic where a magician doesn't have to learn how to cast spells properly, but interact with the very forces of life, coaxing them to perform the magic that he or she desires.

Jump into this new magical world full of drama, romance, action and adventure.

Also by James Cardona

Santa Claus vs. The Aliens

ISBN: 978-0-9850284-6-6

In this fast paced, Children's holiday science fiction adventure, Edwin, a fourteen year old and an odd character dressed as Santa Claus attempt to stop aliens and save the planet in 1950's Manhattan.

When Edwin cuts his finger, dripping a few drops of blood onto a bone-colored tracking device he becomes a target of a group of aliens that think he holds the secret to the human race's defeat. The only person who seems to know what to do is a fat man wearing a Santa Claus suit and he somehow seems to know just a little too much.

Who is he and why does he know so much? Where did the aliens come from and what are they after? Can a Fourteen year old wandering the cold, empty streets of Manhattan late on Christmas Eve and an odd character dressed as Santa Claus stop the aliens, save the planet and discover the true meaning of Christmas?

Readers are calling it "**packed with humor, action**" and "**adventure**" and "**intelligent and thoroughly enjoyable.**" Grab hold of this children's science fiction Christmas adventure and take a wild ride.

One day, Edwin's father, Fundy, witnesses a strange object falling out of the sky. When he realizes a person is in it, he helps the red suited man pull his strange vehicle out of the muck with his horse, Paulo. As Santa flies off, he accidentally drops his ring.

After his encounter with the strange man, Fundy and his wife move to the United States, hoping to find happiness, but instead they eventually get divorced, placing Edwin in a children's home when neither of them could take care of their son. When Edwin is dropped off at the children's home, Fundy gives his son his most prized possession, the Santa's ring.

Several years after his divorce, Fundy has remarried, has a little girl, acquired a decent job, and wishes for Edwin to come back home. Whether for rage or guilt, Edwin cannot bring himself to do this. He feels as though his home is no longer his own, as if a strange woman is living there. Edwin knows that he will no longer see his father and actual mother together ever again, but it's just not right to him.

Called, "an **absolute gem of a story** aimed at our 8 -10 yr olds," it brings "**a wonderful slant to a timeless classic**" that seems to have always lived around

Santa Claus and the gift of Christmas, bringing us closer to that Original Christmas.

As the aliens chase Edwin through the cold, dark streets on Christmas Eve, steadily getting closer and closer, you will run with Edwin as he tries to determine what in the world is going on? Who are those people that are chasing him? Why does Santa seem to know about Edwin being tracked?

Amid the dashing through a city to escape strange people chasing him, our hero discovers things about himself that he has never known and learns just how valuable family really is.

During the fight between Edwin, Santa Claus and the aliens, our hero learns just how much difference loyalty and friendship can make and that family values are the real gifts that Christmas brings.

"There is simply something about the character Edwin that **I really fell in love with and latched on to**. Perhaps it was his family situation and the decision that he had to make when deciding whether to live with his reconstructed family or stay at a children's home that naturally drew me to him." --Annette Huss

A holiday Christmas tale about a dysfunctional family coming together married to a science fiction adventure involving an alien scouting party prior to a full scale alien invasion, this one is sure to please middle grade students and adults alike. Set in a 1950's Manhattan, the book has a retro feel but the situations and family conflicts are timeless. A brisk, fast paced and entertaining novel that constantly engages the reader with new developments, Santa Claus vs the Aliens is full of tense situations interspersed with fun, laughs and comedy.

About the Author

James Cardona has written six books as yet including two non-fiction works, three young adult science fiction novels and one fantasy novel. He is planning on writing many, many more, including the release of the second installment of the Apprentice series in 2015. He is also working on several short stories and two new science fiction novels which he is very excited about.

For his fiction, James tries to make his words come alive by pouring his real-life experiences into his characters such that many of the details described in his books actually happened and are told from the perspective of someone who was there. He also enjoys integrating a hard science approach to his science fiction, feeling that all aspects of his story telling, although perhaps not currently possible, could actually happen once our technology evolves.

James enjoys all things that can unleash the creative process including drawing, painting and creative writing and the not-so-typical such as robot design and writing computer code. He loves tinkering with computers, electronics and building robots and is the Lead Programming Mentor for FIRST Robotics Team 316, a High School Robotics team operating out of Salem Community College.

Additionally James helps organize and run the PSEG Nuclear Salem County Math Showcase which he created back in the year 2000, a math competition for students from grades four through eight, typically attended each year by approximately 500-600 students.

James received his Bachelor's degree in Computer Science from the University of Delaware with a minor in Religious Studies. He lives in Southern New Jersey and works as a Senior Test Engineer for the Laboratory and Testing Services group of the Public Service Electric and Gas Company.

www.ingramcontent.com/pod-product-compliance
Lightning Source LLC
Chambersburg PA
CBHW021433240626
47153CB00001B/139